THE
WIFE
BETWEEN
US

Greer Hendricks spent over two decades as an editor. Prior to her tenure in book publishing, she worked at *Allure Magazine* and earned her Masters in Journalism from Columbia University. Her writing has been published in the *New York Times* and *Publishers Weekly*. Greer lives in Manhattan with her husband, two children, and very needy dog, Rocky. *The Wife Between Us* is her first novel.

Sarah Pekkanen is the internationally and *USA Today* bestselling author of several novels including *Skipping a Beat*. A former investigative journalist and feature writer, her work has been published in *The Washington Post*, *USA Today*, and many others. She is the mother of three sons and lives just outside Washington, D.C.

Praise for *The Wife Between Us*

'Fans of *Gone Girl* and *The Girl on the Train* will adore this classy domestic noir set in New York . . . it has a humdinger of a twist, which I didn't see coming . . . the result is a fast-paced and hugely enjoyable thriller' *Sunday Express*

'Buckle up, because you won't be able to put this one down' *Glamour*

'*The Wife Between Us* delivers a whip-smart, twisty plot in a taut, pacy narrative. It's terrific and troubling. This is one scary love triangle where you won't know who to trust. I loved it'

Gilly Macmillan, *New York Times*
bestselling author of *What She Knew*

'Loved it! What a fantastic story, and the twist completely blind-sided me – and that is rare, believe me!' Mandasue Heller

'Readers who were enthralled by B. A. Paris's *Behind Closed Doors* and Gillian Flynn's *Gone Girl* will love the skewed psychology and shifting perspectives of this domestic thriller' *Library Journal*

'With shocking twists, this intricate thriller proves all is not what it seems for the discarded first wife and the woman about to marry her ex. Addictive' *Woman & Home*

'A scorned woman obsesses over her younger replacement . . . you may think you've heard this one before, there are surprises in store . . . fabulously twisty' *Good Housekeeping*

'Page-flicker . . . keeps you guessing' *Prima*

THE
WIFE
BETWEEN
US

GREER HENDRICKS

AND

SARAH PEKKANEN

PAN BOOKS

First published in the United States 2018 by St Martin's Press, New York

First published in the UK 2018 by Macmillan

This paperback edition published 2018 by Pan Books
an imprint of Pan Macmillan
20 New Wharf Road, London N1 9RR
Associated companies throughout the world
www.panmacmillan.com

ISBN 978-1-5098-4283-4

Visit **www.panmacmillan.com** to read more about all our books
and to buy them. You will also find features, author interviews and
news of any author events, and you can sign up for e-newsletters
so that you're always first to hear about our new releases.

From Greer:
For John, Paige, and Alex, with love and gratitude

From Sarah:
For the ones who encouraged me to write this book

PART
ONE

PROLOGUE

She walks briskly down the city sidewalk, her blond hair bouncing against her shoulders, her cheeks flushed, a gym bag looped over her forearm. When she reaches her apartment building, her hand dips into her purse and pulls out her keys. The street is loud and busy, with yellow cabs racing by, commuters returning from work, and shoppers entering the deli on the corner. But my eyes never stray from her.

She pauses in her entryway and briefly glances back over her shoulder. An electrical charge seems to pulse through me. I wonder if she feels my stare. Gaze detection, it's called—our ability to sense when someone is observing us. An entire system of the human brain is devoted to this genetic inheritance from our ancestors, who relied on the trait to avoid becoming an animal's prey. I've cultivated this defense in myself, the sensation of static rising over my skin as my head instinctively lifts to search out a pair of eyes. I've learned the danger of dismissing that warning.

But she simply turns in the opposite direction, then opens her door and disappears inside, never looking my way.

She is oblivious to what I have done to her.

She is unaware of the damage I have wrought; the ruin I have set in motion.

To this beautiful young woman with the heart-shaped face and lush body—the woman my husband, Richard, left me for—I'm as invisible as the pigeon scavenging on the sidewalk next to me.

She has no idea what will happen to her if she continues like this. None at all.

CHAPTER
ONE

NELLIE COULDN'T SAY what woke her. But when she opened her eyes, a woman wearing her white, lacy wedding gown stood by the foot of her bed, looking down at her.

Nellie's throat closed around a scream, and she lunged for the baseball bat leaning against her nightstand. Then her vision adjusted to the grainy dawn light and the pounding of her heart softened.

She let out a tight laugh as she realized she was safe. The illusion was merely her wedding dress, ensconced in plastic, hanging on the back of her closet door, where she'd placed it yesterday after picking it up from the bridal shop. The bodice and full skirt were stuffed with crumpled tissue to maintain the shape. Nellie collapsed back onto her pillow. When her breathing steadied, she checked the blocky blue numbers on her nightstand clock. Too early, again.

She stretched her arms overhead and reached with her left hand to turn off the alarm before it could blare, the diamond engagement ring Richard had given her feeling heavy and foreign on her finger.

Even as a child, Nellie had never been able to fall asleep easily. Her mother didn't have the patience for drawn-out bedtime rituals, but her father would gently rub her back, spelling out sentences over the fabric of her nightgown. *I love you* or *You're super special,* he'd write, and she would try to guess the message. Other times he'd trace patterns, circles, stars, and triangles—at least until her parents divorced and he moved out when she was nine. Then she'd lie alone in her twin bed under her pink-and-purple-striped comforter and stare at the water stain that marred her ceiling.

When she finally dozed off, she usually slept hard for a good seven or eight hours—so deeply and dreamlessly that her mother sometimes had to physically shake her to awaken her.

But following an October night in her senior year of college, that suddenly changed.

Her insomnia worsened sharply, and her sleep became fractured by vivid dreams and abrupt awakenings. Once, she came downstairs to breakfast in her sorority house and her Chi Omega sister told her she'd been yelling something unintelligible. Nellie had attempted to brush it off: "Just stressed about finals. The Psych Stat exam is supposed to be a killer." Then she'd left the table to get another cup of coffee.

After that, she'd forced herself to visit the college counselor, but despite the woman's gentle coaxing, Nellie couldn't talk about the warm early-fall night that had begun with bottles of vodka and laughter and ended with police sirens and despair. Nellie had met with the therapist twice, but canceled her third appointment and never went back.

Nellie had told Richard a few details when she'd awoken from one of her recurring nightmares to feel his arms tightening around her and his deep voice whispering in her ear, "I've got you, baby. You're safe with me." Entwined with him, she felt a security she realized she'd yearned for her entire life, even before the incident. With Richard beside her, Nellie was finally able to succumb again to the vulnerable state of deep sleep. It was as if the unsteady ground beneath her feet had stabilized.

Last night, though, Nellie had been alone in her old ground-floor brownstone apartment. Richard was in Chicago on business, and her best friend and roommate, Samantha, had slept over at her latest boyfriend's. The noises of New York City permeated the walls: honking horns, occasional shouts, a barking dog . . . Even though the Upper East Side crime rate was the lowest in the borough, steel bars secured the windows, and three locks reinforced the door, including the thick one Nellie had installed after she'd moved in. Still, she'd needed an extra glass of Chardonnay before she'd been able to drift off.

Nellie rubbed her gritty eyes and slowly peeled herself out of bed. She pulled on her terry-cloth robe, then looked at her dress again, wondering if she should try to clear space in her tiny closet so it would fit. But the skirt was so full. At the bridal boutique, surrounded by its poufy and sequin-encrusted sisters, it had looked elegantly simple, like a chignon amidst bouffants. But next to the tangle of clothes and flimsy IKEA bookshelf in her cramped bedroom, it seemed to veer dangerously close to a Disney Princess ensemble.

Too late to change it, though. The wedding was approaching fast and every detail was in place, down to the cake topper—a blond bride and her handsome groom, frozen in a perfect moment.

"Jeez, they even look like you two," Samantha had said when Nellie showed her a picture of the vintage china figurines that Richard had emailed. The topper had belonged to his parents, and Richard had retrieved it from the storage room in his apartment building's basement after he proposed. Sam had wrinkled her nose. "Ever think he's too good to be true?"

Richard was thirty-six, nine years older than Nellie, and a successful hedge fund manager. He had a runner's wiry build, and an easy smile that belied his intense navy-blue eyes.

For their first date, he'd taken her to a French restaurant and knowledgeably discussed white Burgundies with the sommelier. For their second, on a snowy Saturday, he'd told her to dress warmly and had shown up carrying two bright green plastic sleds. "I know the best hill in Central Park," he'd said.

He'd worn a pair of faded jeans and had looked just as good in them as he did in his well-cut suits.

Nellie hadn't been joking when she replied to Sam's question by saying, "Only every day."

Nellie smothered another yawn as she padded the seven steps into the tiny galley kitchen, the linoleum cold under her bare feet. She flicked on the overhead light, noticing Sam had—again—made a mess of the honey jar after sweetening her tea. The viscous liquid oozed down the side, and a cockroach struggled in the sticky amber pool. Even after years of living in Manhattan, the sight still made her queasy. Nellie grabbed one of Sam's dirty mugs out of the sink and trapped the roach under it. *Let her deal with it,* she thought. As she waited for her coffee to brew, she flipped open her laptop and began checking email—a coupon from the Gap; her mother, who'd apparently become a vegetarian, asking Nellie to make sure there would be a meat-free option at the wedding dinner; a notice that her credit-card payment was due.

Nellie poured her coffee into a mug decorated with hearts and the words *World's #1 Teacher*—she and Samantha, who also taught at the Learning Ladder preschool, had a dozen nearly identical ones jammed in the cupboard—and took a grateful sip. She had ten spring parent-teacher conferences scheduled today for her Cubs, her class of three-year-olds. Without caffeine, she'd be in danger of falling asleep in the "quiet corner," and she needed to be on her game. First up were the Porters, who'd recently fretted over the lack of Spike Jonze–style creativity being cultivated in her classroom. They'd recommended she replace the big dollhouse with a giant tepee and had followed up by sending her a link to one the Land of Nod sold for $229.

She'd miss the Porters only slightly less than the cockroaches when she moved in with Richard, Nellie decided. She looked at Samantha's mug, felt a surge of guilt, and used a tissue to quickly scoop up the bug and flush it down the toilet.

Her cell phone rang as Nellie was turning on the shower. She wrapped herself in a towel and hurried into the bedroom to grab her purse. Her phone wasn't there, though; Nellie was forever misplacing it. She eventually dug it out of the folds of her comforter.

"Hello?"

No answer.

Caller ID showed a blocked number. A moment later a voice-mail alert appeared on her screen. She pressed a button to listen to it but only heard a faint, rhythmic sound. Breathing.

A telemarketer, she told herself as she tossed the phone back on the bed. No big deal. She was overreacting, as she sometimes did. She was just overwhelmed. After all, in the next few weeks, she'd pack up her apartment, move in with Richard, and hold a bouquet of white roses as she walked toward her new life. Change was unnerving, and she was facing a lot of it all at once.

Still, it was the third call in as many weeks.

She glanced at the front door. The steel dead bolt was engaged.

She headed to the bathroom, then turned back and picked up her cell phone, bringing it with her. She placed it on the edge of the sink, locked the door, then slung her towel over the rod and stepped into the shower. She jumped back as the too-cold spray hit her, then adjusted the knob and rubbed her hands over her arms.

Steam filled the small space, and she let the water course over the knots in her shoulders and down her back. She was changing her last name after the wedding. Maybe she'd change her phone number, too.

She'd slipped on a linen dress and was swiping mascara over her blond eyelashes—the only time she wore much makeup or nice clothes to work was for parent-teacher conferences and graduation day—when her cell phone vibrated, the noise loud and tinny against the porcelain sink. She flinched, and her mascara wand streaked upward, leaving a black mark near her eyebrow.

She looked down to see an incoming text from Richard:

Can't wait to see you tonight, beautiful. Counting the minutes. I love you.

As she stared at her fiancé's words, the breath that had seemed stuck in her chest all morning loosened. *I love you, too,* she texted back.

She'd tell him about the phone calls tonight. Richard would pour her a glass of wine and lift her feet up onto his lap while they talked. Maybe he'd find a way to trace the hidden number. She finished getting ready, then picked up her heavy shoulder bag and stepped out in the faint spring sunshine.

CHAPTER
TWO

THE SHRIEK OF AUNT Charlotte's teakettle awakens me. Weak sunlight sneaks through the slats of the blinds, casting faint stripes across my body as I lay curled in a fetal position. How can it be morning already? Even after months of sleeping alone in a twin—not the king I once shared with Richard—I still lie only on the left side. The sheets beside me are cool. I am making room for a ghost.

Morning is the worst time because, for a brief moment, my brain is clear. The reprieve is so cruel. I huddle under the patchwork quilt, feeling as if a heavy weight is pinning me here.

Richard is probably with my pretty young replacement right now, his navy-blue eyes fixed on her as his fingertips trace the curve of her cheek. Sometimes I can almost hear him saying the sweet things he used to whisper to me.

I adore you. I'm going to make you so happy. You are my world.

My heart throbs, each steady beat almost painful. *Deep breaths,* I remind myself. It doesn't work. It never works.

When I've watched the woman Richard left me for, I'm always struck by how soft and innocent she is. So like me when Richard and I first met and he would cup my face between his palms, as gently as if it were a delicate flower he was afraid of damaging.

Even in those early, heady months, it sometimes seemed as if it—

he—were a bit scripted. But it didn't matter. Richard was caring, charismatic, and accomplished. I fell in love with him almost immediately. And I never doubted that he loved me, too.

He is finished with me now, though. I've moved out of our four-bedroom colonial home with its arched doorways and rich green sweep of lawn. Three of those bedrooms remained empty throughout our marriage, but the maid still cleaned them every week. I always found an excuse to leave the house when she opened those doors.

The wailing of an ambulance twelve stories below finally prompts me to get out of bed. I shower, then blow-dry my hair, noticing my roots are visible. I pull a box of Clairol Caramel Brown from under the sink to remind myself to touch them up tonight. Gone are the days when I paid—no, when Richard paid—hundreds of dollars for a cut and color.

I open the antique cherrywood armoire that Aunt Charlotte purchased at the GreenFlea Market and refurbished herself. I used to have a walk-in closet bigger than the room in which I now stand. Racks of dresses organized by color and season. Stacks of designer jeans in various states of distressed denim. A rainbow of cashmere lining one wall.

Those items never meant much to me. I usually just wore yoga pants and a cozy sweater. Like a reverse commuter, I changed into a more stylish ensemble shortly before Richard came home.

Now, though, I am grateful that when Richard asked me to leave our Westchester house, I took a few suitcases of my finer clothes. As a sales associate at Saks on the designer-label third floor, I depend on commissions, so it is vital I project an aspirational image. I stare at the dresses lined up in the armoire with an almost military precision and select a robin's-egg-colored Chanel. One of the signature buttons is dented, and it hangs more loosely than the last time I wore it, a lifetime ago. I don't need a scale to inform me I've lost too much weight; at five feet six, I have to take in even my size 4s.

I enter the kitchen, where Aunt Charlotte is eating Greek yogurt with fresh blueberries, and kiss her, the skin on her cheek feeling as soft as talcum powder.

"Vanessa. Sleep well?"

"Yes," I lie.

She stands at her kitchen counter, barefoot and in her loose tai chi outfit, peering through her glasses as she scratches out a grocery list on the back of an old envelope between spoonfuls of her breakfast. For Aunt Charlotte, momentum is the key to emotional health. She's always urging me to join her for a stroll through SoHo, or an art lecture at the Y, or a film at Lincoln Center . . . but I've learned activity doesn't help me. After all, obsessive thoughts can follow you anywhere.

I nibble a piece of whole-grain toast and tuck an apple and a protein bar in my bag for lunch. I can tell Aunt Charlotte is relieved I've landed a job, and not just because it seems as if I am finally getting better. I've disrupted her lifestyle; normally she spends mornings in an extra bedroom that doubles as her art studio, spreading rich oils onto canvases, creating dreamy worlds that are so much more beautiful than the one we inhabit. But she'll never complain. When I was a little girl and my mom needed what I thought of as her "lights-out days," I'd call Aunt Charlotte, my mother's older sister. All it took was the whispered words "She's resting again," and my aunt would appear, dropping her overnight bag on the floor and reaching out with paint-stained hands, folding me into an embrace that smelled of linseed oil and lavender. Without children of her own, she had the flexibility to design her own life. It was my great fortune that she put me at the center of it when I needed her most.

"Brie . . . pears . . ." Aunt Charlotte murmurs as she jots the items on her list, her handwriting full of loops and swirls. Her steel-gray hair is swept up in a messy bun, and the eclectic place setting before her—a cobalt-blue glass bowl, a chunky purple pottery mug, a silver spoon—looks like the inspiration for a still-life painting. Her three-bedroom apartment is expansive since Aunt Charlotte and my uncle Beau, who died years ago, bought in this neighborhood before real-estate prices skyrocketed, but it has the feel of a funky old farmhouse. The wood floors slope and creak, and every room is painted a different color—buttercup yellow, sapphire blue, mint green.

"Another salon tonight?" I ask, and she nods.

Since I've been living with her, I've been as likely to find a group of NYU freshmen as a *New York Times* art critic along with a few studio owners gathered in her living room. "Let me get the wine on my way home," I offer. It is important that Aunt Charlotte not see me as a burden. She is all I have left.

I stir my coffee and wonder if Richard is making his new love coffee and bringing it back to bed, where she's drowsy and warm under the fluffy down comforter we used to share. I see her lips curve into a smile as she lifts the covers for him. Richard and I would often make love in the morning. "No matter what happens during the rest of the day, at least we had this," he used to say. My stomach tightens and I push away my toast. I glance down at my Cartier Tank watch, a gift from Richard for our fifth anniversary, and trace a fingertip over the smooth gold.

I can still feel him lifting my arm to slip it onto my wrist. Sometimes I'm certain I catch on my own clothes—even though they've been cleaned—a whiff of the citrus scent of the L'Occitane soap he washed himself with. He feels linked to me always, as close yet diaphanous as a shadow.

"I think it would be good for you to join us tonight."

It takes a moment for me to reorient myself. "Maybe," I say, knowing I won't. Aunt Charlotte's eyes are soft; she must realize I'm thinking about Richard. She isn't privy to the real story of our marriage, though. She thinks he chased youth, casting me aside, following the pattern of so many men before him. She thinks I'm a victim; just another woman cut down by the approach of middle age.

The compassion would be erased from her expression if she knew of my role in our demise.

"I have to run," I say. "But text me if you need anything else from the store."

I secured my sales job only a month ago, and already I've been given two warnings about my tardiness. I need a better way to fall asleep; the pills my doctor prescribed leave me sluggish in the morning. I haven't worked in almost a decade. If I lose this job, who else will hire me?

I sling my heavy bag over my shoulder with my nearly pristine Jimmy Choos peeking out of the top, lace up my battered Nikes, and put in my earbuds. I listen to psychology podcasts during my fifty-block walk to Saks; hearing about other people's compulsions sometimes pulls me away from my own.

The muted sun that greeted me when I awoke tricked me into thinking it was warming up outside. I brace myself against the slap of a sharp late-spring wind, then begin the trek from the Upper West Side to Midtown Manhattan.

My first customer is an investment banker who introduces herself as Nancy. Her work is consuming, she explains, but her morning meeting was unexpectedly canceled. She's petite, with wide-set eyes and a pixie cut, and her boyish frame makes fitting her a challenge. I'm glad for the distraction.

"I have to dress powerfully or they won't take me seriously," she says. "I mean, look at me. I still get carded!"

As I gently nudge her away from a structured gray pantsuit, I notice her fingernails are bitten to the quick. She sees where my gaze has landed and she tucks her hands into the pockets of her blazer. I wonder how long she'll last in her job. Maybe she'll find another one—something service oriented, perhaps, involving the environment or children's rights—before the field breaks her spirit.

I reach for a pencil skirt and patterned silk blouse. "Maybe something brighter?" I suggest.

As we walk the floor, she chatters about the five-borough bike race that she's hoping to compete in next month, despite her lack of training, and the blind date her colleague wants to set her up on. I pull more items, sneaking glances at her to better gauge her shape and skin tone.

Then I spot a stunning black-and-white floral Alexander McQueen knit and I stop walking. I lift a hand and run it gently down the fabric, my heart beginning to pound.

"That's pretty," Nancy says.

I close my eyes and remember an evening when I wore a dress nearly identical to this one.

Richard coming home with a big white box tied with a red bow. "Wear it tonight," he'd said as I modeled it. "You look gorgeous." We'd sipped champagne at the Alvin Ailey gala and laughed with his colleagues. His hand had rested on my lower back. "Forget dinner," he'd whispered in my ear. "Let's head home."

"Are you okay?" Nancy asks.

"Fine," I reply, but my throat threatens to close up around the words. "That dress isn't right for you."

Nancy looks surprised, and I realize my words came out too harshly.

"This one." I reach for a classic tomato-red sheath.

I walk toward the fitting room, the garments weighing heavily in my arms. "I think we have enough to begin with."

I hang the clothes on the rod lining one wall, trying to focus on the order in which I feel she should try them, beginning with a lilac jacket that will complement her olive skin. Jackets are the best place to start, I've learned, because a customer doesn't need to get undressed to evaluate them.

I locate a pair of stockings and heels so she can better assess the skirts and dresses, then swap out a few 0s for 2s. In the end, Nancy chooses the jacket, two dresses—including the red one—and a navy suit. I call a fitter to hem the suit skirt and excuse myself, telling Nancy I'll ring up her purchases.

Instead I'm drawn back to the black-and-white dress. Three are on the rack. I scoop them into my arms and take them to the stockroom, hiding them behind a row of damaged clothes.

I return with Nancy's credit card and receipt by the time she is slipping into her work clothes.

"Thank you," Nancy says. "I never would have picked these, but I'm actually excited to wear them."

This is the part of my job I actually enjoy—making my customers feel good. Trying on clothes and spending money causes most women to question themselves: *Do I look heavy? Do I deserve this? Is it me?* I know those doubts well because I have been on the inside of the dressing room many times, trying to figure out who I should be.

I slip a hanging bag over Nancy's new clothes and hand her the garments, and for a moment I wonder if Aunt Charlotte is right. If I keep moving forward, maybe my mind will eventually follow my body's propulsion.

After Nancy leaves, I help a few more customers, then head back to the dressing rooms to restock unwanted items. As I smooth clothing on hangers, I overhear two women chatting in adjoining booths.

"Ugh, this Alaïa looks awful. I'm so bloated. I knew that waitress was lying when she said the soy sauce was low sodium."

I recognize the Southern lilt immediately: Hillary Searles, the wife of George Searles, one of Richard's colleagues. Hillary and I attended numerous dinner parties and business events over the years together. I have listened to her opine on public versus private schools, Atkins versus the Zone, and St. Barts versus the Amalfi Coast. I can't bear to listen to her today.

"Yoo-hoo! Is there a salesgirl out there? We need some other sizes," a voice calls.

A fitting-room door flies open and a woman emerges. She looks so much like Hillary, down to the matching ginger locks, that she can only be her sister. "Miss. Can you help us? Our other salesgirl seems to have completely vanished."

Before I can answer, I see a flash of orange and the offending Alaïa is flung over the top of the fitting-room door. "Do you have this in a forty-two?"

If Hillary spends $3,100 on a dress, the commission is worth enduring the questions she'll throw at me.

"Let me check," I reply. "But Alaïa isn't the most forgiving brand, no matter what you've eaten for lunch. . . . I can bring you a forty-four in case it runs small."

"Your voice sounds so familiar." Hillary peeks out, hiding her sodium-bloated body behind the door. She shrieks and it's an effort to keep standing there as she gapes at me. "What are you doing here?"

Her sister chimes in, "Hill, who are you talking to?"

"Vanessa is an old friend. She's married—uh, she used to be married—to one of George's partners. Hang on a sec, girl! Let me just throw on some clothes." When she reappears, she smothers me in a hug, simultaneously engulfing me in her floral perfume.

"You look different! What's changed?" She puts her hands on her hips and I force myself to endure her scrutiny. "For starters, you little wench, you've gotten so thin. You would have no trouble wearing the Alaïa. So, you're working here now?"

"I am. It's good to see you—"

I've never been so thankful to be interrupted by the ring of a cell phone. "Hello," Hillary trills. "What? A fever? Are you sure? Remember the last time when she tricked you by— Okay, okay. I'll be there right away." She turns to her sister. "That was the school nurse. She thinks Madison is sick. Honestly, they send a kid home if they so much as sniffle."

She leans in to give me another hug and her diamond earring scrapes across my cheek. "Let's make a lunch date and properly catch up. Call me!"

As Hillary and her sister click-clack off toward the elevator, I spot a platinum bangle on the chair in the dressing room. I scoop it up and hurry to catch Hillary. I'm about to call her name when I hear her voice wafting back toward me. "Poor thing," she says to her sister, and I detect real pity in her tone. "He got the house, the cars, everything . . ."

"Really? She didn't lawyer up?"

"She turned into a disaster." Hillary shrugs.

It's as if I've slammed into an invisible wall.

I watch as she recedes in the distance. When she presses the button to summon the elevator, I head back to clean her discarded silks and linens off the dressing-room floor. But first, I slip the platinum bracelet onto my wrist.

Shortly before our marriage ended, Richard and I hosted a cocktail party at our home. That was the last time I saw Hillary. The evening began on a stressful note when the caterers and their staff failed to show up on time. Richard was irritated—with them, with me for not booking them an hour earlier, with the situation—but he gamely stepped behind a makeshift bar in our living room, mixing martinis and gin and tonics, throwing back his head and laughing as one of his partners tipped him a twenty. I circulated among the guests, murmuring apologies for the inadequate wheel of Brie and triangle of sharp cheddar I'd set out, promising the real food would soon arrive.

"Honey? Can you grab a few bottles of the '09 Raveneau from the cellar?" Richard had called to me from across the room. "I ordered a case last week. They're on the middle shelf of the wine fridge."

I'd frozen, feeling as if everyone's eyes were on me. Hillary had been at the bar. It was probably she who'd requested that vintage; it was her favorite.

I remember moving in what felt like slow motion toward the basement, delaying the moment when I'd have to tell Richard, in front of all of his friends and business associates, what I already knew: There was no Raveneau in our cellar.

I pass the next hour or so waiting on a grandmother who requires a new outfit for the christening of her namesake and putting together a wardrobe for a woman who is taking a cruise to Alaska. My body feels like wet sand; the flicker of hope I'd experienced after helping Nancy has been extinguished.

This time, I see Hillary before I hear her voice.

She approaches as I'm hanging a skirt on a rack.

"Vanessa!" she calls. "I'm so glad you're still here. Please tell me you found—"

Her sentence is severed as her eyes land on my wrist.

I quickly slip off the bangle. "I didn't . . . I—I was worried about leaving it in the lost and found. . . . I figured you'd return for it, or I was going to call you."

The shadow clears from Hillary's eyes. She believes me. Or at least she wants to.

"Is your daughter all right?"

Hillary nods. "I think the little faker just wanted to skip math class." She giggles and twists the heavy band of platinum onto her wrist. "You saved my life. George only gave it to me a week ago for my birthday. Can you imagine if I had to tell him I lost it? He'd divor—"

A flush blooms on her cheeks as she averts her eyes. Hillary was never unkind, I remember. Early on, she even used to make me laugh sometimes.

"How is George?"

"Busy, busy! You know how it is."

Another tiny pause.

"Have you seen Richard lately?" I aim for a lighthearted tone, but I fail. My hunger for information about him is transparent.

"Oh, now and then."

I wait, but it's clear she doesn't want to reveal more.

"Well! Did you want to try on that Alaïa?"

"I should get going. I'll come back another time, darling." But I sense Hillary won't. What she sees before her—the dented button on the Chanel that is two years old, the hairstyle that could benefit from a professional blowout—is a vision Hillary desperately hopes isn't contagious.

She gives me the briefest of hugs, then begins to leave. But she turns back.

"If it were me . . ." Her brow furrows; she is working through something. Making a decision. "Well, I guess I'd want to know."

What is coming has the feel of an onrushing train.

"Richard is engaged." Her voice seems to float toward me from a great distance away. "I'm sorry. . . . I just thought you might not have heard, and it seemed like . . ."

The roaring in my head suffocates the rest of her words. I nod and back away.

Richard is engaged. My husband is actually going to marry her.

I make it to a dressing room. I lean against a wall and slide down onto the floor, the carpet burning my thighs as my dress rides up. Then I drop my head into my hands and sob.

CHAPTER

THREE

ON ONE SIDE of the old steepled church that housed the Learning Ladder stood three turn-of-the-century grave markers, worn by age and hidden amid a canopy of trees. The other side contained a small playground with a sandbox and a blue-and-yellow climbing structure. Symbols of life and death bookending the church, which had witnessed countless ceremonies honoring both occasions.

One of the headstones was inscribed with the name Elizabeth Knapp. She'd died in her twenties and her grave was set a bit apart from the others. Nellie took the long way around the block, as she always did, to avoid passing the tiny cemetery. Still, she wondered about the young woman.

Her life could have been cut short by disease, or childbirth. Or an accident.

Had she been married? Did she have children?

Nellie set down her bag to unlock the childproof latch on the fence encircling the playground as the wind rustled through the trees. Elizabeth had been twenty-six or twenty-seven; Nellie couldn't remember which. The detail suddenly nagged at her.

She began to walk toward the cemetery to check, but the church's bell rang eight times, the deep, somber chords vibrating through the air and reminding her that her conferences would start in fifteen minutes. A cloud drifted in front of the sun, and the temperature abruptly dropped.

Nellie turned and stepped through the gate, pulling it closed behind her, then rolled back the protective tarp covering the sandbox so it would be ready when the children came out to play. A sharp gust threatened to yank one end away. She fought back against it, then dragged over a heavy flowerpot to secure the edge.

She hurried into the building and down the stairs to the basement, where the preschool was. The earthy, rich scent of coffee announced that Linda, the director, had already arrived. Ordinarily, Nellie would have settled her things in her classroom before greeting Linda. But today she bypassed her empty room and continued down the hall, toward the yellow light spilling out of Linda's office, feeling the need to see a familiar face.

Nellie stepped in and discovered not just coffee but a platter of pastries. Fanning paper napkins beside a stack of Styrofoam cups was Linda, whose shiny dark bob and taupe pantsuit cinched by a crocodile belt wouldn't have been out of place at a board meeting. Linda didn't just dress like this for the parents—even on field day, she looked camera ready.

"Tell me those aren't chocolate croissants."

"From Dean and DeLuca," Linda confirmed. "Help yourself."

Nellie groaned. Just this morning the scale had revealed she still had five—okay, eight—pounds to lose before her wedding.

"Come on," Linda urged. "I got plenty to sweeten up the parents."

"These are Upper East Side parents," Nellie joked. "No one's going to eat sugary carbs." Nellie looked at the platter again. "Maybe just half." She divided one with a plastic knife.

She took a bite as she walked back to her classroom. The space wasn't fancy, but it was roomy, and high windows allowed in some natural light. The soft rug with an alphabet-train pattern running around the edges was where her Cubs sat crisscross—applesauce for story time; in the kitchen area, they donned tiny chef's hats and clattered pots and pans; and the dress-up corner held everything from doctor's coats to ballerina tutus to an astronaut's helmet.

Her mother had once asked Nellie why she didn't want to become a "real" teacher and hadn't understood why Nellie took offense at the question.

The feel of those pudgy, trusting hands in hers; that moment when a child deciphered letters on a page to sound out a word for the first time and looked up at Nellie in wonder; the freshness with which children interpreted the world—how could she explain how precious it all felt?

She'd always just known she wanted to teach, the way some kids feel destined to become writers, or artists.

Nellie licked a buttery flake off her fingertip, then took her planner out of her purse along with a stack of "report cards" she'd be distributing. Parents paid $32,000 a year to send their kids here for a few hours a day; the tepee-link-sending Porters weren't alone in wanting things done a certain way. Every week, Nellie received emails, such as a recent one from the Levines requesting supplemental worksheets for gifted little Reese. Teachers' cell phone numbers were printed in the school directory in case of emergency, but some parents applied loose definitions to the word. Once Nellie fielded a call at five A.M. because Bennett had thrown up during the night and his mother was curious about what he'd eaten at school the previous day.

That sudden shrill ring in the darkness had prompted Nellie to turn on all the lights in her room even after she realized the call was innocuous. She'd burned off her surge of adrenaline by reorganizing her closet and dresser drawers.

"What a diva," her roommate, Sam, had said when Nellie recounted the call. "Why don't you turn off your phone when you go to sleep?"

"Good idea," Nellie had lied, knowing she'd never follow the advice. She didn't listen to loud music while she jogged or commuted to work, either. And she never walked home alone late at night.

If a threat was approaching, she wanted as much warning as possible.

Nellie was scribbling a few final notes at her desk when she heard a knock on the door and looked up to see the Porters, he in a navy pin-striped suit and she in a rose-colored dress. They looked as if they were on their way to the symphony.

"Welcome," she said as they approached and shook her hand. "Please, sit down." She suppressed a smile as they struggled to balance on the child-size chairs around the snack table. Nellie was sitting on one, too, but by now she was used to it.

"So, as you know, Jonah is a wonderful little boy," she began. All of her conferences started with a Lake Wobegon tone, but in Jonah's case, it was true. Nellie's bedroom wall was decorated with paintings created by her favorite students, including Jonah's depiction of her as a marshmallow woman.

"Have you noticed his pencil grip?" Mrs. Porter asked, taking a notebook and pen out of her purse.

"Um, I don't—"

"It's pronated," Mr. Porter interrupted. He demonstrated by grasping his wife's pen. "See how his hand curves in like this? What are your thoughts on whether we should sign him up for occupational therapy?"

"Well, he is only three and a half."

"Three and three-quarters," Mrs. Porter corrected.

"Right," Nellie said. "A lot of kids haven't developed the fine motor skills at that age to—"

"You're from Florida, right?" Mr. Porter asked.

Nellie blinked. "How do you— I'm sorry, why do you ask?" There was no way she had told the Porters where she was from. She was always careful not to reveal too much about her background.

It wasn't difficult to dodge questions once you learned the tricks. When someone asked about your childhood, you told them about the tree house your father built for you, and your black cat that thought he was a dog and would sit up and beg for a treat. If college came up, you focused on the football team's undefeated season and your part-time job at a campus restaurant, where you once started a small fire while making toast and cleared the dining area. Tell colorful, drawn-out stories that deflect attention from the fact that you aren't actually sharing anything. Avoid specifics that will separate you from the crowd. Be vague about the year you graduated. Lie, but only when completely necessary.

"Well, things are different here in New York," Mr. Porter was saying. Nellie looked at him carefully. He was easily fifteen years older than she, and his accent suggested he'd been born in Manhattan. Their paths wouldn't have crossed before now. How could he have known?

"We don't want Jonah to fall behind," Mr. Porter said as he leaned back in his chair, then scrambled to keep from overturning it.

"What my husband is trying to explain," Mrs. Porter interjected, "is that we'll be applying to kindergarten next fall. We're looking at top-tier schools."

"I understand." Nellie pulled her focus back. "Well, it's certainly your decision, but you may want to wait a year." She knew Jonah was already signed up for Mandarin classes, karate, and music lessons. Twice this week she'd seen him yawn and rub his sleepy-looking eyes. At least he had plenty of time to build sand castles and stack blocks into towers while he was here.

"I wanted to let you know about something that happened when one of his classmates forgot to bring lunch," Nellie began. "Jonah offered to share his, which showed such empathy and kindness . . ."

Her voice trailed off when Mr. Porter's cell phone rang.

"Yep," he said. He made eye contact with Nellie, holding her gaze. She'd met him only twice before, at Parents' Night and during the fall conference. He hadn't stared at her or acted peculiarly.

Mr. Porter twirled his hand in rapid circles, indicating she should continue. Who was he speaking to?

"Do you do regular assessments of the kids?" Mrs. Porter asked.

"Sorry?"

Mrs. Porter smiled, and Nellie noticed her lipstick matched the exact hue of her dress. "They do at the Smith School. Every quarter. Academic readiness, small-group pre-reading circles based on ability, early multiplication initiatives . . ."

Multiplication? "I do assess the children." Nellie felt her back straighten.

"You've got to be kidding me," Mr. Porter said into the phone. She felt her gaze being pulled back to him.

"Not on multiplication . . . on, um . . . more basic skills like count-ing and letter recognition," Nellie said. "If you'll look on the back of the report card, you'll see . . . I have categories."

There was a moment of silence as Mrs. Porter scanned Nellie's notes.

"Tell Sandy to get on it. Don't lose the account." Mr. Porter hung up and shook his head. "Are we done here?"

"Well," Mrs. Porter said to Nellie, "I'm sure you're busy."

Nellie smiled, keeping her lips pressed together. *Yes,* she wanted to say. *I am busy. Yesterday I scrubbed that rug after a kid spilled chocolate milk on it. I bought a soft blanket for the quiet corner so your overstressed boy can rest. I pulled three late shifts this week at a restaurant where I waitress because what I earn here won't cover my cost of living—and I still walked through these doors at eight every morning with energy for your children.*

She was heading back to Linda's office to claim the other half of her croissant when she heard Mr. Porter's booming voice: "I forgot my jacket." He reentered her classroom and retrieved it from the back of the tiny chair.

"Why did you think I was from Florida?" Nellie blurted.

He shrugged. "My niece went to school there, too, at Grant Uni-versity. I thought someone mentioned you did as well."

That information wasn't in her bio on the preschool website. She owned nothing with her college's insignia—not a single sweatshirt or key chain or pennant.

Linda must have given her credentials to the Porters—they seemed like the type of parents who would want to know, Nellie told herself.

Still, she looked at him more carefully, trying to imagine his fea-tures on a young woman. She couldn't recall any with the last name Porter. But that didn't mean the woman hadn't sat behind her in class or tried to rush her sorority.

"Well, my next conference is about to begin, so . . ."

He looked at the empty hallway, then back at her. "Sure. See you at graduation." He whistled as he walked back down the hallway. Nellie watched until he disappeared through the door.

Richard rarely talked about his ex, so Nellie knew only a few things about her: She still lived in New York City. She and Richard had split up shortly before he met Nellie. She was pretty, with long dark hair and a narrow face—Nellie had done a Google search and come across a blurry thumbnail photo of her at a benefit.

And she'd been perpetually late, a habit that had irritated Richard.

Nellie sprinted the final block to the Italian restaurant, already regretting the two glasses of Pinot Grigio she'd had with the 3s and 4s teachers as a reward for surviving their conferences. They'd swapped war stories; Marnie, whose classroom was next to Nellie's, was declared the winner because one set of parents had sent their au pair, whose English wasn't very good, to represent them at the meeting.

Nellie had lost track of time until she checked her cell phone on the way to the bathroom. As she'd exited a stall, a woman nearly bumped into her. "Sorry!" Nellie had said reflexively. She'd moved to one side but dropped her bag, scattering its contents across the floor. The woman had stepped over the mess without a word and quickly entered a stall. ("Manners!" the preschool teacher in Nellie had longed to chastise as she knelt to retrieve her wallet and cosmetics.)

She made it to the restaurant eleven minutes late and pulled open the heavy glass door as the maître d' looked up from his leather reservations book. "I'm meeting my fiancé," she panted.

Nellie scanned the dining area, then saw Richard rising from his seat at a corner table. A few fine lines framed his eyes, and at his temples strands of silver were woven through his dark hair. He looked her up and down and gave her a playful wink. She wondered if she'd ever stop feeling a flutter in her stomach at the sight of him.

"Sorry," she said as she approached. He kissed her as he pulled out her chair, and she breathed in his clean citrus scent.

"Everything okay?"

Anyone else would've asked almost as a formality. But Richard's gaze stayed fixed on her; Nellie knew he truly cared about her answer.

"Crazy day." Nellie sat down with a sigh. "Parent conferences.

When we're on the other side of that table for Richard Junior, remind me to say thank you to the teachers."

She smoothed her skirt over her legs as Richard reached for the bottle of Verdicchio cooling on ice in a bucket. On the table, a votive candle burned low, casting a golden circle on the heavy cream-colored tablecloth.

"Just half a glass for me. I had a quick drink with the other teachers after the conferences. Linda treated; she said it was our combat pay."

Richard frowned. "Wish I'd known. I wouldn't have ordered a bottle." He motioned to the waiter, a subtle gesture with his index finger, and requested a San Pellegrino. "You sometimes get a headache when you drink during the day."

She smiled. It was one of the first things she'd ever told him.

She'd been sitting next to a soldier on a flight from South Florida after visiting her mother. She'd moved to Manhattan for a fresh start immediately after graduating from college. If her mom didn't still live in Nellie's hometown, she'd never return.

Before the plane took off, the attendant had approached. "There's a gentleman in first class who would like to offer you his seat," she'd told the young soldier, who stood up and said, "Awesome!"

Then Richard had walked down the aisle. The knot of his tie was loosened, as if he'd had a long day. He held a drink and a leather briefcase. Those eyes had met Nellie's and he'd flashed a warm smile.

"That was really nice of you."

"No big deal," Richard said as he settled down beside her.

Then the safety announcements began. A few moments later the plane lurched upward.

Nellie gripped the armrest as they bounced through an air pocket.

Richard's deep voice, close to her ear, surprised her: "It's just like when your car goes over a pothole. It's perfectly safe."

"I know that logically."

"But it doesn't help. Maybe this will."

He passed her his glass and she noticed his ring finger was bare. She hesitated. "I sometimes get a headache when I drink during the day."

The plane rumbled, and she took a big gulp.

"Finish it. I'll order another . . . or maybe you'd prefer a glass of wine?" He raised his eyebrows questioningly, and she noticed the crescent-shaped silver scar by his right temple.

She nodded. "Thank you." Never before had a seatmate tried to comfort her on a flight; usually people looked away or flipped through a magazine while she fought through her panic alone.

"I get it, you know," he said. "I have this thing about the sight of blood."

"You do?" The plane shuddered slightly, the wings tipping to the left. She closed her eyes and swallowed hard.

"I'll tell you about it, but you have to promise not to lose respect for me."

She nodded again, not wanting his soothing voice to stop.

"So a few years ago one of my colleagues passed out and hit his head on the edge of a conference table in the middle of a meeting. . . . I guess he had low blood pressure. Either that or the meeting bored him into a coma."

Nellie opened her eyes and released a little laugh. She couldn't remember the last time she'd done that on an airplane.

"I tell everyone to step back and I grab a chair and help the guy into it. I was yelling for someone to get water when I see all this blood. And all of a sudden I start getting light-headed, like I'm going to faint, too. I practically kick the injured guy out of the chair so I can sit down, and suddenly everyone is ignoring him and trying to help me."

The plane leveled off. A soft chime sounded, and a flight attendant walked down the aisle, offering headphones. Nellie let go of the armrest and looked at Richard. He was grinning at her.

"You survived, we're through the clouds. It should be pretty smooth from here on out."

"Thank you. For the drink and the story . . . You get to keep your man card, even with the fainting."

Two hours later, Richard had told Nellie about his job as a hedge fund manager and revealed he had a soft spot for teachers ever since one had helped him learn to pronounce his *R*'s: "It's because of her that I didn't introduce myself to you as Wichawd." When she asked him if he had family in New York, he shook his head. "Just an older sister who lives in Boston. My parents died years ago." He bridged his hands and looked down at them. "A car accident."

"My father passed away, too." He glanced back over at her. "I have this old sweater of his. . . . I still wear it sometimes."

They were both silent for a beat, then the flight attendant instructed the passengers to close their tray tables and tilt their seats fully upright.

"Are you okay with landings?"

"Maybe you can tell me another story to get me through it," Nellie said.

"Hmmm. Can't think of one off the top of my head. Why don't you give me your number in case one comes to me?"

He handed her a pen from his suit pocket, and she tilted her head to jot it down on a napkin, her long blond hair falling forward in front of her shoulders.

Richard reached out and gently ran his fingers down the length of it before tucking it back behind her ear. "So beautiful. Don't ever cut it."

CHAPTER
FOUR

I SIT ON THE FLOOR of the dressing room, the lingering perfume of roses reminding me of a wedding. My replacement will be a beautiful bride. I imagine her gazing up at Richard, promising to love and honor him, just as I did.

I can almost hear her voice.

I know how she sounds. I call her sometimes, but I use a burner phone with a blocked number.

"Hi," her message begins. Her tone is carefree, bright. "I'm sorry I missed you!"

Is she truly sorry? Or is she triumphant? Her relationship with Richard is now public, though it began when he and I were still married. We had problems. Don't all couples, after the glow of the honeymoon fades? Still, I never expected him to tell me to move out so quickly. To erase the tracks of our relationship.

It's as though he wants to pretend we were never married at all. As if I don't exist.

Does she ever think about me and feel guilty for what she did?

Those questions batter me every night. Sometimes, when I've lain awake for hours, the sheets twisted around me, I shut my eyes, so close to finally succumbing to sleep, and then her face leaps into my mind.

I sit bolt upright, fumbling for the pills in my nightstand drawer. I chew one instead of swallowing so it takes effect faster.

Her voice-mail greeting gives me no clues about her feelings.

But when I watched her one night with Richard, she looked incandescent.

I'd been walking to our favorite restaurant on the Upper East Side. A self-help book had recommended that I visit painful places from my past, to release their power over me and reclaim the city as my own. So I trekked to the café where Richard and I had sipped lattes and shared the Sunday *New York Times,* and I wandered past Richard's office, where his company held a lavish holiday party every December, and passed through the magnolia and lilac trees in Central Park. I felt worse with every step. It was a horrible idea; no wonder that book was languishing on the discount rack.

Still, I'd pressed on, planning to round out my tour with a drink at the restaurant bar where Richard and I had celebrated our last few anniversaries. That was when I saw them.

Maybe he was trying to reclaim the spot, too.

If I'd been walking just a bit faster, we would have reached the entrance at almost the same moment. Instead I ducked into a storefront and peered around the edge. I caught a glimpse of tanned legs, seductive curves, and the quick smile she flashed at Richard as he opened the door for her.

Naturally my husband wanted her. What man wouldn't? She was as delectable as a ripe peach.

I crept closer and stared through the floor-to-ceiling window as Richard ordered his girlfriend a drink—she had champagne tastes, it seemed—and she sipped the golden liquid from a slim flute.

I couldn't let Richard see me; he wouldn't believe it was a coincidence. I'd followed him before, of course. Or rather, I'd followed them.

Yet my feet refused to move. I greedily drank her in as she crossed her legs so the slit in her dress revealed her thigh.

He was pressed close to her, leaning down as his arm curved over the back of her stool. His hair was longer, brushing the collar of his suit in the back; it suited him. He had the same leonine expression I'd come to recognize when he closed a big business deal, one he'd been pursuing for months.

She tossed back her head and laughed at something he said.

My nails dug into my palms; I'd never been in love with anyone before Richard. At that moment I realized I'd never hated anyone, either.

"Vanessa?"

The voice outside the dressing-room door jars me out of the memory. The British accent belongs to my boss, Lucille, a woman not known for her patience.

I run my fingers under my eyes, aware mascara is probably pooled there. "Just straightening up." My voice has grown husky.

"A customer needs help in Stella McCartney. Sort out the room later."

She is waiting for me to emerge. There is no time to fix my face, to erase the messy signs of grief, and besides, my purse is in the employees' lounge.

I open the door and she takes a step back. "Are you unwell?" Her perfectly arched eyebrows lift.

I seize the opportunity. "I'm not sure. I just . . . I feel a little nauseous. . . ."

"Can you finish the day?" Lucille's tone holds no sympathy, and I wonder if this transgression will be my last. She answers before I can: "No, you might be contagious. You should leave."

I nod and hurry to grab my bag. I don't want her to change her mind.

I take the escalators to the main floor and watch pieces of my ravaged reflection flash in the mirrors I ride past.

Richard is engaged, my mind whispers.

I hurry out the employees' exit, barely pausing for the guard to search my purse, and lean back against the side of the store to slip on my sneakers. I consider a taxi, but what Hillary said is true. Richard got our house in Westchester and the Manhattan apartment he'd kept from his bachelor days, the one he slept in on nights when he had late meetings. The one where he hosted her. He got the cars, the stocks, the savings. I didn't even put up a fight. I'd entered the marriage with nothing. I hadn't worked. I hadn't borne him children. I'd been deceitful.

I hadn't been a good wife.

Now, though, I wonder why I accepted the small lump-sum payment Richard offered me. His new bride will set the table with china I selected. She'll nestle close to him on the suede couch I chose. She'll sit beside him, her hand on his leg, laughing her throaty laugh as he shifts into fourth gear in our Mercedes.

A bus lumbers past and spews hot exhaust. The gray plume seems to settle around me. I push away from the building and walk up Fifth Avenue. A pair of women carrying large shopping bags nearly crowd me off the sidewalk. A businessman strides past, cell phone pressed to his ear, his expression intent. I cross the street and a biker whips by, just inches away. He yells something in his wake.

The city is tightening around me; I need space. I cross Fifty-ninth Street and enter Central Park.

A little girl with pigtails marvels at a balloon animal tied to her wrist, and I stare after her. She could have been mine. If I'd been able to get pregnant, I might still be with Richard. He might not have wanted me to leave. We could be coming here to meet Daddy for lunch.

I'm gasping. I unfold my arms from across my stomach and straighten up. I keep my eyes fixed ahead as I walk north. I focus on the steady rhythm of my sneakers hitting the pavement, counting each step, setting small goals. A hundred steps. Now a hundred more.

At last I exit the park at Eighty-sixth Street and Central Park West and turn toward Aunt Charlotte's apartment. I crave sleep, oblivion. Only six pills are left, and the last time I asked my doctor for a refill, she hesitated.

"You don't want to become dependent upon these," she said. "Try to get some exercise every day and avoid caffeine after noon. Take a warm bath before bed, and see if that does the trick."

But those are remedies for garden-variety insomnia. They don't help me.

I'm almost at the apartment when I realize I've forgotten Aunt Charlotte's wine. I know I won't want to go back out, so I turn and retrace my steps a block, to the liquor store. Four red and two white, Aunt Charlotte had requested. I take a basket and fill it with Merlot and Chardonnay.

My hands close around the smooth, heavy bottles. I haven't tasted wine since the day Richard asked me to go, but I still crave the velvety fruit awakening my tongue. I hesitate, then add a seventh and eighth bottle to my basket. The handles dig into my forearms as I make my way to the cash register.

The young man behind the counter rings them up without comment. Maybe he's used to disheveled women in designer clothes coming in here in the middle of the day to stock up on wine. I used to have it delivered to the house I shared with Richard, at least until he asked me to stop drinking. Then I drove to a gourmet market a half hour away so I wouldn't run into anyone we knew. On recycling day, I took early-morning walks and slipped the empty bottles into neighbors' bins.

"That all?" the guy asks.

"Yes." I reach for my debit card, knowing that if I'd gone for expensive wines rather than fifteen-dollar bottles, the charge wouldn't have cleared my checking account.

He packs the bottles four to a bag, and I push the door open with my shoulder and head for Aunt Charlotte's, the reassuring heft pulling down my arms. I reach our building and wait for the arthritic elevator's doors to creak open. The journey up twelve flights takes an eternity; my mind is consumed with the thought of the first mouthful sliding down my throat, warming my stomach. Blunting the edges of my pain.

Luckily my aunt isn't home. I check the calendar hanging by the refrigerator and see the words *D-three p.m.* Probably a friend she's meeting for tea; her husband, Beau, a journalist, passed away suddenly after a heart attack years ago. He was the love of her life. As far as I know, she hasn't dated anyone seriously since. I set the bags on the counter and uncork the Merlot. I reach for a goblet, then replace it and grab a coffee mug instead. I fill it halfway, and then, unable to wait a moment longer, I raise it to my lips and the rich cherry flavor caresses my mouth. Closing my eyes, I swallow and feel it trickle down my throat. Some of the tightness slowly eases out of my body. I'm not sure how long Aunt Charlotte will be gone, so I pour more into my mug and take it and my bottles into my bedroom.

I slip off my dress, leaving it crumpled on the floor, and step over it. Then I bend down to pick it up and place it on a hanger. I pull on a soft gray T-shirt and fleecy sweatpants and climb into bed. Aunt Charlotte moved a small television into the room when I first arrived, but I rarely use it. Now, however, I'm desperate for companionship, even of the electronic variety. I reach for the remote and flip through channels until I land on a talk show. I cup my mug in my hands and take another long drink.

I try to lose myself in the drama being played out on-screen, but the topic of the day is infidelity.

"It can make a marriage stronger," insists a middle-aged woman who is holding the hand of a man seated beside her. He shifts in his seat and looks down at the floor.

It can also destroy it, I think.

I stare at the man. *Who was she?* I wonder. *How did you meet her? On a business trip, or maybe in line for a sandwich at the deli? What was it about her that drew you in, that compelled you to cross that devastating line?*

I'm clutching my mug so tightly my hand aches. I want to hurl it at the screen, but instead, I refill it.

The man crosses his legs at the ankle, then straightens them. He clears his throat and scratches his head. I'm glad he's uncomfortable. He's beefy and thuggish-looking; not my type, but I can see how he'd appeal to other women.

"Regaining trust is a long process, but if both parties are committed to it, it's very possible," says a woman identified as a couples therapist on the screen below her image.

The drab-looking wife is babbling on about how they've rebuilt trust completely, how their marriage is now their priority, how they lost each other but have found each other again. She sounds as if she's been reading Hallmark cards.

Then the therapist looks at the husband. "Do you agree trust has been reestablished?"

He shrugs. *Jerk,* I think, wondering how he got caught. "I'm workin' on it. But it's hard. I keep picturing her with that—" A beep cuts off his last word.

So I got it wrong. I thought he was the cheater. The clues were present, but I misread them. Not for the first time.

I bang the mug against my front teeth when I go to sip more Merlot. I slide down lower in bed, wishing I'd left the television off.

What separates a fling from a marriage proposal? I thought Richard was just having some fun. I expected their affair to blaze hot and extinguish itself quickly. I pretended not to know, to look the other way. Besides, who could blame Richard? I wasn't the woman he'd married nearly a decade ago. I'd gained weight, I rarely left the house, and I'd begun to search for hidden meanings in Richard's actions, seizing upon clues that I thought indicated he was tiring of me.

She is everything Richard desires. Everything I used to be.

Right after the brief, almost clinical scene that officially ended our seven-year marriage, Richard put our house in Westchester on the market and moved into his city apartment. But he loved our quiet neighborhood, the privacy it afforded. He'll probably buy another place in the suburbs for his new bride. I wonder if she plans to quit work and devote herself to Richard, to trying to become pregnant, just as I did.

I can't believe I have any tears remaining, but more slide down my cheeks as I refill my mug again. The bottle is nearly empty and I spill a few drops on my white sheets. They stand out like blood.

A familiar haze settles around me, the embrace of an old friend. I experience the sensation of blurring into the mattress. Maybe this is how my mother felt when she had her lights-out days. I wish I'd understood better back then; I felt abandoned, but now I know some pain is too fierce to battle. You can only duck for cover and hope the sandstorm passes. It's too late for me to tell her, though. Both of my parents are gone.

"Vanessa?" I hear a gentle knock against my bedroom door and Aunt Charlotte enters. Behind her thick glasses, her hazel eyes look magnified. "I thought I heard the television."

"I got sick at work. You probably shouldn't come any closer." The two bottles are on my nightstand. I hope the lamp is blocking them.

"Can I get you anything?"

"Some water would be great," I say, slurring the *s* slightly. I need to get her out of my room quickly.

She leaves the door ajar as she walks toward the kitchen and I pull myself out of bed, grabbing the bottles and wincing as they clink together. I hurry to my armoire and place them on the floor, righting one when it nearly topples over.

I'm back in the same position when Aunt Charlotte returns with a tray.

"I brought some saltines and herbal tea, too." The kindness in her voice ties a knot in my chest. She places the tray by the foot of my bed, then turns to leave.

I hope she can't smell the alcohol on my breath. "I left the wine in the kitchen for you."

"Thank you, honey. Call if you need anything."

I drop my head back to the pillow as the door closes, feeling dizziness engulf me. Six pills are left. . . . If I let one of the bitter white tablets dissolve on my tongue, I could probably sleep through until morning.

But suddenly I have a better idea. The thought shears through the fog in my mind: *They've only just gotten engaged. It isn't too late yet!*

I fumble for my bag and grab my phone. Richard's numbers are still programmed in. His cell rings twice, then I hear his voice. Its timbre belongs to a bigger, taller man than my ex-husband, a juxtaposition I always found intriguing. "I'll get right back to you," his recorded message promises. Richard always, always keeps his promises.

"Richard," I blurt out. "It's me. I heard about your engagement, and I just need to talk to you. . . ."

The clarity I felt a moment ago wiggles away like a fish through my fingertips. I struggle to grasp the right words.

"Please phone me back. . . . It's really important."

My voice breaks on the last word and I press *End Call*.

I hold the phone to my chest and close my eyes. Maybe I could have avoided the regret ravaging my body if only I'd tried harder to see the warning signs. To *fix* things. It can't be too late. I can't bear the thought of Richard marrying again.

I must have dozed off because an hour later, when my cell vibrates, it jolts me. I look down to see a text:

I'm sorry, but there's nothing more to say. Take care. R.

At that moment a realization seizes me. If Richard had moved on with another woman, I might be able to eventually patch together a life for myself. I could stay with Aunt Charlotte until I'd saved enough to rent my own place. Or I could move to a different city, one with no reminders. I could adopt a pet. Maybe, in time, when I saw a dark-haired businessman in a well-cut suit turning a corner, the sun gleaming off his aviator shades, I wouldn't feel my heart stutter before I realized it wasn't him.

But as long as he is with her—the woman who blithely stepped up to become the new Mrs. Richard Thompson while I pretended to be oblivious—I will never have peace.

CHAPTER
FIVE

WHEN SHE TOOK a good look at her life, Nellie felt as if she'd been splintered into several different women during her twenty-seven years: the only child who'd spent hours playing alone in the creek at the end of her block; the teenager who'd tucked her babysitting charges into bed, promising no monsters lurked in the darkness; and the social director of the Chi Omega sorority who'd sometimes fallen asleep without bothering to lock her door. Then there was the Nellie of today, who'd walked out of a scary movie when the heroine was being cornered, and who made sure she was never the last waitress to close up and leave Gibson's Bistro after the one A.M. final call.

The preschool also saw a version of Nellie: the teacher in jeans who'd memorized every Elephant and Piggie book written by Mo Willems, who dispensed organic animal crackers and cut-up grapes, and who helped children create handprint turkeys for Thanksgiving. Her coworkers at Gibson's knew the waitress who wore black mini-skirts and red lipstick, who would join a tableful of rowdy business-men in tossing back shots to earn a bigger tip, and who could effortlessly palm a tray of gourmet burgers. One of those Nellies be-longed to the day; the other, the night.

Richard had seen her navigate both of her current worlds, though he obviously preferred her preschool-teacher persona. She'd planned to resign from her waitressing job right after they married, and her teaching job as soon as she became pregnant—which she and Richard hoped would happen quickly.

But not long after they'd gotten engaged, he suggested she give notice at Gibson's.

"You mean quit now?" Nellie had looked at him in surprise.

She needed the money, but more than that, she liked the people she worked with. They were a vibrant group—a microcosm of the passionate, creative types who flocked to New York from all over the country, drawn like moths to the bright city. Two fellow waitresses, Josie and Margot, were actresses trying to break into theater. Ben, the headwaiter, was determined to become the next Jerry Seinfeld and practiced comedy routines during slow shifts. The bartender, Chris, a six-foot-three dead ringer for Jason Statham who was probably single-handedly responsible for drawing female customers into the place, wrote scenes for his novel every day before he came to work.

Something about their fearlessness, the way her coworkers exposed their hearts and chased their dreams despite the rejection they continually suffered, spoke to a part of Nellie that had been switched off during her last year in Florida. They were like children in that respect, Nellie realized—they possessed an undaunted optimism. A sense that the world and its possibilities lay open to them.

"I only waitress three nights a week," Nellie had said to Richard.

"That's three more nights you could be with me."

She arched an eyebrow. "Oh, so you're going to stop traveling so much?"

They'd been lounging on the couch at his apartment. They'd ordered in sushi for Richard and tempura for her and had just finished watching *Citizen Kane* because it was his favorite film and Richard had joked that he couldn't marry her until she'd seen it. "It's bad enough that you hate raw fish," he teased. Her legs were slung over his and he was gently massaging her left foot.

"You don't need to worry about money anymore. Everything I have is yours."

"Stop being so wonderful." Nellie leaned over and brushed her lips against his, and though he tried to turn into a deeper kiss, she pulled back. "I like it, though."

"Like what?" Richard's hands were running up the length of her leg. She could see his expression turn intent and his deep-sea eyes darken, the way they always did when he wanted sex.

"My job."

"Baby"—his hands stilled—"I just think of you on your feet all day, then you have to run around and fetch drinks for jackasses all night. Wouldn't you rather come with me on some of my trips? You could have had dinner with me and Maureen last week when I was in Boston."

Maureen was Richard's older sister by seven years; they'd always been close. After his parents died when he was a teenager, he'd moved in with her while he finished his schooling. Maureen now lived in Cambridge, where she was a professor of women's studies at the university, and she and Richard spoke several times a week.

"She's dying to meet you. She was really disappointed when I said you couldn't come."

"I'd love to travel with you," Nellie had said lightly. "But what about my Cubs?"

"Okay, okay. But at least think about taking a painting class at night instead of waitressing. You'd mentioned wanting to do that a while ago."

Nellie hesitated. This wasn't about whether she wanted to take a painting class. She repeated, "I really do like working at Gibson's. It's only for a little while longer, anyway. . . ."

They were quiet for a moment. Richard seemed as if he was about to say something, but instead he reached down and pulled off one of her white socks, waving it in the air. "I surrender." He tickled her foot. She squealed and he pinned her hands above her head and went for her ribs.

"Please don't," she said between gasps.

"Don't what?" he joked as he continued.

"Seriously, Richard. Stop it!" She tried to wriggle away, but he was on top of her.

"Looks like I found your sweet spot."

She felt as if she couldn't get enough oxygen into her lungs. His strong body covered hers, and the remote control dug into her back. Finally, she wrenched her hands free and pushed him away, much harder than she had when he tried to prolong their kiss.

After she caught her breath, she said, "I hate being tickled."

Her tone was sharp—sharper than she'd intended. He looked at her closely. "I'm sorry, sweetheart."

She adjusted her top, then turned to face him. She knew she had overreacted. Richard was only being playful, but the sensation of being trapped had panicked her. She had the same feeling in crowded elevators or going through underground tunnels. Richard was usually sensitive to these issues, but he couldn't be expected to always read her mind. They'd had such a nice night. The dinner. The movie. And he was only trying to be generous and thoughtful.

She wanted to get things back on track. "No, I'm sorry. I'm being grumpy. . . . I just feel like I'm always on the go lately. And my street is so noisy that whenever I open my window, it's impossible to sleep. You're right, it would be nice to relax a little more. I'll talk to my manager this week."

Richard smiled. "Think they can find someone soon? One of our new clients funds a lot of good theater on Broadway. I could get you and Sam house seats to anything you want to see."

Nellie had seen just three shows since moving to New York; tickets were exorbitant. She'd sat in the balcony every time, once behind a man with a severe head cold and the others with a pole partially obscuring her view.

"That would be amazing!" She nestled closer to him.

Someday they'd have an actual fight, but Nellie couldn't imagine being truly mad at Richard. It was more likely her sloppy ways would chafe him. She draped her discarded clothes over her bedroom chair or sometimes left them on the floor; Richard hung up his suits every night, smoothing the fine fabric before tucking them in his closet. Even his T-shirts were shepherded into soldier-straight rows by some sort of clear plastic device that fit into his dresser drawers. The Container

Store probably sold it. More than that, they were sorted by hues: one row for black and gray, one for colors, and one for whites.

His job required intense focus and attention to detail; he had to be organized. And while no one could call teaching preschoolers relaxing, the stakes felt far less intense—not to mention that the hours were shorter and the only travel required was the occasional field trip to the zoo.

Richard took such good care of his things—and of her. He worried about her commuting to the apartment from Gibson's, and he called or texted every night to make sure she'd arrived home safely. He'd bought her a top-of-the-line cell phone. "I'd feel better if you took it with you whenever you go out," he'd said. He'd offered to buy her Mace, too, but she told him she already carried pepper spray. "Good," he said. "There are so many creeps out there."

Don't I know it, Nellie had thought, suppressing a shudder, so grateful for that flight, that young soldier—even for her anxiety about being airborne because it had sparked their first conversation.

Richard had put an arm around her. "Did you like the movie?"

"It was sad. He had that big house, and all that money, but he was so alone."

Richard nodded. "Exactly. That's what I always think when I watch it, too."

Richard loved to surprise her, she was learning.

He had something planned for today—with him, it could be anything from minigolf to a museum—and had told her he was leaving work early to pick her up. She needed to wear something that could cover a range of possibilities, so she decided on her favorite navy-and-white-striped sundress and flat sandals.

Nellie shucked off the T-shirt and cargo pants she'd worn to the Learning Ladder, tossing them in the direction of her laundry basket, then reached into her closet. She shoved aside clothing, searching for the bold stripes, but it was missing.

She went in Samantha's room and spotted it on the bed. She could hardly complain; Nellie had at least two of Sam's tops in her closet. They shared books, clothes, food . . . everything except shoes, because Nellie's feet were a size larger, and makeup, because Samantha was bi-racial, with dark hair and eyes, and Nellie—well, Jonah had chosen a marshmallow to represent her skin tone for a reason.

She dabbed Chanel perfume behind her ears—the scent was a gift from Richard for Valentine's Day, along with a Cartier love bracelet—and decided to head outside to wait for him, since he was due to pick her up any minute.

She exited her apartment and walked down the small hallway, then pulled open the building's main door just as someone else was entering. Nellie reflexively jumped back.

It was only Sam. "Oh! I didn't know you were home! I was just looking for my keys." Sam reached out and squeezed Nellie's arm. "I didn't mean to startle you."

When Nellie had first moved in, she and Sam spent an entire weekend painting the worn old apartment. As they rolled a creamy-yellow hue onto the kitchen cabinets, working side by side, their conversation skimmed over topics such as the rock-climbing group Sam was thinking of joining to meet rugged guys, the father at the preschool who always tried to flirt with the teachers, Sam's therapist mother, who wanted her to go to medical school, and whether Nellie should accept the job at Gibson's or look for weekend shifts at a clothing store.

Then, as darkness fell, Sam uncorked the first of two bottles of wine, and their conversation turned more personal. They'd talked until three A.M.

Nellie always thought of that as the night when they'd become best friends.

"You look nice," Samantha said now. "Maybe a little overdressed for babysitting, though."

"I'm running out first, but I'll be at the Colemans' at six-thirty."

"'K. Thanks again for covering for me. . . . I can't believe I double-booked myself. So unlike me."

"Yeah, what a shocker." Nellie laughed, which had probably been Sam's intention.

"The parents swore they'd be home by eleven, so expect them at midnight. And watch out for Hannibal Lecter when you tell him it's bedtime. Last time he tried to gnaw on my wrist when I took away his Play-Doh."

Sam nicknamed all the kids in her class: Hannibal was the biter, Yoda the tiny philosopher, Darth Vader the mouth breather. But when it came to cajoling a kid out of a tantrum, no one could do it better than Sam. And she'd convinced Linda to spring for rocking chairs so that teachers could soothe kids who suffered from separation anxiety.

A horn tooted and Nellie looked up to see Richard's BMW convertible pulling up. He double-parked next to a white Toyota with a parking ticket on the windshield.

"Nice ride," Sam called out.

"Yeah?" Richard shouted back. "Let me know if you want to borrow it someday."

Nellie caught Sam rolling her eyes. More than once, Nellie had wondered if Sam had a nickname for Richard. But Nellie had never asked. "Come on. He's trying."

Sam squinted as she looked at Richard again.

Nellie hugged her quickly, then hurried down the steps and toward the car as Richard got out to open the passenger-side door.

He wore aviator sunglasses and a black shirt with jeans, a look Nellie loved. "Hi, beautiful." He gave her a long kiss.

"Hi yourself." As she got into the car and twisted around to grab her seat belt, she noticed Samantha hadn't moved from the doorway. Nellie waved, then turned back to Richard. "Are you going to tell me where we're going?"

"Nope." He started the car and pulled away from the curb, heading east onto the FDR Drive.

Richard was quiet during the ride, but Nellie kept seeing the edges of his mouth curl up.

When they exited the Hutchinson River Parkway, he reached into the glove compartment and pulled out a sleep eye-mask. He tossed it onto her lap. "No peeking until when we get there."

"This feels a little kinky," Nellie joked.

"Come on. Put it on."

She stretched the elastic band across the back of her head. It was too tight for her to peek out the bottom.

Richard made a sharp turn and she was pressed against the door. Without visual clues, she couldn't brace her body against the vehicle's movements. And Richard was driving fast, as usual.

"How much longer?"

"Five or ten minutes."

She felt her pulse quicken. She'd tried to wear a sleep mask on an airplane before, hoping it would help ease her fear. But it had the opposite effect: She'd felt more claustrophobic than ever. Sweat pricked her armpits and she realized she was clutching the door handle. She almost asked Richard if she could just shut her eyes, but then she remembered the way he'd smiled—that boyish grin—as he tossed the mask on her lap. Five minutes. Sixty times five was three hundred. She tried to distract herself by counting the seconds in her head, visualizing the second hand of a clock sweeping around in a circle. She let out a gasp when Richard squeezed her knee. She knew he'd meant it affectionately, but her muscles were tense and his fingers had dug into sensitive spots right above her kneecap.

"Just another minute," he said.

The BMW stopped abruptly and she heard the motor die. She reached to rip off the mask, but Richard's voice stopped her: "Not yet."

She heard him open his door, then he came around to let her out, taking her arm to guide her as they walked on something that felt hard beneath her shoes. Not grass. Pavement? A sidewalk? Nellie was so accustomed to the noise constantly surrounding her in the city that its absence was jarring. A bird started to trill, then its notes abruptly died. They'd only been driving for thirty minutes or so, but she felt as if they'd traveled to a different planet.

"Almost there." Richard's breath was warm against her ear. "Ready?"

She nodded. She'd have agreed to anything to take off the mask.

Richard lifted it up and Nellie blinked as sharp sunlight blinded her. When her eyes adjusted, she found herself staring up at a large brick house with a SOLD! sign staked in the front yard.

"It's your wedding present, Nellie." She turned to look at him. He was beaming.

"You bought this?" She gaped.

The house was set back from the street and sprawled across a lot that was at least an acre. Nellie didn't know much about homes—the modest single-floor brick house she'd grown up in in South Florida could be described as "rectangular"—but this one was obviously luxurious. The details as much as the size were the giveaways: an enormous wood door with a stained-glass window and brass handle, manicured gardens rimming the lawn, tall lanterns flanking the walk like sentries. Everything looked pristine, untouched.

"I'm . . . speechless."

"Never thought I'd see that," Richard joked. "I was going to save it until after the wedding, but the settlement went through early, and I couldn't wait."

He handed her the key. "Shall we?"

Nellie walked up the front steps and fit it into the lock. The door glided open and she stepped into a two-story foyer, hearing her footsteps echo against the glossy floor. To her left she could see a wood-paneled study with a gas fireplace. To her right, an oval-shaped room with a deep window seat.

"There's a lot still to be done. I want you to feel like a part of this, too." Richard took her hand. "The best part is the back. The great room. Come on."

He led the way as Nellie followed, trailing her fingertips along the floral wallpaper until she caught herself and yanked them away before she left a smudge.

The room's name was an understatement. The kitchen, with its sand-colored granite counters and bar featuring a flush cooktop and wine refrigerator, flowed into a dining area capped with a modern cut-glass chandelier. The sunken living room had a recessed ceiling with wood detail, a stone fireplace, and wainscoting on the walls. Richard unlocked the back door and led her to the second-story deck. In the distance, a double hammock swayed under a tree.

Richard was looking at her. "Do you like it?" A crease formed between his eyebrows.

"It's . . . unbelievable," she managed. "I'm scared to touch anything!" She gave a little laugh. "It's so perfect."

"I know you wanted to live in the suburbs. The city is so loud and stressful."

Had she told him that? Nellie wondered. She'd complained about the chaos of Manhattan but couldn't recall saying she wanted to move. Maybe she had, though, when she'd talked about growing up on a residential street; she'd probably mentioned a desire to replicate that environment for their children.

"My Nellie." He walked over and enveloped her in his arms. "Wait till you see the upstairs."

He took her hand and led her up the split staircase, then down a hallway past several smaller bedrooms. "I thought we could turn this one into a guest room for Maureen." He pointed. Then he opened the door to the master suite. They stepped through side-by-side walk-in closets, then into the skylight-filled master bathroom. Beneath a row of windows was a Jacuzzi for two, and the separate shower was enclosed in glass.

One hour ago, she'd been inhaling the smell of the onions her neighbor was frying and stubbing her toe on the case of Diet Coke Samantha had left inside their door. She, who was thrilled when she got a 25 percent tip or discovered a cute pair of Hudson jeans at a secondhand store, had somehow wandered into yet another life.

She looked out the bathroom window. A row of thick green hedges blocked the view of the neighbors' house. In New York, she could hear through the radiator the couple who lived one floor above arguing about the Giants game. Here, the sound of her own breathing seemed loud.

She shivered.

"Are you cold?"

She shook her head. "Just someone walking over my grave. Creepy expression, right? My father used to say that."

"It's so quiet." Richard took in a slow, deep breath. "So peaceful." Then he gently turned her toward him. "The alarm company is coming next week."

"Thank you." Of course Richard had thought of that detail.

She wrapped her arms around him and felt herself relax against his solid chest.

"Mmmm." He began to kiss her neck. "You smell so good. Want to test out the Jacuzzi?"

"Oh, babe . . ." Nellie slowly pulled away. She became aware that she was twisting her engagement ring around on her finger. "I love that idea, but I really need to get going. Remember, Sam asked me to take her babysitting job. . . . I'm so sorry."

Richard nodded and put his hands in his pockets. "I guess I'll just have to wait, then."

"It's amazing. I can't believe this is going to be our home."

After a moment, he pulled out his hands and squeezed her close again. His face was tender as he looked down at her. "Don't worry about tonight. We can celebrate every night for the rest of our lives."

CHAPTER
SIX

My head throbs. A sour taste coats my mouth. I reach for the water glass on my nightstand, but it is empty.

As if in defiance of my mood, the sun shines brightly through my open blinds, assaulting my eyes. My clock informs me it is nearly nine. I need to call in sick again, making it another day of work—and of commissions—I'll miss. Yesterday I was so hungover that my raspy voice convinced Lucille I really was ill. I stayed in bed and drank my second bottle of wine, then polished off the half bottle left over from Aunt Charlotte's salon, and when the visions of Richard entwined with her refused to be blotted from my mind, I took a pill as well.

As I reach for the phone, my stomach heaves and I stumble toward the bathroom instead. I fall to my knees but can't throw up. My abdomen is so empty it feels concave.

I pull myself up and twist the sink tap, gulping the metallic-tasting water greedily. I splash handfuls on my face and look at my reflection.

My long dark hair is tangled and my eyes are swollen. New hollows have formed beneath my cheekbones, and my collarbone stands out sharply. I brush my teeth, trying to scrub away the taste of old alcohol, and pull on a bathrobe.

I fall back into bed and reach for the phone. I dial Saks and ask to be put through to Lucille.

"It's Vanessa." I'm grateful that my voice still sounds gravelly. "I'm sorry, but I'm still pretty sick. . . ."

"When do you think you might be back in?"

"Tomorrow?" I venture. "Definitely the day after."

"Right." Lucille pauses. "We're starting presales today. It's going to be very busy."

She lets the implication hang. Lucille has probably never missed a day of work in her life. I've seen the way she appraises my shoes, my clothes, my watch. The way her mouth tightens when I come into work late. She thinks she knows me, that this job is a lark; she is certain she waits on my type every single day.

"I don't have a fever, though," I say quickly. "Maybe I can give it a try?"

"Good."

I hang up and reread Richard's text, even though every word is branded into my memory, then force myself to get into the shower, turning the knob as far left as possible to make it steaming hot. I stand there while my skin flushes red, then I towel off. I dry my hair and pull it into a twist to hide the roots, promising myself I'll cover them tonight. I slip on a simple gray cashmere sweater set, black trousers, and a pair of black ballerina flats. I pat on extra concealer and blush to camouflage my sallow complexion.

When I go into the kitchen, Aunt Charlotte isn't there, but she has set a place for me at the counter. I sip the coffee and nibble the banana bread she left me. I can tell it's homemade. My stomach protests after a few bites, so I wrap the remains of my slice in a paper towel and dump it in the trash, hoping she will think I ate it.

The front door closes behind me with a metallic clank. It seems that in the past two days the weather has undergone a seismic change. I realize immediately that I am overdressed. It's too late for me to put on another outfit, though; Lucille is waiting. Besides, the subway stop is only four blocks away.

The air slams into me as I head down the sidewalk: hot, muggy, rank with smells from the waffle vendor on the corner, the garbage that hasn't been picked up, the wisp of cigarette smoke drifting toward my face. Eventually, I reach the entrance to the subway and descend the stairs.

The sun is blotted out instantly and the humidity feels even thicker down here. I swipe my MetroCard and push through the turnstile, feeling the hard bar resisting against my waist.

A subway car thunders into the station, but it's not my line. The crowd presses forward, near the edge, but I remain by the wall, away from the lethal electric rail. Some people fall to their deaths here; some are shoved. Occasionally, police can't determine which has occurred.

A young woman comes to stand beside me by the wall. She is blond and petite, and very pregnant. Tenderly, she rubs her stomach, her hand moving in slow circles. I watch, mesmerized, and it is as if a centrifugal force commands my thoughts, spinning my mind back to the day I sat on the cold tile of my bathroom floor, wondering if one blue line or two would emerge on the pregnancy test.

Richard and I wanted children. A baker's dozen, he liked to joke, though privately we'd agreed on three. I'd stopped working. We had a maid come every week. This was my only job.

At first I'd worried about the kind of mother I'd be, the unconscious lessons I'd absorbed from my own role model. Some days I'd come home from school to see my mother using a toothpick to excavate crumbs from the cracks in our dining room chairs. Other times, the mail would still be scattered on the floor beneath the slot in the door and dishes would be piled in the sink. I learned early on to not knock on my mother's bedroom door on her lights-out days. When my mother forgot to pick me up from after-school art classes or playdates, I became adept at making excuses and suggesting that my father be called instead.

I started packing my own lunches when I was in the third grade. I'd see other kids dip spoons into thermoses of homemade soup or Tupperware containers of pasta shaped like stars—some parents even included notes with jokes or loving messages—while I tried to gobble my daily sandwich fast, before anyone noticed the bread was torn because I'd spread the peanut butter on while it was still cold.

But as the months passed, my yearning for a child surpassed my trepidation. I'd mothered myself; certainly I could care for a child. As I lay beside Richard at night, I would fantasize about reading Dr. Seuss books to a little boy with those long-lashed eyes, or clinking miniature teacups with a daughter who had his endearing lopsided smile.

I'd watched, feeling numb, as a single blue line emerged on the pregnancy test, as vivid and straight as the slash of a knife. Richard had been in the bedroom that morning, easing one of his charcoal wool suits out of the dry-cleaning bag. Waiting for me to emerge. I knew he'd read the answer in my eyes and I'd see the echo of disappointment in his own. He'd stretch out his arms and whisper, "It's okay, baby. I love you."

But with this negative test—my sixth in a row—my time was officially up. We had agreed if it didn't happen after six months, Richard would go for a test. My ob-gyn had explained it was less invasive to count sperm. All Richard would have to do was stare at a *Playboy* and reach into his pants. He'd joked that his teenage years had prepared him well. I knew he was trying to make me feel better. If Richard didn't have any issues—and I was certain he didn't, the problem lay within me—then it would be my turn.

"Sweetheart?" Richard had knocked on the bathroom door.

I stood up and smoothed my sleeveless pale pink nightgown. I opened the door, my face wet.

"I'm sorry." I held the stick behind my back, as if it were something shameful to hide.

He hugged me as tightly as ever and said all the right things, but I felt a subtle shift in the energy between us. I recalled how we took a walk in the park near our home shortly after our wedding and had seen a father playing catch with his son, who looked to be about eight or nine. They wore matching Yankees baseball caps.

Richard had paused, staring at them. "I can't wait to do that with my boy. Hope he has a better arm than I do."

I'd laughed, aware that my breasts were just the tiniest bit tender. It happened before my period, but it was also a sign of pregnancy, I'd read. Already, I was taking prenatal vitamins. I filled my mornings with long walks and I'd bought a beginner's yoga video. I'd stopped eating unpasteurized cheeses and drinking more than a single glass of wine at dinner. I was doing everything the experts recommended.

But nothing worked.

"We'll just have to keep trying," Richard had said early on, back when we were still optimistic. "That's not so bad, is it?"

I'd thrown the sixth pregnancy test into the bathroom trash can, covering it with a tissue, so I wouldn't have to see it.

"I was thinking," Richard had said. He moved away from me to look in the mirror above the dresser as he knotted his tie. On the bed behind him was an open suitcase. Richard traveled frequently, but usually just short trips, for a night or two. Suddenly I knew what he was going to say: He was going to invite me to come with him. I felt the darkness start to lift as I imagined escaping our beautiful, empty home, in a charming neighborhood where I had no friends. Of putting distance between me and my latest failure.

But what Richard said was "Maybe you should stop drinking altogether?"

The pregnant woman moves away from me and I blink hard, reorienting myself. I watch as she heads toward the tracks and the roar of the approaching subway car. The wheels screech to a halt and the doors slide open with a weary exhale. I wait until the crowds have pushed inside, then I walk forward, feeling a tinge of unease.

I step over the threshold and hear the warning chime signaling the doors are closing. "Excuse me," I say to the guy in front of me, but he doesn't move. His head bobs in time to the music blasting over his headphones; I can feel the vibrations of the bass. The doors close, but the train remains still. It is so hot I can feel my trousers sticking to my legs.

"Seat?" someone offers, and an older man stands up to give his to the pregnant woman. She flashes a smile as she accepts. She's wearing a plaid dress; it's simple and cheap looking, and her full breasts strain against the thin fabric as she reaches up to lift her hair off the back of her neck and fan herself with one hand. Her skin is flushed and dewy; she is radiant.

Richard's new love can't be pregnant, can she?

I don't think it's possible, but suddenly I imagine Richard standing behind her, his hands reaching around to cup her full belly.

I suck in shallow breaths. A man in a white undershirt with yellowed armholes is holding on to the pole by my head. I tilt my face away but I can still smell his pungent sweat.

The car lurches and I fall against a woman reading the *Times*. She doesn't even look up from her paper. A few more stops, I tell myself. Ten minutes, maybe fifteen.

The train rumbles along the tracks, sounding angry, threading through the dark tunnel. I feel a body press against mine. Too close; everyone is too close. My sweaty hand slips off the pole as my knees buckle. I collapse against the doors, crouching with my head close to my knees.

"Are you okay?" someone asks.

The guy in the undershirt leans close to me.

"I think I'm sick," I gasp.

I begin to rock, counting the rhythmic whirring of the wheels along the track. *One, two . . . ten. . . . twenty . . .*

"Conductor!" a woman calls out.

"Yo! Is anyone here a doctor?"

. . . fifty . . . sixty-four . . .

The train stops at Seventy-ninth and I feel arms around my waist, helping me up. Then I am half carried through the doors, onto the solid platform. Someone leads me to a bench a dozen yards away.

"Can I call anyone?" asks a voice.

"No. The flu . . . I just need to get home. . . ."

I sit there until I can breathe again.

Then I walk fourteen blocks back to the apartment, counting all 1,848 steps aloud, until I can crawl into bed.

CHAPTER
SEVEN

Nellie was late, again.

She felt perpetually a beat behind these days, groggy from her relentless insomnia and jittery from the extra coffee she drank to offset it. It seemed as if she was always trying to cram in one more thing. Take this afternoon: Richard had suggested they drive back to their new home as soon as preschool ended to meet the contractor who was building a patio off the English basement.

"You can pick the color of the stones," Richard had said.

"They come in shades other than gray?"

He laughed, not realizing she was serious.

She agreed, feeling guilty about cutting short their first trip to see the house. That meant canceling the blowout she'd been planning to splurge on with Samantha in preparation for the bachelorette party Sam was throwing her that evening, though. Her friends from both the Learning Ladder and Gibson's were attending—one of the few times Nellie's divergent worlds would collide. *Sorry!* Nellie had texted Sam, hesitated, then added, *Last minute wedding errand* . . .

She couldn't think of a way to explain it that wouldn't make it look as if she was choosing her fiancé over her best friend.

"I just have to be home by six to get ready for the party," she'd told Richard. "We're meeting everyone at the restaurant at seven."

"Always with the curfew, Cinderella," he'd said, lightly kissing the tip of her nose. "Don't worry, you won't be late."

But they had been. Traffic was awful, and Nellie didn't walk into her apartment until close to six-thirty. She knocked on Sam's door, but her roommate had already left.

She stood there for a moment, taking in the white Christmas lights Samantha had wound through the slats of her bed's headboard, and the fuzzy green-and-blue rug the two of them had found rolled up by the curb of a posh apartment building on Fifth Avenue. "Is someone actually throwing this out?" Samantha had asked. "Rich people are nuts. It still has a price tag on it!" They'd lifted it onto their shoulders and carried it home, and when they passed a cute guy waiting to cross the street, Sam winked at Nellie, then deliberately turned so the end of the carpet swung into his chest. Sam ended up dating him for two months; it was one of her longer relationships.

Nellie had thirty minutes to make it to the restaurant, which meant she'd have to skip a shower. Still, she poured a half glass of wine to sip while she got ready—not the expensive stuff Richard always ordered for her, but she couldn't really taste the difference anyway—and cranked up Beyoncé.

She splashed cold water on her face, then smoothed on tinted mois-turizer and began to line her green eyes with a smoky-gray pencil. Their bathroom was so small that Nellie was forever banging into the sink or the edge of the door, and every time she opened the medicine cabinet, a tube of Crest or can of hair spray tumbled out. She hadn't taken a bath in years; the apartment had only a tiny shower stall that barely afforded her enough room to bend over to shave her legs.

In the new home, the master bath's shower featured a bench and a rain-forest spray nozzle. Plus, that Jacuzzi.

Nellie tried to imagine soaking in it, after a long day spent . . . doing what? Gardening in the backyard, maybe, and putting together din-ner for Richard.

Did Richard realize that she'd drowned the only houseplant she'd ever owned, and that her cooking repertoire was limited to heating up Lean Cuisines?

As they headed back to the city, she'd stared out the window of the car, taking in the scenery. There was no denying her new neighborhood's beauty: the grand houses, the blossoming trees, the pristine sidewalks. Not a single piece of litter marred the smoothly paved roads. Even the grass seemed greener than in the city.

As they'd exited and passed the guard's station, Richard had given the uniformed man a little wave. Nellie had seen the name of the development on an arched sign, the letters thick and ornate: CROSSWINDS.

Of course, she'd still commute into Manhattan every day with Richard. She'd have the best of both worlds. She'd meet Sam for happy hours and drop by Gibson's to grab a burger at the bar and see how Chris's novel was progressing.

She'd turned around to peer through the rear windshield. She hadn't seen even one person walking down the sidewalk. No cars had been in motion. She could have been staring at a photograph.

But if she got pregnant soon after the wedding, she probably wouldn't return to the Learning Ladder in the fall, she'd thought as she watched her new neighborhood recede in the distance. It would be irresponsible to leave the children mid-year. With Richard traveling every week or two, she'd be alone in the house so much of the time.

Maybe it would make sense to wait a few months before she went off her birth control pills. She could teach for another year.

She'd looked at Richard's profile, taking in his straight nose, his strong chin, the slim, silvery scar above his right eye. He'd gotten it when he was eight and tumbled over the handlebars of his bike, he'd told her. Richard had one hand low on the wheel and the other reaching for the radio's button.

"So, I—" she began, just as he turned on WQXR, his favorite classical station.

"This piece by Ravel is wonderful," he said, increasing the volume. "You know, he composed a smaller body of work than most of his contemporaries, but many regard him as one of France's greatest."

She nodded. Her words were lost in the opening notes of the music, but maybe it was just as well. It wasn't the time for this conversation.

As the piano reached a crescendo, Richard pulled up at a stoplight and turned to her. "Do you like it?"

"I do. It's . . . lovely." She needed to learn about classical music and wine, she decided. Richard had strong opinions on both, and she wanted to be able to discuss the subjects knowledgeably with him.

"Ravel believed that music should be emotional first and intellectual second," he'd said. "What do you think?"

That was the problem, she realized now as she dug through her purse, searching for her favorite Clinique soft-pink lip gloss. She gave up—she hadn't been able to find it the last time she'd looked, either—and put on a peachy shade instead. Intellectually, she knew the changes ahead were wonderful. Enviable, even. But emotionally, it all felt a little overwhelming.

She thought of the dollhouse in her classroom, the one Jonah's parents wanted to replace with a tepee. Her students loved to rearrange the furniture in the darling little home, then move the dolls from room to room, positioning them in front of the fake fireplace, folding them into chairs around the table, and laying them down to sleep in their narrow wooden beds.

The idea invaded her mind like a school-yard taunt from a bully: *Dollhouse Nellie.*

Nellie took a gulp of wine and opened her closet door, pushing aside the wrap dress she'd been planning to wear and pulling out a pair of fitted black leather pants she'd bought on sale at Bloomingdale's when she'd first come to New York. She winced as she sucked in her stomach to pull up the zipper. They'll stretch, she assured herself. Still she partnered the pants with a low-cut, loose-fitting tank in case she needed to release the top button later.

She wondered if she would wear either of the items ever again. She imagined Dollhouse Nellie with a sensible bob dressed in khakis, a cashmere cable-knit sweater, and brown suede loafers as she held out a tray of cupcakes.

Never, she promised herself, digging around for her black high heels and finally finding them under her bed. She and Richard would have a houseful of children, and the elegant rooms would be softened by laughter and pillow forts and little shoes piled in baskets by the front door. They'd play Candy Land and Monopoly by the fire. They'd take family ski trips—Nellie had never skied, but Richard had promised to teach her. A few decades from now, she and Richard would sit side by side on the porch swing, linked by their happy memories.

In the meantime, she'd definitely bring along her own artwork to adorn the walls. She had several original commissions by her preschoolers, including Jonah's marshmallow-woman portrait of her and Tyler's cerebral painting aptly titled *Blue on White*.

She finished getting ready ten minutes after she should have left. She started to exit the apartment, then turned back and grabbed two ropes of colorful beads hanging on a hook by the front door. She and Samantha had each bought a strand at a Village street fair a few years ago. They called them their happy beads.

She slipped one of them around her neck, then scanned the street for a cab.

"Sorry, sorry," Nellie called as she hurried toward the women sitting at the long rectangular table. Her Learning Ladder colleagues lined one side, and her Gibson's coworkers the other. But Nellie could see a cluster of shot glasses, as well as glasses of wine in front of everyone, and all of the women seemed comfortable. She circled the table, giving each of her friends a hug.

When she reached Sam, she looped the beads around her roommate's neck. Sam looked gorgeous; she must have gone for the blowout alone.

"Drink first, talk second," instructed Josie, one of her waitress pals, handing Nellie a shot of tequila.

She tossed it back neatly, earning cheers.

"And now it's my turn to give you something to put on." Samantha glided a comb fixed to a giant glitter-and-tulle veil through the crown of Nellie's hair.

Nellie laughed. "Subtle."

"What do you expect when you ask a preschool teacher to be in charge of the veil?" asked Marnie.

"So what did you have to do today?" asked Samantha

Nellie opened her mouth to speak, then looked around. The other women all worked at low-paying jobs, yet they were splurging at a restaurant famous for its wood-burning-stove pizzas. Nellie could also see a pile of gifts on the empty chair at the end of the table. She knew Sam was searching for a new roommate because she couldn't afford the rent on her own. Suddenly, the last thing Nellie felt like talking about was her showplace of a house. Besides, it hadn't technically been a wedding errand. Maybe Sam wouldn't understand.

"Nothing exciting," Nellie said lightly. "Is it time for another shot?"

Samantha laughed and signaled the waiter.

"Has he told you where you're going for the honeymoon yet?" Marnie asked.

Nellie shook her head, wishing the waiter would hurry up with the fresh round of tequila. The problem was, Richard wanted to keep the destination a surprise. "Buy a new bikini" was all he'd say when she begged for a hint. What if Richard was taking her to a beach in Thailand? She couldn't endure twelve hours on a plane; even the thought made her heart pound.

In the past weeks, in two of her unsettling dreams, she'd been trapped aboard turbulent flights. In the latest one, a panicked attendant had raced down the aisle, yelling for everyone to tuck themselves into the crash position. The images were so vivid—the attendant's wide eyes, the bouncing jet, the thick roiling clouds outside her tiny window—that Nellie had awoken gasping.

"A stress dream," Sam had said the next morning as she applied mascara in their tiny bathroom and Nellie reached over her to grab her body lotion. Sam, always the therapist's daughter, loved analyzing her friends. "What are you anxious about?"

"Nothing. Well, flying, obviously."

"Not the wedding? Because I'm thinking the flying is a metaphor."

"Sorry, Sigmund, but this cigar is just a cigar."

A fresh shot of tequila appeared in front of Nellie and she downed it gratefully.

Sam caught her eye across the table and smiled. "Tequila. It's always the answer."

The next line in their routine sprang from Nellie's lips instantly: "Even if there isn't a question."

"Let me get another look at that rock." Josie grabbed Nellie's hand. "Does Richard have a hot, rich brother? Just, you know, asking for a friend."

Nellie pulled her hand back, hiding the three-carat diamond under the table—she always felt uncomfortable when her friends made a fuss over it—then laughed. "Sorry, only an older sister."

Maureen was coming to New York for the summer, as she had in past years, to teach a six-week course at Columbia. Nellie was finally going to meet her in a couple days.

An hour later, the waiter had cleared their plates and Nellie was opening her presents.

"This one's from Marnie and me," said Donna, an assistant 4s teacher, handing Nellie a silver box with a bright red bow. Nellie pulled out a black silk teddy as Josie released a wolf whistle. Nellie held it up against her body, hoping it would fit.

"Is that for her or Richard?" asked Sam.

"It's gorgeous. I'm sensing a sexy-night theme here, ladies." Nellie laid it next to the Jo Malone perfume, position-of-the-day playing cards, and body-massage candles she'd already unwrapped.

"Last but not least." Sam handed Nellie a gift bag containing a silver picture frame. Inside was a thick piece of ecru paper and a poem printed in italics. "You can take the paper out and put in a wedding photo."

Nellie began to read aloud:

I remember the day I met you, the way you won my affection
You gave me Advil for my hangover at the Learning Ladder; we had
an instant connection
It was your first job in New York City, and your path I did lead

Showing you the best spin studios and where to find the closest Duane Reade

I taught you the ropes, like how to stay on Linda's good side

And about the secret supply closet, for when you just needed to hide

We soon became roomies in an apartment with bugs

Overflowing with makeup, magazines, and kids' decorated mugs

You were late with the rent—let's face it, you're not good with money

And I'm a bit messy—always leaving out my mugs and honey

Over the years you've taught kids how to count and to write

And how to use their words, not their hands, when they begin to fight

Every day we worked hard—couldn't the parents tell we were trying?

Still sometimes we'd get yelled at, and then we'd just start crying

We've been together for an amazing five years

We know each other so well—our hopes and our fears

You got engaged and Linda bought you a fancy cake with many calories

How ironic that it cost more than our combined salaries

You're moving out soon and I worry I might sink

At the very least I'm sure it will drive me to drink (ahem, more)

But when you're walking down the aisle wearing something old and new

Please know that you'll always be my best friend and I really love you.

Nellie could barely finish the poem. It brought her back to her early days in the city, when she'd been desperate to put distance between herself and all that had happened in Florida. She'd traded palm trees for pavement, and a loud, busy sorority house for an impersonal apartment building. Everything was different. Except the memories had followed her across the miles, draping around her like a heavy cloak.

If it hadn't been for Sam, she might not have stayed. She could still be running, still trying to find a place that felt safe. Nellie leaned over the table and gave her roommate a tight hug, then wiped her eyes. "Thanks, Sam. I love it." She paused. "Thanks to all of you. I'm going to miss you. And . . ."

"Oh, stop, don't get sappy. You'll only be a train ride away. We'll see you all the time. Only now you'll always pick up the tab," said Josie.

Nellie let out a small laugh.

"Come on. Let's get out of here." Samantha pushed back her chair. "The Killer Angels are playing at Ludlow Street. Let's go dance."

Nellie hadn't smoked a cigarette since her last year of college, but now, three Marlboro Lights, three tequila shots, and two glasses of wine later, she had been dancing for hours and could feel a trickle of sweat running down her back. Maybe leather pants hadn't been the wisest choice. Across the room, a cute bartender was wearing Samantha's veil and flirting with Marnie.

"I almost forgot how much I love to dance," Nellie shouted over the pulsing music.

"And I almost forgot what a terrible dancer you are," shouted back Josie.

Nellie laughed. "I'm enthusiastic!" she protested. She lifted her arms over her head and did an exaggerated shimmy before spinning around in a circle. Halfway through her spin, she froze.

"Heya, Nick," Josie said as a tall, slim guy in a faded Rolling Stones concert, circa 1979, T-shirt and dark wash jeans walked up to them.

"What are you doing here?" Nellie asked, belatedly realizing her arms were still above her head. She pulled them down and folded them across her chest, aware of how her damp tank top was clinging to her body.

"Josie invited me. I moved back a few weeks ago."

Nellie glared at her friend, and Josie made a mock-innocent face and shrugged, then melted away in the crowd.

Nick had waited tables alongside Nellie for a year, until he moved to Seattle with his band. Slick Nick, they'd all called him, although a few heartbroken women in his wake had modified it to Nick the Prick. He was the hottest guy Nellie had ever dated—although "dated" wasn't an accurate description of their encounters, since most took place in a bedroom.

Nick's black hair was shorter now, emphasizing his sharp cheekbones. Any one of his features—his blunt nose, his heavy eyebrows, his wide mouth—might have been overpowering alone, but together, they all worked. They worked even better than Nellie had remembered.

"I can't believe you're engaged. It seems like we were just hanging out. . . ." He reached over and slowly ran his hand up her bare arm.

Her body responded instantly, even though she pulled her arm away and took a step back.

How predictable that Nick was interested in her again now that she was taken. He'd stopped answering her texts about two minutes after he left the city. He'd always liked a challenge.

"*Happily* engaged. The wedding is next month."

Nick's heavy-lidded eyes appeared amused. "You don't look like someone who's about to get married."

"What does that mean?"

Someone bumped into her from behind, pushing her closer to Nick. He curved an arm around her waist. "You look hot," he said softly, his lips so close to her ear that the dark stubble on his chin tickled her skin. "The girls in Seattle don't compare to you."

She felt a tug in her lower stomach.

"I've missed you. Missed us." His fingers slipped beneath the fabric of her shirt to rest against her lower back. "Remember that rainy Sunday when we stayed in bed all day?"

He smelled like whiskey and she could feel the heat of his taut body through his T-shirt.

The pulsing music and heat of the crowded room made her feel dizzy. A strand of her hair fell into her eyes and Nick smoothed it away.

He bent his head slowly, keeping his eyes locked on hers. "One last kiss? For old times' sake?"

Nellie arched her back to look up at him and offered him her cheek.

He gently cupped her chin, turned her mouth toward his, and kissed her softly. His tongue grazed her lips and she parted them. He pulled her tightly against him and she let out an involuntary groan.

She hated to admit it even to herself, but although sex with Richard was always good, with Nick, it had been great.

"I can't." She pushed him away, breathing harder than when she'd been dancing.

"C'mon, baby."

She shook her head and walked toward the bar, squeezing between people and flinching as a man's elbow bumped into her right temple. She stumbled over someone's foot.

Eventually, she reached Marnie, who flung an arm around her shoulders. "Tequila time?"

Nellie winced. She'd been so busy talking at dinner that she'd only eaten one slice of pizza, and she'd had just a salad for lunch. She felt a little nauseous, and her feet ached from dancing in heels. "Water first." Her cheeks were burning and she fanned herself with one hand. The bartender nodded, his veil bobbing, and began to fill a tall glass from a spigot.

"Did Richard find you?" Marnie asked.

"What?"

"He's here. I told him you were dancing."

Nellie whipped around, scanning the surrounding faces before she finally spotted him across the room.

"Be right back," she said to Marnie, who was leaning over the bar, clinking a shot glass with the bartender.

"Richard!" Nellie called out. She hurried toward him, slipping on the sticky floor just as she reached him.

"Whoa." He grabbed her arm to steady her. "Someone's had a lot to drink."

"What are you doing here?"

A purple light washed across his face as the band launched into a new song. Nellie couldn't read Richard's expression.

"I'm leaving." He let go of her arm. "Are you coming with me?" He'd seen. She knew by the way he held himself; his body was still, but she could sense energy churning within him.

"Yes. Let me just say good-bye. . . ." She'd last noticed Sam and Josie on the dance floor, but now she couldn't spot them anywhere.

She glanced back toward Richard and saw he was already headed for the exit. She ran to catch up with him.

He didn't speak once they were outside—not even after he'd hailed a cab and given the address of his apartment.

"That guy—I used to work with him."

Richard stared straight ahead so that she was looking at his profile, just as she had on the drive only a few hours earlier. But then his hand had been resting on her thigh; now he sat with his arms folded rigidly across his chest.

"Do you greet all your former colleagues with such enthusiasm?" Richard's tone was so formal it chilled her.

Nausea rose in her gut as the cabdriver lurched through traffic. She put a hand over her stomach, then pushed the button to roll down her window a few inches. The wind whipped at her hair, slapping it across her cheek.

"Richard, I pushed him away. . . . I didn't . . ."

He turned and faced her. "You didn't what?" he asked, enunciating every word again.

"Think," she whispered. She'd been wrong: He wasn't furious. He was hurt. "I am so sorry. I walked away from him and I was about to call you."

That part was a lie, but Richard would never know.

Finally, his face softened. "I could forgive you for just about anything." She began to reach for his hand. His next words stopped her: "But do not ever cheat on me."

Even when he'd been on contentious business calls, she'd never heard him sound so absolute.

"I promise," she whispered. Tears sprang to her eyes. Richard had picked out an exquisite home for her. He'd sent her an email earlier that day asking if she thought their guests would like passed hors d'oeuvres or a buffet at the cocktail reception between the wedding ceremony and the dinner. *Or both?* he'd written. He'd worried when she hadn't answered his text—he knew she wouldn't feel secure entering her dark apartment alone late at night. So he'd come to find her and make sure she was safe.

And in response she'd kissed Nick, who'd dated half the women at Gibson's and who probably couldn't remember her last name.

Why had she risked so much?

She wanted to marry Richard; this wasn't cold feet.

But Nick had been unfinished business. In spite of his practiced charm, Nellie knew Nick had a tender side. She'd heard him at Gibson's talking on the phone to his grandmother. He hadn't known Nellie was rolling silverware into napkins just around the corner. He'd promised to bring his nana chocolate-chip cannoli and watch *Wheel of Fortune* with her the next night.

Nick was also the first man she'd slept with since leaving college. She'd stopped thinking about him even before she met Richard. But when Nick had leaned toward her on the dance floor, she'd relished that glorious moment of knowing how much he wanted her. Of feeling the power shift into her hands.

She wished it was as simple as blaming it on the shots. The truth wasn't pretty.

For a brief, rebellious moment, she'd embraced spontaneity over steadiness. She'd wanted one last taste of the city before she settled into the suburbs.

"I'm so glad you came and got me," she said, and at last she felt Richard's arm wrap around her.

She drew in a deep breath.

She'd always regret certain decisions in her life, but choosing Richard would never be one of them.

"Thank you," she said, leaning her head against his chest. She heard his steady heartbeat, the one that lulled her to sleep when nothing else could.

She'd had the sense for a while now that a deep pain was in his past, one he held so closely he hadn't yet shared it with her. Perhaps it had to do with his ex, or maybe his heart had been broken even earlier.

"I won't ever do anything to hurt you." She knew that even on their wedding day, she'd never make a more sacred vow.

CHAPTER
EIGHT

I TURN MY HEAD to see the silhouette of Aunt Charlotte, backlit by the hallway globe, as she stands in my doorway. I don't know how long she has been there, or if she noticed I've been staring blankly at the ceiling.

"Feeling better?" She walks into the room and pulls open the blinds. Sunlight floods in, and I wince and cover my eyes.

I told her I had the flu. But Aunt Charlotte understands the intertwining of emotional and physical health—how the former can ensnare the latter, suffocating it like a thick vine. After all, she had taken care not only of me, but of my mother during her episodes.

"A little." But I make no move to get up.

"Should I be worried?" Her tone navigates the edge between playfulness and sharpness. It is familiar; I remember it from when she'd help my mother out of bed and into the shower. "Just for a little while," she'd cajole, her arm around my mom's waist. "I need to change the sheets."

She would've been a wonderful parent, Aunt Charlotte. But she never had children; I suspect all those years of nurturing my mother and me had something to do with why.

"No, I'm going to work."

"I'll be in my studio all day. I've got a commission for a private portrait. This woman wants a nude of herself to give to her husband to hang over her fireplace."

"Seriously?" I try to inject energy into my tone as I sit up. Like a throbbing toothache, thoughts of Richard's fiancée dominate every other aspect of my life.

"I know. I don't even like the communal dressing area at the Y."

I muster a smile as she starts to leave the room. But then she bangs her hip against the edge of the dresser by the doorway and releases a little cry.

I leap out of bed, and now it's me with my arm around Aunt Charlotte's waist, guiding her toward a chair.

Aunt Charlotte brushes off my arm and my concern. "I'm fine. Old people are clumsy."

And suddenly, the realization pierces me: She is getting old.

I get her ice for her hip over her protests, then I make us some scrambled eggs, mixing in cheddar cheese and scallions. I wash the dishes and wipe down the counters. And I hug Aunt Charlotte tightly before I leave for work. The thought strikes me again: I have no one in the world but her.

I'm dreading seeing Lucille, but to my surprise, she greets me with concern: "I shouldn't have encouraged you to come in yesterday."

I notice Lucille's eyes linger on my Valentino tote. Richard brought it home for me one night just before he left for a business trip to San Francisco. The leather is slightly worn around the clasp; the bag is four years old. Lucille is the type of woman to observe such details. I see her take it in, then look at my old Nikes and my bare ring finger. Her eyes sharpen. It's as if she is really seeing me for the first time.

I'd called her after my breakdown on the subway. I can't remember our entire conversation, but I do remember crying.

"Let me know if you need to leave a bit early," she says now.

"Thank you." I drop my head, feeling ashamed.

It is busy today, especially for a Sunday, but not busy enough. I thought coming in to work might distract me, but visions of her crowd my mind. I imagine her hands on her swollen belly. Richard's hands on her swollen belly. Him reminding her to take vitamins, urging her to get enough sleep, holding her close at night. If she gets pregnant, he'll probably assemble a crib and perch a teddy bear inside.

Even when I was struggling to become pregnant, a soft, smiling teddy bear waited in the room we'd designated for a baby. Early on, Richard had called it our good-luck charm.

"It'll happen," Richard had said, shrugging off my worry.

But after those six months of failed tests, he went to a doctor to have his sperm analyzed. His semen count was normal. "The doctor said I've got Michael Phelps swimmers," he joked, while I tried to smile.

So I set up an appointment with a fertility specialist, and Richard said he'd try to reschedule a meeting to attend.

"You don't have to." I'd attempted to keep my voice light. "I can fill you in after."

"You sure, sweetheart? Maybe if my client leaves early, I can meet you for lunch, as long as you'll be in the city. I'll have Diane book a table at Amaranth."

"Lunch sounds perfect."

But an hour before the appointment, just as I was stepping onto the train, he called to say he'd come to the doctor's office. "I put off my client. This is more important."

I was grateful he couldn't see my expression.

The fertility specialist would ask me questions. Questions I didn't want to answer in front of my husband.

As my train sped toward Grand Central Terminal, I stared out the window at the bare trees and graffiti-littered buildings with boarded-up windows. I could lie. Or I could try to get the doctor alone and explain. The truth was not an option.

A sharp pain made me look down. I'd been picking at my cuticles and had torn one below the quick. I put my finger in my mouth, sucking away the blood.

The train screeched into the terminal before I'd come up with a plan, and far too soon a taxi delivered me to an elegant Park Avenue building.

When Richard met me in the lobby, he didn't seem to notice my agitation. Or maybe he thought I was just anxious about the appointment. I felt as if I were sleepwalking as he pressed the button for the fourteenth floor in the elevator, then stepped back so I could exit first.

Richard's urologist had referred us to Dr. Hoffman. A graceful slender woman in her mid-fifties, she greeted us with a smile shortly after we'd signed in and led us to her consult room. Under her lab coat I saw a flash of fuchsia. We followed her down the hall, and even though she was wearing three-inch heels, I struggled to match her pace.

Richard and I sat side by side on an upholstered couch facing her uncluttered desk. I twisted my hands in my lap, fidgeting with the slender gold bands on my finger. At first, Dr. Hoffman was hesitant to even indulge our insecurities as she explained that it took many couples more than six months to conceive. "Eighty-five percent of couples are pregnant within a year," she assured us.

I mustered a smile. "Well, then . . ."

But Richard interjected. "We don't care about statistics." He reached for my hand. "We want to get pregnant now."

I should have known it wouldn't be that easy.

Dr. Hoffman nodded. "There's nothing to prevent you from exploring fertility treatments, but they can be time-consuming and expensive. There are also side effects."

"Again, with all due respect, these are not issues that concern us," Richard said. I caught a glimpse of what he must be like at work—commanding, persuasive. Impossible to resist.

Why had I ever thought I could hide something so significant from him?

"Baby, your hands are icy." Richard rubbed mine between his.

Dr. Hoffman turned her head to look directly at me. Her hair was swept into a fashionably loose twist, and her skin was smooth and unlined. I wished I had worn something more elegant than simple black pants and a cream turtleneck sweater, which I'd just noticed had a small bloodstain by the cuff. I tucked the material under the finger I'd injured and tried to curve my lips upward.

"Okay, then. Let me start by asking Vanessa some questions. Richard, perhaps you'd like to take a seat in the waiting room?"

Richard looked at me. "Sweetheart, would you like me to go?"

I hesitated. I knew what he wanted me to say. He'd taken off work to accompany me. Would it be a bigger betrayal if I asked him to leave and he found out anyway? Maybe Dr. Hoffman would be ethically bound to tell him, or a nurse might glance at my chart and slip up someday.

It was so hard to think.

"Honey?" Richard prompted.

"I'm sorry. Of course, it's fine if you stay."

The questions began. Dr. Hoffman's voice was low and modulated, but each query felt like a bullet: How frequent are your periods? How long do they last? What methods of birth control have you used? My stomach clenched like a fist. I knew where this was heading.

Then Dr. Hoffman asked, "Have you ever been pregnant?"

I stared down at the thick carpet—gray with small pink squares. I started counting the shapes.

I could feel the heat of Richard's stare. "You've never been pregnant," he said. It was a statement.

I still thought about that time in my life, but the memories had remained locked inside me.

This was so important.

I couldn't lie, after all.

I looked up at Dr. Hoffman. "I have been pregnant." My voice sounded squeaky and I cleared my throat. "I was only twenty-one."

I recognized the "only" as a plea directed at Richard.

"You had an abortion?" I couldn't read the expression in Richard's voice.

I looked up at my husband again.

And I knew I couldn't tell the full truth, either.

"I, ah, I had a miscarriage." I cleared my throat again and avoided his stare. "I was only a few weeks along." That part, at least, was true. Six weeks.

"Why didn't you tell me?" Richard leaned back, away from me. Shock flitted across his face, then something else. Anger? Betrayal?

"I wanted to. . . . I just—I guess I couldn't figure out how." It was such an inadequate response. I'd been so stupid to hope he'd never find out.

"Were you ever going to tell me?"

"Listen," Dr. Hoffman interrupted. "These conversations can get emotional. Do you two need a moment?"

Her tone was calm, the thick silver pen she'd been jotting notes with poised in midair, as if this were a normal interlude. But I couldn't imagine that many other wives had kept the same kind of secrets from their husbands as I had. I knew I'd have to privately tell Dr. Hoffman the full truth at some point.

"No. No. We're fine. Let's keep going?" Richard said. He smiled at me, but a few seconds later he crossed his legs and released my hand.

When the questions were finally over, Dr. Hoffman conducted my physical and blood work while Richard sat in the waiting area, thumbing through emails on his BlackBerry. Before she left the room, Dr. Hoffman put a hand on my shoulder and gave it a gentle squeeze. It felt like a motherly gesture, and my throat convulsed as I tried to hold back tears. I'd hoped Richard and I would still go to lunch, but he said he had postponed the client meeting to one o'clock and he needed to get back to the office. We rode the elevator downstairs in silence along with a few strangers, all of us staring straight ahead.

When we stepped outside, I looked up at Richard. "I'm sorry. I should have . . ."

He'd silenced his phone during our appointment, but now it began to buzz with an incoming call. He checked the number, then kissed me on the cheek. "I need to take this. I'll see you at home, sweetheart."

As he walked down the street, I stared at the back of his head and willed him to turn around and give me a smile or a wave. But he just rounded a corner and disappeared.

That wasn't the first time I'd betrayed Richard, and it wouldn't be the last. Nor would it be the worst—not even close.

I'd never been the woman he thought he'd married.

During a lull in customers at Saks I duck into the break room for coffee. My stomach has settled but a dull ache lingers between my temples. Lisa, a salesperson from the shoe department, is sitting on the couch, nibbling a sandwich. She is in her twenties, blond and pretty in a wholesome way.

I pull my gaze away.

One of my psychology podcasts featured the Baader-Meinhof phenomenon. It's when you become aware of something—the name of an obscure band, say, or a new type of pasta—and it seems to suddenly appear everywhere. Frequency illusion, it's also called.

Young blond women are surrounding me now.

When I came into work this morning, one was trying on lipstick at the Laura Mercier counter. Another was touching fabrics in the Ralph Lauren section. Lisa raises her sandwich for a bite and I see the ring gleaming on her left hand.

Richard and his fiancée are getting married so quickly. *She can't possibly be pregnant, can she?* I wonder again. I feel the familiar hitch in my breath and the cold seep into my body, but I force myself to ward off the panic.

I need to see her today. I need to know for certain.

She lives not too far away from where I stand right now.

Sometimes you can learn a lot about people online—everything from whether they had sour cream on their lunchtime burrito to their upcoming wedding date. Other people are harder to track. But with almost everyone, you can determine a few baseline facts: Their address. Their phone number. Where they work.

You can learn other details by watching.

One night, back when we were still married, I followed Richard to her place and stood outside her apartment. He was carrying a bouquet of white roses and a bottle of wine.

I could have pounded on the door, pushed my way in behind him, screeched at Richard, and demanded he come home.

But I didn't. I returned to our house, and a few hours later, when Richard arrived, I greeted him with a smile. "I left dinner for you. Should I heat it up?"

They say the wife is always the last to know. But I wasn't. I just chose to look the other way. I never dreamed it would last.

My regret is an open wound.

Lisa, the pretty young saleswoman, is gathering up her things quickly, even though some of her sandwich is still left. She tosses the remains in the trash, sneaking glances at me. Her forehead is creased.

I have no idea how long I've been staring.

I exit the break room, and for the rest of my shift, I greet customers pleasantly. I fetch clothing. I nod and give an opinion when asked about the suitability of dresses and suits.

All the while, I bide my time, knowing I'll soon be able to satisfy my growing need.

When at last I can leave, I find myself being pulled back to her apartment.

To her.

CHAPTER

NINE

NELLIE BENT OVER the toilet, her stomach heaving, then slumped down on the marble floor in Richard's bathroom.

Images from the previous night began to surface: The shots. The smoking. The kiss. And the look on Richard's face in the taxi as they made their way back to his apartment. She couldn't believe she'd nearly sabotaged her future with him.

Across from her, a full-length mirror reflected her image: mascara smeared under her eyes, silver glitter from the veil dotting her hair—and a crisp New York City Marathon T-shirt, courtesy of Richard.

She struggled to her feet and reached for a towel to wipe her mouth, then hesitated. They were all snow-white with royal-blue trim. Like everything else in Richard's apartment, they were starkly elegant—everything but her, Nellie thought. She grabbed a Kleenex instead, then tossed it in the toilet. Richard never seemed to have garbage in his trash bins; she wasn't going to leave her soiled tissue behind.

She brushed her teeth and washed her face in icy water that left her skin pale and blotchy. Then, even though she craved a retreat back under Richard's luxurious down comforter, she steadied herself to find him and endure whatever he had to say to her.

Instead of her fiancé, she discovered a bottle of Evian and a container of Advil on the gleaming granite kitchen counter. Beside them rested a note on thick ecru paper embossed with his initials: *I didn't want to wake you. I'm off to Atlanta. Back tomorrow. Feel better. Love you, R.*

The clock on the oven read 11:43. How had she slept so late?

And how could she have forgotten Richard's travel schedule? She didn't even recall his mentioning Atlanta.

As she shook out two tablets and downed the still-cool water, she studied Richard's neat block letters and tried to gauge his mood. Last night's images were jagged and incomplete, but she recalled him tucking her in, then leaving the room and shutting the door. If he'd eventually returned and climbed into bed beside her, she hadn't noticed.

She picked up the cordless phone on his counter and dialed his cell, but it went straight to voice mail. "I'll get right back to you," he promised.

Hearing his voice made her feel the ache of missing him.

"Hi, honey." She fumbled for words. "Um . . . just wanted to say I love you."

She headed back to the bedroom, passing a few large framed photographs lining the hallway. Her favorite was of Richard as a boy, his small hand clasped in Maureen's, as they stood at the ocean's edge. Maureen had towered over him. Richard was five feet eleven inches now, but he hadn't had a growth spurt until he was sixteen, he'd told Nellie. The next photograph was a posed shot of Richard and Maureen with their parents. Nellie could see that Richard had inherited his piercing eyes from his mother and full lips from his father. At the end was a black-and-white picture of his mom and dad on their wedding day.

It said so much about Richard that he decorated his walls with images of family, that these were the faces he wanted to see every day. She wished his parents were still alive, but at least Richard had his sister. Nellie would get to meet Maureen tomorrow at dinner at one of Richard's favorite restaurants.

Her reverie was interrupted by the house phone ringing. *Richard,* she thought, feeling a rush of joy as she ran back into the kitchen and grabbed the receiver.

But the voice that greeted her was feminine: "Is Richard there?"

"Um, no." Nellie hesitated. "Is this Maureen?"

Silence. Then the woman replied, "No. I'll call him back." Then came the dull, unbroken note of the dial tone.

Who would phone Richard on a Sunday and not want to leave a message?

Nellie hesitated, then checked caller ID. The number was blocked.

She had come to Richard's apartment on many occasions. But this was the first time she'd ever been here alone.

Behind her, in the living room, a wall of windows afforded a stunning view of Central Park as well as several other residential buildings. She walked over and looked out, her eyes sweeping over the apartments. Many were dark or shuttered by blinds or curtains. But others had nothing covering the panes of clear glass.

From certain angles, she thought she could see the shadowy outlines of furniture or figures inside.

Which meant anyone in those buildings also had a view into Richard's apartment.

She'd seen Richard close the blinds before at night—a complicated electronic system on that wall wired his lighting and shades. She jabbed at a button and the recessed overhead lights turned off. It was so gloomy outside that the apartment was plunged into shadows.

She pushed the button again and the bulbs flashed on. She exhaled slowly, then tried another button. This time she managed to do it correctly and the blinds glided down. Even though a doorman was stationed in the lobby, Nellie quickly walked to the front door to check the lock. It was engaged. Richard would never leave her unprotected, no matter how annoyed he might be, she thought.

Nellie took a shower, washing her body with Richard's citrus-scented L'Occitane soap and shampooing the smell of stale smoke out of her hair. She tilted back her head and closed her eyes to rinse the suds, then shut off the water and wrapped herself in Richard's robe, thinking of the soft voice on the phone.

The woman had no accent. It was impossible to discern her age.

Nellie opened Richard's medicine cabinet and took out gel, combing a bit through her damp hair and securing it in a ponytail. She changed into the exercise clothes she kept at the apartment since she occasionally used the gym in the building, then found her crumpled top and leather pants neatly folded on top of a small canvas tote by the foot of the bed. She tucked her belongings into the bag and left the apartment, rattling the door to make sure the lock clicked into place.

As she walked toward the elevator, the only other neighbor on Richard's floor, Mrs. Keene, stepped out of her apartment, holding the leash of her bichon frise. Whenever they bumped into her in the lobby, Richard pretended he needed to collect his mail or came up with another excuse to avoid her. "She'll talk you to death if you let her," Richard had warned.

Nellie suspected she was lonely, so she gave the woman a smile as she pressed the call button for the elevator.

"I've been wondering why you haven't been around lately, dear!"

"Oh, I was just here a few days ago," Nellie said.

"Well, next time, knock on my door and I'll have you in for tea."

"Your dog is adorable." Nellie gave its puffy white fur a quick stroke. The woman and her dog looked as if they shared a hairstylist, Nellie thought.

"Mr. Fluffles likes you. So, where's your paramour?"

"Richard had to go to Atlanta for work."

"Work? On a Sunday?" The dog sniffed Nellie's shoe. "He's so busy, isn't he? Always racing off to catch a plane. I've offered to keep an eye on his place while he's gone, but he said he'd never impose on me. . . . So where are you off to now?"

Lonely and gossipy, Nellie thought. The elevator arrived and Nellie held the door open with her forearm until Mrs. Keene and her dog were safely inside.

"I'm actually going to work, too. I teach at a preschool and I need to clean out my classroom for the end of the year."

Graduation was tomorrow, and though traditionally teachers sorted through the rooms a few days after the students left, making it something of a party, complete with smuggled-in wine, Nellie needed to do it now because she was leaving for Florida at the end of the week.

Mrs. Keene nodded approvingly. "How lovely. I'm glad Richard found himself a nice young lady. That last one wasn't very friendly."

"Oh?"

Mrs. Keene leaned closer. "I saw her talking to Mike, the doorman, just last week. She was quite agitated."

"She was here?" Richard hadn't mentioned this.

A glint in Mrs. Keene's eyes told Nellie how much she was enjoying being the conveyer of such news. "Oh, yes. And she handed Mike a bag—Tiffany's, I recognized that distinctive blue—and said he should give it back to Richard."

The elevator doors opened again and Mrs. Keene's dog lunged toward another neighbor who'd just walked into the building with her pug.

Nellie stepped out into the lobby, which resembled a small art gallery: A large orchid graced the glass table between two low-backed sofas, and the cream-colored walls were enlivened by abstract paintings. Frank, the Sunday doorman with a thick Bronx accent, greeted her. He was her favorite of the white-gloved men who kept watch over the residents of this Upper East Side building.

"Hi, Frank," Nellie said, grateful to see his wide, gap-toothed smile. She glanced back at Mrs. Keene, who was in animated conversation with another neighbor. It sounded as if Richard's ex had simply returned something he'd once given her, and that he hadn't even seen her. Who even knew what was in the bag? Obviously their split had been acrimonious.

Many were, Nellie told herself. Yet she still felt unsettled.

Frank winked at her, then pointed outside. "Looks like it's gonna rain. Do you have an umbrella, hon?"

"Three of them. Back at my apartment."

He laughed. "Here, borrow one." He reached into the brass stand by the door.

"You're the best." She extended her left hand to accept it. "Promise I'll bring it back."

She noticed him glance at her ring and do a quick double take before he caught himself and looked away. He'd known of their engagement, but Nellie usually twisted the diamond to the inside of her hand so it would be hidden when she walked around the city. Richard had suggested it, reminding her that one couldn't be too careful.

"Thanks," she said to Frank, feeling a flush creep over her cheeks. It felt a little ostentatious wearing something that probably cost as much as Frank earned in a year—that cost as much as *she* made in a year, too.

Did Richard's ex live nearby? Nellie wondered. Perhaps she'd even passed her on the street.

She didn't realize she was fidgeting with the release button on the umbrella until it sprang open. Her father's voice rang through her mind: *Don't ever open an umbrella inside. It's bad luck.*

"Stay dry," Frank said as Nellie stepped outside into the swollen gray air.

Sam wore her long sleep shirt—the one with WHAT A BEAUTIFUL MESS written in script across the front.

Nellie rustled the paper bag containing poppy-seed bagels with egg, cheddar, bacon, and ketchup—their favorite hangover remedy—in the air. "Good afternoon, sunshine."

Sam's sandals from last night were kicked off just inside the front door, followed by her purse, then, a few feet later, her miniskirt. "The trail of Sam," Nellie joked.

"Hey." Sam poured coffee into a mug but didn't turn around to look at her. "What happened to you last night?"

"I went to Richard's. Too much tequila."

"Yeah, Marnie said he showed up." Sam's tone was curt. "Nice of you to say good-bye."

"I—" Nellie burst into tears. She'd managed to upset Sam, too.

Sam spun around. "Whoa. What's going on?"

Nellie shook her head. "Everything." She choked back a sob. "I'm so sorry I didn't tell you I was leaving. . . ."

"Thank you for saying that. I have to admit I was pissed, especially since you showed up late to dinner."

"I didn't want to leave, but Sam . . . I kissed Nick."

"I know. I saw."

"Yeah, Richard saw, too." Nellie dried her eyes with a paper napkin. "He was really upset. . . ."

"Did you work it out?"

"Sort of. He had to go to Atlanta this morning, so we didn't get to talk much. . . . But Sam, this woman called his apartment this morning when I was there alone. She wouldn't give her name. And then Richard's neighbor told me his ex came by last week."

"What? He's still seeing her?"

"No," Nellie said quickly. "She just came to return something. She left it with the doorman."

Sam shrugged. "That sounds innocent enough."

Nellie hesitated. "But it ended between them months ago. Why is she returning it now?" She wasn't sure why she hadn't revealed to Sam that she suspected the item was actually a gift Richard had given his ex when they were together. And if it was from Tiffany's, it was likely expensive.

Sam took a sip of coffee, then handed the mug to Nellie, who also took a sip. "Why don't you ask Richard about it?"

"I guess . . . I feel like it shouldn't bother me."

"Huh." Sam took a bite of bagel and chewed. Nellie's stomach clenched when she began to unwrap her own sandwich. Her appetite had vanished.

"I thought she was completely out of the picture. This is totally random, okay? But those weird phone calls I've been getting . . ."

"It's her?"

"I don't know," Nellie whispered. "But isn't it a coincidence that they started right after I got engaged to Richard?"

Sam didn't seem to have an answer for that.

"And there was this moment this morning after I said hello when all I could hear was breathing. It was just like those other calls. Then this woman asked for Richard, so . . . I sound sort of crazy when I say it aloud."

Sam put down her bagel and gave Nellie a quick, hard hug. "You're not crazy, but you need to talk to Richard. They were together a long time, right? Don't you deserve to know about that part of his life?"

"I've tried."

"It isn't fair that he shuts you down like that."

"He's a guy, Sam. He doesn't feel the need to talk things to death like we do." *Like* you *do*, Nellie thought.

"Sounds like you haven't talked about it at all."

Nellie let that go. She and Sam rarely argued. Nellie didn't want to dig into this. "He told me they just grew apart. It happens, right?"

But Richard had said one more thing. It seemed especially significant now.

She wasn't who I thought she was.

Those had been his exact words. Nellie had been taken aback by the disgust twisting Richard's face when he'd uttered them.

Her roommate would certainly have some thoughts on that.

But Sam was wearing the same inscrutable expression that had come over her features when Nellie told her about the house Richard had bought. She'd worn that look the day Nellie came home wearing the engagement ring, too.

"You're right," Nellie said lightly. "I'll ask him again."

She could tell Sam wasn't through with the conversation, but Nellie felt protective of Richard. She'd wanted Sam to reassure her about Richard's ex, not point out the flaws in Nellie's relationship with him.

Nellie grabbed a few shopping bags that were wedged into the narrow slot between the refrigerator and the wall. "I need to run to the school. I've got to start packing up my classroom. Want to come?"

"I'm wiped out. Think I'll nap."

Things still weren't right between them.

"Sorry again I bailed on you. It was a really great party." Nellie nudged her best friend with her shoulder. "Hey, are you around tonight? We can do face masks and watch *Notting Hill*. Order in Chinese. My treat . . ."

Sam still wore that look, but she accepted the unspoken truce. "Sure. Sounds fun."

What *was* Richard's ex like?

Slim and glamorous, Nellie thought as she approached the Learning Ladder. Maybe his ex enjoyed classical music and could identify the top notes in a bottle of wine. And Nellie bet his ex was confident about the pronunciation of *charcuterie,* unlike Nellie, who'd had to point at it on her menu once.

Nellie had brought her up soon after she met Richard, curious about the woman he'd shared his life with before her. They'd been trading sections of the *Times* on a lazy Sunday morning after they'd made love and showered together. Nellie had used the extra toothbrush Richard had bought for her, and she was wearing a T-shirt she'd left behind on an earlier visit. It had made her wonder why there weren't any traces of Richard's ex left in the apartment. They'd been together for years, yet no lone elastic hair band had been forgotten in the cabinet under the bathroom sink, or tin of herbal tea languished in the back of the pantry, or pretty throw cushion softened the severe lines of Richard's suede couch.

The apartment was completely masculine. It was as if his ex had never spent time in it at all.

"I was thinking. . . . We haven't talked much about your ex. . . . Why did it end?"

"It wasn't any one thing." Richard had shrugged and turned a page of the business section. "We grew apart. . . ."

That's when he'd spoken the line that Nellie couldn't get out of her head now: *She wasn't who I thought she was.*

"Well, how did you guys meet?" Nellie playfully batted down the newspaper he was reading.

"Come on, sweetheart. I'm with you. The last thing I want to talk about is *her.*" His words were gentle, but his tone wasn't.

"Sorry . . . I was just wondering."

She'd never brought her up again. After all, Nellie had topics from her past she didn't want to talk about with him, either.

Richard would have landed in Atlanta by now, Nellie thought as she unlatched the gate encircling the playground and walked toward the preschool. He might be in a meeting or alone in his hotel room. Was he consumed by images of Nellie's ex, just as she was fixating on his?

She couldn't imagine how wrenching it would feel to see Richard kiss another woman. She wondered if Richard thought Nellie might turn out to be a different person from what he thought she was, too.

She reached for her cell phone to call him, then stopped. She'd already left a message. And she wasn't going to question him about his ex's visit. He'd earned her trust, but she'd shaken his.

"Hey there!"

Nellie looked up to see the church's youth leader holding open the door for her. "Thanks," she said, hurrying toward him. She gave him a big smile to compensate for not remembering his name.

"I was about to lock up. Didn't think anyone from the school would be here on a Sunday."

"I was going to start cleaning out my classroom."

He nodded, then glanced up at the sky. Thick, shifting clouds blotted out the sun. "Looks like you just beat the rain," he said cheerfully.

Nellie headed into the basement, flicking on the overhead light as she descended the stairs. She wished she'd come here straight from Richard's, when the church would've been full of parishioners. She hadn't expected it to be empty.

As she entered her classroom, she nearly stepped on a lone paper crown. She bent over and picked it up, smoothing out the creases. Brianna's name was on the inside, written in the shaky letters Nellie had taught her to form. "Remember, the B has two big bellies that stick out," Nellie had told her when the little girl kept reversing the direction. Brianna had been so proud when she'd mastered it.

The Cubs had made the crowns to wear during the graduation ceremony. They'd stand in a wiggling line behind a curtain until Nellie put her hand on their little shoulders one by one and whispered, "Go!" Then they'd march down a makeshift aisle while their parents stood up and cheered and snapped photos.

Brianna would be upset she'd lost hers; she'd spent a long time affixing stickers to it and had used a half bottle of glue to attach a different-colored pom-pom to each point. Nellie would call Brianna's parents to let them know she'd found it.

She tucked the crown in one of her shopping bags, then stood in the atypical quiet.

Her classroom was modest, and the toys were basic compared to the ones most of the children had at home, but her students still bounded in every morning, tucking their lunches into cubbies and hanging their little jackets and sweaters on hooks. Nellie's favorite part of the day was show-and-tell, which was predictably unpredictable. Once Annie had brought in a miniature Frisbee she'd found in the medicine cabinet. Nellie had returned the diaphragm to Annie's mother at pickup. "At least it wasn't my vibrator," the mother had joked, instantly endearing her to Nellie. Another time Lucas had opened his lunchbox, revealing a live hamster, which had immediately seized its chance at freedom and leaped out. Nellie hadn't been able to find it for two days.

She hadn't thought it would hurt this much to leave.

She began to pull off the walls the construction-paper butterflies the children had made and tuck them into folders that she would send home with each child. She winced as the edge of one cut into the soft tip of her index finger.

"Fudge." She hadn't sworn properly in years, ever since she'd shocked little David Connelly and had to scramble to convince him she'd merely been pointing out a toy truck. She put her finger in her mouth and reached into her supply closet, taking out an Elmo Band-Aid.

She was wrapping it around her finger when she heard a noise in the hallway.

"Hello?" she called.

No answer.

She walked to the doorway and peeked out. The narrow corridor was empty, the linoleum floors reflecting the gleam of the overhead lights. The other classrooms were dark, and their doors were pulled shut. The church's old bones creaked sometimes; it must have been a floorboard settling.

In the absence of the laughter and chaos, the school felt off-kilter.

Nellie reached into her purse and pulled out her cell. Richard hadn't phoned yet. She hesitated, then texted him: *I'm at the Learning Ladder. . . . Call if you can. I'm here alone.*

Sam knew where she was, but Sam was napping. Nellie would just feel better if Richard knew, too.

She started to put her cell back in her bag but tucked it in the waistband of her Lycra pants instead. She peeked out into the hallway again and listened for a long moment.

Then Nellie resumed pulling artwork off the walls, working quickly, until they were bare. She took down from an easel the activity schedule printed in big letters. She reached up to strip a large calendar from a bulletin board. Velcro cards attached to it listed the day of the week and a symbol for the weather. A smiling sun was still affixed to Friday.

Nellie glanced out the window. The first drops of rain had started to softly patter down.

She almost didn't notice the woman standing just behind the gate.

A tall climbing structure partially obstructed her view. Nellie could only make out a tan raincoat and a green umbrella blocking the person's face. And long brown hair whipping in the wind.

Maybe it was someone out walking her dog.

Nellie craned her head to see at a different angle. There was no dog.

Could it be a prospective parent checking out the school?

But it wouldn't make sense for someone to come on a Sunday, when the Learning Ladder was closed.

It could be a parishioner . . . although the service had ended hours ago.

Nellie pulled her phone out of her pocket, then pressed her face close to the window. The woman suddenly moved, hurrying away, blending in with the trees. Nellie spotted the woman round the corner by the three gravestones.

Toward the entrance on the opposite side of the church.

Sometimes that door was propped open by a heavy brick when nighttime activities, such as an AA meeting, were scheduled.

Something about the way the person abruptly turned away—that quick, jerky motion—reminded Nellie of the woman who'd caused her to drop her purse in the bathroom on parent-conference day.

Nellie couldn't be there for another minute. She grabbed her bags, leaving papers still scattered across her desk, and headed for the door. Her cell phone buzzed in her hand and she flinched. It was Richard.

"I'm so glad it's you," she gasped.

"Are you okay? You sound upset."

"I'm just alone at the school."

"Yeah, you told me in your text. Are the church doors locked?"

"I'm not sure, but I'm leaving now." Nellie hurried up the stairs. "It feels sort of creepy for some reason."

"Don't be scared, baby. I'll stay with you on the phone."

She glanced behind her as she exited the building, then slowed down and caught her breath. She reached the end of the block, opened her umbrella, and began to walk toward the busier cross street. Now that she was outside, she knew she'd overreacted.

"I miss you so much. And I feel horrible about last night."

"Look, I've been thinking about it, and I saw you push him away. I know you love me." He really was too good to be true.

"I wish I could've been with you today." She didn't want Richard to know she'd forgotten about his trip. "After graduation, I'm all yours."

"You have no idea how happy that makes me." His voice felt like safety.

In that moment, she decided she didn't want to continue teaching. She'd travel with Richard in the fall. She'd still be around children—*their* children.

"I need to get back to my client. Are you feeling better now?"

"Much."

Then Richard spoke the words that would stay with her forever: "Even when I'm not there, I'm always with you."

CHAPTER

TEN

SHE LIVES ON an active street. New York City has dozens of blocks like hers—not ritzy, not poverty-stricken, but falling somewhere in the wide swath of the middle.

It reminds me of the neighborhood I lived in when I first met Richard.

Despite the torrential burst of rain that has just ended, enough people are around so I don't stand out. A bus stop is on her corner, next to a deli, and two doors down from her building is a small hair salon. A father pushing a stroller crosses paths with a couple walking hand in hand. A woman juggles three bags of groceries. A Chinese-food delivery guy splashes through a puddle and splatters me with a few drops, the aroma of the meals stacked on the back of his bicycle wafting in his wake. In the past, my stomach would have been tempted by the succulent smells of chicken fried rice or sweet-and-sour shrimp.

I wonder how well she knows her neighbors.

She might've knocked on the door of the apartment above hers, handing over a UPS delivery box that was mistakenly left by her door. Maybe she picks up fruit and bagels at the deli, where the owner mans the cash register and greets her by name.

Who will miss her when she disappears?

I'm prepared to wait quite a while. My appetite is nonexistent. My body feels neither hot nor cold. There is nothing I need. But before long—at least I think I have not waited very long—I feel a quickening in my pulse, a hitch in my breath, as she rounds the corner.

She is carrying a bag. I squint and make out the logo of Chop't, the takeout salad place. It swings as she walks, matching the gentle sway of her high ponytail.

A cocker spaniel darts in front of her and she pauses to avoid becoming entangled with the leash. The owner reels in the dog, and I see her nod and say something, then she bends down to stroke its head.

Does she know how Richard feels about dogs?

I'm holding my cell phone to my ear, my body half turned away from her, my umbrella tilted to cover my face. She continues walking toward me and I soak her in. She wears yoga capris and a loose white top, with a Windbreaker tied around her waist. Salad and exercise; she must want to look her best in her wedding gown. She pauses in front of her building, reaching into her purse, and a moment later, she vanishes inside.

I let my umbrella drop and massage my forehead, trying to focus. I tell myself I'm acting crazy. Even if she were pregnant—which I don't believe is a possibility—she probably wouldn't be showing yet.

So why did I come here?

I stare at her closed door. What would I even say if I knocked and she answered? I could beg her to call off the wedding. I could warn her that she'll regret it, that he cheated on me and he'll do the same to her—but she'd probably just slam the door and phone Richard.

I don't want him to ever know I've followed her.

She thinks she's safe now. I imagine her rinsing her plastic salad bowl and putting it into the recycling bin, applying a mud mask, maybe calling her parents to talk about last-minute wedding details.

There is still a little time. I cannot be impulsive.

I have a long walk home. I round the corner, retracing her steps. A block later I pass Chop't and I turn around to go in. I study the menu, trying to guess what she might have craved, so I can order the same thing.

When the server hands me my salad—in a plastic bowl and

tucked in a white paper bag alongside a fork and napkin—I smile and thank her. Her fingers brush mine and I wonder if she also waited on my replacement.

Before I am even out the door, I'm suddenly overwhelmed by acute hunger pangs. All the dinners I've slept through, the breakfasts I've skipped, the lunches I've tossed in the trash—they converge upon me now, fueling a nearly savage desire to fill the emptiness inside me.

I step to one side, where there is a counter and stools, but I can't wait long enough to put down my things and settle into a seat.

My fingers tremble as I open the container and begin to fork in mouthful after mouthful, holding the container close to my chin so I don't spill any, devouring the tangy greens, chasing bits of egg and tomato around the slippery container with my fork.

I'm queasy as I swallow the final bite, and my stomach feels distended. But I am as hollow as ever.

I throw away the empty bowl and begin to walk home.

When I enter the apartment, I see Aunt Charlotte splayed on the couch, her head angled against a cushion, a washcloth draped over her eyes. Usually on Sunday nights she teaches an art-therapy class at Bellevue; I haven't known her to ever miss one.

I've also never seen her nap before.

Worry pierces me.

She lifts her head at the thump of the door closing and the washcloth slips off, into her hand. Without her glasses, her features seem softer.

"Are you okay?" I recognize the irony: It's an echo of the words she has repeated to me ever since a cab deposited me on the curb outside her building with three suitcases stacked behind me.

"Just a killer headache." She grips the edge of the sofa and stands. "I overdid it today. Check out the living room. I think I cleared away twenty years of clutter after my subject left."

She is still wearing her painting uniform—jeans topped by one of her late husband's blue oxford shirts. By now the shirt is soft and worn, decorated with layers of drips and splatters. It's a work of art in itself; a visual history of her creative life.

"You're sick." The words seem to propel themselves out of me. My voice is high and panicky.

Aunt Charlotte walks over and puts her hands on my shoulders. We are nearly the same height and she looks directly into my eyes. Her hazel eyes are faded by age, but they are as alert as ever.

"I am not ill."

Aunt Charlotte has never shied away from difficult conversations. When I was younger, she explained my mother's mental-health issues to me in simple, honest terms, ones I could understand.

Even though I believe my aunt, I ask, "Promise?" My throat thickens with tears. I cannot lose Aunt Charlotte. Not her, too.

"I promise. I'm not going anywhere, Vanessa."

She hugs me and I inhale the scents that grounded me as a girl: linseed oil from her paints, the lavender she dabs on her pulse points.

"Have you eaten? I was going to throw something together. . . ."

"I haven't," I lie. "But let me make dinner. I'm in the mood to cook."

Maybe it's my fault she is exhausted; maybe I've taken too much from her.

She rubs her eyes. "That would be great."

She follows me to the kitchen and sits on a stool. I find chicken and butter and mushrooms in the refrigerator and begin to pan-sear the meat.

"How did the portrait go?" I pour us each a glass of sparkling water.

"She fell asleep during our session."

"Really? Naked?"

"You'd be surprised. Overprogrammed New Yorkers often find the process relaxing."

As I whisk together a simple lemon sauce, Aunt Charlotte leans over and inhales. "It smells delicious. You're a much neater cook than your mother."

I pause in rinsing off the chopping board.

I am so used to masking what I feel that it's easy to slip on a smile and chat with Aunt Charlotte. But the reminders are everywhere, as always—in the white wine I dash into my sauce, and the salad greens I push aside to reach the mushrooms in the refrigerator's vegetable bin. I fall into light conversation with my aunt, gliding above the thoughts roiling through my mind, like a swan whose churning feet are hidden as he floats across the water.

"Mom was a tornado," I say, even conjuring a smile. "Remember how the sink was always overflowing with pots and pans, the counters coated with olive oil or bread crumbs? And the floor! My socks would practically stick to it. She didn't exactly subscribe to the belief that you should tidy up as you went along." I reach into the big ceramic bowl on the counter and pull out a Vidalia onion. "Her food was great, though."

On her good days, my mother would create elaborate three-course meals. Worn volumes by Julia Child, Marcella Hazan, and Pierre Franey lined our bookshelves, and I would often find her reading one the same way that I might devour Judy Blume.

"You were probably the only fifth grader who would get home-made beef bourguignonne and a lemon torte on an ordinary Tuesday night," Aunt Charlotte says.

I flip the chicken breasts, the uncooked side crackling against the hot pan. I can see my mother now, her hair wild from the heat seeping from the oven, clattering pots onto burners and mincing garlic, and singing loudly. "Come on, Vanessa!" she'd say when she caught sight of me. She'd twirl me around, then shake salt into her hand and throw it into a pot. "Never follow a recipe exactly," my mother always said. "Give it your own flair."

I knew a crash would come soon after those nights, when my mother's energy had burned itself out. But something in her freedom was glorious—her unfiltered, stormlike joy—even though it frightened me as a child.

"She was something else," Aunt Charlotte says. She leans an elbow on the blue tile countertop and rests her chin in her hand.

"She was." I'm glad my mother was still alive when I married, and in a way, I'm grateful she isn't around to see how I've ended up.

"Do you like cooking now, too?" Aunt Charlotte is watching me carefully. Almost studying me, it seems. "You look so much like her, and your voice is so similar sometimes I think it's her in the other room. . . ."

I wonder if another, unspoken question is in her mind. My mother's episodes grew more severe in her thirties. Around the same age I am now.

I lost touch with Aunt Charlotte during my marriage. That was my fault. I was even more of a mess than my mother, and I knew Aunt Charlotte couldn't just swoop in to help me. I was too far gone for that. The hopeful, buoyant young woman I was when I married Richard is almost unrecognizable to me now.

She turned into a disaster, Hillary had said. She was right.

I wonder if my mother also suffered from obsessive thoughts during her episodes. I'd always imagined her mind was blank—numb—when she took to her bed. But I'll never know.

I choose to answer the simpler question. "I don't mind cooking."

I hate it, I think as my knife comes down and severs the onion cleanly.

When Richard and I first married, I didn't know my way around a kitchen at all. My single-girl dinners consisted of Chinese takeout or, if the scale was mistreating me, a microwaved Lean Cuisine. Some nights I skipped dinner altogether and munched on Wheat Thins and cheese as I sipped a glass of wine.

Still, the unspoken arrangement was that once Richard and I married, I would cook for him every weeknight. I'd quit working, so it seemed more than reasonable. I rotated between chicken, steak, lamb, and fish. They weren't fancy meals—a protein, a carb, and a vegetable—but Richard seemed appreciative of my efforts.

The day we first visited Dr. Hoffman—the day Richard learned I'd been pregnant in college—was my first attempt at making something special for him.

I wanted to try to ease the tension between us, and I knew Richard loved Indian food. So after I left Dr. Hoffman's office, I looked up a recipe for lamb vindaloo, searching for the one that seemed the least complicated.

It's funny how certain details stick in the memory, such as how the wheel of my shopping cart needed to be adjusted, causing it to squeak every time I turned down a new aisle. I wandered through the market, searching for cumin and coriander, trying to forget how Richard's face had looked when he learned I'd gotten pregnant by another man.

I'd called Richard to tell him I loved him, but he hadn't replied. His disappointment—worse, the thought of his disillusionment—upset me more than any argument could. Richard didn't yell. When angry, he seemed to coil into himself until he regained control over his emotions. It didn't usually take him long, but I worried I'd pushed him too far this time.

I remember driving home on the quiet streets, the new Mercedes sedan Richard had purchased for me purring past the stately colonials constructed by the same builder who'd sold Richard our house. Occasionally I saw a nanny out with a young child, but I'd yet to make a friend in our neighborhood.

I was hopeful when I began to cook dinner. I cut the lamb into even chunks, following the recipe carefully. I remember how sunlight glowed through the large bay windows in our living room, as it did toward the end of every day. I'd found my iPod and scrolled down to the Beatles. "Back in the U.S.S.R." twanged through the speakers. The Beatles always lifted my spirits because my father used to blast John, Paul, George, and Ringo in our old sedan when he took me out for ice cream or to the movies during my mom's lighter episodes, the ones that only lasted a day or two and didn't require Aunt Charlotte's assistance.

I'd allowed myself to imagine that after I served Richard his favorite meal, we would cuddle in bed and talk. I wouldn't tell him everything, but I could admit a few of the details. Maybe my revelation would even bring us closer. I'd let him know how terribly sorry I was, how I wished I could erase what had happened and start again.

So there I was, in my exquisite kitchen, stocked with Wüsthof knives and Calphalon pots and pans, cooking dinner for my new husband. I was happy, I think, but I wonder now if my memory is playing tricks on me. If it is giving me the gift of an illusion. We all layer them over our remembrances; the filters through which we want to see our lives.

I'd tried to follow the recipe exactly, but I'd neglected to buy the fenugreek because I had no idea what it was. And when it came time to add the fennel, I couldn't find it, even though I swore I'd put it in the cart. The fragile emotional peace I'd tried to build began to crumble. I, who had been given everything, couldn't even manage to make a proper meal.

When I opened the refrigerator door to put back the coconut milk and saw a half-full bottle of Chablis, I hesitated, staring at it.

Richard and I had agreed that I'd stopped drinking, but surely a few sips wouldn't hurt. I poured myself a half glass. I'd forgotten how good the crisp minerality tasted on my tongue.

I retrieved our pressed blue linen place mats and matching napkins from the big oak armoire in the dining room. I laid out the nice china Hillary and George had given us as a wedding gift. When we first got married, I'd had to consult an online etiquette site to learn how to set a formal table. Despite my mother's extravagant meals, she was uninterested in the dining ambience; sometimes when all the dishes were dirty, we'd eat off paper plates.

I set candlesticks in the middle of the table and switched the music to classical, selecting Wagner, one of Richard's favorite composers. Then I retreated to the couch, wineglass by my side. By now our house had more furniture—sofas in the living room, splashes of artwork on the walls, including the portrait Aunt Charlotte had done of me as a child, and an Oriental rug in vivid blues and reds in front of the fireplace—but the rooms still felt a bit characterless to me. If only we'd had a high chair in the dining room, a few soft toys scattered on the rug . . . I stilled my hand when I realized I was tapping my fingernails against my glass and making little chiming sounds.

Richard usually arrived home around eight-thirty, but it wasn't until after nine that I finally heard his key turn in the lock and the thunk of his briefcase on the floor.

"Honey," I called. No answer. "Sweetie?"

"Give me a second."

I listened to his footsteps climbing the stairs. I didn't know if I should follow him, so I stayed on the couch. When I heard him begin to descend, I caught sight of my wineglass. I ran to the sink, rinsing it out quickly and putting it back in the cabinet still wet, before he could see.

It was impossible to decipher his mood. He could have been upset with me, or he could have just had a tough day at work. Richard had seemed tense all week; I knew he was dealing with a difficult client. During dinner I tried to make conversation, my lighthearted tone masking the worry underneath.

"This is good."

"I remembered you told me once lamb vindaloo was your favorite dish."

"I said that?" Richard bent his head to take a forkful of rice.

I'd felt puzzled. Hadn't he?

"I'm sorry I didn't tell you about my . . ." My voice trailed off. I couldn't say the word.

Richard nodded. "It's forgotten," he said quietly.

I'd steeled myself for questions. His words came almost as a letdown. Maybe I'd wanted to share that part of my life with him, after all.

"Okay" was all I said.

As I cleared the table, I noticed half his plate was still full. By the time I'd finished cleaning, Richard was already asleep. I curled up next to him, listening to his steady breaths, until I drifted off, too.

The next morning, Richard left early for the office. Midway through the day, as I was at the hair salon getting highlights, my phone pinged with an incoming email from the local French culinary institute.

The note read, *Ma cherie. Je t'aime. Richard.* When I opened the attachment, I saw a gift certificate for ten cooking lessons.

"Honey?" Aunt Charlotte's voice is concerned.

I wipe my eyes and gesture to the cutting board. "Just the onion." I can't tell if she believes me.

After dinner, Aunt Charlotte goes to bed early and I clean the kitchen. Then I retreat to my room and listen to the sounds of the old apartment settling in for the night—the sudden hum of the refrigerator, a door slamming in the unit below. Sleep is elusive now, as if I've stockpiled enough of it over my lost months to suppress my natural circadian rhythm.

My mind wanders to the topic of a recent podcast: obsession.

"Our genes are not our destiny," insisted the speaker. But he acknowledged that addiction is hereditary.

I think of the way my mother left a trail of destruction.

I think of the way my mother dug her nails into her palms when she was agitated.

And I think, as always, of her.

A plan begins to form in my mind. Or maybe it has been there all along, waiting for me to catch up to it. To become strong enough to carry it out.

I see her again, bending down to stroke the head of the little dog in her path. I see her crossing her shapely legs and leaning close to Richard at the bar—*our* bar. And I see her on the day I came to his office to surprise him for lunch, back when we were still married. The two of them were walking out of the building. She wore a blush-colored dress. His hand gently touched the small of her back as he allowed her to exit the door first. *She's mine,* the gesture seemed to say.

He used to touch me that way. I told him once I loved the subtle, sexy feel of his fingers there.

I get up, moving quietly in the darkness, and retrieve my burner phone and my laptop from the bottom dresser drawer.

Richard cannot marry again.

I begin to make preparations. The next time I see her, I will be ready.

CHAPTER
ELEVEN

NELLIE LAY IN THE DARKNESS, listening to the sounds of the city waft through the bars of her open window: A honk; the shouted lyrics to "Y.M.C.A."; a car alarm wailed in the distance.

The suburbs were going to seem so quiet.

Sam had left a few hours earlier, but Nellie had decided to stay in. If Richard called, she wanted to be at the apartment. Besides, the tumult of the past twenty-four hours had left her feeling depleted.

When she'd gotten home from the Learning Ladder, she and Sam had plastered on cobalt-blue algae masks while they waited for their Chinese food to arrive—spareribs, pork dumplings, sweet-and-sour chicken, and, in a token nod to Nellie's wedding diet, brown rice.

"You look like a Blue Man Group reject," Sam had said as she smoothed the paste over Nellie's cheeks.

"You look like Sexy Smurf."

After the morning's tension and the inexplicable menace she'd felt at the school, it was so good to laugh with Sam.

Nellie had grabbed plastic forks from the drawer beside the sink, the one that was also crammed with packets of hot sauce and mustard and mismatched paper napkins. "I'm using the good silver tonight," she joked. It hit her that this would likely be the last meal they shared alone before the wedding.

When the food arrived, they washed off their masks. "Ten bucks wasted," Sam proclaimed as she examined her skin. Then they flopped on the couch and dug in, chatting about everything except what was really on Nellie's mind.

"Last year the Straubs gave Barbara a Coach bag after graduation," Sam said. "Think I'll score something good?"

"Hope so." Richard had presented Nellie with a Valentino bag the previous week after he noticed an ink stain on the one she usually carried. It was still under her bed in its protective dustcover; no way was she going to risk a kid finger-painting it. She hadn't mentioned the purse to Sam.

"Sure you don't want to join me?" Sam had asked as she shimmied into Nellie's AG jeans.

"I haven't recovered from last night."

Nellie had wanted Sam to stay in and watch a movie with her, but she knew Sam had to maintain her other friendships. After all, Nellie would be gone in a week.

Nellie had thought about calling her mother, but their conversations often left Nellie feeling a bit on edge. Her mother had met Richard only once, and she'd immediately honed in on the age difference. "He's had time to sow his oats and travel and *live*," she told Nellie. "Don't you want to do the same before you settle down?" When Nellie responded that she wanted to travel and *live* with Richard, her mother shrugged. "Okay, lovey," she said, but she didn't sound completely convinced.

It was now after midnight but Sam was still out; maybe with a new boyfriend, or maybe with an old one.

Despite Nellie's exhaustion and the rituals she'd tried—chamomile tea and her favorite meditation music—she kept listening for the scrape of Sam's key in the lock. She wondered why it was always on the nights one most craved sleep that it was elusive.

She found her thoughts returning to Richard's ex. When she was in Duane Reade earlier picking up the face masks, she'd stood in line behind a woman who was talking on her cell phone, making plans to meet someone for dinner. The woman was petite and yoga toned, and her laughter spilled out like bright coins during the call. Would she be Richard's type?

Nellie's own cell phone waited within reach on her nightstand. She kept looking at it, steeling herself in case it erupted with another unsettling hang-up. As the night stretched on, its silence began to feel more ominous, as if it were mocking her. Eventually, she got up and walked over to her dresser. Moogie, her childhood stuffed dog, was perched atop it, listing to one side, his brown-and-white fuzz worn but still soft. Even though she felt silly, she lifted him up and brought him back into bed with her.

She managed to doze off at some point, but at six A.M., a jackhammer erupted just outside her apartment. She staggered out of bed and closed her window, but the insistent sputtering continued.

"Shut that fucking thing off!" Nellie's neighbor bellowed, his words carrying through the radiator.

She pulled her pillow over her head, but it was futile.

She took a long shower, rolling her head around in circles to try to ease the ache in her neck, then put on her robe and rifled through her closet searching for her light blue dress with the little yellow flowers—it would be perfect for graduation—only to remember that it was still at the dry cleaner's, along with half a dozen other items.

Picking them up had been on the to-do list she'd scribbled on the back of a spin-class schedule, along with *Move books to Richard's storage bin* and *Buy bikini* and after *Change mailing address at post office*. She'd yet to make it to a spin class this month, either.

Her phone rang at seven on the dot.

"I got a deodorant commercial! I'm Sweaty Girl Three!"

"Josie?"

"I'm sorry, I'm sorry, I didn't want to call so early, but I've tried everyone else. Margot can do the first half of my shift. I just need someone to take over at two."

"Oh, I—"

"I'll have a line! I can get my SAG card after this!"

Nellie should have said no for so many reasons. Graduation wouldn't end until one. She still had to finish packing her things. And tonight was the dinner with Richard and Maureen.

But Josie was such a good friend. And she'd been trying to get her SAG card for two years.

"Okay, okay, break a leg. Or is it break a sweat?"

Josie laughed. "Love you!" she shouted.

Nellie rubbed her temples. A faint headache began to pulse between them.

She opened her laptop and typed herself an email with the subject line *TO DO!!!!!!*: *Dry cleaner, pack up books, Gibson's at 2, Maureen at 7.*

A ding announced she had new messages waiting: Linda, reminding the teachers to come in early to set up for graduation. An old sorority sister, Leslie, who still lived in Florida, congratulating her on her engagement. Nellie paused, then deleted that email without replying. Her aunt, asking if Nellie needed any last-minute wedding help. A notification that her automatic monthly charity donation was being deducted from her checking account. Then an email from the wedding photographer: *Should I refund your deposit or do you think you'll reschedule?*

Nellie frowned, the words making no sense. She reached for her cell phone and dialed the number at the bottom of his note.

The photographer picked up on the third ring, sounding sleepy.

"Hang on," he said when she asked about the email. "Let me go to my office."

She could hear his footsteps, then papers shuffling.

"Yeah. Here's the message. We got a call last week that the wedding was being postponed."

"What?" Nellie began to pace in her small bedroom, passing her wedding gown with every few steps. "Who called?"

"My assistant took the message. She told me it was you."

"I didn't call! And we haven't ever changed the date!" Nellie protested, sinking down on the bed.

"I'm sorry, but she's worked with me for almost two years, and nothing like this has ever happened before."

She and Richard had both wanted an intimate wedding with a small guest list. "If we do it in New York, I'd have to invite all my colleagues," Richard had said. He'd found a breathtaking resort in Florida not far from her mother's home—a white-columned building facing the ocean, encircled by palm trees and red and orange hibiscus—and was paying for the entire bill, including the guests' rooms, the food, and the wine. He was even picking up the airfare for Sam and Josie and Marnie.

When they viewed the photographer's website, Richard had admired the journalistic-style images: "Everyone else goes for the stiff posed shots. This guy captures emotion."

She'd been saving money for weeks, wanting the photographs to be her wedding gift to him.

"Look . . ." Her voice lilted the way it always did when she was on the verge of tears. Maybe the resort could find another photographer, but it wouldn't be the same. "I don't mean to be difficult, but this was clearly your mistake."

"I'm staring at the message right now. But hang on, let me check something. What time is your ceremony again?"

"Four o'clock. We were going to do pictures before, too."

"Well, I've already booked another shoot for three. But I'll work something out. It's an engagement portrait, so I bet they won't mind being bumped an hour or so."

"Thank you," Nellie breathed.

"Hey, I get it, it's your wedding day. Everything should be perfect."

Her hands shook as she hung up the phone. The assistant must have messed up and the photographer was covering for her, Nellie decided. She'd probably confused their ceremony with another couple's. But if the photographer hadn't emailed, blurry shots from her mother's cheap camera would have been the only pictures they would have had.

The photographer was right, she thought. Everything *should* be perfect.

Everything *would* be perfect. Except . . . She went to her top dresser drawer and pulled out a small satin pouch that held a light blue monogrammed handkerchief. It had been her father's, and since her dad wouldn't be able to walk her down the aisle, Nellie planned to wrap it around her bouquet. She wanted to feel his presence on that symbolic journey.

Her dad had been stoic. He hadn't cried even as he told her about his diagnosis of colon cancer. But when Nellie graduated from junior high school, she'd seen his eyes grow damp. "Thinking about all the things I'll miss," he'd said. He'd kissed the top of her head, and then the mist disappeared from his eyes, like a morning fog evaporating in the sun. Six months later, he was gone, too.

Nellie smoothed out the soft handkerchief, winding it through her fingers. She wished her father could have met Richard. Her dad would have approved, she was certain. "You done good," he would have said. "You done good."

She touched the handkerchief to her cheek, then put it back in the pouch.

She checked the clock on the kitchen stove. The dry cleaner would open at eight; graduation was at nine. If she left right now, she'd have just enough time to pick up the flowered dress, change, and make it to school to set up.

Nellie leaned against the bar, waiting for Chris to finish making the dirty martinis destined for Table 31, a group of lawyers celebrating a birthday. She fidgeted with the new bracelet on her wrist. The beads were thick and bright, fastened with a clumsy knot. Jonah had given it to her at graduation.

It was her table's third round, and it was almost six—the time she'd planned to leave. Nellie hadn't told Richard she was covering Josie's shift and couldn't be late to meet Maureen.

It had been slow at the restaurant initially. She'd chatted with a white-haired couple visiting from Ohio, recommending a great bagel place and suggesting they check out a new exhibit at the Met. They'd pulled out pictures of their five grandchildren and mentioned that the youngest was having trouble learning to read, so Nellie jotted down a list of books that might help.

"You're a doll," the woman had said, tucking the sheet of paper into her purse. Nellie had noticed the gold band on her left hand and wondered how it would feel, decades from now, to have photographs of her own grandchildren to show to new acquaintances. By then her engagement ring would surely feel as if it were a part of her, ingrained into her very skin, rather than the weighty, new object on her finger.

But toward the end of her shift, the restaurant was full of clusters of twenty- and thirtysomethings.

"Can you close out my tables?" Nellie asked Jim, another waiter, as he passed by the bar.

"How many do you have left?"

"Four. They don't want to eat, they're just parking."

"Damn, I'm in the weeds right now. Give me a few?"

She looked at her watch again. She'd been hoping to get home to take a shower and put on her black eyelet dress. She always smelled like french fries when she left Gibson's. But now she'd have to change back into the flowered sundress she'd worn for graduation.

She was about to lift up the tray of dirty martinis destined for the lawyers when someone draped an arm over her shoulders. She turned to see a tall guy who'd probably just turned twenty-one crowding in next to her. He was accompanied by a few friends, who emanated the rowdy energy of athletes before a big game. Normally groups of guys were her favorite customers; unlike women, they never asked for separate checks, and they tipped her well.

"How do we get in *your* section?" The guy was wearing a Sigma Chi T-shirt, the Greek letters close to her face.

She wrenched her eyes away. "Sorry, but I'm leaving in a few minutes." She ducked out from beneath his arm.

As she grabbed the drinks and spun away, she heard one of the guys say, "If I can't get in her section, how do I get in her pants?"

She fumbled the tray and it flipped, soaking her in gin and olive juice. Glasses shattered against the floor, and the guys burst into applause.

"Damn it!" Nellie cried, wiping her face with her sleeve.

"Wet T-shirt contest!" one of the guys hooted.

"Settle down, boys," Jim said to the guys. "You okay? I was just coming to say I could cover for you."

"I'm fine." A busboy approached with a broom as she hurried to the back office, holding her soaked shirt away from her chest. She grabbed her gym bag and went into the bathroom, peeling off her clothes and mopping her skin with a handful of paper towels. She wet another paper towel and rubbed herself down as best she could, then reached into her bag for her flowered dress. It was a little rumpled, but at least it was clean.

She stared at her image in the mirror, not seeing her flushed cheeks or messy hair.

She saw herself at the age of twenty-one, waking up in the sorority house the morning after everything had changed: her throat raw from crying, her body shivering despite her warm pajamas and quilt.

She exited the bathroom, planning to cut a wide berth around those assholes.

They were clustered in a circle by the bar, holding bottles of beer, laughing raucously.

"Aw, we didn't want to make you leave," one of the guys said. "Kiss and make up?" He held out his arms. His back was to the bar, as were the other guys'—probably so they could ogle the women in the room.

Nellie glared at him, wanting to throw a drink in his face. Why not? It wasn't as if she'd get fired.

But as she moved closer, she noticed something on the bar, just behind him. "Sure," she said sweetly. "I'll give you a hug."

Nellie plopped her gym bag on the bar, then leaned in and endured the feel of his body pressing against hers.

"Have a fun night, boys," she said, picking up her things.

She quickly hailed a cab. Once she was ensconced in the back, she opened the slim leather check holder she'd scooped up when she took her gym bag off the bar. The one with the edge of the credit card poking out of the top.

A block later, when the cab had stopped at a red light, she casually dropped it out the window, into a busy intersection.

CHAPTER
TWELVE

"WERE YOU AT SAKS?" Aunt Charlotte asks when I arrive home. "For some reason I thought you had the day off. . . . Anyway, a package came from FedEx. I put it in your room."

"Really?" I say, feigning interest as I skim past her question. I wasn't at work today. "I didn't order anything."

Aunt Charlotte is standing on a stool in the kitchen, reorganizing the cabinets. She steps down, leaving the bowls and mugs she has been sorting through lined up on the counter. "It's from Richard. I saw his name on the return address when I signed for it." She is staring at me, waiting for my reaction.

I keep my expression calm. "Probably just some things I left behind." She can't know how I feel about Richard and his engagement. I don't want her to blame herself later for not doing more to help me.

"I picked us up some salads for dinner." I hold up a white paper bag decorated with black letters and dancing greens. I've vowed to pitch in more. Besides, Chop't was a convenient stop. "I'll just stick these in the fridge and then go change." I'm desperate to open the box.

The package is waiting on my bed. My hands begin to tremble when I see the neatly printed numbers and letters written in all capitals. Richard used to leave me notes in that handwriting nearly every day before he left for work: *You are so beautiful when you're asleep.* Or, *I can't wait to make love to you tonight.*

The tenor of the notes changed as time passed. *Try to get some exercise today, sweetheart. It'll make you feel better.* And near the end of our marriage, the notes were replaced by emails: *I just phoned and you didn't answer. Are you sleeping again? We need to talk about this tonight.*

I use scissors to slice through the masking tape and open up my past.

Our wedding album is on top. I lift the heavy satin keepsake. Beneath it I see some of my clothes, neatly folded. When I left, I took mostly cold-weather outfits. Richard has sent ensembles suitable for summertime. He has selected the pieces that always looked the best on me.

At the bottom is a padded black jewelry box. I open it and see a diamond choker. It's the necklace I could never bear to wear because Richard gave it to me after one of our worst fights.

This isn't all I've left behind, of course. Richard probably donated the rest of my things to charity.

He knows I never cared much about clothes. What he really wanted me to have is the album and the necklace. But why?

There's no note in the box.

But he is sending me a message with its contents, I realize.

I open the album and stare at a young woman in a lacy gown with a full skirt, smiling up at Richard. I barely recognize myself; it's like looking at an image of a different person.

I wonder if his new fiancée will take his last name: Thompson. It is still my name, too.

I see her turning her face up to Richard as the minister unites them. She is beaming. Will he think of me briefly and remember how I looked in that moment, before he pushes the memory away? Does he ever call her my name by accident? Do they talk about me, the two of them, when they're cuddling in bed?

I pick up the album and hurl it across the room. It leaves a mark on the wall before it falls to the floor with a thud. My entire body is shaking now.

I've been putting on an act for Aunt Charlotte. But my costume can no longer camouflage what I've become.

I think of the liquor store down the street. I could buy a bottle or two. A drink might help douse the rage inside me.

I shove the box into my wardrobe, but now I'm imagining Richard lifting her chin and clasping a diamond choker around her neck, then leaning in to kiss her. I can't bear the image of his lips on her mouth, of his hands on her.

My time is running out.

I need to see her. I waited outside of her apartment for hours today, but she never appeared.

Is she scared? I wonder. *Does she sense what is coming?*

I elect to allow myself a final bottle of wine. I'll drink it and go over my plan again. But I choose to do one thing before going to the liquor store. And miraculously, because of that simple act, an unexpected chance drops into my lap.

I decide to call Maureen. Even after all these years, she is the person with whom Richard is the closest.

We haven't talked in a while. Our relationship began pleasantly enough, but during my marriage to her brother, her feelings toward me seemed to shift. She grew distant. I'm sure Richard confided in her. No wonder she was wary of me.

But early on, I tried to form an independent relationship with her. It seemed important to Richard that we be close. So I called her every week or two. But we quickly ran out of things to talk about. Maureen had a Ph.D. and ran the Boston Marathon each spring. She rarely drank, other than a single glass of champagne on special occasions, and she rose at five A.M. to practice the piano, an instrument she'd taken up as an adult.

Shortly after my wedding, I accompanied Maureen and Richard on the annual ski trip they took for her birthday. They whipped down black diamonds with ease, and I only held them up. I ended up leaving the slopes at lunchtime and curling up by the fireplace with a hot toddy until they returned, pink cheeked and exhilarated, to collect me for dinner. They always invited me to come, but I never joined them after that first trip, staying home while they went to Aspen or Vail, and on their week-long trip to Switzerland.

Now I dial her cell number.

She answers on the third ring: "Hang on a sec." Then I hear a muffled "Ninety-second and Lexington, please."

So she is in town already; she comes here in the summer to teach a course at Columbia.

"Vanessa? How are you?" Her tone is measured. Neutral.

"I'm okay," I lie. "How about you?"

"Fine."

One of my podcasts recounted a psychology experiment in which a researcher flashed different faces from a projector and students had to quickly identify the emotions portrayed. It was astonishing. In less than a second, with no clues but a subtle shifting of features, almost everyone could accurately differentiate between disgust and fear and surprise and joy. But I've always thought voices reveal just as much expression, that our brains are capable of deciphering and categorizing almost imperceptible nuances in tone.

Maureen wants nothing to do with me. She is going to end the call quickly.

"I was just wondering . . . could we meet for lunch tomorrow? Or coffee?"

Maureen exhales. "I'm a little busy now."

"I can come to you. I was wondering . . . the wedding. Is Richard—"

"Vanessa. Richard has moved on. You need to do the same."

I try again. "I just need to—"

"Please stop. Just stop. Richard told me you've been calling all the time. . . . Look, you're upset things ended between you two. But he's my brother."

"Have you met her?" I blurt. "He can't marry her. He doesn't love her—he can't—"

"I agree it's very sudden." Maureen's voice is kinder when she speaks again. "And I know it's hard to see him with another woman. To think of him with anyone but you. But Richard has moved on."

Then the last, frayed thread tying me to Richard is severed with the click of the phone.

I stand there, feeling numb. Maureen was always protective of Richard. I wonder if she'll befriend his new bride, if the two of them will go to lunch . . .

Then clarity sweeps through my cloudy brain like an arcing windshield wiper. Ninety-second and Lexington. That's where Sfoglia is. Richard used to love that restaurant. It's almost seven o'clock—dinnertime.

Maureen must have been giving the address to a cabdriver. The restaurant is a long way from Columbia, but it's close to Richard's apartment. Could she be going to meet him—*them*—there?

I have to get her alone, where Richard can't see.

If I leave now, maybe I can be waiting on the corner when she arrives. If not, I can ask for a table by the ladies' room and follow her if she uses it.

Two minutes is all I require.

I glance at my reflection in the beveled glass mirror beside my armoire. Although I must get there quickly, I need to appear presentable so I blend in. I take a moment to brush my hair and apply my lipstick, belatedly realizing the shade is too dark for my chalky complexion. I dab concealer under my eyes and smooth on blush.

As I locate my keys, I call out to tell Aunt Charlotte that I need to dash out for an errand. I don't wait for her response before I hurry out the door. The elevator is too slow, so I spiral down the stairs, my purse banging against my side. Inside it is everything I need.

The streets are clogged with traffic. It's rush hour. No buses are in sight. Maybe a cab? As I head toward the East Side, I scan the yellow vehicles, but they all seem full. It's a twenty-minute walk. So I break into a run.

THIRTEEN

By the end of the taxi ride, Nellie had pushed away the oppressive sensation of the frat guys' touching her. It wasn't too difficult; she'd long ago learned to compartmentalize the sorts of feelings they'd conjured in her. Still, she wanted to take a moment alone in the restaurant bathroom. She suspected she could use a fresh swipe of lip gloss, not to mention a spritz of perfume.

However, when she arrived, the maître d' informed her another woman was waiting at her table. "Shall I take your bag?"

Nellie relinquished the electric-blue-and-yellow Nike satchel containing her damp uniform, feeling like a rube. She wondered if she was supposed to tip him. She'd have to ask Richard; she was far more familiar with restaurants that featured a hostess offering oversize menus along with crayon packets for children.

Nellie was led through the bar area, past a silver-haired man in a tuxedo playing a grand piano, then through the high-ceilinged dining room. Her stomach clenched. Maureen was sixteen years her senior and a college professor, and here was Nellie, a slightly disheveled preschool teacher who smelled like a deep fryer.

This introduction couldn't have come on a worse night.

But the moment Nellie saw Maureen, she exhaled. Richard's sister looked like the photonegative of him. Her hair was cut in a classic bob, and she wore a simple pantsuit. She was peering at *The Economist* through reading glasses, biting her lower lip the way Richard always did when he was concentrating.

"Hi!" Nellie said, leaning over to give Maureen a hug. "Was that weird? I just feel like we are going to be sisters . . . and I've never had a sister."

Maureen smiled and tucked her magazine into her purse. "It's wonderful to meet you."

"I'm sorry I look like a mess." Nellie slid into the chair across from Maureen, feeling chatty, a side effect of the tension that had been brewing inside her. "I just came from work."

"At the preschool?"

Nellie shook her head. "I waitress, too . . . or I did. I actually quit. I was just covering for a friend. I'm a little frazzled because I was worried I'd be late."

"Well, you look just fine to me." Maureen was still smiling, but her next words caught Nellie off guard. "And you're totally Richard's type."

Hadn't Richard's ex been a brunette? "What do you mean?" Nellie reached for the bread basket. The last thing she'd consumed was a banana on the way to graduation more than ten hours ago. On the table rested a shallow bowl of olive oil topped with a floating purple flourish of vinegar and a sprig of thyme. She tore off a small piece of a roll and tried to delicately dip it without ruining the ornamentation.

"Oh, you know. Sweet. Pretty." Maureen folded her hands and leaned forward.

Richard had said Maureen was honest almost to a fault; it was one of the things he most appreciated about her. Maureen's remark wasn't intended to sound demeaning, Nellie told herself—no one would consider being called sweet and pretty an insult.

"Tell me all about yourself," Maureen said. "Richard mentioned you're from Florida?"

"Um-hmm . . . But I should be asking *you* questions, like what Richard was like when he was younger. Share a story he wouldn't have told me." The roll was warm and studded with herbs, and Nellie gobbled another bite.

"Oh, where to begin?"

Before Maureen could say anything more, Nellie caught sight of Richard heading to their table, his eyes fixed on her. She hadn't seen him since he tucked her into bed after her bachelorette party. Without hesitating, he bent down and gave her a kiss on the lips. *It's really okay,* she thought. *He has forgiven me.*

"Sorry." He gave his sister a quick peck on the cheek. "Flight was delayed."

"Actually, you're too early. Maureen was just about to tell me all of your deep, dark secrets," Nellie joked.

As soon as Nellie spoke, she saw Richard's features briefly tighten, then he smiled. She expected him to come back around the table to sit next to her, but he took the chair to Maureen's right, diagonally across from Nellie.

"Right, all those controversial summers at the golf course at the club." Richard shook out his napkin and placed it in his lap. "And there was that incident when I was elected vice president of the debating team."

"Shameful," Maureen joined in. She brushed a piece of lint off Richard's lapel. It struck Nellie as a maternal gesture. Even though Richard was an orphan, at least he had a big sister who clearly adored him.

"I bet you looked cute in your preppy golf outfits," Nellie said.

Instead of replying, Richard gestured for the waiter. "I'm starving. But first we need drinks."

"Sparkling water with lemon, please," Maureen told the waiter.

"Could I get the wine list for my fiancée?" Richard winked at Nellie. "I've never known you to turn down a drink."

Nellie laughed but was aware of how this might sound to Maureen. Nellie had been concerned about the odor of grease. But had she smelled like gin when she greeted Richard's sister?

"Just a glass of Pinot Grigio, thanks." Nellie tried to cover her embarrassment by dipping the last bite of her bread into the tangy olive oil.

"I'll have a Highland Park on the rocks," Richard said.

There was a little pause after the waiter left, then Nellie blurted, "I came here straight from Gibson's. Some idiot spilled a drink on me. My wet uniform is in my gym bag, so . . ." Was she babbling again?

"I thought you quit," Richard said.

"I did. I was just covering for Josie. She landed her first commercial and couldn't find anyone else. . . ." Nellie let her words trail off, unsure of why she felt the need to explain.

When the waiter brought their beverages, Richard lifted his toward Maureen. "How's your hamstring?"

"Getting better. A few more physical-therapy sessions and I should be able to get back to my longer runs."

"Were you injured?" Nellie asked.

"Just a pulled muscle. It's been bothering me off and on since the marathon."

"I could never run a marathon!" Nellie said. "Three miles and I'm done. That's really impressive."

"It's not for everyone," Maureen joked. "Just us type A's."

Nellie reached into the bread basket and pulled out another roll, then put it back, realizing no one else was eating any. She tried to discreetly brush away the crumbs around her plate.

"I enjoyed your article on gender stratification and intersection theory," Richard said to Maureen. "Interesting angle. What's the reaction been like?"

As they talked, Nellie nodded and smiled and fiddled with the beads on Jonah's bracelet, but couldn't find a way to contribute to the conversation.

She glanced at the surrounding tables and saw a flash of green as a waiter scooped up a credit card sitting atop a silver tray.

It made her think of the AmEx she'd dropped out the taxi window. By now that card was hopefully in the hands of a thief making the rounds at Best Buy and P.C. Richard. Or better yet, a poor mother stocking up on food for her children.

She was relieved when their server delivered their entrées so she could pretend to focus on her chicken and couscous.

Maureen seemed to notice and turned to Nellie. "Early education is so important. What drew you to it?" Maureen elegantly twirled her tagliatelle on her fork and took a bite.

"I've always loved children."

Nellie felt Richard's leg touch hers beneath the table. "Ready to be an aunt?" he asked Maureen.

"Absolutely."

Nellie wondered why Maureen had never married or had children. Richard had told Nellie he thought she intimidated men because she was so intelligent. And, Nellie supposed, she'd been a mother to Richard already.

Maureen looked at Nellie. "Richard was an adorable baby. He learned to read when he was barely four."

"I can't take all the credit for that. She's the one who taught me."

"Well, we've already picked out your guest room," Nellie said. "You'll have to come visit all the time."

"And likewise. I'll show you around my town. Have you ever been to Boston?"

Nellie had just taken a forkful of couscous, so she shook her head and swallowed as quickly as possible. "I haven't traveled much. Only to a few states in the South."

She didn't elaborate or explain that she'd only driven through them when she left Florida for New York. The thousand-mile trip had taken two days; she'd wanted to put her hometown behind her as quickly as possible.

Maureen spoke fluent French, Nellie recalled, and guest-taught at the Sorbonne a few years ago.

"Nellie just got her first passport," Richard said. "I can't wait to show her Europe."

Nellie smiled at him gratefully.

They chatted a bit about the wedding—Maureen mentioned that she loved to swim and couldn't wait to take a dip in the ocean—then, after the waiter cleared their plates, Maureen and Richard declined dessert, so Nellie pretended she was too full for the blood-orange mousse she secretly craved. Richard had just stood up to pull back Nellie's chair when she exclaimed, "Oh, Maureen, I nearly forgot. I have something for you."

It had been an impulse buy. Nellie had been walking through the Union Square market the previous week when she saw a vendor displaying jewelry. A necklace had caught her eye. Its light purple and blue glass beads were suspended by gossamer-thin silver wire, so they appeared to be floating. The clasp was fashioned to look like a butterfly. She couldn't imagine anyone not feeling joy when it was fastened around her neck.

Richard had asked if Maureen could be Nellie's maid of honor, and even though she would've preferred Samantha, she'd said yes. Because the wedding was so small, Maureen was going to be their only attendant. Maureen was planning to wear a violet dress. The necklace would look perfect against it.

The artist had nestled the necklace into a fluffy cotton bed in a brown cardboard box (recycled, she'd explained) and tied a bow around it with a ropy string. Nellie hoped Maureen would like it and also hoped Richard would understand it was more than a necklace. It was a gesture that meant Nellie wanted to be close to his sister, too.

She reached into her purse for the small box. Two of the corners were slightly bent and the bow had wilted.

Maureen carefully unwrapped the present. "It's charming." She lifted it up to show Richard.

"I thought you could wear it at the wedding," Nellie said.

Maureen immediately put it on, despite the fact that it clashed with her gold earrings. "How thoughtful."

Richard squeezed Nellie's hand. "Sweet."

But Nellie dipped her head so they wouldn't see the blush staining her cheeks. She knew the truth. The necklace that had looked craftsy and pretty just last week suddenly appeared flimsy and a little childish around Maureen's neck.

CHAPTER
FOURTEEN

I HURRY ACROSS TOWN, ignoring the man who tries to shove a flyer into my hand. My legs feel shaky, but I press on toward the entrance to Central Park.

I make it to the next crosswalk just as the light blinks red, and I stand on the corner, breathing hard. Maureen is probably at the restaurant by now. Richard would have ordered a nice wine; savory bread would be placed on the table. Perhaps the three of them are clinking glasses, toasting to the future. Under the table, Richard's hand might be squeezing his fiancée's. His hands always felt so strong when they were on me.

The light turns and I bolt across the street.

We went to Sfoglia many times together—until one night when we abruptly stopped.

I remember that evening so vividly. It was snowing and I'd marveled at the way the fat white flakes had transformed the city, dusting the streets, erasing the rough edges and grime. Richard would be coming from the office and had asked me to meet him at the restaurant. I'd stared out the taxi window, smiling as I caught sight of a little boy in a striped hat sticking out his tongue to catch a taste of winter. I'd felt a yearning tug in my chest; Dr. Hoffman still couldn't pinpoint why I hadn't been able to get pregnant, and I had just scheduled another round of tests.

Richard had called as my taxi pulled up in front of the restaurant. "I'm running a few minutes late."

"Okay. I guess you're worth waiting for."

I heard his deep chuckle, then I paid the driver and exited the cab. I stood on the sidewalk for a moment, absorbing the energy. I always looked forward to meeting Richard in the city.

I made my way to the bar, where there was one open stool. I ordered a mineral water and eavesdropped on the conversations around me.

"He's going to call," the young woman to my right reassured her friend.

"What if he doesn't?" her friend asked.

"Well, you know what they say: The best way to get over one guy is to get under another."

The women burst into laughter.

I hadn't seen my girlfriends much lately; it had made me miss them. They still worked full-time, and on the weekends, when they went out and commiserated about the men they were seeing, I was always with Richard.

After a few minutes, the bartender set a glass of white wine down in front of me. "Compliments of the gentleman at the end of the bar."

I looked over and saw a man lift his cocktail in my direction. I remember raising the wineglass with my left hand, hoping he'd see my wedding ring, and taking a tiny sip before pushing it away.

"Not a fan of Pinot Grigio?" a voice asked a few moments later. The guy was short but muscular, with curly hair. The opposite of Richard.

"No, it's good . . . thanks. I'm just waiting for my husband." I took another sip to remove any potential sting from my rebuff.

"If you were my wife, I wouldn't keep you waiting in a bar. You never know who might hit on you."

I laughed, still holding on to the glass of wine.

I glanced at the door and locked eyes with Richard. I saw him take it all in—the man, the wine, my high-pitched, nervous giggle—then he came toward me.

"Honey!" I cried, standing up.

"I thought you'd be at the table. I hope they're still holding it for us."

The curly-haired man melted away as Richard signaled the hostess.

"Do you want to take your glass of wine with you?" she asked.

I shook my head mutely.

"I wasn't really drinking it," I whispered to Richard as we walked to the table.

His jaw tightened. He didn't respond.

I'm so lost in the memory that I don't even realize I've stepped into traffic until someone grabs my arm and yanks me back. A second later a delivery truck speeds past, blaring its horn.

I wait on the corner for another moment, until the light turns green. I imagine Richard ordering the squid ink pasta for his new love, telling her she has to try it. I see him half rise when she excuses herself to go to the restroom. I wonder if Maureen will lean toward Richard with an approving nod that says, *She's better than your last one.*

On the night when the stranger bought me a glass of wine and I'd taken a few sips to avoid being rude, our meal had been ruined. The restaurant was so charming, with its exposed brick wall and intimate rooms, but Richard barely talked to me. I tried to make conversation, to comment on the food, to ask him about his day, but after a while, I stopped.

When he finally spoke, after I'd pushed away my plate of half-eaten pasta, his words felt like a hard pinch.

"That guy in college, the one who got you pregnant. Are you still in touch with him?"

"What?" I gasped. "Richard, no . . . I haven't talked to him in years."

"What else haven't you told me?"

"I don't—nothing!" I stuttered.

His tone was incongruous with our elegant surroundings and the smiling server approaching with the dessert menu. "Who was that guy you were flirting with at the bar?"

My cheeks heated up at the fresh accusation. I realized his words had been taken in by the couple at the next table, and they were now looking at us.

"I don't know who he was. He bought me a drink. That was it."

"And you drank it." Richard's lips tightened and his eyes narrowed. "Even though it might hurt our baby."

"There is no baby! Richard, why are you so angry with me?"

"Anything else you want to reveal while we're learning more about each other, sweetheart?"

I blinked against the sharp sting of tears, then I abruptly pushed back my chair, the wooden legs scraping against the floor. I grabbed my coat and fled into the still-falling snow.

I stood outside, tears streaming down my cheeks, wondering where I could go.

Then he appeared. "I'm sorry, honey." I knew he truly meant it. "I had a horrible day. I should never have taken it out on you."

He reached out his arms, and after a moment, I leaned into them.

He stroked my hair, and my sobs dissolved into a loud hiccup. He laughed quietly then. "My love." All the venom had disappeared from his tone, replaced by a velvety tenderness.

"I'm sorry, too." My voice was muffled because my head was pressed against his chest.

After that night, we never went back to Sfoglia.

I'm almost there now. I've crossed the park and have just three more blocks to travel. My chest feels tight. I'm gasping. I yearn to sit down, just for a minute, but I can't miss my chance to see her.

I force myself to run faster, to avoid the subway grates that want to snag at my heels, to weave around the hunched-over man with the cane. Then I reach the restaurant.

I throw open the door and hurry down the narrow entranceway, past the hostess stand. "Hello," the young woman holding menus calls after me, but I ignore her. I scan the bar area and the people sitting at tables. They aren't here. But there's another room, and it's where Richard prefers to sit because it's quieter.

"Can I help you?" The hostess has followed me.

I rush toward the back room, stumbling down a step and grabbing at the wall to steady myself. I look at each table, then check again.

"Was a dark-haired man here with a young blond woman?" I'm panting. "There might have been a second woman with them, too."

The hostess blinks and takes a step back, away from me. "We've had a lot of people come through tonight. I don't—"

"The reservations!" I almost shout. "Please check. . . . Richard Thompson! Or it might be under his sister's name—Maureen Thompson!"

Someone else approaches. A heavyset man in a navy suit, his brow furrowed. I see the hostess exchange a look with him.

He takes me by the arm. "Why don't we go outside? We don't want to disturb the other diners."

"Please! I have to know where they are!"

The man walks me toward the exit, his grip firm.

I feel myself start to shake. *Richard, please don't marry her. . . .*

Have I said it aloud? The restaurant is suddenly silent. People are staring.

I'm too late. But how is that possible? There wouldn't have been time for them to eat. I try to recall Maureen's instructions to the cabdriver. Could she have said something else entirely? Or did my mind betray me by telling me what I wanted to hear?

The man in the suit deposits me on the street corner. I'm crying again, my sobs raw and uncontrollable. But this time, no arms are around me. No gentle hands stroking my hair away from my face.

I'm completely alone.

CHAPTER
FIFTEEN

NELLIE THOUGHT SHE'D BEEN in love once before, back in college. In the evening he'd drive up around the corner from her sorority house and she'd run across the quad to meet him, the grass spongy under her feet, the air warm against her bare legs. He'd pull a soft cotton blanket out of the back of his old Alfa Romeo and shake it out onto the beach, then pass her a flask of bourbon. She'd put her mouth where his had been moments earlier as the amber liquid heated a trail down her throat and into her belly.

After the sun sank, they'd pull off their clothes and race into the ocean, then wrap up in the blanket. She loved the taste of salt on his skin.

He quoted poetry and pointed out constellations in the night sky. He was addictively inconsistent, phoning her three times in a day, then ignoring her for a weekend.

None of it had been real.

It didn't bother her when he disappeared for a day or two at a time—until that night in October when she needed him. She'd called him over and over, leaving increasingly urgent messages. But he never answered.

Days later he showed up holding a cheap bouquet of carnations, and she let him comfort her. She hated him for failing her. She hated herself more for crying when he said he had to go.

She'd be smarter the next time, she'd vowed. She'd never again be with a man who'd look away when she started to fall.

But Richard did more than that.

Somehow, he caught her before she even realized she was about to stumble.

"Maureen's terrific," Nellie told Richard as they strolled hand in hand toward his apartment.

"I can tell she liked you a lot." Richard squeezed her hand.

They chattered a while longer, then Richard pointed at the gelato shop across the street. "I know you secretly wanted dessert."

"My heart says yes but my diet says no," Nellie moaned.

"It was your last day of work, right? You deserve to celebrate. How was graduation?"

"Linda asked me to give a little talk. I got choked up at the end of it, and Jonah thought I was having trouble reading my notes. So he shouted, 'Just sound it out! You can do it!'"

Richard laughed and leaned in to kiss her just as her cell phone erupted with *"When the sun shines, we'll shine together."* Rihanna's "Umbrella"—the ringtone she'd assigned to Sam.

"Aren't you going to answer?" Richard didn't seem irritated the moment had been interrupted, so Nellie did.

"Hey, are you coming back here tonight?" Sam asked.

"I wasn't planning on it. What's up?"

"Some woman came to check out the apartment. She said she heard I was looking for a new roommate. After she left, I couldn't find my keys."

"You left them inside a grocery bag a few weeks ago and almost threw them away."

"But I've looked everywhere. She was outside the apartment when I came home, and I swear I put them right back in my purse."

Not until Richard whispered, "Everything okay?" did Nellie realize she'd stopped walking.

"What did she look like?" she blurted.

"Totally normal. Thin, dark hair, a little older than us, but she said she was newly single and was starting over. It was so dumb, but I had to pee desperately and she kept asking all these questions, like she really wanted it. She was only alone in the kitchen for two seconds."

Nellie cut her off. "Are you by yourself now?"

"Yeah, but I'm going to have Cooper come over and stay the night just in case. I'll have him drag something over to block the door. Shit, it's going to cost a fortune to get a locksmith here. . . ."

"What is it?" Richard whispered.

"Hang on," Nellie told Sam.

Richard pulled out his cell phone before Nellie had even finished recounting the story. "Diane?" Nellie recognized the name of his long-time secretary, a competent woman in her sixties whom she'd met on several occasions. "I'm sorry to bother you at this hour. . . . I know, I know, you always tell me that. . . . Yeah, a personal one—can you get an emergency locksmith over to re-key an apartment as soon as possible tonight? . . . No, not mine. . . . Sure, let me give you the address. . . . Whatever it costs. Thank you. Come in late tomorrow if you'd like."

He hung up and tucked the phone back into his pocket.

"Sam?" Nellie said into her receiver.

"I heard him. Wow . . . that was really nice. Please tell him thanks."

"I will. Call me when the locksmith comes." Nellie hung up.

"There are a lot of crazy people in New York," Richard said.

"I know," Nellie whispered.

"But odds are Sam misplaced them again." Richard's voice had the same soothing cadence as when they'd first met on the airplane. "Why would she have taken the keys and not Sam's wallet?"

"You're right." Nellie hesitated. "But Richard . . . all those hang-ups I've been getting?"

"Only three."

"There was another one. Not exactly the same, but a woman called your apartment after you left for Atlanta. I thought it was you, so I answered without thinking. . . . She wouldn't leave her name, and I—"

"Sweetheart, that was just Ellen from the office. She reached me on my cell phone."

"Oh." Nellie's body sagged with the release of tension. "I thought—I mean, it was a Sunday, so . . ."

Richard kissed the tip of her nose. "Gelato. Then Sam will probably call to say she found her keys in the refrigerator."

"You're right." Nellie laughed.

Richard moved to take the side next to the curb, between her and traffic, as he always did. He wrapped his arm around her and they continued walking.

After Sam called to say the locksmith had come and gone, Nellie went to the bathroom to change into her gauzy sleeveless nightgown and brush her teeth. Richard was already in bed, wearing his boxer briefs. As she climbed in next to him, she noticed the silver-framed photograph on his nightstand was tilted away so it faced the wall. It was a picture of her sitting on a bench in Central Park wearing jean shorts and a tank top; Richard always said he liked to see her when he woke up on mornings when she wasn't there.

Richard noticed, too, and reached to turn it back around. "The maid was here."

He picked up the remote and turned off the television, then pressed his body against hers. At first she thought his touch meant what it usually meant when he reached for her under the sheets. But then he released her and rolled onto his back.

"I need to tell you something." His tone was serious.

"Okay," Nellie said slowly.

"I didn't play golf until I was in my twenties."

She couldn't see his face in the darkness. "So . . . those summers at the club?"

He exhaled. "I was a caddy. A waiter. A lifeguard. I carried clubs.

I picked up wet towels. When kids ordered hot dogs that cost as much as I made in an hour, I served them. I hated that fucking club. . . ."

Nellie traced her fingers down his arm, smoothing the dark hairs under her fingertips. She'd never heard him sound so vulnerable before. "I'd always assumed you'd grown up with money."

"I told you my dad was in finance. He was an accountant. He did the taxes for the neighborhood plumbers and handymen."

She remained silent, not wanting to interrupt.

"Maureen got a college scholarship, then helped pay for me to go." Richard's body felt rigid under her touch. "I lived with her to save money, and I took out a lot of loans. And I worked my ass off."

She sensed Richard hadn't shared this part of himself with many people.

They lay together in silence for a few minutes as Nellie slowly became aware that Richard's revelation pieced together something for her.

His manners were so flawless they seemed almost choreographed. Dropped into any conversation, he could hold his own—whether he was talking to a cabdriver or a Philharmonic violinist at a charity event. He knew how to wield silverware gracefully and change the oil in his car. His nightstand held magazines ranging from *ESPN* to *The New Yorker* as well as a stack of biographies. She'd thought he was a chameleon, the sort of person who could effortlessly fit in anywhere.

But he must have taught himself those skills—or perhaps Maureen had taught him some of them.

"Your mother?" Nellie asked. "I know she was a homemaker. . . ."

"Yeah. Well, a Virginia Slims smoker and soap opera watcher, too." It could have been a joke, except no humor was in his tone. "My mom never went to college. Maureen was the one who helped me with homework. She pushed me; she told me I was smart enough to do anything I put my mind to. I owe her everything."

"But your parents—they loved you." Nellie thought of the photographs on Richard's wall. She knew his parents had died in the car crash when he was just fifteen and that he'd gone to live with Maureen then, but she hadn't realized how deeply formative a role his big sister had played in his life.

"Sure," he said. Nellie was about to ask more about his parents, but Richard's voice stopped her. "I'm beat. Let's drop this, okay?"

Nellie laid her head on his chest. "Thank you for telling me." Knowing he'd struggled—that he'd been a waiter, too, and hadn't always been sure of himself—conjured feelings of tenderness in her.

He was so quiet she thought he'd fallen asleep, but then he flipped over on top of her and began to kiss her, his tongue slipping between her lips as his knee spread apart her legs.

She wasn't ready for him and sucked in a breath as he entered her, but didn't ask him to stop. He pressed his face into her neck, his arms on either side of her head. He finished quickly and lay on top of her, breathing hard.

"I love you," Nellie said softly.

She wasn't sure if he'd heard, but then he lifted his head and kissed her gently on the lips.

"Do you know what I thought the first time I saw you, my Nellie?" He smoothed back her hair.

She shook her head.

"You were smiling down at a little boy in the airport; you looked like an angel. And I thought you could save me."

"Save you?" she echoed.

His words were a whisper: "From myself."

CHAPTER

SIXTEEN

YEARS AGO, SHORTLY AFTER I'd first moved to New York, I was walking to work, taking in the sights: towering buildings, snatches of conversations in multiple languages, yellow taxis darting through the streets, and calls from vendors hawking everything from pretzels to fake Gucci purses. Then the flow of foot traffic abruptly stopped. Through the crowd, I could see a few police officers gathered ahead, near a gray blanket someone had left crumpled on the sidewalk. An ambulance idled at the curb.

"A jumper," someone said. "Must've just happened."

I realized then the blanket covered a shattered body.

I'd stood there for a minute, feeling as if it was somehow disrespectful to cross the street and walk past the scene, even though the police were directing us to do so. Then I saw a shoe by the curb. A low-heeled, sensible blue pump, lying on its side, its sole slightly worn. The kind of shoe a woman might reach for to wear to a job that required her to dress professionally but also be on her feet for long stretches. A bank teller, maybe, or desk clerk at a hotel. A police officer was bending down to place the shoe in a plastic bag.

I couldn't stop thinking about that shoe, or the woman it belonged to. She must have gotten up that morning, gotten dressed, and stepped out of a window into the air.

I searched the newspapers the following day, but there was only a tiny mention of the incident. I never knew what had made her commit such a desperate act—if she'd been planning it, or if something inside her had suddenly snapped.

I think I've figured out the answer, all these years later: It was both. Because something inside me has finally cracked open, but I've come to realize I've also been heading toward this moment all along. The phone calls, the watching, the other things I've done . . . I've been circling around my replacement, drawing closer to her, assessing her. Preparing.

Her life with Richard is beginning. My life feels as if it is ending.

Soon she will step into her white dress. She will smooth makeup over her clear young skin. She will wear something borrowed and something blue. The musicians will lift their instruments to serenade her as she slowly makes her way down the aisle, toward the only man I ever truly loved. Once she and Richard look into each other's eyes and say "I do," there will be no point of return.

I must stop the wedding.

It is now four A.M. I haven't slept. I've been staring at the clock, going over what I need to do, playing out the various scenarios.

She hasn't moved out of her apartment yet. I've checked.

I will be waiting to intercept her today.

I imagine her eyes widening, her hands flying up to protect herself.

It's too late! I yearn to scream at her. *You should have stayed away from my husband!*

When it's finally light outside, I rise and go to my armoire, and without hesitation I select Richard's favorite emerald silk dress. He loved the way it brought it out the green in my eyes. Once it hugged my body, but now it is so loose I clasp a slim gold chain-link belt around my waist to cinch it. With a precision I have not attempted in years I apply my makeup, taking time to blend my foundation, curl my lashes, and apply two coats of mascara. Then I remove the new tube of Clinique lip gloss from my purse and run the sticky, soft pink wand over my lips. I slip on my highest pair of nude heels so my legs look long and lean. I text Lucille that I will be out today, aware that her response will almost certainly be that I should not come in ever again.

I have one stop to make before I go to her apartment. I've booked an early appointment at the Serge Normant salon on the Upper East Side. I will be finished and at her place in plenty of time.

It wasn't difficult to find her schedule; I know what her plans are for today. I slip out quietly, without leaving a note for Aunt Charlotte.

When I arrive at the salon, the colorist greets me. I see her eyes go to my roots, which I never did touch up. "What are you looking for today?"

I hand her a picture of a beautiful young woman and tell her to match the warm, buttery shade.

The colorist looks from the photo to me and back again. "Is this you?"

"Yes," I say.

CHAPTER
SEVENTEEN

Soon the musicians would play Pachelbel's Canon as she walked down the aisle with her father's handkerchief—something blue—wrapped around a bouquet of white roses. "Have and hold . . . honor and cherish . . . till death do you part," the minister would say.

Nellie was leaving for the airport in a few hours. She tucked her new red bikini into one of her two suitcases and checked her to-do list. Her wedding gown had been shipped ahead to the resort by FedEx, and the concierge had confirmed its arrival. Her toiletries were all that remained to pack.

Faint white rectangles showed on the walls where her pictures had hung. She was leaving behind her bed, dresser, and a lamp. Sam had a lead on a new roommate, a Pilates instructor who was coming by tomorrow. If the new roommate didn't want Nellie's furniture, she had promised she'd arrange to have the items hauled away. "I'm going to pay rent until someone else moves in, too," she'd insisted.

She could tell Sam didn't want to accept the offer, especially since Richard was paying for her trip to Florida and had just covered the cost of the locksmith.

Nellie knew Sam couldn't afford the apartment on her own. "Come on," Nellie had said as Sam sat on Nellie's bed, watching her finish packing. "It's only fair."

"Thanks." Sam had given Nellie a quick, hard squeeze. "I hate good-byes."

"I'll see you in a few days," Nellie protested.

"That's not what I mean."

Nellie nodded. "I know."

A moment later, Sam was gone.

As Nellie wrote out that month's rent check, the phone rang. She'd been staring at her signature, realizing she might never again sign her old last name. *Mr. and Mrs. Thompson,* she thought. It sounded so dignified.

Nellie checked caller ID before answering. "Hey, Mom."

"Hi, lovey, just wanted to double-check your flight number. It's American, right?"

"Yeah. Hang on." Nellie opened her laptop and scrolled down through her emails to find the airline's confirmation, then read the information aloud. "It gets in at seven-fifteen."

"Will you have had dinner?"

"Only if you consider a package of peanuts a meal."

"I can cook for you."

"Let's keep it simple—why don't we just pick up something on the way home? . . . By the way, did you pick out your spa treatments yet? Richard booked us massages and facials, but you need to let them know if you want a deep-tissue or Swedish or whatever. . . . Did you see the brochure he emailed you?"

"He doesn't need to do that for me. You know I have trouble sitting still for those kinds of things."

It was true; Nellie's mom's preferred form of relaxation would be taking a walk on the beach at sunset, rather than lying facedown on a masseuse's table. But Richard hadn't known that. He'd wanted to do something special. How could Nellie tell him her mother had rejected his gesture?

"Try it. I bet you'll like it more than you think."

"Just sign me up for whatever you're getting."

Nellie knew she was far from the only daughter who chafed at what seemed to be veiled maternal barbs. "So much processed sugar," her mother had murmured the last time Nellie ate a bag of Skittles in front of her, and she'd asked more than once how Nellie could stand the "claustrophobia" of Manhattan.

"Please at least act excited about it in front of Richard."

"Lovey, you seem so concerned by what he thinks all the time."

"I'm not concerned. I'm appreciative! He's so good to me."

"Did he ask if you wanted to spend the day before your wedding getting a facial?"

"What? Why does that even matter?" Only Nellie's mother could get her so riled up about a stupid spa treatment. No, not stupid! It was Richard's gift.

"Let me just say something. You've told me that facials make you break out. Why wouldn't you tell that to Richard? And he bought a house you hadn't even seen. Do you want to live in the suburbs?"

Nellie exhaled through her teeth but her mother continued, "I'm sorry, but he seems like he has such a strong personality."

"You've only met him once!" Nellie protested.

"You're still so young, though. I'm worried you might fade away. . . . I know you love him, but please stay true to yourself, too."

Nellie was not going to do this; she'd walk away from the fight her mother seemed determined to pick. "I have to finish packing. But I'll see you in a few hours." *After some wine on the plane has fortified me.*

Nellie hung up the phone and went into the bathroom to gather up her toiletries. She arranged her cosmetics, toothpaste, and lotions in her travel kit, then glanced in the mirror above the sink. Despite the fact that she hadn't been sleeping, her skin looked perfect.

She strode back into the bedroom, picked up the phone, and called the resort's salon to cancel her facial. "Can I get a seaweed body wrap instead?"

She was only spending a few days with her mother before Richard would fly down and they headed to the resort for the wedding; she'd be able to get through it. Plus, Sam and her aunt would be flying in a day early and could help serve as buffers.

She laid the toiletry kit in the still-open suitcase and tried to close it. But she could barely zip it halfway.

"Dammit!" She tried to force down the lid.

The problem was, she still had no idea where they'd be going for the honeymoon. She'd guessed someplace tropical because of Richard's comment about the bikini, but even warm-weather islands could turn chilly at night. She'd packed casual dresses, beach cover-ups, athletic wear, a few evening outfits in case there was a dress code, as well as heels and flip-flops.

She'd have to start over. She began pulling out of her suitcase all the items she'd carefully folded. Three fancy outfits instead of four, she decided, also tossing one of the pairs of heels into the brown packing box by her closet. And the floppy beach hat that had looked so cute in the J.Crew catalog might not make the cut.

She should've figured this out sooner; her plane was leaving in three hours and Richard was on his way to pick her up and drive her to the airport. She refolded her clothes and managed to fit everything but the floppy hat in her bag. She stuck it on top of the dresser; she'd leave it for Sam. Now she just needed to double-check that she hadn't forgotten anything, since she wouldn't be returning to her apartment again, and—

Her father's handkerchief.

A few mesh pockets lined the inside of her suitcase, and she was certain she'd tucked it into one. But she hadn't seen it when she'd unpacked the bag.

She unzipped her suitcase again and felt around for the soft pouch, her movements growing frantic.

All her clothes were getting wrinkled, but she shoved them aside to grope inside the mesh pockets. She couldn't find the pouch; her socks and bras and panties were still there, but nothing else.

She sat on the edge of her bed and dropped her head into her hands. She'd packed most of her things a few nights ago. She'd been so conscious of that blue square of fabric; it was the one irreplaceable item she was bringing for the wedding.

A knock on her open bedroom door made her gasp. Her head jerked up.

"Nellie?"

It was only Richard.

She hadn't heard him come in; he must have used the new key she'd given him.

"I can't find my dad's handkerchief!" she cried.

"Where did you last see it?"

"In my suitcase. But it isn't there anymore. I tore everything apart, and we have to leave for the airport, and if I can't—"

Richard looked around the room, then lifted up the suitcase. She saw the square of blue and closed her eyes.

"Thank you. Did I really not see it? I thought I looked there, but I was so frazzled, I just . . ."

"It's okay now. And you have a plane to catch."

Then Richard walked over to the dresser and picked up her new beach hat, spinning it around on his index finger. He placed it on her head. "Are you wearing this on the flight? You look adorable."

"I am now." It even went with her jeans and striped T-shirt and the slip-on Converse sneakers she always wore when she flew, to save time during the security check.

Her mother didn't get it. Richard fixed everything. She'd be safe with him no matter where they lived.

He lifted up her suitcases and headed for the door. "I know you had some good memories in this place. We'll make new ones, though. Better ones. Ready?"

She was stressed and tired, her mother's comments still stung, and she'd never lost those damn eight pounds. But Nellie nodded and followed him out the door. Richard was sending a mover to pick up the brown packing boxes she'd left stacked in her closet, as well as the things she'd put in his apartment building's storage unit, and deliver them to the new house.

"I parked a couple of blocks away." Richard set her bags down near the curb. "Be back in two minutes, babe."

He strode off, and Nellie looked around her street. A delivery van idled a few doors down and a couple of men were wrestling an oversize chair out of its back.

But other than for those guys and a woman waiting at the bus stop with her back to Nellie, the street was quiet.

Nellie closed her eyes and tilted back her head. Feeling the early-afternoon sun against her cheeks. Waiting for the sound of her name to tell her it was time to go.

CHAPTER
EIGHTEEN

MY REPLACEMENT DOESN'T SEE ME coming.

By the time she senses my approach and shock fills her eyes, I am very close.

She looks around wildly, probably trying to find an escape.

"Vanessa?" Her voice is incredulous.

I am surprised she recognizes me so swiftly. "Hello."

She is younger than me, and her curves are more generous, but now that my hair is back to its natural hue, we could be sisters.

I've anticipated this moment for so long. Remarkably, I don't feel any panic.

My palms are dry. My breathing is steady.

I am finally doing it.

I am a very different woman today than when Richard and I fell in love all those years ago.

Everything about me has transformed.

At the age of twenty-seven, I was a buoyant, chatty preschool teacher who hated sushi and loved the movie *Notting Hill*.

I palmed trays of burgers at my part-time waitressing job and rummaged through secondhand-clothing stores and went out dancing with my friends. I had no idea how lovely I was. How *lucky* I was.

I had so many friends. I've lost every one of them. Even Samantha. Now all I have left is Aunt Charlotte.

In my old life, I even had another name.

The first time we met, Richard nicknamed me Nellie. That was all he ever called me.

But to everyone else, I was always—and am still—Vanessa.

I can still hear Richard's deep voice as he would tell the story—*our* story—whenever people asked how we met.

"I spotted her in the airport lounge," he'd say. "Trying to roll her suitcase with one hand and holding her purse and a bottle of water and a chocolate-chip cookie in the other."

I was returning to New York from visiting my mother in Florida. The trip had been a good one, despite that going home always conjured painful memories for me. I missed my father more than ever when I went back to my old house. And I could never escape the recollections of my time at college. But at least my mother's erratic moods had somewhat stabilized thanks to a new medicine. Still, I hated to fly and I felt especially anxious about being in the air that day, even though the sky was a swath of azure dotted with only a few cottony clouds.

I noticed him right away. He wore a dark suit and a crisp white shirt and was frowning at his laptop while he typed.

"This little kid started pitching a tantrum," Richard would continue. "His poor mom had a baby in a car seat and was at her wit's end."

I had that cookie, so I gestured to the mother, asking if I could give it to the crying boy. She nodded gratefully. I was a preschool teacher; I knew the power of a well-timed bribe. I bent down and gave the child his treat and his tears evaporated. When I glanced in Richard's direction a minute later, he'd disappeared.

As I boarded the plane, I passed him, seated in first class—naturally. He sipped a clear liquid from a glass. His tie was loose around his neck.

He'd spread a newspaper open on his tray but was watching the passengers file in. I felt a magnetic pull when his gaze stopped on me.

"I watched her thumping that suitcase down the aisle," Richard would say, drawing out the story. "Not a bad view at all."

I wheeled my blue suitcase to row twenty. I settled into my seat and performed my usual preflight superstitious rituals: I slipped off my Converse sneakers, closed the window shade, and wrapped a cozy scarf around myself.

"She was sitting next to a young Army private," Richard would continue, winking at me. "And suddenly I felt quite patriotic."

The attendant approached to say a first-class passenger had offered to trade seats with the soldier sitting next to me. "Awesome!" the soldier had said.

Somehow I'd known it was him.

When the plane lumbered into the sky, I gripped the armrest and swallowed hard.

He offered me his drink. His ring finger was bare. I was surprised he wasn't married—he was thirty-six—but later I'd learn he had an ex, a dark-haired woman he'd lived with. She'd been upset when they broke up.

After Richard proposed, her existence haunted me. I felt her presence everywhere. And I was right—someone was following me. It just wasn't Richard's ex.

"I got her tipsy," Richard would tell his enthralled listener. "Figured that way I'd have a better chance of getting her number."

I'd sipped the vodka tonic he'd passed me, very aware of the heat of his body.

"I'm Richard."

"Vanessa."

Here was the part of the story where Richard would turn away from our audience and glance at me tenderly. "She doesn't look like a Vanessa, does she?"

Richard had smiled at me that day on the plane. "You're much too sweet and soft for such a serious name."

"What sort of name should I have, then?"

The plane bumped through another air pocket and I gasped.

"It's just like going over a pothole. You're perfectly safe."

I took a big gulp of his drink and he laughed.

"You're a nervous Nellie." His voice was unexpectedly gentle. "That's what I'm going to call you: Nellie."

The truth is I always disliked the nickname. I thought it sounded old-fashioned. But I never told that to Richard. He was the only one who ever called me Nellie.

We talked for the rest of the flight.

I couldn't believe someone like Richard was so interested in me. When he took off his jacket, I caught a citrus scent that I'd forever associate with him. As we began our descent, he asked for my phone number. While I jotted it down, he reached out to stroke the length of my hair. A shiver ran down my spine. The gesture felt as intimate as a kiss.

"So beautiful," he said. "Don't ever cut it."

From that day on—all through our whirlwind courtship in New York City, our wedding at the resort in Florida, and our years spent living in the new house Richard had bought for us in Westchester—I was always his Nellie.

I'd expected my life to unfurl gracefully. I thought he would always keep me safe. I'd become a mother and would resume teaching when our children were grown. I dreamed of dancing at our silver wedding anniversary.

But of course, none of that happened.

And now Nellie is gone forever.

I am only Vanessa.

"Why are you here?" my replacement asks.

I can tell she is gauging whether she can be quick enough to duck around me and run down the street.

But she is wearing strappy high-heeled sandals and a fitted skirt. I know she is heading to her bridal fitting today; her schedule was easy to obtain.

"All I want is two minutes." I spread open my empty hands to convince her I mean no physical harm.

She hesitates and looks up and down the block again. A few people mill past, but no one stops. What is there to see? We're just two well-dressed women standing in front of an apartment building on a busy street, near a deli and down the block from a bus stop.

"Richard will be here any second. He's just locking up my apartment."

"Richard left twenty minutes ago." I was worried he might drop her off at the fitting, but I watched him flag down a cab.

"Please just listen," I say to the beautiful young woman with the heart-shaped face and lush body that Richard left me for. She needs to know the story of how I transformed from buoyant, chatty Nellie into the shattered woman I am today. "I need to tell you the truth about him."

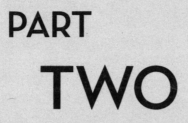

PART
TWO

CHAPTER
NINETEEN

HER NAME IS EMMA.

"I used to be you," I begin as I look at the young woman before me.

Her blue eyes widen as she takes in my appearance. She examines my changed hair, then the dress draped over my too-thin frame. It is clear my reflection is not an image she can imagine superimposed on herself.

I've lain in bed so many nights rehearsing what I'll say to her. She was Richard's assistant; that is how they met. Less than a year after she was hired to replace his secretary Diane, he left me for her.

I don't need to reach for the printed copy of my speech in my bag, my backup in case words failed me. "If you marry Richard, you will regret it. He will hurt you."

Emma frowns. "Vanessa." Her voice is even and measured. It's as if she is talking to a small child. It's the tone I used when I told my Cubs it was time to put away their toys or finish up their snacks. "I realize the divorce was hard on you. It was hard on Richard, too. I saw him every day; he really tried to make it work. I know you've had your troubles, but he did everything he could." I sense some accusation in her gaze; she believes I'm to blame.

"You think you know him," I interrupt. I'm going off script, but I press on. "But what did you see? The Richard you work for isn't the real man. He's careful, Emma. He doesn't let people in. If you go through with the wedding—"

She interrupts me now. "I feel horribly about everything. I want you to know he started opening up to me as a colleague, as a friend. I'm not the kind of woman who ever thought she'd have an affair with a married man. We didn't expect to fall in love."

I believe this. I saw their attraction spark shortly after Richard hired Emma to manage his calls, proofread his correspondence, and keep his schedule.

"It just happened. I'm sorry." Emma's round eyes are earnest. She reaches out and touches my arm gently. I flinch as her fingertips gently graze my skin. "I do know him. I'm with him ten hours a day, five days a week. I've seen him with his clients and our coworkers. I've seen him with the other assistants, and I saw him with you back when you were married. He's a good man."

Emma pauses for a moment, as if debating whether to go on. She is still staring at my lighter hair color. My naturally blond roots finally blend in well. "Maybe it's you who never knew him." Her tone has an edge.

"You have to listen to me!" I am shaking now, desperate to convince her. "Richard does this! He confuses things so we can't see the truth!"

"He said you might try something like this." Contempt has replaced the sympathy in her voice. She folds her arms and I know I am losing her. "He told me you were jealous, but this has gotten out of control. I saw you outside my building last week. Richard said if you pull something like that again, we'll file a restraining order."

Beads of sweat run down my back, and more gather on my upper lip. My long-sleeved dress is too warm for the weather. I imagined I'd planned everything out so carefully, but I've stumbled, and now my thoughts are as thick and muggy as this June day.

"Are you trying to get pregnant?" I blurt. "Did he tell you he wants to have children?"

Emma takes a step back, then moves to the side and passes me. She walks to the curb and lifts up her hand to signal a cab.

"Enough," she says, without turning to look back at me.

"Ask him about our last cocktail party." Distress makes my voice shrill. "You were there. Remember how the caterers showed up late and there wasn't any Raveneau? That was Richard's fault—he didn't order it. It was never delivered!"

A taxi slows. Emma turns to me. "I was there. And I know the wine was delivered. I'm Richard's assistant. Who do you think placed the order?"

This I never expected. She opens the door of the cab before I can recover.

"He blamed me," I shout. "After the party, it got bad!"

"You really need help." Emma slams the door shut.

I watch as the cab pulls Emma away from me.

I stand on the sidewalk outside her apartment, as I've done so many times before, but for the first time I truly wonder if everything Richard said about me is true. Am I crazy, like my mother, who battled mental illness her entire life—at times more successfully than others?

My nails are digging into my palms. I cannot stand the thought of them together tonight. She will tell him everything I've said. He'll lift her legs over his and massage her feet and promise he will keep her safe. From me.

I hope she will listen. That she will believe me.

But Richard suspected I would try this, after all. He told her so.

I know my ex-husband better than anyone else. I should have remembered he also knows me.

It rained the morning of our wedding.

"That's good luck," my father would have said.

By the time I walked down the royal-blue silk runner spread on the grand patio of the resort, flanked by my mother and Aunt Charlotte, the sky had cleared. The sun caressed my bare arms. Waves provided a gentle melody.

I passed Sam and Josie and Marnie, seated in chairs tied with white

silk bows, then Hillary and George and a few of Richard's other partners. And up front, by the rose-draped archway, Maureen stood next
to Richard in her capacity as maid of honor. She wore the glass-bead
necklace I'd given her.

Richard watched me approach and I couldn't stop beaming. His
expression was intent; his eyes looked nearly black. After we joined
hands and the minister pronounced us man and wife, I saw his lips
tremble with emotion before he leaned down to kiss me.

The photographer captured the enchantment of the evening:
Richard slipping a ring onto my finger, our embrace at the end of the
ceremony, and our slow dance to "It Had to Be You." The album I
ordered contains a shot of Maureen straightening Richard's bow tie,
Sam raising her glass of champagne, my mother walking barefoot on
the beach at sunset, and Aunt Charlotte hugging me good-bye at the
end of the evening.

My life had been so filled with uncertainty and turmoil—with my
parents' divorce, my mother's struggles, my father's death, and, of
course, the reason I'd fled my hometown—but on that night, my future
seemed as straight and seamless as the blue silk runner that had led me
to Richard.

The next day we flew to Antigua. We reclined in first class, and
Richard ordered us both mimosas before the wheels ever left the
ground. The nightmares I'd experienced never came to fruition.

It wasn't flying I needed to fear.

Our honeymoon wasn't documented in an album, but when I think
back, that's how I remember it, too: as a series of snapshots.

Richard cracking open my lobster and grinning suggestively as I
sucked the sweet meat out of a claw.

The two of us getting a couple's massage as we lay side by side on
the beach.

Richard standing behind me, his hands on mine, as I helped release the sail on a catamaran we'd rented for the day.

Each night, our private butler drew us a bath perfumed with rose petals and rimmed with lit candles around the curved edge. Once, we crept down in the moonlight to the beach and, hidden amid the billowing curtains designed to block out the sun, we made love in a cabana. We soaked in our private Jacuzzi, sipped rum-spiked drinks by the infinity pool, and napped in a double hammock.

On our last full day Richard signed us up for scuba diving. We weren't certified, but the resort staff told us that if we took a private lesson in the pool, we could do a shallow dive with an instructor.

I didn't enjoy swimming, but I was all right in the placid, chlorinated water. Other guests splashed nearby, sunlight illuminated the surface just a few feet above my head, and the edge of the pool was merely a few strokes away.

I took a deep breath as we climbed into the motorboat and tried to make my voice sound calm and carefree. "How long will we be down?" I asked the instructor, Eric, a young guy on summer break from UC Santa Barbara.

"Forty-five minutes. Your tank has more oxygen that that, so we can push it a little if you want."

I gave him a thumbs-up, but as we sped away from land, toward a hidden coral reef, pressure built in my chest. The heavy oxygen tank was strapped to my back, and fins pinched my feet.

I looked at the plastic face mask atop Richard's head, feeling an identical one tugging the sensitive hairs at my temples. Eric cut the motor, and the silence felt as vast and absolute as the water surrounding us.

Eric jumped off the edge of the boat, pushing his shaggy hair out of his face after he surfaced in the water. "The reef's about twenty yards away. Follow my fins."

"Ready, baby?" Richard seemed so excited to see the blue-and-yellow angelfish, the rainbow-colored parrot fish, and the harmless sand sharks. He pulled down his mask. I tried to smile as I did the same, feeling the rubber seal tightening the skin around my eyes.

I can come back up anytime, I told myself as I began to climb down the ladder, where the heavy equipment would help drag me beneath the surface. *I won't be trapped.*

Moments after I sank into the cool, salty ocean, everything was blotted out.

All I could hear was breathing.

I couldn't see; Eric had said that if fog formed on the inside of our masks, we should simply tilt them just enough to allow a stream of water to clear the condensation. "Hold up one hand if something's wrong; that'll be our emergency signal," he'd said. But all I could do was kick and flail, trying to maneuver to the surface. The straps of my equipment compressed my body, binding my chest. I tried to suck in oxygen as my mask grew cloudier.

The noise was awful. Even now, I can hear jagged, tortured gasps filling my ears and feel the tightness in my chest.

I couldn't spot Eric or Richard. I spun alone in the ocean, my limbs churning, a scream building in my lungs.

Then someone gripped my arm and I felt myself being pulled. I went limp.

I broke the surface and spit out my mouthpiece, then yanked off my mask, feeling a burst of pain as it ripped away a few strands of my hair.

Gasping and coughing, I tried to draw more air into my lungs.

"The boat's right here," Eric said. "I've got you. Just float."

I reached out and grabbed a rung of the ladder. I was too weak to climb it, but Eric hauled himself up onto the boat, then leaned down for my hand. I collapsed on a bench, so dizzy I had to put my head between my legs.

I heard Richard's voice from below. "You're safe. Look at me."

The pressure in my ears made him sound like a stranger.

I tried to do as he said, but he was still bobbing in the water. Seeing the blue ripples made me nauseous.

Eric knelt next to me, unhooking the straps from around my body. "You'll be okay. You panicked, right? This happens sometimes. You're not the only one."

"I just couldn't see," I whispered.

Richard climbed up the ladder and hoisted himself over the side, his equipment clanging as he landed. "I'm here. Oh, sweetheart, you're shaking. I'm so sorry, Nellie. I should have known."

The mask had left a red imprint encircling his eyes.

"I've got her," he said to Eric, who finished unstrapping my tank, then moved aside. "We'd better head in."

Richard held me close as the speedboat skipped over the waves. We returned to the resort in silence. After Eric docked, he reached into a cooler and handed me a bottle of water. "How do you feel now?"

"Much better," I lied. I was still trembling, and the bottle of water in my hand shook. "Richard, you can go back out. . . ."

He shook his head. "No way."

"Let's get you onto land," Eric said. He jumped onto the dock and Richard followed him. Eric reached down for my hand again. "Here." My legs were unsteady, but I managed to stretch out my arm for him to take.

But Richard said, "I've got her." He gripped my upper left arm and pulled me out of the boat. I winced at the feel of his fingers pressing into my soft flesh as he held me tightly to stabilize me.

"I'm going to take her to the room," Richard told Eric. "You'll return our equipment?"

"No problem." Eric looked worried, maybe because Richard's voice was a little clipped. I knew Richard was only concerned about me, but perhaps Eric thought we'd make a complaint.

"Thanks for helping me," I told him. "Sorry I freaked out."

Richard wrapped a fresh towel around my shoulders, and we walked off the dock, through the soft sand, toward our room.

I felt better after I'd changed out of my wet bikini and wrapped myself in a fluffy white robe. When Richard suggested we return to the beach, I pleaded a headache, but insisted that he go.

"I'll just rest for a little while," I said.

My temples did throb mildly—a side effect of the dive, or maybe just residual tension. As soon as I heard the door close behind Richard, I walked into the bathroom. I reached for the Advil in my toiletries bag, then hesitated. Next to it was the orange plastic prescription bottle of Xanax I'd obtained in case of a long flight. I hesitated, thinking of my mother as I always did when I swallowed a pill, then shook out one of the oval white tablets and gulped it down with some of the bottled

Fiji water the maid replenished twice a day. I closed the heavy drapes, blotting out the sun, then crawled into bed and waited for the drug to take effect.

Just as I was drifting off to sleep, I heard a knock on the door. Thinking it was the maid, I called, "Can you come back later?"

"It's Eric. I've got your sunglasses. I'll just leave them out here."

I knew I should've gotten up to thank him, but my body felt so heavy it was weighing me down. "Okay. I appreciate it."

My cell phone rang a moment later. I reached for it on the nightstand. "Hello."

No answer.

"Richard?" My tongue already felt thick from the sedative.

Again, no response.

I knew what I'd see even before I looked down at my phone: *Blocked number.*

I bolted upright, my hand gripping the receiver, suddenly wide awake. All I could hear was the rush of cold air whirling through the vent in our room.

I was a thousand miles away from home, yet someone was still tracking me.

I pressed *End Call* and pulled myself out of bed. I yanked aside the blinds and peered out the sliding glass doors to our balcony. No one was there. I looked across the room, at the closed door of our closet. Had it been open when we'd left?

I walked over and reached for the handle, tugging it toward me.

Nothing.

I looked at my cell phone on my bed, the blue screen glowing. I grabbed it and threw it against the tile floor. A piece snapped off, but the display was still illuminated. I picked it up and plunged it into our ice bucket, reaching down until I felt the shock of the freezing water.

But I couldn't leave it there; the maid would certainly find it when she refilled the bucket. I dug through the ice again and pulled it out, then looked frantically around the room until I saw the wastebasket containing that morning's newspaper and a few tissues. I wrapped my phone in the sports section and crammed the papers back into the bin.

The cleaning crew would whisk it all away. The phone would end up in a giant Dumpster along with the trash of a hundred other guests. I'd tell Richard I'd lost it, that it must have fallen out of my beach bag. He'd bought it for me right after we got engaged, saying he wanted me to have the best-quality device, and I knew he'd simply bring home a new one for me. I'd already disrupted our vacation enough; there was no need to worry him more.

My breathing slowed down; the pill was conquering my fear. Our suite was airy and spacious, with purple orchids in a low vase on the glass table, blue tile floors, and whitewashed walls. I walked to the closet again and selected my flowing orange sundress and gold high-heeled sandals. I hung the dress on the back of the closet door and placed the shoes neatly beneath it; I'd wear the outfit tonight. Our mini-refrigerator held a bottle of champagne. I pulled it out and nestled it in the ice bucket, then arranged two delicate flutes beside it.

My eyelids were heavy now. I took a last glance around. Everything looked lovely; everything was in place. I slipped back under the covers. I curled onto my left side and winced. When I looked at my upper arm, I saw a red mark that was the beginning of a bruise forming where Richard had gripped me to pull me out of the boat.

I had a light sweater that would go with my sundress. I'd wear it to cover the mark.

I turned onto my other side. A short nap, I told myself, and then, when Richard came back, I'd suggest that we open the champagne and get ready for dinner together.

We were flying back to New York tomorrow; our honeymoon was almost over. I needed to erase the memory of this afternoon. I wanted one more perfect night before we went home.

CHAPTER
TWENTY

I WATCH THE BARTENDER POUR a clear stream of vodka into my glass and top it with a foamy spritz of tonic. She wedges a lime on the edge and slides it across the smooth wood, then removes the empty glass from in front of me.

"Do you want some water, too?"

I shake my head. Damp strands of hair stick to my neck, and my thighs feel sweaty against the vinyl chair. My shoes rest on the floor beneath me.

After Emma dismissed me and disappeared into the taxi, I stood on the street corner for a long moment, not knowing where to go. There was simply no one I could turn to. No one who would understand how spectacularly I had failed.

Then, because I couldn't think of an alternative, I began to walk. With each step, my anguish grew wider, like a yawn I could not contain. A few blocks later, I found the Robertson Hotel bar.

The bartender silently pushes yet another glass in front of me. Water. I look up, wondering if I did actually shake my head or just imagined doing so, but she avoids my gaze. She moves away, straightening the stack of newspapers on a corner of the countertop.

I catch sight of myself in the large mirror behind her, the one that reflects the rows of Absolut, Johnnie Walker, Hendrick's Gin, and reposado tequila.

Now I see what Emma saw.

I'm looking into a fun-house mirror. The image I wanted to project—the old me, Richard's Nellie—is distorted. My hair is brittle from overprocessing; more straw than butter. My eyes look sunken in my gaunt face. The makeup I'd so carefully applied is smudged. No wonder the bartender wants me to stay sober; I'm in the lobby of a fine hotel, one that hosts international businesspeople and offers two-hundred-dollar snifters of Scotch.

I feel the vibration of my phone again. I force myself to pull it out of my purse and see five missed calls. Three from Saks, beginning at ten A.M. Two from Aunt Charlotte in the past thirty minutes.

Only one thing can break through the dull ache engulfing me: the thought of Aunt Charlotte worrying. So I answer.

"Vanessa? Are you okay?"

I have no idea how to respond.

"Where are you?"

"At work."

"Lucille called me when you didn't show up." My aunt is my emergency contact; I put her home number down on my application.

"I just needed—I'm going in late."

"Where are you?" my aunt repeats, her tone firm.

I should tell her that I'm on my way home, that my flu has returned. I should make excuses to ease her worry. But the sound of her voice—the only safe thing I know—unravels me. So I give her the name of the hotel.

"Don't move," she says, and hangs up.

By now, Emma has arrived at her dress fitting. I wonder if she called Richard to tell him I intercepted her. I think of how the pity in her eyes transformed into scorn; I'm not sure which made me feel worse. I recall her shapely legs folding up into the cab, the door shutting, her image receding as I stared after her.

I wonder if Richard will reach out to me now.

Before I can even order another drink, I hear Aunt Charlotte's Birkenstocks slap against the floor as she approaches. I see her absorb my new hair color, my empty cocktail glass, and my bare feet.

I wait for her to speak, but she just takes the stool next to me.

"Can I get you anything?" the bartender asks.

Aunt Charlotte peers at the cocktail menu. "A sidecar, please."

"Sure, that's not on the menu, but I can whip one up."

My aunt waits while the woman pours the cognac and orange liqueur over ice and squeezes in a lemon.

Aunt Charlotte swallows a sip, then puts down her frosted glass. I brace myself for more questions, but they never come.

"I can't make you tell me what is going on. But please stop lying to me." A bit of yellow paint stains the knuckle of her index finger—just a small dot—and I stare at it.

"Who was I after I got married?" I ask after a moment. "What did you see?"

Aunt Charlotte leans back and crosses her legs. "You changed. I missed you."

I missed her, too. Aunt Charlotte didn't meet Richard until just before our wedding, since she was doing a yearlong apartment swap with a Parisian artist friend. After she returned to New York, we saw each other—more frequently in the beginning and then much less often as the years passed.

"I first noticed something the night of your birthday. You just didn't seem like your old self."

I know exactly which night she is talking about. It was August, shortly after our first anniversary. I nod. "I'd just turned twenty-nine." A couple of years older than Emma is now. "You brought me a bouquet of pink snapdragons."

She'd given me a small painting, too, about the size of a hardcover book. It was of me on my wedding day. Instead of a portrait, Aunt Charlotte had captured me from behind as I began to walk toward Richard. The bell shape of my dress and my gauzy veil stood out against the vivid blue Floridian sky; it was almost as if I were walking off into infinity.

We'd invited Aunt Charlotte to Westchester for a drink followed by dinner at our club. I'd already started taking fertility pills, and I remember I couldn't zip up the skirt I was planning to wear. The silk A-line was one of the many new items filling my enormous closet. I'd napped that afternoon—the Clomid left me woozy—and was running late. By the time I'd changed into a more forgiving dress, Richard had greeted Aunt Charlotte and poured her a glass of wine.

I'd heard their conversation as I approached the library. "They were always her favorite flowers," Aunt Charlotte was saying.

"Really?" Richard said. "They were?"

When I entered, Aunt Charlotte set the cellophane-wrapped snapdragons down on a side table so she could hug me.

"I'll put these in a vase." Richard discreetly took one of our linen cocktail napkins and wiped away a drop of water from the blackwashed mango wood; the piece had been delivered just the previous month. "There's mineral water for you, sweetheart," he said to me.

Now I reach for the glass of water on the bar in front of me and take a long sip. Aunt Charlotte had known I was trying to get pregnant, and when she smiled at Richard's remark, I'd realized she might have drawn the wrong impression from my thickening waistline and the nonalcoholic beverage.

I'd shaken my head slightly, not wanting to say the words to correct her. At least not then, in front of Richard.

"Beautiful place," Aunt Charlotte says now, but I'm not tracking the conversation. Is she talking about our old house or the club?

Everything in my life looked beautiful back then: the new furnishings I'd picked out with the help of an interior decorator, the sapphire earrings Richard had presented to me earlier that day, the long driveway winding through lush golf greens and past a duck-filled pond as we approached the club, the explosion of crape myrtles and creamy dogwoods surrounding the white-columned entrance.

"The other people at the club all seemed so . . ." She hesitates. "Settled, I guess. It's just that your friends in the city were so energetic and young."

Aunt Charlotte's words are gentle, but I know what she means. The men wore jackets in the dining room—a club rule—and the women seemed to have unspoken edicts of their own governing how to look and to act. Most of the couples were much older than me, too, but that wasn't the only reason why I felt I didn't fit in.

"We sat at a booth in the corner," Aunt Charlotte continues. Richard and I attended lots of events at the club—the Fourth of July fireworks, the Labor Day barbecue, the December holiday dance. The corner booth was Richard's favorite because it afforded him a view of the room and was quiet.

"I was surprised by the golf lessons," Aunt Charlotte says.

I nod. They'd been a surprise to me, too. Richard had given them to me, of course. He wanted to play together and had mentioned a trip to Pebble Beach once I'd mastered my fairway drive. I'd talked about the way I'd learned to tell my seven from my nine iron, how I always shanked my shot when I didn't spend enough time taking practice swings, and what fun it was to drive the golf cart. I should have known Aunt Charlotte would see through my lively chatter.

"When the waiter appeared, you asked for a glass of Chardonnay," Aunt Charlotte says. "But I saw Richard touch your hand. Then you changed your order to water."

"I was trying to get pregnant. I didn't want to drink."

"I understand that, but then something else happened." Aunt Charlotte takes a sip of her sidecar, holding the thick glass with both hands, then sets it carefully back onto the bar. I wonder if she is reluctant to continue, but I need to know what I did.

"The server brought you a Caesar salad." Aunt Charlotte's voice is soft. "You told him you'd wanted the dressing on the side. It wasn't a big deal, but you insisted you'd ordered it that way. I just thought it was strange because you'd been a waitress, honey. You know how easy it is for mistakes to happen."

She pauses. "The thing is, you were wrong. I ordered a Caesar salad, too, and you just said you'd have the same. You didn't say anything about the dressing."

I feel my brow crease. "That was all? I mis-ordered?"

Aunt Charlotte shakes her head. I know she will be honest with me. I also know I may not like what I hear next.

"It was the way you said it. You sounded . . . agitated. He apologized, but you made it into a bigger deal than it needed to be. You blamed the waiter for something that wasn't his fault."

"What did Richard do?"

"He was finally the one to tell you not to worry, that you'd have a new salad in a minute."

I don't remember my exact exchange with the waiter—although I do recall other, more fraught restaurant meals during my marriage—but I'm certain of one thing: My aunt has an excellent memory; she has spent her entire life cataloging details.

I wonder how many other unpleasant moments Aunt Charlotte witnessed during those years and has held close out of love for me.

Although we were still newlyweds, my transformation had already begun.

CHAPTER
TWENTY-ONE

I ALWAYS KNEW my life with Richard wouldn't resemble my old one.

I imagined my changes would be external, though—additions to who I already was and what I already had. I'd become a wife. A mother. I'd create a home. I'd find new friends in our neighborhood.

But in the absence of the daily scramble that composed my existence in Manhattan, it was too easy to focus on what was missing. I should have been waking three times a night to breast-feed, and scheduling Mommy & Me classes. I should have been steaming carrots into mush and reading *Goodnight Moon*. I should have been washing onesies in Dreft and icing teething rings to soothe little swollen gums.

My life was on hold. I felt suspended between my past and my future.

I used to agonize over the balance in my checking account, the sound of footsteps behind me at night, and whether I would make it onto the subway car before the doors closed so I could get to Gibson's on time. I worried about the little girl in my class who bit her nails even though she was only three, about whether the cute guy I'd given my number to would ever call, and if Sam had remembered to unplug her flatiron after straightening her hair.

I guess I thought marrying Richard would erase my concerns.

But my old anxieties simply yielded to new ones. The whirl and noise of the city were replaced by the incessant churning of my thoughts. My peaceful new surroundings didn't soothe my interior world. If anything, the constant stillness, the empty hours, seemed to taunt me. My insomnia returned. I also found myself circling back home to make sure I'd locked the door when I went on an errand, even though I could see myself pulling it shut and turning the key. I left a dental appointment before I'd gotten my teeth cleaned, convinced I'd left on the oven. I double-checked closets to make sure the lights were off. Our weekly housekeeper left everything spotless, and Richard was incredibly tidy by nature, but I still wandered through the rooms, seeking a brown leaf to pinch off a potted plant, a book jutting out a bit farther than the others on our shelves to tuck back into alignment, towels to refold into perfect thirds in our linen closet.

I learned to stretch out a simple chore like taffy; I could orient my entire day around a meeting at the club for the junior volunteer committee. I was constantly checking the clock, counting down the hours until Richard would come home.

Shortly after my twenty-ninth birthday and the night at the club with Aunt Charlotte, I went to the grocery store to get chicken breasts for dinner.

It was almost Halloween, which had always been my favorite holiday when I'd taught the Cubs. I doubted we'd get many trick-or-treaters—we hadn't the previous year since the houses in our neighborhood were so spread out. Still, at the market, I picked up a few bags of mini Kit Kats and M&M's, hoping I wouldn't eat more than I'd distribute. I also added a box of Tampax to my cart. When I accidentally turned down the aisle that held Pampers and baby food, I abruptly retreated, taking the longer route to the cash registers.

As I set the table for dinner, just two plates in a corner of the wide stretch of mahogany, loneliness pierced me. I poured myself a glass of wine and dialed Sam's number. Richard still didn't like it when I drank, but on a few days every month, I needed the consolation—so I made sure to brush my teeth and bury the empty bottle in the bottom of our recycling bin. Sam told me she was getting ready to go on a third date with a guy, and she actually seemed excited about him. I could picture her wiggling into her favorite jeans, the ones I no longer borrowed, and applying cherry-red lip stain.

I sipped my Chablis as I soaked in her happy chatter and suggested we get together in the city soon. Sam had only come out to see me once since the wedding. I didn't blame her; Westchester was boring to a single woman. I made it to Manhattan more often, and I would try to meet Sam near the Learning Ladder for a late lunch.

But I'd had to postpone our last lunch because I'd caught a stomach bug, and Sam had canceled the dinner we'd scheduled before that because she'd forgotten her grandmother's ninetieth birthday party was on the same evening.

We hadn't seen each other in ages.

I'd vowed to stay in close contact with Sam after the wedding, but nights and weekends—Sam's free times—were also my only chances to be with Richard.

Richard never put constraints on my schedule. Once, when he picked me up at the train station after I'd met Sam for Sunday brunch at Balthazar, he asked if I'd had fun.

"Sam is always fun," I'd said, laughing as I told him how after we left the restaurant, we'd come across a movie scene being filmed a few blocks away, and Sam had grabbed my hand and pulled me into the crowd of extras. We'd been asked to leave, but not before she managed to grab a big bag of trail mix from the craft-services table.

Richard had laughed with me. But at dinner that night, he mentioned that he would be working late almost every evening that week.

Before we got off the phone, Sam told me to pick a time for us to get together. "Let's drink tequila and go dancing like we used to."

I hesitated. "Let me just check Richard's calendar. It might be easier if I come in when he's out of town."

"You planning to bring a boy home?" Sam joked.

"Why only one?" I bantered, trying to change the focus, and she laughed.

I was in the kitchen a few minutes later, chopping tomatoes for a salad, when our burglar alarm began to shriek.

As promised, Richard had a sophisticated alarm system installed right before we moved into the Westchester home. It was a comfort during the days when he was at work, and especially on the nights when he traveled.

"Hello?" I called. I went into the hallway, flinching as the high-pitched warning pulsed through the air. But our heavy oak door remained shut.

Our house had four vulnerable areas, the alarm-company contractor had said, holding up an equal number of fingers to emphasize his point. The front door. The basement entrance. The big bay window in the eat-in kitchen area. And especially the double glass doors off the living room that overlooked our garden.

All of those entrances were wired. I ran to the double glass doors and glanced out. I couldn't see anything, but it didn't mean no one was there, wasn't hiding in the shadows. If someone was breaking in, I'd never hear the noise over the blaring alarm. Instinctively, I bolted upstairs, still holding the butcher knife I'd been using to cut the tomatoes.

I grabbed my cell phone from the nightstand, grateful I'd put it back in its charger. As I burrowed into the back of my closet, behind a row of slacks, I dialed Richard.

"Nellie? What's wrong?"

I clutched the phone tightly as I huddled on the floor of my closet. "I think someone's trying to break in," I whispered.

"I can hear the alarm." Richard's voice was tense and urgent. "Where are you?"

"My closet," I whispered.

"I'll call the police. Hang on."

I imagined him on the other line giving our address and insisting that they should hurry, that his wife was alone in the house. I knew the alarm company would alert the police, too.

Our home phone was ringing now, as well. My heart pounded, the frantic throbbing filling my ears. So many sounds—how could I know if someone stood on the other side of the closet door, twisting the knob?

"The police will be there any second," Richard said. "And I'm already on the train, at Mount Kisco. I'll be at the house in fifteen minutes."

Those fifteen minutes lasted an eternity. I curled into a tighter ball and began to count, forcing myself to slowly mouth the numbers. Surely the police would come by the time I reached two hundred, I thought, remaining motionless and taking shallow breaths so that if someone came through the closet door, they might not detect my presence.

Time slowed down. I was acutely aware of every detail of my surroundings, my senses intensely heightened. I saw individual flecks of dust on the baseboards, the slight variation in the hue of the wood floor, and the tiny ripple my exhalations made in the fabric of the black slacks hanging an inch from my face.

"Hang on, baby," Richard said as I reached 287. "I'm just getting off the train."

That was when the police finally arrived.

The officers searched but found no sign of an intruder—nothing taken, no doors jimmied, no windows broken. I cuddled next to Richard on the sofa, sipping chamomile tea. False alarms weren't uncommon, the police told us. Faulty wiring, animals triggering a sensor, a glitch in the system—it was probably one of those things, an officer said.

"I'm sure it was nothing," Richard agreed. But then he hesitated and looked at the two officers. "This probably isn't related, but when I left this morning, there was an unfamiliar truck parked at the end of our street. I figured it belonged to a landscaper or something."

I felt my heart skip a beat.

"Did you get the license plate number?" the older officer, the one who did most of the talking, asked.

"I didn't, but I'll keep an eye out for it." Richard drew me in closer. "Oh, sweetheart, you're trembling. I promise I will never let anything happen to you, Nellie."

"You're sure you didn't see anyone, though, right?" the officer asked me again.

Through the windows I watched the flashing blue and red lights revolve atop the cruisers. I closed my eyes but I could still visualize those frantic colors spinning through the darkness, pulling me back into that long-ago night when I was in senior in college.

"No. I didn't see anyone."

But that wasn't completely true.

I had seen a face, but not in one of our windows. It was visible only in my memory. It belongs to someone I last encountered in Florida, someone who blames me—who wants me punished—for the cataclysmic events of that fall evening.

I had a new name. A new address. I'd even changed my phone number.

I'd always feared it wouldn't be enough.

The tragedy began to unfold during a beautiful day, also in October. I was so young then. I'd just started my senior year in college. The blistering heat of the Florida summer had yielded to a mellow warmth; the girls in my sorority wore light sundresses or tank tops and shorts with CHI OMEGA stamped across the butt. Our house was filled with a happy energy; the new pledges would be initiated after sunset. As social director, I'd planned the Jell-O shots, the blindfolding, the candles, and the surprise plunge into the ocean.

But I woke up exhausted and feeling queasy. I nibbled on a granola bar as I dragged myself to my early-child-development seminar. When I pulled out my spiral-bound planner to write down the next week's assignment, a realization stilled my pencil on the page: My period was late. I wasn't ill. I was pregnant.

When I looked up again, all the other students had packed up and were leaving the classroom. Shock had stolen minutes from me.

I cut my next class and walked to a pharmacy on the edge of campus, buying a pack of gum, a *People* magazine, some pens, and an e.p.t test as if it were just another casual item on my shopping list. A McDonald's was next door and I huddled in a stall, listening as two preteen girls brushed their hair in the mirror and talked about the Britney Spears concert they were dying to attend. The plus sign confirmed what I already suspected.

I was only twenty-one, I thought wildly. I hadn't even finished school. My boyfriend, Daniel, and I had been together for just a few months.

I stepped out of the stall and went to the row of sinks, running cold water over my wrists. I glanced up and the two girls fell silent when they caught sight of my face.

Daniel was in a sociology class that let out at twelve-thirty; I'd memorized his schedule. I hurried to his building and paced the stretch of sidewalk in front of it. Some students sat on the steps, smoking, while others sprawled on the green—a few eating lunch, others forming a triangle and throwing a Frisbee. A girl rested with her head on a guy's lap, her long hair draped over his thigh like a blanket. The Grateful Dead blared from a boom box.

Two hours earlier, I would've been one of them.

Students began to trickle out the door and I scanned their faces, frantically searching for Daniel. He wouldn't be the guy wearing flip-flops and a Grant University T-shirt, or the one burdened by a cumbersome saxophone case, or even the one with a backpack shrugged onto a shoulder.

He didn't look like any of them.

After the crowd had thinned, he appeared at the top of the stairs, folding his glasses into the pocket of his oxford shirt, a messenger bag slung crosswise over his chest. I lifted my hand and waved. When he saw me, he faltered, then continued down the steps to where I stood.

"Professor Barton!" A girl intercepted him, probably with a question about his class. Or maybe she was flirting.

Daniel Barton was in his mid-thirties, and he made the Frisbee-throwing jocks, with their leaps and hoots when they caught the disk, look like puppies. He kept glancing at me while he talked to the other girl. His anxiety was palpable. I'd violated our rule: Don't acknowledge each other on campus.

He could be fired, after all. He'd given me an A during my junior year, a few weeks before our affair began. I'd earned it—we'd never shared a personal conversation, let alone a kiss, until I bumped into him after being separated from my friends at a Dave Matthews beach concert—but who would believe us?

When at long last he drew close to me, he whispered, "Not now. I'll call you later."

"Pick me up at the usual spot in fifteen."

He shook his head. "Today won't work. Tomorrow." His brusque tone stung me.

"It's really important."

But he was already moving past me, hands in his jeans pockets, toward the old Alfa Romeo that had taken us to the beach on so many moonlit nights. I watched him go, feeling stunned and deeply betrayed. I'd stuck to our agreement; he should have realized this was urgent. He tossed his bag onto the passenger's seat—my seat—and sped off.

I clutched my arms around my stomach and watched as his car turned a corner and disappeared. Then I slowly made my way back to the sorority house, where everybody was busy preparing.

I just had to get through the rest of the day, I told myself, blinking hard at the tears that filled my eyes. Then I could talk to Daniel. We'd come up with a plan together.

"Where were you?" asked our chapter's president as I walked through the door, but she didn't wait for an answer. Twenty new pledges would officially join our house tonight. The evening would start out with a dinner and rituals: the house song and a sorority trivia game about our founders and important dates. Each girl would then take a candle and repeat sacred vows. I'd stand behind my "little sister," Maggie, whom I'd been paired with for the year. The hazing would begin around ten P.M. Although it would last several hours, nothing bad would be done to the girls. Nothing dangerous. Certainly no one would be hurt.

I knew this because I was the one to plan it.

Bottles of vodka for the Jell-O shots lined the dining room table, along with grain alcohol for the Dirty Hunch Punch. *Did we need so much liquor?* I wondered. I remember because of everything that happened afterward. Those flashing blue and red police lights. The high-pitched screaming that sounded like an alarm.

But as I climbed the steps to my room, it was just a fleeting thought, winging past like a moth, quickly replaced by my worry over the pregnancy. The feeling of sickness radiated out from my core, encompassing my entire being.

Daniel hadn't even glanced back at me as he'd driven off. I kept remembering the way he'd walked right past me, whispering, "Not now." He'd treated me with less respect than the student who'd intercepted him before he reached me.

I slipped into my room and quietly shut the door, then pulled out my cell phone. I lay down on my bed, hugging my knees to my chest, and called him. After four rings, I heard his outgoing message. The second time I dialed, it went directly to voice mail.

I could see Daniel glancing down at his phone as the code name he'd given me—Victor—flashed. His long, tapered fingers, the ones that caressed my leg whenever I sat beside him, picking up the phone and pressing *Decline*.

I'd seen him do the exact same thing to other callers when we were together, never thinking he'd do it to me.

I dialed his number again, hoping he'd see it and realize how desperately I needed to talk to him. But he ignored me.

My pain was being overtaken by anger. He must have known something was wrong. *He'd said he cared about me, but if you truly cared for someone, wouldn't you at least answer her fucking call?* I'd thought.

I'd never been to his place because he lived with two other professors in faculty housing. I knew his address, though.

I'd thought, *Tomorrow isn't good enough.*

CHAPTER
TWENTY-TWO

AFTER AUNT CHARLOTTE comes to get me at the Robertson bar, I take a cool shower, scrubbing off my sweat and makeup. Wishing I could rinse away the day as easily and have a fresh chance with Emma.

I'd planned my words so carefully; I'd anticipated that Emma would be skeptical at first. I would have been, too—I still remember how I'd bristled when Sam seemed suspicious of Richard, or when my mother expressed concern that I seemed to be losing my identity.

But I'd assumed Emma would at least listen to me. That I would have the opportunity to plant doubts that might prompt her to take a closer look at the man she was choosing to spend the rest of her life with.

But clearly she'd already formed a strong opinion of me, one that tells her I'm not to be trusted.

Now I recognize how foolish I was to think this could end so easily.

I will have to find another way to make her understand.

I notice my left arm is red and slightly raw from where I've been aggressively scrubbing it. I turn off the shower and smooth lotion on my tender skin.

Then Aunt Charlotte knocks on my bedroom door. "Up for a walk?"

"Sure." I'd rather not, but it's my inadequate concession to her for the worry I've caused.

So the two of us head over to Riverside Park. Usually Aunt Charlotte sets a brisk pace, but today she strolls slowly. The steady, repetitive movement of my arms and legs and the soft breeze from the Hudson River help me feel more grounded.

"Do you want to continue our conversation?" Aunt Charlotte asks.

I think about what she requested: *Please stop lying to me.*

I'm not going to lie to her, but before I can tell Aunt Charlotte the truth, I need to figure out what it is for myself.

"Yes." I reach for her hand. "But I'm not ready yet."

Although at the bar we only dissected a single evening of my marriage, talking with my aunt has released some of the pressure that has built up inside me. The full story is far too tangled and complex to unravel in one afternoon. For the first time, though, I have someone else's recollections to rely on other than my own. Someone I can trust as I absorb the aftershocks of my life with Richard.

I take Aunt Charlotte to the Italian restaurant near her apartment, and we order minestrone soup. The waiter brings us warm, crusty bread, and I drink three glasses of ice water, realizing I'm parched. We talk about the biography of Matisse that she is reading, and a movie I pretend to want to see.

Physically I feel a little better. And the superficial chat with my aunt distracts me. But the moment I'm back in my room, closing my blinds as dusk falls, my replacement returns. She is an uninvited guest I can never turn away.

I see her at her dress fitting, twirling before a mirror, the new diamond glinting on her finger. I imagine her pouring Richard a drink and bringing it to him, kissing him as he takes it from her hand.

I am pacing back and forth in the small bedroom, I realize.

I walk to my desk and locate a yellow legal pad in a drawer. I bring it and a pen back to my bed and stare at the blank page.

I begin to form her name, my pen lingering over the edges and curves in her letters: *Emma.*

I have to get the words exactly right. I must make her understand.

I realize I am pressing the pen into the paper so deeply that the ink has bled through the page.

I don't know what to write next. I don't know how to start.

If I could only figure out where my demise began, I might be able to explain it to her. Was it with my mother's mental illness? My father's death? My inability to conceive a child?

I am growing more and more certain the origin lies within that October night in Florida.

I can't tell Emma about that, though. The only part of my story she needs to understand is Richard's role in it.

I tear away the paper and begin again with a clean one.

This time I write, *Dear Emma.*

Then I hear his voice.

For a moment, I wonder if my mind has conjured it, until I realize he's in the apartment, and that Aunt Charlotte is calling my name. Summoning me to Richard.

I leap to my feet and glance in the mirror. The afternoon sun and walk have left me pink cheeked, and my hair is swept into a low ponytail. I'm wearing Lycra shorts and a tank top. Dark circles mark my eyes, but the soft, forgiving light is kind to my body's sharp angles. Earlier today I dressed up for Emma, but in this moment I look more like the Nellie my husband fell in love with than I have in years.

I walk barefoot into the living room, and my body reacts instinctively, my vision tunneling until he is all I can see. He is broad shouldered and fit; his runner's build filled out during the years we were married. Richard is one of those men who grow more attractive with age.

"Vanessa." That deep voice. The one I still hear in my dreams all the time. "I'd like to talk."

He turns to Aunt Charlotte. "May we have a moment?"

Aunt Charlotte looks at me and I nod. My mouth is dry. "Of course," she says, retreating to the kitchen.

"Emma told me you went to see her today." Richard is wearing a shirt I don't recognize, one he must have bought after I left. Or maybe one Emma bought for him. His face is tanned, the way it always gets in the summer because he runs outside in good weather.

I nod, knowing it's futile to deny it.

Unexpectedly, his expression softens and he takes a step toward me. "You look terrified. Don't you know I'm here because I'm worried about you?"

I gesture to the sofa. My legs feel shaky. "Can we sit down?"

Throw pillows are piled at either end of the couch, which means we end up closer to each other than either of us might have expected. I smell lemons. I feel his warmth.

"I'm marrying Emma. You have to accept this."

I don't have to, I think. *I don't have to accept you marrying anyone.* But instead I say, "It all happened so fast. Why the rush?"

Richard won't indulge my question. "Everyone asked me why I stayed with you all those years. You complained that I left you alone at home too much, but when we socialized, you were . . . The night of our cocktail party—well, people still talk about it."

I don't realize a tear is rolling down my cheek until he gently wipes it away.

His touch sets off an explosion of sensation inside me; it has been months since I've felt it. My body clenches.

"I've been thinking about this for a while. I never wanted to say it because I knew it would hurt you. But after today . . . I don't have any choice. I think you should get help. An inpatient stay somewhere, maybe the place where your mom went. You don't want to end up like she did."

"I'm doing better, Richard." I feel a flash of my old spirit. "I've got a job. I'm getting out more and meeting people. . . ." My voice trails off. The truth is visible to him. "I'm not like my mother."

We've had this conversation before. It's clear he doesn't believe me.

"She overdosed on painkillers," Richard says gently.

"We don't know that for sure!" I protest. "It could have been a mistake. She might have gotten her pills mixed up."

Richard sighs. "Before she died, she told you and Aunt Charlotte she was doing better. So when you just said that to me . . . Look, do you have a pen?"

I freeze, wondering how he senses what I was doing in the moment before he arrived.

"A pen," he repeats, furrowing his brow at my reaction. "May I borrow one?"

I nod, then stand up and return to my bedroom, where the legal pad with Emma's name sits on my bed. I glance over my shoulder, suddenly gripped by the fear that he has followed me. But the space in my wake is empty. I turn over the pad and pick up the pen, then I notice our wedding album still splayed on the floor. I put it on the floor of my armoire, then go back into the living room.

My knee gently bumps against Richard's when I sit back down next to him.

He tilts toward me on the couch as he reaches for his wallet. He withdraws the single blank check he always carries. I watch as he writes a number and adds several zeros.

I gape at the amount. "What is this for?"

"You didn't get enough in the settlement." He puts the check on the coffee table. "I liquidated some stock for you and let the bank know there would be a large withdrawal from my checking account. Please use this to get some help. I couldn't live with myself if something happened to you."

"I don't want your money, Richard." He fixes his eyes on me. "I never did."

I've known people with hazel eyes that morph from green to blue to brown based on the light, or what they're wearing. But Richard is the only person I've ever met whose irises shift solely through shades of blue—from denim to Caribbean sea to a beetle's wing.

Now they are my favorite shade, a soft indigo.

"Nellie"—it is the first time he has called me this since I moved out—"I love Emma."

A sharp pain bursts in my chest.

"But I will never love anyone as much as I loved you," he says.

I continue to look into his eyes, then I jerk away my gaze. I am stunned by his admission. But the truth is, I feel the same way about him. The silence in the air hangs like an icicle about to crack.

Then he leans forward again, and shock robs me of the ability to think coherently as his soft lips find mine. His hand cups the back of my head, pulling me in closer. For just a few seconds, I am Nellie again and he is the man I fell in love with.

Then I'm jolted back to reality. I push him away, wiping my mouth with the back of my hand. "You shouldn't have done that."

He looks at me for a long moment, then stands up and leaves without a word.

CHAPTER
TWENTY-THREE

SLEEP ELUDES ME AGAIN that night as I recall every detail of my encounter with Richard.

When I finally drift off, he visits me in my dream, too.

He approaches me as I lie in bed. His fingertips trace my lips, then he kisses me tenderly, slowly, first on my mouth and then working his way down my neck. He lifts up my nightgown with one hand, then moves his mouth lower. My hips begin to move involuntarily. I choke back a groan as my body betrays me by growing warm and pliant.

Then he pins me to the mattress, his torso crushing mine, his hands trapping my wrists. I try to push him off, to make him stop, but he's too strong.

Suddenly, I realize it isn't me beneath Richard—it isn't my hands being held down, or my lips parting.

It is Emma.

I jerk awake and sit upright. My breath comes in choppy gasps. I look around my bedroom, desperate to center myself.

I hurry to the bathroom and splash cold water on my face to erase the sensations that linger from my dream. I grip the hard edges of the sink until my breathing finally slows.

———

I climb back into bed, thinking of how my heart clattered and my skin tingled when I was dreaming of Richard. I still feel the aftereffects of that treacherous response to him.

How could I have been aroused by him, even in a dream?

Then I recall one of my recent psychology podcasts on the part of the brain that processes emotions.

"The human body often responds in the same way to two over-arching emotional states—romantic arousal and fear," a scientist had explained. I close my eyes and try to recall exactly what the expert said. "Consider the pounding in the chest, the dilating of the pupils, the increase in blood pressure. These are sensations that appear in both terror and arousal."

This, I know well.

The expert had said something else about how our thought processes change during both states. When we are in the throes of romantic love, for example, the neural machinery responsible for making critical assessments of other people can be compromised.

Is that what Emma is experiencing? I wonder. *Is that what I encountered, too?*

I am too shaken to fall back asleep.

I lie there as images of Richard's visit batter my mind. It was both vivid and fleeting—like a mirage—and as the long night stretches on, I begin wonder if it actually happened, or if it also was just part of my dream.

Was anything of the previous evening real? I wonder.

I walk in the first shimmer of morning gold, as if in a trance, to my armoire. I slide open the top drawer. The check is nestled among my socks.

As I put it back, I look down and see the white satin cover of our wedding album. This is the only physical documentation of my marriage that I have.

I can't imagine I will ever want to view the photographs again after today, but I need to view them a final time. Our other photos are all in the Westchester house, unless Richard has already moved them into the storage unit in the basement of his city apartment's building or destroyed them. I imagine he has; Richard would have disposed of every trace of me before Emma could stumble upon the unsettling reminders.

Aunt Charlotte told me a bit of what she'd witnessed during my marriage. Sam also told me what she'd seen during our last conversation— which turned into a worse fight than I could ever have imagined us having. But now I want to look for myself, with fresh eyes.

I sit cross-legged on my bed and turn to the first page. In the opening shot I'm in the hotel room, fastening the clasp on an antique pearl bracelet—my "something borrowed" from Aunt Charlotte. Beside me she artfully ties my father's blue handkerchief around my bouquet. I turn another page and glimpse Aunt Charlotte, my mother, and me walking down the aisle together. My fingers are interlaced with my mother's, while Aunt Charlotte has her arm looped through mine on the other side, since my left hand is grasping the bundle of white roses. Aunt Charlotte's face is flushed pink and her eyes have a sheen of tears. My mother's expression is difficult to decipher, although she is smiling for the camera. She is also set a bit apart from me and Aunt Charlotte; had we not been holding hands, I could take a pair of scissors and easily crop her out of the photograph.

If I showed this picture to strangers and asked them to guess which woman was my mother, they would likely choose Aunt Charlotte, even though physically I resemble my mother more strongly.

I've always told myself that I only received superficial traits from my mother, such as her long neck and green eyes. That on the inside, I was my father's daughter; that I was more like my aunt.

But now Richard's words boomerang back.

During our marriage, whenever he told me I wasn't acting rationally, that I was being illogical, or, in more heated moments, when he yelled, "You're crazy!" I denied it.

"He's wrong," I would whisper to myself as I paced the sidewalks in our neighborhood, my body rigid, my footsteps pounding the cement.

I'd slam down my left foot: *He's*—then my right foot—*wrong.*

He's wrong. He's wrong. He's wrong. I'd repeat those words dozens, even hundreds, of times. Maybe I'd thought if I said them enough, they would bury the persistent worry worming through my brain: *What if he was right?*

I flip to another photo of my mother standing up to give a toast. On a table directly behind her was our three-tiered wedding cake adorned with Richard's heirloom topper. The porcelain bride's painted-on smile is serene, but I remember feeling anxious in that moment. Luckily, my mother's speech at my wedding dinner had been coherent, even if it rambled on too long. Her meds were doing their job that day.

Perhaps I had inherited more from my mother than I'd allowed myself to believe.

I grew up with a woman who inhabited a different world from the station-wagon-driving, grilled-cheese-making mothers of my friends. My mom's feelings were like intense colors—fiery reds and sparkling, soft pinks and the deepest slate grays. Her shell was fierce, yet on the inside, she was fragile. Once, when a manager at the drugstore was berating an elderly cashier for moving too slowly, my mother yelled at the manager, calling him a bully, and earning applause from the other customers in line. Another time, she knelt down suddenly on the sidewalk, soundlessly weeping over a monarch butterfly that could no longer fly because its wing had been torn.

Had I absorbed some of her skewed vision, her impulsively dramatic reactions? Were the genes that dictated my destiny influenced more by her, or by my steady, patient father's composition? I desperately wanted to know which invisible attributes I'd inherited from each of them.

During the life span of my marriage, I became gripped by a growing urgency to capture the truth. I chased it in my dreams. I worried my memories would fade like an old color photograph that's been bleached by light, so I tried to keep them alive. I began to write everything down in a kind of diary—a black Moleskine notebook that I hid from Richard under the mattress of the bed in our guest room.

It's ironic now, because I've surrounded myself with lies. Sometimes I am tempted to succumb to them. It might be simpler that way, to quietly sink into the new reality I've created as though it were quick-sand. To disappear beneath its surface.

It would be so much easier to just let go, I think.

But I cannot. Because of her.

I set aside the album and walk to the small desk in the corner of my room. I retrieve my legal pad and pen and start again.

Dear Emma,

I would never have listened to anyone who told me not to marry Richard. So I understand why you're resisting me. I haven't been clear because it's hard to know where to begin.

I write until I fill the page. I consider adding one final line—*Richard visited me last night*—but leave it out when I realize she may think I'm trying to make her jealous, to create the wrong kinds of doubts in her.

So I simply sign the letter and fold it into thirds and tuck it into the top drawer to read one more time before I give it to her.

A little later that morning, I have showered and dressed. I am tracing lipstick over my mouth, covering up the imprint of Richard's touch, when I hear Aunt Charlotte yell. I run into the kitchen.

Black smoke curls toward the ceiling. Aunt Charlotte is batting a dish towel at orange flames dancing on the surface of the stove.

"Baking soda!" she cries.

I grab a box from the cabinet and toss it on the flames, dousing them. Aunt Charlotte drops the dish towel and turns on the kitchen tap to cold. I see the angry red mark on her forearm as water courses over it.

I remove the pan of burning bacon from the stove and grab an ice pack from the freezer. "Here." When she moves her arm away from the water, I turn off the tap. "What happened? Are you okay?"

"I was pouring the bacon drippings into the old coffee can." I pull out a stool for her and she sits down heavily. "I missed. Just a little grease fire."

"Do you want to go to a doctor?"

She pulls away the ice pack and peers at her arm. The burn is the width of a finger and about two inches long. Luckily it isn't blistering. "It's not that bad," she says.

I look at the overturned box of Domino sugar on the counter, grains spilling out onto the stove.

"I threw sugar on it by accident. Maybe that made it worse."

"Let me get you some aloe." I hurry to her bathroom and find a tube in the medicine cabinet, behind her old tortoiseshell glasses and a bottle of ibuprofen. I bring the painkillers back to the kitchen, too, and shake three tablets into my hand, then pass them to her.

She sighs as she smooths on some aloe. "That helps." I pour her a glass of water and she swallows the pills.

I look at the thick new glasses that sit on the bridge of Aunt Charlotte's nose, then I sit down heavily on the stool next to hers.

How could I have missed it?

I've been so fixated on potential clues about Emma and Richard's relationship that I haven't caught on to what has been unfolding right in front of me.

Her clumsiness and headaches. The appointment with D—for "doctor." The furniture clearing, for easier movement through the apartment. My aunt peering at the menu at the Robertson bar, then ordering a drink that isn't on it. Her more tentative pace on our walk along the Hudson. And the square box of sugar that doesn't look anything like the baking soda, but would feel similar to someone in a rush. Someone who is reaching for it through a thin veil of smoke.

Someone who is losing her eyesight.

A sob thickens my throat. But I cannot have her be the one to comfort me. I reach for her hand with its papery-thin skin.

"I'm going blind," Aunt Charlotte says softly. "I just had a second appointment to confirm it. Macular degeneration. I was going to tell you soon. But maybe not in such a dramatic fashion."

I think of how she once spent a week layering hundreds of strokes of paint onto a canvas to replicate the bark of an ancient redwood. How, when she took me to the beach during one of my mother's lights-out days, we lay on our backs looking up into the sky, and she explained that although we perceive the glow from the sun as white, it is really made up of all the colors of the rainbow.

"I'm so sorry," I whisper.

I am still thinking of that day—of the turkey-and-cheese sandwiches and thermos of lemonade my aunt packed, of the deck of cards she'd brought along in her purse to teach me how to play gin rummy—when she speaks again.

"Do you remember when we read *Little Women* together?"

I nod. "Yes." I'm already wondering what she can and can't see.

"In the book, Amy said, 'I'm not afraid of storms, for I'm learning how to sail my ship.' Well, I've never feared bad weather, either."

Then my aunt does one of the bravest things I have ever seen. She smiles.

CHAPTER
TWENTY-FOUR

I HATE IT when I can't see.

Maggie, the shy seventeen-year-old pledge from Jacksonville, had said those exact words to me the night of our sorority initiation.

But I hadn't listened to her. I was too fixated on how Daniel had brushed me off. *Tomorrow isn't good enough,* I'd thought as my anger mounted.

Somehow I managed to participate in most of the evening's rituals. I hovered behind Maggie as she stood in the circle of girls in our living room, their faces illuminated by candlelight. When all of the sisters had gathered together to vote after rush week, Maggie hadn't been on our original list of the twenty selected. The other pledges were pretty, lively, and fun—the sort of girls who would be asked to fraternity formals and enhance the spirit of the house. But Maggie was different. When I'd talked to her during one of our social events, I'd learned that during high school, she had started a volunteer program aimed at helping animals in a shelter near her family's home.

"I didn't have a lot of friends when I was growing up," Maggie had told me, shrugging. "I was kind of an outsider." She'd grinned, but I'd seen vulnerability in her eyes. "I guess helping animals kept me from feeling alone."

"That's amazing. Can you explain how you started that program? I want to get our house more involved in service."

Her face had lit up as she described the three-legged dachshund named Ike that had sparked her idea. I decided that no matter what the other girls in the house thought, Maggie needed to be one of our pledges.

But as I stood behind her, listening to the voices of my sorority sisters rise in song, I wondered if I'd made a mistake. Maggie was dressed in a childish white cotton top printed with a pattern of little cherries and matching shorts, and she had barely said a word all night. She'd told me she was looking forward to a fresh start in college, that she wanted to form connections with the other girls here. But she wasn't putting forth any effort to bond with the sisters. She hadn't memorized our anthem; I could see her pretending to mouth the words. She'd taken a sip of the Dirty Hunch Punch and spat it back into her cup. "Gross," she'd said, leaving the cup on the table instead of throwing it out, then reaching for a Jell-O shot.

It was my job to watch over Maggie, to make sure she was completing her tasks—including the scavenger hunt through the house— and, especially, to track her during the ocean plunge. Even we college kids knew that drinking and swimming in the choppy waves at night could be treacherous.

I couldn't focus on Maggie, though. I was too aware of the change in my body, the silent phone in my pocket. When she complained that she couldn't locate the brass rooster we jokingly called our mascot and had hidden in the house, I shrugged and ticked it off her list anyway. "Just find what you can," I said, then I checked my phone again. Daniel still hadn't called.

It was nearly ten o'clock by the time our sorority president led the way down to the beach for our final initiation rite. The girls were blindfolded and holding on to one another, giggling drunkenly.

I saw Maggie peeking out from under her blindfold, violating another rule. "I hate it when I can't see. It makes me feel claustrophobic."

"Put it back on," I instructed. "It's only for another few minutes."

As we passed by fraternity houses on Greek Row, guys clapped and cheered, "Go, Chi O!"

Jessica, the wildest girl in our sorority, lifted up her shirt and flashed her hot-pink bra, earning a standing ovation. I was pretty sure Jessica would end up sleeping out tonight; she'd been matching the pledges shot for shot.

Beside me was Leslie, one of my closest friends. Her arm was linked through mine, and she was singing along to "99 Bottles of Beer on the Wall" with all the other girls. Normally I would have been shouting the lyrics along with them, but I hadn't had a sip of alcohol. How could I, knowing a little life was inside me?

I thought about the beach. The place where Daniel and I had likely conceived. I couldn't go there.

"Hey," I whispered. "I feel like crap. Can you do me a favor? Watch Maggie at the ocean?"

Leslie made a face. "She's kind of a dud. Why'd we vote her in?"

"She's just shy. She'll be fine. And she's a good swimmer, I already asked."

"Whatever. Feel better. And you owe me."

I found Maggie and told her I was ill. She lifted up her blindfold again, but this time I let it slide.

"Where are you going? You can't leave me."

"You'll be okay." I was annoyed at the whine in her tone. "Leslie will look out for you. Just tell her if you need anything."

"Which skinny blonde is she?"

I rolled my eyes and pointed in Leslie's direction. "She's our vice president."

I peeled away from the group as they turned the corner and began to march the last two blocks to the ocean. The faculty housing was on the other side of campus, a fifteen-minute walk if I cut across the quad. I tried Daniel a final time. Straight to voice mail, again. I wondered if he'd turned off his phone.

I thought back to the girl who'd approached him after class this afternoon. I'd been so focused on Daniel that I hadn't paid attention to her. But now, as if I were watching a movie and the camera was panning back to encompass her, I saw her anew. She was quite attractive. How close had she stood to him?

Daniel had told me I was the first student he'd ever slept with. I'd never doubted that until this moment.

He could be out with her for all I knew.

I didn't realize I'd quickened my step until I began to breathe more heavily from exertion.

The faculty homes were all in a row, just like the Greek houses. They lined the very edge of campus, back behind the Agriculture Department's greenhouse. The two-story redbrick structures weren't fancy, but they were rent-free—a great perk for a college professor.

His Alfa Romeo was parked in the driveway of house number nine.

My plan had been to knock on a door and ask where Daniel—no, Professor Barton—lived. I was going to say I had a paper I had to turn in, that I'd given him the wrong draft in class. But the car eliminated that need. Now I knew exactly where he lived. And he was home.

I pressed the buzzer, and one of Daniel's professor roommates answered. "Can I help you?" She tucked her wheat-colored hair behind an ear. A calico cat sauntered into the room and rubbed its head against her ankle.

"It's the stupidest thing. Is Professor Barton here? I just realized I, um, gave him the wrong—"

The woman was turning around to look at someone descending the stairs. "Honey? One of your students is here."

He almost ran down the final steps. "Vanessa! What brings you to my home so late at night?"

"I—I gave you the wrong paper." I knew my eyes were wild as they flicked between Daniel and the woman who'd called him "honey."

"Oh, no problem," Daniel said quickly. He was smiling too brightly. "Just submit a new version tomorrow."

"But I—" I blinked hard against tears as he began to shut the door on me.

"Wait a minute." The woman reached out to stop the door's movement, and that's when I saw the gold band wrapped around her finger. "You came all the way out here to talk about a paper?"

I nodded. "You're his wife?" I was still hoping it was a roommate, that this was some kind of misunderstanding. I tried to keep my voice even and casual. But it broke.

"I am. I'm Nicole."

She looked at my face more carefully. "Daniel, what is going on?"

"Nothing." Daniel's blue eyes widened. "I guess she turned in the wrong paper."

"Which class is this?" his wife asked.

"Family Sociology," I said quickly. It was the class I took last semester. I didn't lie to protect Daniel. I did it for the woman standing in front of me. She was barefoot and wore no makeup. She looked tired.

I think she wanted to believe me. Maybe she would have. She might have closed the door and heated up oil for popcorn and cuddled with Daniel on the couch while they watched *Arrested Development*. Daniel could have explained me away, as if I were a mosquito to be batted aside. "These kids are so stressed about grades," he might've said. "Remind me, how long until I can retire?"

Except for one thing.

At the exact same moment that I said, "Family Sociology," Daniel said, "Senior Seminar."

His wife didn't react immediately.

"That's right!" Daniel snapped his fingers theatrically. Overcompensating. "I'm teaching five classes this semester. It's nutty! Anyway, it's late. Let's let this poor girl go home. We'll sort it out tomorrow. Don't worry about the paper, it happens all the time."

"Daniel!"

At his wife's shout, he fell silent.

She jabbed a finger at me. "Stay away from my husband." Her lower lip quivered.

"Sweetie," Daniel pleaded. He wasn't looking at me; he didn't see me at all. Two broken women stood in front of him. But he only cared about one.

"I am so sorry," I whispered. "I didn't know."

The door slammed and I could hear her yell something. As I walked down the front steps, I had to grip the railing to keep from stumbling when I saw a yellow tricycle in the grass. A tree had hidden it from my view when I approached the house. Near it was a pink jump rope.

Daniel already had children.

Much later, after I'd returned to the sorority house and cursed Daniel and sobbed and raged; after Daniel had brought me a bouquet of inexpensive carnations and an equally cheap apology, saying he loved his family and that he couldn't start a new one with me; after I'd gone alone to a clinic an hour away, an experience so wrenching I was never able to talk about it with anyone; after I'd completed my senior year with honors and had set out for New York, desperate to put Florida behind me—even after all that, whenever my mind returns to that warm October night, the moment I always remember the most vividly is this:

When the pledges returned from the ocean, Maggie was missing.

Maggie and Emma have nothing in common. Except for me. These two young women have forever changed the course of my existence. But one is now gone from my life, and the other is ever present.

I used to spend as much time thinking about Maggie as I now do Emma. Maybe that is why they are beginning to blur together in my mind.

But Emma is not like Maggie, I remind myself.

My replacement is stunning and confident. Her radiance draws the eye.

The first time I saw her, she rose from behind her desk to greet me in a fluid, elegant motion. "Mrs. Thompson! I'm so happy to *finally* meet you!"

We'd spoken on the phone, but her throaty voice hadn't prepared me for her youth and beauty.

"Oh, call me Vanessa." I felt ancient even though I was only in my mid-thirties.

It was December, the night of Richard's office holiday party. We'd been married seven years by then. I wore a black A-line dress in an attempt to hide my extra pounds. It looked funereal next to Emma's poppy-red jumpsuit.

Richard came out of his office and kissed me on the cheek.

"Are you heading upstairs?" he asked Emma.

"If my boss says it's okay!"

"Your boss says it's an order," Richard joked. So the three of us rode the elevator together to the forty-fifth floor.

"I love your dress, Mrs.—I mean Vanessa." Emma gave me a toothpaste-ad smile.

I looked down at my plain outfit. "Thank you."

A lot of women might have been threatened by the possibilities of an Emma: those late nights at the office when Chinese food was ordered in and bottles of vodka pulled from a partner's bar, the overnight trips to see clients, her daily proximity to my husband's corner office.

But I never was. Not even when Richard called me to say he was working late and would crash in the city apartment.

Back when we were first dating—back when I was Richard's Nellie—I remember wondering about the sterile quality of that apartment. Another woman had lived there with Richard before he met me. All he told me about her was that she still resided in the city and was perpetually late. I stopped worrying she was somehow a threat to me once Richard and I were married; she was never an intrusion in our lives, even though I became more curious about her as the years went by.

But I never made a mark on the apartment, either. It remained much as it had during Richard's bachelor days, with the brown suede sofa and complicated lighting system and tidy row of family photographs lining the hallway, plus one of me and Richard on our wedding day, in a simple black frame that matched those of the other images.

During those months when Richard and Emma thought they were having a secret affair—when he took her to the apartment or visited hers—I actually relished his being gone. It meant I didn't have to change out of my sweats. I could empty a bottle of wine and not worry about where to hide the evidence. I didn't have to concoct a story about what I'd done that day or come up with a new way to avoid having sex with my husband.

His affair was a reprieve. A vacation, really.

If only it had remained just that—an affair.

I've spent most of the morning talking with Aunt Charlotte. She has agreed to allow me to accompany her to the doctor to learn more about how I can help her, but she insisted on going to meet a friend for a lecture at MoMA, as she'd planned.

"My life isn't going to stop," Aunt Charlotte had said, brushing off my offer to skip work and go with her or, at the very least, call her a cab.

After I clean the kitchen, I open my laptop and type in the words *macular degeneration*. I read, *The condition is caused by the deterioration of the central portion of the retina.* If the eye is a camera, the macula is the central and most sensitive area of the so-called film, the website explains. A working macula collects highly detailed images at the center of the field of vision and sends them up the optic nerve to the brain. When the cells of the macula deteriorate, images are not received correctly.

It sounds so clinical. So sterile. As if these words have no connection to how my aunt will no longer be able to blend together blues and reds and yellows and browns to replicate the skin on a hand, the veins and creases, the gentle dips and swells of the knuckles.

I close my laptop and retrieve two things from my room: Richard's check, which I put into my wallet to cash later this week. He'd told me to use it to get help, and I will. Help for Aunt Charlotte. Her medical bills, audiobooks and other supplies, and whatever else she needs.

I also pull Emma's letter from the desk drawer and read it a final time.

Dear Emma,

   I would never have listened to anyone who told me not to marry Richard. So I understand why you're resisting me. I haven't been clear because it's hard to know where to begin.

I could tell you what really happened the night of our party, when there was no Raveneau in our cellar. But I am certain Richard will erase any doubt I might create in you. So if you won't talk to me—if you won't see me—then please just believe this one thing: A part of you already knows who he is.

There's a reptilian inheritance in each of our brains that alerts us to danger. You've almost certainly felt it stirring by now. You've dismissed it. I did, too. You've made excuses. So did I. But when you are alone, please listen for it; listen to it. There were clues before our wedding that I ignored; hesitations I waved away. Don't make the same mistake I did.

I couldn't save myself. But it is not too late for you.

I fold up the letter again, then go to look for an envelope.

CHAPTER
TWENTY-FIVE

ONE OF THE FIRST CLUES surfaced even before we were married. I held it in my hand. Sam saw it. So did everyone else at our wedding.

A blond bride and her handsome groom, frozen in a perfect moment.

"Jeez, they even look like you two," Sam had said when I showed her the cake topper.

When Richard took it out of the storage unit in his apartment building's basement, he told me it had belonged to his parents. At that time, I had no cause to question this.

But a year and a half after our wedding, on a night when I went into the city to see Sam, two things happened. I realized how distant my best friend and I had already become. And I began to find reasons to doubt my husband.

I was so looking forward to seeing Sam. It felt like forever since we'd had more than a quick lunch together. We set a date for a Friday night, when Richard was at a work conference in Hong Kong. It was scheduled to last only for three days, so even though he'd invited me to come, we agreed it didn't make sense. "You won't even recover from jet lag by the time we'll be heading home," Richard had said. As with everything else, Richard adapted easily to new time zones. But I knew the combination of the Xanax I'd need for the long plane ride and the Clomid I was taking to get pregnant would leave me so groggy I wouldn't enjoy the brief stay in Asia.

Impulsively, I booked a table at Pica, deciding to treat Sam. I took the train in, planning to spend the night at Richard's city apartment. Even after all this time, and even though I still kept some toiletries and a few items of clothes there, I always thought of it as his place.

Sam and I had agreed to meet at the apartment we used to share. She greeted me at the door and we hugged hello. She loosened her arms, but I held on a beat longer, savoring her warmth. I'd missed her even more than I'd realized.

She wore a fitted sleeveless suede dress and high boots. Her hair had a few more layers than the last time I had seen her, and her arms looked more sculpted than ever.

"Is Tara here?" I followed Sam through the tiny entranceway and kitchen and into her bedroom. Beyond it, the door was shut to my old room—Tara's bedroom now.

"Yeah," Sam said as I plopped down on the bed. "She just got back from the studio. She's in the shower."

I could hear the water running through the old pipes, the ones that would occasionally scald me without warning. White lights were still woven through Sam's headboard, and clothes were scattered across the floor. Everything was exactly the same, yet different. The apartment seemed smaller and shabbier; I felt the same sensation of alienness I'd experienced when I visited my old elementary school as a teenager.

"I guess there are benefits to rooming with a Pilates instructor. You look amazing."

"Thanks." She reached for a thick chain bracelet on her dresser and fastened it on her wrist. "Don't take this the wrong way, but you look . . . how do I put this delicately? Sort of terrible."

I grabbed a pillow and threw it at her. "Is there a right way to take that?" My tone was light, but I felt hurt.

"Oh, shut up, you're still gorgeous. But what the heck are you wearing? I love the necklace, but you kinda look like you're on the way to a PTA meeting."

I looked down at my black slacks (slimming) and lacy gray chiffon top that I'd left untucked. I'd accessorized the outfit with my happy beads.

Sam peered more closely at my blouse. "Oh my God . . ." She began to giggle. "That shirt . . ."

"What?"

Sam laughed harder. "Mrs. Porter was wearing the exact same one at the holiday cookie party!" she finally managed.

"Jonah's mom?" I flashed back to the prissy woman who'd come to my conference wearing lipstick that precisely matched her rose-hued dress. "No, she wasn't!"

"I swear." Sam wiped her eyes. "Jonah's little sister is in my class, and I remember because a kid smeared frosting on it and I had to help her clean it off. Come on, we're not going to tea at the Ritz." She dug through the clothes heaped over the back of a chair. "I've got this new pair of Jeggings from Anthropologie—hang on, they'll look great on you." She found them and tossed them at me, along with a black scoop-neck top.

Sam had seen me dress and undress hundreds of times. I'd never been modest around her, but that night I felt self-conscious. I knew I wouldn't fit into her pants, no matter how much Lycra they contained.

"I'm fine." I wrapped my arms around my knees, recognizing I was doing so in an effort to look smaller. "It's not like I'm trying to impress anyone."

Sam shrugged. "Okay. Want a glass of wine before we head out?"

"Sure." I jumped off the bed and followed her to the kitchen. The cabinets were still painted the creamy shade we'd applied together when I first moved in, but the color was now faded, with a few chips showing by the handles. The countertops were lined with boxes of herbal tea: chamomile, lavender, peppermint, nettle leaf. Sam's ever-present honey jar was there, but it had been changed to a squirt container.

"You cleaned up your act." I picked it up.

When Sam opened the refrigerator door, I noticed containers of hummus and bags of organic baby carrots and celery. Not a single left-over Chinese-food container in sight. They'd always adorned our fridge, even days after they should have been discarded.

Sam grabbed two glasses from the cabinet and filled them, then handed me one.

"I meant to bring some wine," I said, suddenly remembering the bottle I'd left in our home's vestibule.

"I've got plenty." We clinked glasses and each took a sip. "It's probably not as good as the stuff you drink with the Prince, huh?"

I blinked. "Who's the Prince?"

Sam hesitated. "You know, Richard." She paused again. "Your Prince Charming."

"You say that like it's a bad thing."

"Of course it's not a bad thing. He is, isn't he?"

I looked down into my glass of wine. It tasted a little sour—I wondered how long it had been uncorked in Sam's fridge—and looked more like apple juice than the pale gold liquid I'd grown used to drinking. The blouse I was wearing, the one Sam had mocked, cost more than my monthly rent had here.

"No more Diet Coke." I gestured toward the empty spot by the front door. "Are you drinking nettle tea instead now?"

"I haven't gotten her to try that yet," a soft, airy voice said. I turned around to see Tara. The photos Sam had shown me on her phone didn't do Tara justice. She was brimming with good health—her teeth were white and straight, her skin glowed, and her eyes were bright. I could see the sleek, rectangular bulge of thigh muscles through her leggings. She didn't wear a stitch of makeup. She didn't need it.

"Tara read me the ingredients in Diet Coke one day. Remember?"

Tara laughed. "By the time I got to potassium benzoate, she had her hands over her ears."

Sam picked up the story. "I was so hungover, and it almost made me throw up."

I gave a little laugh. "You used to guzzle that stuff. Remember how we'd always stub our toes on the cases?"

"I've got her drinking water now." Tara reached up to twist her damp hair into a knot on the top of her head. "I infuse it with parsley. It gets rid of the natural inflammation in the body."

"So that's why your arms look so good," I told Sam.

"You should try it," Sam said.

Because I'm puffy? I finished my wine quickly. "Ready? We've got a reservation. . . ."

Sam rinsed our glasses in the sink, then put them on the drying rack that hadn't been there when this was our apartment. "Let's hit it." She turned to Tara. "Text me later if you want to meet us for a drink."

"Yeah, that would be fun," I added. But I didn't want Tara there, talking about her parsley-infused water and laughing with Sam.

We took a cab to the restaurant and I gave my name to the maître d'. We walked through the thickly carpeted entranceway into the dining room. Nearly every table was full—this place had gotten a great write-up in the *Times*. It was why I'd chosen it.

"Nice," Sam said as the waiter held her chair. "Maybe you were right not to change into the Jeggings."

I laughed, but as I looked around, I realized this type of restaurant— with its ten-page wine list in a thick leather folder, and napkins intricately folded on the plates—was the sort of place Richard would take me to. It wasn't Sam's style. I suddenly wished I'd suggested sitting on her bed and ordering in spring rolls and Szechuan chicken, the way we used to.

"Get anything you want," I told Sam as we opened our menus. "Remember, this is on me. Should we share a bottle of white Burgundy?"

"Sure. Whatever."

I went through the wine-tasting routine, and we decided to split a rustic goat cheese and tomato tart and a watercress and grapefruit salad for appetizers. I then ordered the filet mignon, medium rare, with the sauce on the side. Sam chose the salmon.

A server came by the table holding a basket with four artfully arranged bread selections. He described each one and my stomach rumbled. The scent of warm bread has always been my kryptonite.

"None for me," I said.

"I'll take hers, then. Can I have the rosemary focaccia and the multigrain?"

"Does Tara eat bread?"

Sam dunked a piece in olive oil. "Sure. Why are you asking?"

I shrugged. "She just seems so healthy."

"Yeah, but she's not a zealot about it. She drinks and she even smokes weed once in a while. Last time we did it, we went to Central Park and rode the carousel."

"Wait, you get high now?"

"Like, once a month, maybe. No big deal." Sam lifted the bread to her mouth and I noticed her defined biceps again.

After a little pause, the waiter brought our salad and tart and we each took some.

"So, are you still dating that guy—the graphic designer?" I asked.

"Nah. But tomorrow night I'm going on a blind date with one of Tara's client's brothers."

"Yeah?" I took a bite of salad. "What's his story?"

"His name is Tom. He sounded great on the phone. He runs his own business. . . ."

I tried to feign enthusiasm as Sam told me about Tom, but I knew that the next time we spoke, Tom would be a vague memory of hers.

Sam reached for a spoon and added more tart to her plate. "You're not eating much."

"Just not that hungry."

Sam looked me straight in the eye. "So why'd we come here?"

I'd always loved and hated her directness. "Because I wanted to treat you to something nice," I said lightly.

Sam's spoon made a clink as she dropped it back onto the plate. "I'm not a charity case. I can buy my own dinner."

"You know that's not what I meant." I laughed, but for the first time, the cadence of our conversation seemed bumpy.

The waiter came by the table and topped off our wineglasses. I gratefully drank a bit more, then my phone vibrated. I pulled it out of my purse and saw Richard's text: *What are you up to, sweetheart?*

Dinner with Sam, I texted back. *We're at Pica. What are you doing?*

Heading to the golf course with clients. You're taking a car home, right? Remember to set the alarm before you go to bed.

I will. Love you! I hadn't mentioned that I was intending to sleep in the city. I wasn't sure why. Maybe I thought Richard might suspect I was planning a long, late night of drinking, as I'd done before I met him.

"Sorry." I put the phone back onto the table. But I laid it there face-down. "It was Richard. . . . He wanted to make sure I'd be okay getting home."

"To the apartment?"

I shook my head. "I didn't tell him I might sleep there. . . . He's in Hong Kong, so—it just didn't seem like a big deal."

I saw Sam register that, but she didn't comment.

"So!" Even I could hear the false note of cheer in my voice. Luckily the server appeared to clear our appetizers and bring the main courses.

"How is Richard? Tell me what you've been up to."

"Well . . . he's still traveling a lot, obviously."

"And you're drinking, so you're not pregnant."

"Yeah." I felt the sting of tears and I drank more wine to buy time to compose myself.

"Are you okay?"

"Sure." I tried to smile. "It's just taking longer than we thought, I guess." I felt a pang of nostalgia for the child I didn't yet have.

I looked around at the other diners—couples leaning in toward each other across tables, and larger groups chatting animatedly. I wanted to talk to Sam the way we used to, but I didn't know how to begin. I could bring up the interior designer who'd helped me select new upholstery for our dining room chairs. I could mention the hot tub Richard wanted to install in our backyard. I could show her all of the enviable bits of my life, the superficial things Sam wouldn't have any interest in.

Sam and I had fought before—over stupid things, like when I lost one of her favorite hoop earrings, or when she forgot to mail our rent check. But tonight we weren't fighting. It was worse than that. A distance was between us that wasn't simply caused by time apart and geographical separation.

"Tell me about your kids this year." I cut off a piece of steak and watched the juice seep onto the plate. Richard always ordered his steak medium rare, but in truth I preferred mine more pink than red.

"They're mostly great. James Bond is my favorite—that kid has serious style. I'm stuck with Sleepy and Grumpy, though."

"Could be worse. You could have the evil stepsisters."

Sam's nickname for Richard flashed in my mind again. The Prince. The blandly handsome guy who rides in to save the day, to give the heroine a luxurious new life.

"Is that how you see Richard? As my rescuer?"

"What?"

"Earlier. You called him the Prince." I put down my fork. Suddenly I truly wasn't hungry. "I always wondered if you had a nickname for him." I was acutely aware of my expensive top, of the cost of the wine we were drinking, of my Prada handbag slung over the back of my chair.

Sam shrugged. "Don't turn it into a big deal." She cast her eyes down at her plate and focused on shaking pepper onto her salmon.

"Why don't you ever want to come out to the house?" I wondered why she had chosen this moment to avoid being straightforward. The one time she'd been over, Richard had greeted her with a hug. He'd grilled burgers. He'd remembered Sam hated sesame seeds on her bun. "Just admit it. You've never really liked him."

"It's not that I don't like him. I don't—I feel like I don't know him at all."

"Do you even want to get to know him? He's my husband, Sam. You're my best friend. It's important to me."

"Okay." But she left it there and I knew she was holding something back. Sam and Richard had never connected in the way that I had hoped. I'd told myself it was just because they were so different. I almost pressed her for more, but the reality was, I didn't want to hear it.

Sam broke our eye contact to duck her head and take a forkful of salmon. Maybe it wasn't simply Richard she didn't want to get to know, I thought. Maybe it was me as Richard's wife she was avoiding.

"Anyway, let's figure out where to go next," Sam said. "Up for dancing? I'll text Tara and tell her we're finishing up."

I didn't go out with them, after all. By the time I'd paid the check, I felt exhausted, even though I'd done nothing that afternoon but fold laundry and wait for the plumber to fix a leaky faucet, while Sam had worked a full day and managed to squeeze in a spin class. Besides, I wasn't dressed for dancing—as Sam had said, I looked as if I were on my way to a PTA meeting.

I dropped Sam off at the club where Tara was waiting and took a cab back to Richard's place. It was only ten o'clock. *We made it an early night. I'm just about to get into bed,* I texted Richard. I reasoned that I wasn't really lying.

A new doorman was on duty and I introduced myself. Then I took the elevator upstairs, creeping by the door of nosy neighbor Mrs. Keene, and entered Richard's apartment using the key he'd given me long ago. I walked through the hallway, passing the family photographs lining the wall.

I'd never told Sam about Richard's upbringing, about his checked-out mother and his father, the neighborhood accountant. Richard had revealed it during a private moment, and I'd felt it was his story to tell. If Sam would actually ask Richard about himself rather than categorize him as she did her children, maybe she would've seen him differently, I'd thought.

Sam didn't like who I was when I was with Richard—that was clear now. But I also knew Richard didn't like the way I acted when I was with Sam.

I headed into the living room, noticing how the configuration of lighting—the darkness of the room combined with the bright kitchen globe behind me —turned the wall of glass windows overlooking Central Park into a mirror. I saw my blurry image, as wispy and insubstantial as a cloud. As if I were a figure trapped inside a snow globe.

In my black-and-gray outfit, I looked drained of color. I seemed to be fading away.

I wished I'd gone with Richard on his trip. I wished I'd handled dinner with Sam better. I desperately craved something solid to hold on to. Something more real to touch than the pristine furniture and glossy surfaces of this apartment.

I went into the kitchen and opened the refrigerator. It was empty except for a few bottles of Perrier and one of Veuve Clicquot champagne. I knew the cabinets held pasta, a few cans of tuna, and espresso pods. In the living room, the latest issues of *New York* magazine and *The Economist* were on the coffee table. Dozens of books lined the shelves in Richard's office, mostly biographies and a few classics by Steinbeck, Faulkner, and Hemingway.

I began to walk back down the hallway to the bedroom to turn in for the night. I passed the family photographs again.

Then I stopped.

One was missing.

Where was the picture of Richard's parents on their wedding day? I could still see the small hole where the nail had been.

I knew it wasn't in the Westchester house. I checked the other walls of the apartment, even looking in the bathroom. The picture was too big to tuck in a drawer, but I searched anyway. It wasn't anywhere.

Had Richard put it in the storage unit? I wondered. Other photographs were down there, including some of Richard as a child.

I wasn't tired, not anymore. I reached into my purse for my keys and retraced my steps to the elevator.

The storage units made available to the building's tenants were in the basement. I'd been there with Richard once, shortly before our wedding, when I'd brought a few boxes to his place to keep until our move. His was the fifth unit on the left. After he'd spun the dial of the thick padlock and put away my things, he'd opened one of his big blue plastic bins stacked along the wall. He'd pulled out a dozen or so photos—four-by-six glossies, tucked in a faded yellow envelope that said *Kodak*. They were all taken on the same day, a series of shots of Richard at baseball practice. The photographer seemed to be trying to get a picture of Richard swinging and connecting with the ball, but in every shot, he or she had clicked at the wrong moment.

"How old were you in these?" I'd asked.

"About ten or eleven. Maureen took them."

"Can I have one?" I loved the intent expression on Richard's face, the way his little nose was wrinkled up in concentration.

He laughed. "I was going through a dorky phase. I'll find you a better picture."

But he hadn't, not on that day. We'd been in a rush to meet George and Hillary for brunch, so Richard put the pictures back atop a pile of identical yellow envelopes and clicked the padlock into place, and we ascended in the elevator to the lobby.

Maybe he'd stored his parents' wedding photo in that bin. As I stepped into the elevator, I told myself I was merely curious.

Now, with the benefit of hindsight, I wonder if my subconscious was guiding me. If it was urging me to learn more about my husband on a night when he had no idea where I actually was. On a night when he was as physically far away from me as possible.

Even in the daytime, the basement was a dismal place, the under-belly of the elegant structure atop it. Overhead lightbulbs illuminated the area and it was clean, but the walls were dishwater gray and the individual units were separated by thick grids of wire fencing. It looked like a prison for the belongings people didn't require for everyday use.

Richard used the combination of Maureen's birthday. It was the same temporary code he always installed in the safes in our hotel rooms whenever we traveled, so I knew it well. I spun the dial, the metal pad-lock cool and dense in my palm, and it fell open.

I stepped inside. The units on either side were filled with a mish-mash of objects—furniture, skis, a plastic Christmas tree. But Richard's was characteristically tidy. Other than the pair of green sleds we'd used on our second date, the unit held only a half dozen identical big blue bins, stacked in pairs, lining a wall.

I knelt down, the concrete floor rough against my knees, and opened the first one. School yearbooks, a baseball trophy with the gold paint peeling off the player, a folder with a few report cards—he'd struggled with cursive and had been a quiet student, his second-grade teacher reported—and a stack of old birthday cards, all signed by Maureen. I opened one with Snoopy holding a balloon on the cover. *To my little brother,* she'd written. *You're a superstar! This is going to be your best year yet. I love you.* I wondered where the cards from his parents were. I began to work my way through the bins, setting aside the envelopes of photos I wanted to take upstairs and linger over. But I was careful not to remove too much, and to remember exactly where every item had been so I could return it all in the morning.

The third bin held a pile of old tax documents and warranties, a deed to Richard's previous apartment, the titles to his cars, and other paperwork. I replaced it all and reached for the lid of the next bin.

I heard a rumbling sound in the distance, like heavy mechanical gears shifting into motion.

Someone was calling the elevator.

I froze, listening for the sound of the doors opening around the corner from where I crouched. But no one came.

Probably just a resident who was traveling from the lobby to his or her apartment, I realized.

I knew I should go back upstairs, and not only because the new doorman might mention to Richard that I'd been here.

But I felt compelled to continue.

When I pulled the lid off the fourth bin, I saw a large flat object wrapped in thick layers of newspaper. I peeled back the protective covering, revealing the faces of Richard's parents.

Why had he moved it down here? I wondered.

I studied his father's lanky build and full lips, his mother's piercing eyes that Richard had inherited, and her dark hair curling around her shoulders. The date of their marriage was written in ornate script at the bottom.

Richard's father's arm was around his wife's waist. I'd assumed Richard's parents had had a happy marriage, but the wedding photo was so posed it didn't provide any insight. In the absence of any real information, my mind had filled in the blanks, creating the picture I had wanted to see.

Richard had never told me much more about his parents. When I asked, he always said it was too painful to think about them. Maureen seemed to subscribe to the same unspoken rule of focusing on the present with Richard, instead of their shared past. Maybe they talked more about their childhood when they were alone on their annual ski trips or when Richard went to Boston on business and met her for dinner. But when Maureen came to visit us, our conversations always revolved around his work and hers, their running regimes, travel plans, and world events.

Talking about my father made me still feel connected to him, but I'd been able to say good-bye to him, and to tell him I loved him in his final moments. I understood why Richard and Maureen might want to block the memories of the sudden, violent deaths of their parents in the car accident.

When it came to the darkest and most painful pieces of my own past, I also edited a few of the details while sharing the stories with my husband. I'd shaped my narrative carefully, leaving out the bits I knew he might find sordid. Even after Richard discovered I'd gotten pregnant in college, I never revealed that the professor was married. I didn't want him to think I'd been foolish, that I was somehow to blame. And I hadn't been truthful about how my pregnancy ended.

As I knelt in the storage unit, I considered whether that had been a mistake. I recognized marriage didn't guarantee a storybook ending, the happily ever after stretching past the final page, the words echoing into infinity. But wasn't this most intimate relationship supposed to be a safe place, where another person knew your secrets and faults and loved you anyway?

A sharp, tinny sound to my left jerked me out of my thoughts.

I twisted my head around and peered into the dim light. The unit next to Richard's was packed with furniture; it blocked my vision.

This was an old prewar building, I told myself. The noise was only a pipe clanging. Still, I shifted so that I faced the opening of the storage unit. That way I could glimpse anyone who might be approaching.

I quickly folded the newspaper back around the wedding picture. I'd found what I had come here for; I should go. But I felt compelled to see what else was tucked away, hidden from the orbit of Richard's everyday life. I wanted to continue digging through the stratum of Richard's past.

I reached into the bin again and pulled out a small wooden plaque with a heart and the word *Mom* etched by the top. Richard's name was on the back; he must've made it for his mother, perhaps in a wood-shop class at school. There was also a crocheted yellow blanket, and a pair of bronzed baby shoes.

Toward the bottom of the bin was a small photo album. I couldn't identify any of the people, but I thought I recognized his mother's smile on one of the girls holding the hand of a woman in pedal pushers and a halter top. Maybe the album had belonged to her, I'd thought. The next item I touched was the white box that held our wedding-cake topper.

I lifted the lid and picked it up. The porcelain felt delicate and smooth; the colors were soft pastels.

Ever think he's too good to be true? Sam had asked the day I showed her the cake topper. I wished she'd never asked that question.

I looked down at the handsome groom and the flawless bride with her light blue eyes. Absently, I caressed the figures as I turned them over and over in my hand.

Then the figurine slipped from my fingers.

I frantically fumbled for it, desperate to prevent the cake topper from shattering against the concrete.

I caught it two inches from the floor.

I closed my eyes and released my breath.

How long had I been down here? A few minutes, or had it been closer to an hour? I'd completely lost track of time.

Perhaps Richard had texted me back. He'd be worried if I didn't respond. Just as the thought struck me, I heard a faint noise, again to my left. The pipe? Or maybe it was a footstep.

I suddenly became aware that I felt trapped in this metal cage. I'd left my cell phone upstairs, in my purse. No one knew where I was.

Would sound even travel up to the doorman in the lobby if I screamed?

I held my breath, my pulse quickening, waiting for a face to appear from around the corner.

No one came.

Only my imagination, I told myself.

Still, my hand shook when I began to return the topper to its box. As I laid it flat, I noticed some tiny numbers embossed on the bottom. I looked closer, squinting to make out the numerals in the dim light. A date: 1985. That must have been when the topper was sculpted.

No, that couldn't be right, I thought.

I pulled out the figurines again and peered more closely at the numbers. They were unmistakable.

But Richard's parents had already been married for years by then. He would've been a teenager in 1985.

Their wedding was held more than a decade before the cake topper existed. It couldn't have belonged to them.

Maybe his mother had simply found the figurine at an antiques store and had purchased it because she'd thought it was pretty, I reasoned as I rode the elevator back up to Richard's floor. Or maybe this was my fault. It could be I'd simply misunderstood Richard.

I could hear my cell phone ringing inside the apartment as I fit my key into the lock. I rushed to grab my purse, but it fell silent before I could dig it out.

Then the apartment line began to shrill.

I ran into the kitchen and snatched it up.

"Nellie? Thank God. I've been trying to reach you."

Richard's voice sounded higher than usual—stressed. I knew he was on the other side of the world, but the connection was so clear, he could have been in the next room.

How had he known I was here?

"I'm sorry," I blurted. "Is everything okay?"

"I thought you were at home."

"Oh, I was going to, but then I was so tired—I just thought—I figured it would be easier for me to stay at the apartment," I blurted.

Silence crackled between us.

"Why didn't you tell me?"

I didn't have an answer. At least not one I felt I could share with him.

"I was going to . . ." I stalled. For some reasons tears filled my eyes and I blinked them away. "I just figured I'd explain tomorrow rather than send you a long text while you're with clients. I didn't want to bother you."

"*Bother* me?" He made a sound that wasn't quite a laugh. "It bothered me far more to imagine that something had happened to you."

"I'm so sorry. Of course, you're right. I should have told you."

He didn't respond for a beat.

Then he finally said, "So why didn't you answer your cell? Are you alone?"

I'd made him angry. His clipped tone was the giveaway. I could almost see his eyes narrowing.

"I was in the bath." The lie just shot out of me. "Of course I'm alone. Sam went out dancing with her roommate but I didn't want to, so I just came here."

He exhaled slowly. "Listen, I'm just glad you're safe. I should probably get back to the golf course."

"I miss you."

When he spoke again, his voice was gentle. "I miss you, too, Nellie. I'll be home before you know it."

Being in that basement—and being caught in my deception—had unsettled me, I realized as I changed into my nightgown, then double-checked that I'd secured the dead bolt on the front door.

I went into Richard's bathroom, using his toothpaste and extra washcloth as I prepared for bed. The smell of lemons was so strong it unnerved me, until I realized Richard's terry-cloth robe, the one he always stepped into after showering, was hanging on a hook directly next to me. The scent of his soap lingered on the absorbent fabric.

I turned off the light, then hesitated and flicked the switch back up, closing the door partway so it wouldn't shine in my eyes. I pulled back the fluffy white comforter on Richard's bed, wondering what he was doing at that exact moment. Probably socializing with important business associates on the greens. Perhaps a cooler of cold beers and bottled water would be in the golf cart, and an interpreter on hand to facilitate conversation. I could picture Richard concentrating on his chip shot, his face creased, his expression an echo of the one he wore when he was a little boy playing baseball.

I'd searched the bins to better understand Richard. I was still yearning for more answers about my husband.

But as I climbed between the crisp, ironed sheets in his king-size bed, I realized he understood me well enough to guess exactly where I was when he hadn't been able to reach me at home.

He knew me better than I knew him.

CHAPTER
TWENTY-SIX

THE LETTER TO EMMA feels heavy in my hand, its weight disproportionate to its actual material heft. I fold the note again, then look for an envelope in Aunt Charlotte's room, where my aunt likes to sit at a rolltop desk to do paperwork and pay bills. I find an envelope but ignore the stamps. I need to hand-deliver this; I can't rely on the mail to get it there in time.

Atop the pile of papers on her desk, I also see a photograph of a dog. A German shepherd with soft brown and black fur.

Gasping, I reach for it. *Duke.*

But of course, it isn't him. It's only a promotional postcard from a group that provides guide dogs for the blind.

It just looks so much like the picture I still carry in my wallet.

I need to get this letter to Emma. I need to investigate ways to help Aunt Charlotte. I should be moving forward right now. But all I can do is collapse onto her bed as the images come hard and fast, crashing over me like waves. Dragging me into the undertow of memory again.

My insomnia returned when Richard came back from Hong Kong.

He found me in our guest room at two A.M., the light on and a book splayed open across my lap. "Can't sleep."

"I don't like being in bed without you." He stretched out his hand and led me back to our room.

Feeling his arms wrapped around me and his steady breaths warm in my ear no longer helped, though. I began to wake up most nights, easing myself out of bed quietly, tiptoeing down the hall to the guest room, then I'd sneak back into our bed before dawn.

But Richard must have known.

On a bone-chillingly frigid Sunday morning, Richard was reading the *Times* Week in Review in the library and I was searching for a new recipe for cheesecake. We were hosting my mother and Maureen for dinner the following weekend to celebrate Richard's birthday. My mother hated the cold and had never before come up north during the winter months. Instead, she visited every spring and fall to see me and Aunt Charlotte. During those trips, she spent most of her time touring art galleries and walking the city streets to soak up the atmosphere, as she put it. I didn't mind that we spent so little time together; being with my mom required deep reservoirs of patience as well as unlimited energy.

I was unsure of her motivation for changing that pattern.

But I suspected it was due to a conversation we'd had in a recent call. She'd caught me on a bad day—a lonely day—when I hadn't even left the house. The streets were crusted with old snow and patches of ice, and since I had no experience driving in winter weather, I wasn't comfortable taking out the Mercedes Richard had bought me. When my mother phoned in the early afternoon and asked what I was doing, I was honest. I'd let down my guard with her.

"I'm still in bed."

"Are you sick?"

I realized I'd already revealed too much. "I didn't sleep well last night." I thought that would appease my mother.

But it only made her ask more questions. "Does this happen often? Is there anything bothering you?"

"No, no. I'm fine."

There was a pause. Then: "You know what? I was thinking I'd like to come up for a visit."

I tried to talk her out of it, but she was resolute. So finally I suggested she time it for Richard's birthday. Maureen would be joining us to celebrate, as she did every year, and perhaps her presence would help dilute my mother's focus.

When the doorbell rang that Sunday morning, my first thought was that my mother had decided to surprise us by arriving a few days early or had gotten the dates wrong. It wouldn't have been out of character.

But Richard put down his paper and stood up. "That's probably your present."

"My present? You're the one with a birthday coming up."

I was a few steps behind him. I heard Richard greet someone, but his body blocked my view. Then he bent down. "Hey there, boy."

The German shepherd was massive. I could see his shoulder muscles rolling as Richard took his leash and led him into the house, followed by the man who'd delivered the dog.

"Nellie? Meet Duke. This big guy is the best security you could ever ask for."

The dog yawned, revealing his sharp teeth.

"And this is Carl." Richard laughed. "One of Duke's trainers. Sorry about that."

"No worries, I'm used to Duke getting top billing." Carl must have noticed my unease. "He looks fierce, but remember, he's going to look that way to everyone else, too. And Duke knows it's his job to protect you."

I nodded. Duke probably weighed almost as much as I did. If he stood on his hind legs, he'd be my height.

"He spent a year at the Sherman Canine Academy. He understands a dozen commands. Here—I'll tell him to sit." At Carl's word, the dog sank down on its haunches. *"Up,"* Carl instructed, and the dog rose fluidly.

"Try it, sweetheart," Richard urged.

"Sit." My voice sounded scratchy. I couldn't believe the dog would obey, but he fixed his brown eyes on me and touched his bottom to the floor.

I averted my gaze. Rationally I knew the dog had been trained to follow orders. But hadn't he also been trained to attack when he perceived a threat? Dogs could sense fear, I remembered, shrinking back against the wall.

I was fine around little dogs, the fluffy breeds that were common in New York City, sometimes tucked into purses or dancing along on the end of brightly colored leashes. I even stopped sometimes to offer them a pat, and I'd never minded sharing the elevator in Richard's apartment with Mrs. Keene and her bichon frise with the matching hairstyle.

Big dogs like this one were rare in the city; apartment sizes simply didn't make them practical. I hadn't been near one in years.

But when I was a child, my next-door neighbors in Florida had owned two rottweilers. They were kept behind a chain-link enclosure, and whenever I rode my bike past their yard, they lunged at me and crashed into the fence as if they wanted to break through it. My dad told me they were just excited, that the dogs were friendly. But their deep, throaty barks and the sound of that rattling metal terrified me.

Duke's unnatural stillness was even more unnerving.

"Do you want to pet him?" Carl asked. "He loves being scratched behind the ears."

"Sure. Hey there, Duke." I reached out and gave him a quick stroke. His black-and-brown fur was softer than I'd expected.

"I'll go grab his supplies." Carl headed back to his white truck.

Richard gave me a reassuring smile. "Remember what the security guy told us. Dogs are the number one deterrent to intruders. Better than any alarm system you can buy. You'll sleep well when he's around."

Duke was still sitting on the floor, staring up at me. Was he waiting for me to tell him he could stand again? I'd only ever owned a cat, back when I was a child.

Carl returned, his arms full of a bag of food and a bed and bowls. "Where would you like me to set him up?"

"The kitchen's probably best," Richard said. "It's through here."

At another clipped word from Carl, the dog followed them, his big paws padding almost soundlessly on our wood floors. Carl drove off a few minutes later, leaving behind his card and a laminated list of the words Duke knew—*Come. Stay. Attack.* He'd explained that Duke would react to those words only when they were directed at him by Richard or me in a commanding tone.

"He's a smart boy." Carl had given Duke's head a final rub. "You picked a good one."

I'd smiled weakly, dreading the next morning when Richard would leave for work and I'd be alone with the dog who was supposed to make me feel safe.

I kept to the other side of the house for the first few days, only entering the kitchen to grab a banana or dump some food into Duke's bowl. Carl had instructed us to walk him three times a day, but I didn't want to fumble with the leash's catch around Duke's throat. So I simply opened the back door and told him to *Go*—another of his commands—and then I cleaned up after him before Richard came home.

On the third day, as I read in the library, I looked up and saw Duke standing silently in the entryway, watching me. I hadn't even heard his approach. I still feared meeting his gaze—didn't dogs interpret locked eyes as a challenge?—so I stared back at my book, wishing he'd go away. Richard, right before he went to sleep every night, took Duke for a short walk. Duke had plenty to eat, fresh water, and a comfortable bed. I had no reason to feel guilty. Duke had a great life, with everything he could possibly want.

He padded over and flopped down next to me, putting his head between his big paws. He looked up at me and sighed heavily. It was such a human sound.

I snuck a peek at him over the top of my novel and saw furrows form above his chocolate-brown eyes. He looked sad. I wondered if he was used to being around other dogs, to being surrounded by activity and noise. *Our house must seem so strange to him,* I thought. Tentatively I reached down and patted the spot behind his ear, the way his trainer had said Duke liked. His bushy tail thumped once, then stilled, as if he didn't want to make too much of a commotion.

"You like that? It's okay, boy. You can wag as much as you want."

I slid off my chair to sit beside him as I continued to stroke his head, finding a rhythm he seemed to enjoy. It soothed me, too, to feel my fingers gliding along the warm, thick fur.

A little later, I stood up and went into the kitchen and found his leash.

Duke followed me.

"I'm going to put this on you. Be a good dog and *sit,* okay?"

For the first time, I equated his stillness with gentleness. Still, I attached the silver clip to his collar as quickly as possible so I could withdraw my hand from the vicinity of his teeth.

The crisp winter air pinched the tip of my nose and my ears as soon as we stepped outside, but it wasn't so chilly that I was in a rush to return home. Duke and I probably walked close to three miles that day, exploring corners of our neighborhood I'd never before seen. He matched my pace, standing by my side the entire time, only stopping to sniff grass or relieve himself when I paused.

Unclipping his leash wasn't as intimidating when we arrived home. I filled his water bowl and poured a glass of iced tea for myself, drinking it down thirstily. My legs felt pleasantly heavy from the walk, and I realized I'd needed it as much as Duke had. I began to return to the library, then paused in the doorway and looked at Duke.

"*Come.*"

He ambled over and sat down beside me.

"You're such a good boy."

On Richard's birthday, we picked up my mother at the airport and brought her back to the house. By the time Maureen arrived a few hours later, my mother had already scattered her belongings through the rooms—her purse in the kitchen, her shawl slung over the back of a dining room chair, and her book splayed open on Richard's favorite ottoman—and had turned up the heat an extra five degrees. I could tell this irked Richard, even though he didn't say a word.

Dinner went smoothly enough, even though my mother kept slipping Duke pieces of her steak—she'd already abandoned vegetarianism—under the table.

"He's an unusually intuitive dog," she declared.

Maureen shifted her chair a bit farther away from Duke and my mother, then asked Richard a question about a stock she was considering buying. She wasn't a dog person, she explained, though she'd gamely given Duke a pat.

After I served the cheesecake, we all went into the living room to open gifts. Richard opened mine first. I'd gotten him a framed Rangers hockey jersey signed by all the players—and a matching Rangers collar for Duke.

My mother presented Richard with the new Deepak Chopra book. "I know you work so hard. Maybe you can read this on your commute?"

He politely opened it and flipped through a few pages. "This is probably exactly what I need." When my mom went to find the card she'd left in her purse, he winked at me.

"I'll get you the CliffsNotes version in case she asks you about it," I joked.

Maureen gave him two floor seats to a Knicks game the next night. "We've got a sports theme going here," she laughed. She and Richard were both basketball fans.

"You should take Maureen to the game," I said.

"That was my plan all along," Maureen replied lightly. "I remember Richard tried to explain goaltending to you once and I saw you zone out."

"Guilty as charged."

My mother's eyes flitted from Maureen to Richard, then they landed on me. "Well, it's a good thing I'm up here. Otherwise you'd be left home alone, Vanessa. Why don't you and I go into the city tomorrow and we can have dinner with Aunt Charlotte?"

"Sure." I could tell my mother was surprised Maureen hadn't gotten three tickets. Maybe she thought I felt left out, but the truth was, I was happy Richard's sister wanted to be with him. He had no other family.

My mother stayed for two more days, and although I braced myself for her usual unfiltered declarations, they never emerged. She came with me whenever I took Duke on his walks, and she suggested we give him his first bath. Duke submitted to it with his usual dignity, though his brown eyes seemed reproachful, and he got revenge by shaking water on us after he stepped out of the tub. Laughing with my mother then was the highlight of her trip for me. I think it may have been for her, too.

When we said good-bye at the airport, she hugged me for much longer than she usually did when we parted.

"I love you, Vanessa. I'd like to see you more. Maybe you could come to Florida in a month or two?"

I'd dreaded her visit, but I found myself surprisingly comforted by her embrace. "I'll try."

And I intended to. But then everything changed again.

I quickly grew used to Duke's solid presence in the house, to our brisk morning walks, to chatting with him as I cooked dinner. I brushed his fur for long stretches while he rested his head on my leg, and I wondered how I'd ever been frightened of him. When I took a shower, he waited like a sentry just outside the bathroom. Whenever I came home, he was stationed in the hallway just inside the front door, his ears perked up into triangles. He seemed relieved when I was back in his sights.

I was so grateful to Richard. He must have known that Duke would provide more than security. In the absence of the baby we so desperately wanted, Duke was my companion.

"I love Duke so much," I told Richard one night a few weeks later. "You were right. He really does make me feel safe." I recounted the story of how Duke and I had been strolling down our sidewalk, a dozen yards from our house, when the mailman suddenly emerged from a gap in the hedges surrounding a neighbor's yard. Duke had quickly positioned himself between the two of us, and I heard a low rumbling in his throat. The mailman gave us a wide berth and continued on his way, and so did we. "That's the only time I've seen that side of him."

Richard nodded as he picked up a knife and buttered his roll. "It's good to remember it's always there, though."

When Richard left for an overnight business trip the following week, I brought Duke's bed upstairs and placed it next to mine. When I awoke in the night, I looked down to see that he was awake, too. I let my arm drape over the side of the bed so I could touch his head, then I fell back asleep quickly. I slept deeply and dreamlessly, better than I had in months.

I'd told Richard I was doing tons of walking with Duke to get rid of the extra pounds I'd put on since moving to the suburbs. It wasn't just the fertility pills. In the city, I could easily trek four miles a day, but now I drove even to buy a half gallon of milk. Plus, we ate dinner so late. Richard had never commented on my weight, but he stepped on the scale every morning and worked out five times a week. I wanted to look good for him.

When Richard returned, I didn't have the heart to move Duke back downstairs, to our cold, sterile kitchen. Richard couldn't believe how quickly my attitude toward Duke had changed. "Sometimes I think you love that dog more than me," he joked.

I laughed. "He's my buddy. When you're not around, he keeps me company." The truth was, the love I felt toward Duke was the purest, most uncomplicated affection I had ever known.

Duke was more than just a pet. He became my ambassador to the world. A jogger we often ran into during our daily walks stopped to ask if he could pet Duke, and we ended up chatting. The gardeners brought him a bone, shyly asking me if it was okay. Even the mailman grew to love him, once I told Duke the mailman was a *friend*—another of the words Duke understood. On my weekly calls with my mother, I gushed about our latest adventures.

Then, on one of those early-spring days when every tree and flower seems about to burst into bloom, I took Duke to a hiking trail a few towns over.

Looking back, I would think of it as the last good day—Duke's, and mine—but as we sat on a big flat rock, my fingers absently weaving through Duke's fur, the sun warming us, it just seemed like a perfect afternoon.

When Duke and I returned home, my cell phone rang. "Sweetheart, did you get to the dry cleaner's?"

I'd forgotten Richard had asked me to pick up his shirts. "Oh, shoot. I just need to pay the gardeners and then I'll run out."

The team of three had grown especially fond of Duke, and sometimes if the weather was nice, they would stay a little late to play fetch with him.

I was gone thirty, maybe thirty-five minutes tops. When I returned home, the gardeners' truck was gone. The moment I opened our front door, I felt a coldness rush through my body.

"Duke," I called out.

Nothing.

"Duke!" I yelled again, my voice trembling.

I ran to the backyard to look for him. He wasn't there. I called the gardening service. They swore they'd closed the back gate. I ran around the neighborhood, calling for him, then phoned the Humane Society and the local vets. Richard rushed home and we drove through the streets, shouting Duke's name through the open car windows until our throats were raw. The next day Richard didn't go into work. He held me while I cried. We put up posters. We offered a huge reward. Every night I stood outside, calling for Duke. I imagined someone taking him or Duke jumping the fence to go after an intruder. I even googled wild-animal sightings in our area, wondering if Duke could have been attacked by a larger animal.

A neighbor claimed she had seen him on Orchard Street. Another thought he'd spotted him on Willow. Someone called the number on our poster and brought by a dog that wasn't Duke. I even phoned a pet psychic, who told me Duke was in an animal shelter in Philadelphia. None of the tips materialized. It was as if the ninety-pound canine had vanished from my life as magically as he had appeared.

Duke was so well trained; he wouldn't have just run off. And he would've attacked anyone who'd tried to take him. He was a guard dog.

But that wasn't what I thought about at three A.M. when I crept down the hallway, putting distance between me and my husband.

Right before Duke vanished, Richard had called to ask me about the shirts. I'd assumed he was calling from work, although I had no way to verify that; he'd never given me the passwords to his cell phone and BlackBerry, and I'd never asked him, so I couldn't check his call records.

But when I'd gone to the dry cleaner's, Mrs. Lee greeted me with her usual exuberance: *So good to see you! Your husband just called a little while ago, and I told him his shirts were ready, light starch, like always.*

Why would Richard have phoned the cleaner's to make sure I hadn't gotten the shirts, then called me to see if I'd picked them up?

I didn't ask him about it immediately. But soon it was all I could think about.

I grew hollow eyed from insomnia. On the nights when I managed to catch a little sleep, I often awoke with my arm dangling over the side of the bed, my fingers touching the empty space where Duke used to lie. Much of the time I was numb. I rose with Richard and made him coffee, downing several extra cups myself. I kissed my husband good-bye when he walked out the door to work, staring after him as he strolled to his car, humming.

A few weeks after Duke disappeared, when I was listlessly planting flowers in our backyard, I came across one of his favorite toys, a green rubber alligator he loved to chew. I clutched it to my chest and bawled as I hadn't since my father's funeral.

When I finally quelled my tears, I went inside. I stood in the mannered quiet with the alligator still in hand. Then I walked through our living room, not caring that I might be tracking mud on our pristine rug, and placed Duke's toy on the table in the hallway where Richard always put his keys. I wanted him to see it the moment he came home.

Here's what I didn't do next: I didn't change out of my dirty clothes. I didn't tidy up the newspapers and fold the laundry and put away the gardening tools. I didn't prepare the swordfish, snap peas, and tortellini I had planned to make for dinner.

Here's what I did instead: I made myself a vodka and tonic and sat in the den. I waited as the light dwindled to dusk. Then I poured myself more vodka, this time without the tonic. I hadn't been drinking much other than an occasional glass or two of wine. I could feel the strong alcohol coursing through my body.

When at last Richard walked in the door, I remained silent.

"Nellie," he called.

For the first time in our marriage, I didn't reply "Hi, honey" or hurry to greet him with a kiss.

"Nellie?" This time my name was a question, not a statement.

"I'm in here," I finally said.

He appeared in the doorway, holding Duke's muddy alligator with the tail half missing. "What are you doing sitting in the dark?"

I lifted my tumbler and drained the rest of my vodka.

I saw him take in my clothes—the faded jeans with dirt on the knees and the old, oversize T-shirt. I set down my glass, not caring that I hadn't used a coaster.

"Sweetheart, what's wrong?" He walked over and put his arms around me.

I felt his solid warmth and my resolve began to melt. I'd been so angry with him all afternoon, but now what I wanted most was to have the man who'd caused my distress to comfort me. The accusations that had been forming in my mind grew blurry; how could Richard have done such a horrible thing? None of it made sense again.

Instead of saying what I'd planned to, I blurted out, "I need a break."

"A break?" He pulled back. "From what?" His brow furrowed.

I wanted to say, *From everything,* but instead I replied, "From the Clomid."

"You're drunk. You don't mean that."

"Yeah, I guess I am a bit tipsy, but I do mean it. I'm not going to take it anymore."

"Don't you think this is something we should discuss as a couple? It's a joint decision."

"Was it a joint decision to get rid of Duke?"

With the release of those words, I knew I'd crossed a line in our relationship.

What stunned me was how good it felt. Our marriage, like every

marriage, had unspoken rules, and I'd broken one of the most important ones: Don't challenge Richard.

Now I realize my adherence to that mandate had prevented me from
asking why he'd bought a house without showing it to me, and why
he never wanted to discuss his childhood, as well as other questions
I'd tried to push out of my mind.

Richard hadn't made that rule alone; I'd been a willing accomplice.
How much easier it was to just let my husband—the man who'd always
made me feel safe—take charge of the direction of our lives.

I didn't feel safe anymore.

"What are you talking about?" Richard's voice was cold and measured.

"Why did you call Mrs. Lee and ask if your shirts were ready? You
knew I hadn't picked them up. Were you trying to get me out of the
house?"

"Jesus!" Richard stood up abruptly.

I had to tilt my head to look up at him as he loomed over me in my
chair.

"Nellie, you're being completely irrational." I could see his hand
gripping the alligator, mangling its shape. His features seemed to
tighten, his eyes narrowing and his lips folding inward; it was as if my
husband was disappearing behind a mask. "What the fuck does the
cleaner's have to do with Duke? Or with us having a baby? Why would
I want you out of the house?"

I was losing my way, but I couldn't back down. "Why would you
ask me if I'd gotten your shirts when you already knew I hadn't?" My
voice was shrill.

He threw the alligator to the ground. "What are you suggesting?
You're acting crazy. Mrs. Lee is old and always in a rush. You must've
misunderstood."

He closed his eyes briefly. When he opened them, he was Richard
again. The mask was gone. "You're depressed. We've had a huge loss.
We both loved Duke. And I know the fertility treatments are hard on
you. You're right. Let's take a little break."

I was still so angry at him; why did it feel as if he were forgiving me?

"Where is Duke?" I whispered. "Please tell me he's alive. I just need to know he's safe. I'll never ask you again."

"Baby." Richard knelt down beside me and wrapped me in his arms. "Of course he's safe. He's so smart and strong. He's probably just a few towns over, living with a new family that loves him as much as we did. Can't you see him chasing a tennis ball in a big backyard?" He wiped away the tears running down my cheeks. "Let's get you out of these dirty clothes and into bed."

I watched Richard's full lips move as he talked; I tried to read his eyes. I had to make a decision, perhaps the most important one I'd ever confronted. If I didn't let go of my suspicions, it would mean everything I'd believed about my husband and our relationship was false, that every moment of the past two years was a hideous lie. I wouldn't just be doubting Richard, I'd be dismantling my own instincts, my judgment, my deepest truth.

So I chose to accept what Richard told me. Richard loved Duke and knew how much I did, too. He was right; I had been crazy to think he'd do anything to our dog.

All the tension slipped out of my body, leaving me feeling as dense and heavy as cement.

"I'm sorry," I said as Richard led me upstairs.

When I came out of the bathroom after changing, I saw he had drawn down the covers and put a glass of water on my nightstand.

"Do you want me to lie here with you?"

I shook my head. "You must be hungry. I feel bad that I didn't make dinner."

He kissed me on the forehead. "Don't worry about that. Get some rest, sweetheart."

It was as if none of it had ever happened.

The next week, I signed up for a new cooking class—this one Asian themed—and joined a children's literacy committee at the club. We collected books to distribute to schools in underserved areas in Manhattan. The group met at lunchtime. Wine was always served during those meals, and I was often the first to empty my glass and request a refill. I kept a bottle of Advil in my purse to offset the headaches that daytime drinking sometimes gave me. I looked forward to the meetings because I would take a nap afterward, filling a few more hours. My breath was minty and Visine had erased any redness from my eyes by the time Richard arrived home.

I thought about suggesting we get another dog, maybe a different breed. But I never did. And so our home—no pets, no children—shrank back to being just a house.

I began to loathe it, the constant silence that never let up.

CHAPTER
TWENTY-SEVEN

I PLACE THE POSTCARD with the German shepherd back on Aunt Charlotte's desk. I have missed so much work. I can't be late again. I tuck the letter to Emma in my purse. I will deliver it after my shift. I imagine I can feel its weight pulling down the strap on my shoulder as I begin my walk to Midtown.

I'm halfway there when my phone rings. For a brief moment, I think, *Richard*. But when I look down, the number flashing is Saks.

I hesitate, then answer and blurt out, "I'm almost there. Another fifteen minutes, tops." I pick up my pace.

"Vanessa, I hate to have to do this," Lucille says.

"I'm so sorry. I lost my cell phone, and then . . ." She clears her throat and I fall silent.

"But we need to let you go."

"Give me one more chance," I say desperately. With Aunt Charlotte's condition, I need to work now more than ever. "I was going through a rough time, but I promise, I won't— Things are turning around."

"Being late is one matter. Repeated absences are another. But concealing merchandise? What were you planning to do with those dresses?"

I'm going to deny it, but something in her voice tells me not to bother. Maybe someone saw me remove the three black-and-white floral knit Alexander McQueen dresses and hide them in the stockroom.

It's futile. I have no defense.

"I have your final check. I'll mail it to you."

"Actually, can I come in to pick it up?" I hope I can convince Lucille to give me another chance in person.

Lucille hesitates. "Fine. We're a little busy at the moment. Stop by in an hour."

"Thank you. That's perfect."

Now I have time to deliver the letter to Emma's office instead of waiting until after work and leaving it at her home. It's only been twenty-four hours since I last saw Richard's fiancée, but that means it's a day closer to her wedding.

I should be using this time to plan my speech to Lucille. But all I can think of is how I can linger outside in the courtyard and see if Emma steps out for a coffee or to run an errand. Maybe I'll be able to discern from her expression if Richard told her about his visit.

The last time I entered this sleek high-rise building was for Richard's office party. The night it all began.

But I have so many other memories of this place: coming here from the Learning Ladder to meet Richard and watching him conclude a business call, his voice so intent it was almost stern, while he made goofy faces at me above the phone receiver; commuting in from Westchester to join Richard and his colleagues for dinner; stopping by to surprise Richard and having him lift me off my feet into a joyful hug.

I push through the revolving door and approach the security guard's desk. At ten o'clock, the lobby isn't busy, for which I'm grateful. I don't want to bump into anyone I know.

I vaguely recognize the guard, so I keep my sunglasses on. I hand over the envelope with Emma's name printed on it. "Can you deliver this to the thirty-second floor?"

"Just a moment." He touches a screen on his desk and types in her name. Then he looks up at me. "She no longer works here." He pushes the envelope back to me across the desk.

"What? When did she—did she quit?"

"I don't have that information, ma'am."

A UPS deliverywoman walks up behind me, and the guard shifts his attention.

I take the envelope and walk back through the revolving door. In the nearby courtyard is a little bench where I planned to wait for Emma. Now I collapse onto it.

I shouldn't be so surprised. After all, Richard wouldn't want his wife working, particularly not for him. I briefly wonder if she has taken another job, but I know she wouldn't do that right before her wedding. I am equally certain she won't return to work after she is married, either.

Her world is beginning to shrink.

I need to get to her right away. She threatened to call the police if I approached her apartment again, but those are not consequences I can focus on now.

I stand up and go to put the letter in my purse. My fingers graze my wallet. The one containing Duke's picture.

I pull the small color photograph out from its protective plastic covering. Rage descends over me; if Richard were here now, I would fly at him, clawing his face, screaming obscenities.

But I force myself to return, yet again, to the security guard's desk.

"Excuse me," I say politely. "Do you have an envelope?"

He hands me one without comment. I put Duke's photo inside, then I search my purse for a pen. I come up with a gray eyeliner and use it to write *Richard Thompson* on the envelope. The blunt-tipped, soft liner leaves a trail of progressively messier letters, but I don't care.

"Thirty-second floor. I know he still works there."

The guard raises an eyebrow but otherwise remains impassive, at least until I leave.

I need to go to Saks, but as soon as I am through there, I intend to walk directly to Emma's apartment. I wonder what she is doing at this precise moment. Packing up her things in preparation for the move? Buying a sexy nightgown for her honeymoon? Having a final coffee with her city friends, promising she'll be back all the time to see them?

My left foot hits the pavement. *Save.* My right foot comes down.

Her. I walk faster and faster, the words echoing in my brain. *Saveher-savehersaveher.*

I was too late once before, when I was in my final year in Florida at the sorority. That will not happen again.

On the night Maggie vanished, I came home from Daniel's just as the pledges were returning to the house, wet and giggling, smelling like the sea.

"I thought you were sick!" Leslie yelled.

I pushed through the cluster of pledges and headed upstairs to my room. I was shattered, unable to think straight. I don't know what made me look back at the girls, who were by then drying themselves with the towels someone was throwing over the top of the staircase.

I spun around. "Maggie."

"She's right—she's right—" Leslie spluttered. Those two syllables echoing as my sorority sisters scanned the room, their laughter fading as they checked faces, searching for the one who wasn't there.

The story of what happened on the beach emerged in frantic shards and fragments; memories distorted by alcohol and exuberance that had turned to fear. Some fraternity boys had crept along behind the girls as they'd marched to the beach, perhaps galvanized by the flash of that hot-pink bra. The pledges had all stripped, as instructed, then run into the ocean.

"Check her room!" I shouted to our sorority president. "I'll go to the beach."

"I saw her come out of the water," Leslie kept saying as we ran back to the ocean.

But so had the guys. By then the boys had run onto the sand, hooting and laughing, scooping up the discarded clothing and dangling it just out of reach of the naked girls. It was a prank; not one we'd planned, though.

"Maggie!" I screamed as we sprinted now onto the beach.

The girls had been screaming, too, with some of the clothed sisters chasing the boys. The pledges tried to cover themselves with shirts or dresses the guys dropped as they withdrew farther back onto the sand. The girls had eventually gotten back the clothing and had run to the house.

"She isn't here!" Leslie yelled. "Let's go back to the house in case we missed her on the way."

Then I saw the white cotton top with little cherries and matching shorts strewn on the sand.

Blue and red lights churning. Divers searching the ocean, dragging nets through the water. A spotlight dancing across the waves.

And the high, drawn-out scream when a body was pulled from the ocean. It came from me.

The police questioned us one by one, methodically forming a narrative. The local newspaper filled four pages with articles and sidebars and photographs of Maggie. A news station from Miami filmed footage of our sorority house and aired a special report about the dangers of pledge-week drinking. I was the social director; I was Maggie's big sister. These details were reported. My name was printed. So was my photo.

In my mind, I always see skinny, freckled Maggie retreating into the ocean, trying to hide her body. I see her going out too far, losing her footing in the unsteady sand. A wave breaks over her head. Maybe she cries out, but her voice blends into the other shrieks. She gulps salt water. She spins around, disoriented, in the inky black. She can't see. She can't breathe. Another wave drags her under.

Maggie vanished. But maybe she wouldn't have if I hadn't disappeared first.

Emma will disappear, too, if she marries Richard. She will lose her friends. She will become estranged from her family. She will disconnect from herself, just as I did. And then it will get so much worse.

Save her, my mind chants.

CHAPTER
TWENTY-EIGHT

I WALK THROUGH THE EMPLOYEES' door and take the elevator to the third floor. I find Lucille refolding sweaters. She's been shorthanded because of me; she is doing my job.

"I really am sorry." I reach for the pile of pewter cashmere. "I need this job, and I can explain what's been going on. . . ."

She turns to me as my voice trails off. I try to read her expression as she appraises my appearance: confusion. Did she think I would simply pick up my check and leave? Her gaze halts at my hair, and I instinctively turn to the mirror alongside the sweaters. Of course she's perplexed; she has only known me as a brunette.

"Vanessa, it's I who am sorry, but I gave you several second chances."

I'm going to beg some more, but then I see the floor is filled with customers. A few other saleswomen are watching us. Perhaps it was even one of them who told Lucille about the dresses.

It's futile. I put down the sweaters.

Lucille retrieves my check and hands it to me. "Good luck, Vanessa."

As I walk back to the elevator, I see the black-and-white intricately patterned gowns hanging in their rightful place on the rack. I hold my breath until I've safely passed them.

————

That dress had fit me like a glove, as if it were custom-made for my curves.

Richard and I had been married for several years by then. Sam and I were no longer speaking. Duke's disappearance had never been resolved. My mother had also unexpectedly canceled her upcoming spring trip to visit us, saying she wanted to go on a group tour to New Mexico.

But instead of withdrawing from life, I'd begun to ease back into it.

I hadn't had a sip of alcohol in nearly six months, and the puffiness had dissipated from my body like helium slowly leaking from a balloon. I'd begun to rise early each morning to jog through the broad streets and gentle hills in our neighborhood.

I had told Richard I was focusing on getting healthy again. I thought he believed me, that he simply accepted my new behavior as a positive shift. After all, he was the one who'd printed out the itemized bills the country club emailed to him every month before they charged his credit card. He'd begun to leave them on the kitchen table for me with the liquor charges highlighted. Turns out, I had never needed to bother with the Visine and breath mints; he'd known exactly how much I'd been drinking during those committee lunches.

But I was changing more than just my physical health. I'd also begun a new volunteer job. On Wednesdays, I commuted on the train with Richard, then caught a cab to the Lower East Side, where I read to kindergarteners at a Head Start program. I'd gotten to know the program's organizers while delivering books for the club's literacy program. I only worked with the children for a few hours each week, but it gave me purpose. Stepping back into the city was rejuvenating, too. I was feeling more like my old self than I had since my honeymoon.

"Open it," he had said the night of the Alvin Ailey gala as I looked down at the glossy white box tied with a red bow.

I untied the silk, lifted the lid. Since marrying Richard, I'd grown to appreciate the textures and detailing that separated my old H&M staples from fine designer pieces. This dress was among the most elegant I'd ever seen. It also contained a secret. From a distance, it appeared to be a simple black-and-white pattern. But that was an illusion. Up close, every thread was deliberately placed, stitch upon stitch creating a floral wonderland.

"Wear it tonight," Richard said. "You look gorgeous."

He put on his tuxedo and I brushed aside his hand when he began to tie his bow.

"Let me." I smiled. Some men in black tie look like boys on their way to the prom, with their slicked-back hair and glossy shoes. Others seem like pompous posers, the wannabe one percenters. But Richard owned it. I straightened the wings of his bow tie and kissed him, leaving a trace of pink glossing his bottom lip.

I can see us that night as if from above: Exiting our Town Car into the lightly falling snow and walking arm in arm into the gala. Finding our table card that said *Mr. and Mrs. Thompson: Table 16* in flowing script. Posing for a photo, laughing. Accepting flutes of champagne from a passing server.

And, oh, that first sip—those golden bubbles crushing in my mouth, that warmth trickling down my throat. It tasted like exhilaration in a glass.

We had watched the dancers leap and soar, their sinewy arms and muscular legs whirling, their bodies twisting into impossible shapes, while drums frantically throbbed. I didn't realize I was swaying back and forth and lightly clapping until I felt Richard's hand give my shoulder a gentle squeeze. He was smiling at me, but I felt a flush of embarrassment. No one else was moving to the music.

When the performance ended, there were more cocktails and passed hors d'oeuvres. Richard and I chatted with some of his colleagues, one of whom, a white-haired gentleman named Paul, sat on the board of the dance company and had bought a table for the dinner benefit. We were there as his guests.

Dancers mingled among us, their bodies rippling sculptures, looking like gods and goddesses who'd descended from the sky.

Usually at these types of social events, my face hurt from smiling by the end of the night. I always tried to look engaged and cheerful to compensate for my not having much to say, especially in the dull silence following the inevitable question, the one strangers always think is so harmless: "Do you have children?"

But Paul was different. When he asked what I'd been up to and I mentioned volunteering, he didn't say, "How nice," and seek out a more accomplished person. Instead he asked, "How did you get into that?" I found myself telling him about my years as a preschool teacher and my volunteer work with Head Start.

"My wife helped get the funding for a wonderful new charter school not too far from here," he said. "You should think about getting involved with it."

"I would love that. I miss teaching so much."

Paul reached into his breast pocket and pulled out a business card. "Call me next week." He leaned in a bit closer and whispered, "When I say my wife helped with their funding, I mean my wife told me to write them a big check. They owe us a favor." His eyes crinkled at the corners and I grinned back. I knew he was one of the most successful men in the room and that he was still happily married to his high school sweetheart, a white-haired woman who was chatting with Richard.

"I'll make introductions," Paul continued. "I bet they can find a spot for you. If not now, maybe at the start of the school year."

A waiter offered us glasses of wine from a tray, and Paul handed me a fresh one. "Cheers. To new beginnings."

I'd misjudged the force of our glasses connecting. The delicate, thin rims collided with a crash, and I was left holding a jagged stem while wine coursed down my arm.

"I'm so sorry!" I blurted as the waiter rushed back to me, offering his stack of cocktail napkins and removing the broken stem from my hand.

"Completely my fault," Paul said. "I don't know my own strength! I'm the one who's sorry. Hold on, don't move, there's glass on your dress."

I stood there while he plucked a few shards out of the fine knit, putting them on the waiter's tray. The conversations around us had halted for a moment, but now they resumed. Still, I felt everyone's heightened awareness of me. I wanted to melt into the carpet.

"Let me help," Richard said, coming to stand next to me. He blotted my damp dress. "Good thing you weren't drinking red."

Paul laughed, but it sounded forced. I could tell he was trying to remove some of the awkwardness from the moment. "Well, now I really owe you a job." Paul looked at Richard. "Your lovely wife was just telling me how much she misses teaching."

Richard crumpled up the damp napkin in his hand, put it on the waiter's tray, and said, "Thanks," dismissing the man. Then I felt Richard touch the small of my back. "She's great with kids," he told Paul.

Paul's attention was caught by his wife, waving him over. "You have my number," he told me. "Let's talk soon."

The moment he left, Richard leaned closer to me. "How much have you had to drink, sweetheart?" His words were innocuous, but his body held an unnatural stillness.

"Not that much," I said quickly.

"By my count you had three glasses of champagne. And all that wine." His hand increased its pressure on my lower back. "Forget dinner," he whispered in my ear. "Let's head home."

"But—Paul bought a table. Our seats will be empty. I promise I'll stick to water."

"I think it would be better if we left," Richard said quietly. "Paul will understand."

I went to get my wrap. While I was waiting, I saw Richard approach Paul and say something, then clap him on the shoulder. Richard was making excuses for me, I thought, but Paul would perceive the subtext: Richard needed to get me home because I was far too tipsy to stay for dinner.

But I wasn't drunk. Richard only wanted everyone to think I was.

"All set," Richard said to me when he returned. He'd already called for our car, which was waiting just outside the building.

The snow was coming down more heavily now. Even though our

driver proceeded slowly through the mostly empty streets, I felt nauseated. I closed my eyes and leaned as far back against the door as my seat belt would allow. I feigned sleep, but I'm pretty sure Richard knew I didn't want to face him.

He might've let it go—let me walk upstairs and fall into our bed.

But as I climbed the steps toward our front door, I stumbled and had to catch myself on the railing.

"It's these new heels," I said desperately. "I'm not used to them."

"Of course it is," he said sarcastically. "It couldn't be all those drinks on an empty stomach. This was a work event, Nellie. It was an important night for me."

I stood silently behind him as he unlocked the front door. Once inside, I sat on the tufted bench in our entranceway and removed my shoes. I placed them side by side on the bottom stair, aligning the heels precisely, then I removed my wrap and hung it in the closet.

Richard was still there when I turned around. "You need to eat something. Come on."

I followed him into the kitchen, where he pulled a bottle of mineral water out of the refrigerator and silently handed it to me. He opened a cabinet and took out a box of Carr's water crackers.

I ate one quickly. "I feel better. You were right to bring me home. . . . You must be hungry, too. Do you want me to cut you up some Brie? I just bought it today at the farmers' market."

"I'm fine." I could tell Richard was about to disappear as he had done during other arguments that I'd tried to forget; he was struggling to keep his anger from surfacing. From swallowing him.

"About the job," I said quickly, trying to defuse it. "Paul just offered to introduce me to people at the charter school. It could be part-time or it might not even happen."

Richard nodded slowly. "Is there a special reason you want to be in the city more frequently?"

I stared at him; of all the things he could say, I didn't expect this. "What do you mean?"

"One of the neighbors mentioned seeing you at the train station the other day. All dressed up, he said. Funny, but when I called you that morning, you said you'd been swimming laps at the club and that's why you hadn't answered the phone."

I couldn't deny it; Richard, with his laser-quick mind, would trip me up if I tried to lie. *Which neighbor?* I wondered. *The station had been nearly empty at that time of day.*

"I did swim that morning. But then I went to see Aunt Charlotte. Just for a short visit."

Richard nodded. "Of course. Another cracker? No?" He slid the cardboard tab back into the slot of the box. "There's no reason why you shouldn't visit your aunt. How was she?"

"Good," I blurted as the pounding of my heart softened. He was going to let this go. He believed me. "We had tea at her apartment."

Richard opened the cabinet to return the crackers, the wood door swinging between us and momentarily hiding his face.

When he closed it, he was looking at me. He was very near. His narrowed eyes seemed to sear through mine. "What I can't figure out is why you waited until I left for work, got all dressed up, took the train into the city, came home in time to cook dinner, and sat there eating lasagna with me but never once thought to mention that you'd visited your aunt." He paused for a moment. "Where did you really go? Who were you with?"

I heard a sound like a bird's cry and realized I'd made it. Richard was gripping my wrist. Twisting it as he spoke.

He looked down and instantly let go, but white ovals from his fingertips remained, like a burn.

"I'm sorry." He took a step back. Ran a hand through his hair. Exhaled slowly. "But why the fuck did you lie to me?"

How could I tell him the truth? That I wasn't happy—that everything he'd given me wasn't enough? I'd wanted to meet someone to discuss my concerns about my marriage. The woman I'd sought out had listened intently to me and asked a few thought-provoking questions, but I knew one session with her wouldn't be enough. I was planning to sneak back into the city to see her again next month.

But it was too late to conjure a plausible excuse for my deception. Richard had caught me.

I didn't even see his open palm coming until it connected with my cheek with a loud crack.

For the next two nights, I hardly slept. My head throbbed and my throat felt raw from crying. I covered the scattering of bruises on my wrist with long sleeves and dotted extra concealer over the dark half-moons under my eyes. All I could think of was whether I should stay with Richard or try to leave him.

Then, while I was attempting to read in bed but not absorbing any of the words on the page, Richard gently tapped on the open guest-room door. I looked up to tell him to come in, but at the expression on his face, my words dissolved.

He was cradling the cordless house phone. "It's your mother." His face creased. "It's Aunt Charlotte, I mean. She's calling because . . ."

It was eleven o'clock at night, past the hour my aunt usually retired. The last time I'd talked to my mother, she'd said she'd been doing well—but she hadn't returned my most recent calls.

"I'm so sorry, baby." Richard held out the phone.

Reaching for it was one of the hardest things I've ever had to do.

CHAPTER
TWENTY-NINE

RICHARD WAS EVERYTHING I needed him to be after my mother died.

We flew to Florida with Aunt Charlotte for the burial, and he rented a hotel suite with adjoining rooms so we could all stay together. I remembered how my mom had looked when she was happiest—in the kitchen, clattering pans and tossing spices into a dish, or on her good mornings, singing me a goofy song to wake me up, or laughing as she wiped away the water Duke had splashed on her face after we'd bathed him. I tried to picture her on the night of my wedding, walking barefoot in the sand, her face turned toward the setting sun, as I said that final good-bye. But another image kept intruding: my mother as she'd died—alone, on the couch, with an empty bottle of pills by her side and the television blaring.

There was no note, so we were left with questions that could never be answered.

When Aunt Charlotte broke down at the gravesite, blaming herself for not knowing that my mother had taken a bad turn, Richard comforted her: "None of this is your fault; it isn't anyone's fault. She was doing so well. You were always there for your sister, and she felt your love."

Richard also sorted through the paperwork and arranged for the

sale of the little brick rambler where I'd grown up, while Aunt Charlotte and I went through my mother's personal belongings.

The rest of the house was relatively neat, but my mother's room
was a mess, with books and clothes piled on every surface. Crumbs on
her bed told me she'd recently been taking most of her meals there. Old
coffee mugs and water glasses crowded her nightstand. I saw Richard's
eyebrows lift in surprise when he noticed the disorder, but the only
thing he said was "I'll have a cleaning service come."

I didn't take many of my mother's belongings: Aunt Charlotte suggested we each select a few of my mother's scarves, and I chose a few
pieces of her costume jewelry as well. The only other possessions I
wanted were our old family photographs, and two of my mother's battered, beloved cookbooks.

I also knew I needed to clear out a few things from my old bedroom, which had been turned into the guest room. I'd deliberately left
some items on the shelf in the back of my closet. While Aunt Charlotte wiped down the refrigerator and Richard was on the phone
with a real-estate agent, I brought in a step stool and reached onto the
dusty ledge. I tossed a sorority pin in a trash bag, then threw in my
college yearbook and my final transcripts. I put my early-childhood-
development honors paper into the trash bag as well. I reached to the
very back of the shelf for my diploma, still rolled into a cylinder and
tied with a faded bow.

I threw it away without even looking at it.

I wondered why I'd even saved any of it, after all these years.

I couldn't look at the pin or yearbook without thinking of Maggie. I
couldn't look at the diploma without thinking about what had happened
on the day I graduated.

I was knotting the top of the bag when Richard entered my old
bedroom. "I thought I'd run out and pick up some dinner." He looked
at the bag. "Want me to toss that for you?"

I hesitated, then handed it to him. "Sure."

I watched him cart away the last remnants of my college days, then I
looked around the empty room. The water stain still marred the ceiling;

if I closed my eyes, I could almost picture my black cat curled up beside me on my pink-and-purple-striped comforter while I read a Judy Blume book.

I knew I would never see this house again.

That night back in our hotel, as I soaked in a hot bath, Richard brought me a cup of chamomile tea. I took it gratefully. Despite the heat of the Florida day, I couldn't seem to get warm.

"How are you holding up, sweetheart?" I knew he wasn't just referring to my mother's death.

I shrugged. "Okay."

"I worry you haven't been happy lately." Richard knelt beside the tub and reached for a washcloth. "All I want is to be a good husband to you. But I know I haven't always been. You're lonely because I work such long hours. And my temper . . ." Richard's voice grew husky. He cleared his throat and began to gently clean my back. "I'm sorry, Nellie. I've been stressed. . . . The market's been crazy, but nothing is as important as you. As *us*. I'm going to make it up to you."

I could tell how hard he was trying to reach me, to bring me back. But I still felt so chilled and alone.

I stared at the water dripping slowly from the bath tap as he whispered, "I want you to be happy, Nellie. Your mother wasn't always happy. Well, mine wasn't, either. She tried to act like she was, for me and Maureen, but we knew. . . . I don't want that to happen to you."

I looked at him then, but his gaze was distant, his eyes cloudy, so I stared at the silvery scar above his right eye.

Richard never talked about his parents. This admission meant more than all of his promises.

"My dad wasn't always good to my mom." His palm kept moving in circles on my back, in a gesture a parent would make to soothe a child who was upset. "I could live with anything except being a bad husband to you. . . . I have been, though."

It was the most honest conversation we'd ever had. I wondered why it had taken my mother's death to bring us to this place. But maybe it hadn't been her overdose. Maybe it had been what happened two days before we'd learned about it, when we'd come home from the Alvin Ailey gala.

"I love you," he said.

I reached out for him then. His shirt grew damp from the bathwater transferred to it by my wet arms.

"We're both orphans now," he said. "So we'll always be each other's family."

I held on to him tightly. I held on to hope.

That night we made love for the first time in a long while. He cupped my cheeks between his palms and stared into my eyes with such tenderness and yearning that I felt something inside me, something that felt like a tight, hard knot, release. As he held me afterward, I thought about Richard's gentle side.

I recalled how he'd paid for my mother's medical bills, how he'd attended Aunt Charlotte's gallery openings, even if it meant skipping a client dinner, and how he always came home early each year on the anniversary of my father's death with a pint of rum raisin ice cream in a white paper bag. It was my father's favorite flavor, the one he ordered when we went for drives together on my mother's lights-out days. Richard would serve us each a scoop, and I'd tell him details about my father that would otherwise grow dusty and forgotten, such as how despite his superstitions, he'd let me adopt the black cat I'd fallen in love with as a little girl. The ice cream would melt on my tongue, filling my mouth with sweetness, on those nights. I thought about how Richard had generously tipped waiters and taxi drivers and donated to a variety of charities.

It wasn't hard to focus on the goodness in Richard. My mind fell easily into those reminiscences, like a wheel latching comfortably into the grooves of a track designed for its rotations.

As I lay in his arms, I looked over at him. His features were barely perceptible. "Promise me something," I whispered.

"Anything, my love."

"Promise things won't get bad for us again."

"They won't."

It was the first promise to me he'd ever broken. Because things got even worse.

As our plane lifted off and began to head toward New York the next morning, I stared out the window at the topography that grew ever smaller and shuddered. I was so grateful to be leaving Florida. Death surrounded me here like concentric rings. My mother. My father. Maggie.

The sorority pin I'd thrown away hadn't belonged to me. I was supposed to give it to Maggie after she was officially initiated into our house. But instead of the celebratory brunch we'd planned to throw for the end of pledge week, my sisters and I attended her funeral.

I'd never told my mother what happened after Maggie's service; her reaction would have been too unpredictable. I'd called Aunt Charlotte instead, but I hadn't confided that I'd been pregnant. Richard only knew part of the story, too. Once when I woke up in his bed after a nightmare, I explained why I wouldn't walk home alone at night; why I carried pepper spray and slept with a bat by my side.

As I'd lain in Richard's arms, I described how I'd gone to offer condolences to Maggie's family. Her parents had merely nodded, so dazed they appeared incapable of forming speech. But her older brother, Jason, who was a senior at Grant University like me, had gripped my outstretched hand. Not to shake it. To pin me in place.

"It's you," he breathed. I smelled stale liquor on his breath; the whites of his eyes were streaked through with crimson. He had Maggie's pale skin, Maggie's freckles, Maggie's red hair.

"I'm so sor—" I began, but he squeezed my hand more tightly. It felt as if he were grinding the bones together. Someone had reached out to hug Maggie's brother, and he released his grip, but I felt his eyes following me. My sorority sisters stayed on for the reception in the church's community room, but I slipped away after a few minutes and stepped outside.

As I walked through the door, I encountered exactly what I'd sought to avoid: Jason.

He stood alone on the front steps, tapping a pack of Marlboro Reds against his palm. They made a steady smacking sound. I tried to duck my head and move past him, but his voice stopped me.

"She told me about you." He flicked a lighter and inhaled deeply as he lit his cigarette. He exhaled a stream of smoke. "She was scared to go through pledge week, but you said you'd help her. You were her only friend in the sorority. Where were you when she died? Why weren't you there?"

I remember stepping back and feeling Jason's eyes hold me, just as his grip had done.

"I'm sorry," I said again, but it didn't douse the rage in his expression. If anything, my words seemed to fuel it.

I began to retreat slowly, clutching the railing so I wouldn't fall as I edged down the stairs. Maggie's brother kept his eyes on me. Just before I reached the sidewalk, he called out to me, his voice harsh and raw.

"You will never forget what you did to my sister." His words landed with as much force as fists. "I'll make sure of it."

I didn't need his threat to hold on to Maggie, though. I thought about her constantly. I never went back to that beach again. Our sorority had been put on probation for the rest of the year, but that wasn't why I took a job waitressing at a campus pub on Thursday and Saturday nights. Fraternity parties and dances held no more appeal for me. I set aside part of my tips, and when I had a few hundred dollars, I tracked down the animal shelter, Furry Paws, where Maggie had volunteered and started anonymously donating in Maggie's honor. I promised to keep sending money every month.

I didn't expect my small donations to absolve me of my culpability, my role in Maggie's death. I knew I would always carry it with me, would always wonder what would have happened if I hadn't veered away from the group of girls walking to the ocean. If I'd waited even just one more hour to confront Daniel.

Exactly a month after Maggie's death, I awoke to hear one of my sorority sisters shrieking. I ran downstairs in my boxers and T-shirt and saw the overturned chairs, the shattered lamp, the obscenities spray-painted in black across our living room wall. *Bitches. Whores.*

And the message I knew was meant for me only: *You killed her.*

I sucked in my breath and stared at the three words proclaiming my guilt for everyone to see.

More girls came downstairs as our chapter president called campus security. One of the freshmen burst into tears; I saw two other girls pull away from our group and whisper to each other. I thought they were sneaking glances at me.

The smell of stale cigarette smoke permeated the room. I saw a butt on the floor and I knelt down to look at it. Marlboro Red.

When the guard arrived, he asked us if we had any guesses as to who might have vandalized our house. He knew about Maggie's death—by then most people in Florida did.

Jason, I thought, but I couldn't say it.

"Maybe one of her friends?" someone ventured. "Or her brother? He's a senior, right?"

The guard looked around the room. "I'm going to need to call the police. That's procedure. Back in a minute."

He stepped outside, but before he reached for his car radio, I intercepted him. "Please don't get him in trouble. If it was her brother, Jason . . . we don't want to press charges."

"You think it was him?"

I nodded. "I'm sure it was."

The guard sighed. "Breaking and entering, destruction of property . . . that's pretty serious. You girls should start locking your doors."

I looked back at our house. If someone came in and climbed the stairs, my room was the second one on the left.

Maybe being questioned by the police would inflame Jason even more. He might blame me for that, too.

After the police came and took photographs and collected evidence, I put on shoes so the glass from the smashed lamp wouldn't cut my feet and helped my sisters clean up the mess. As hard as we scrubbed, we couldn't remove the ugly words from the wall. A few of us went to the hardware store to pick up paint.

As my sisters considered the various shades, my cell phone rang. I reached into my pocket. Undisclosed number, the screen said, which probably meant the call originated at a pay phone. In the instant before the dial tone sounded in my ear, I thought I could hear something.

Breathing.

"Vanessa, what do you think of this color?" one of my sisters asked.

My body was rigid and my mouth dry, but I managed to nod and say, "Looks great." Then I walked directly to another aisle, the one containing locks. I bought two, one for my bedroom door and one for my window.

Later that week, a pair of police officers came to the house. The older of the two officers informed us that they had questioned Jason, who'd admitted to the crime.

"He was drunk that night and he's sorry," the officer said. "He's working out a deal to get counseling."

"As long as he never comes around here again," one of my sisters said.

"He won't. That was part of the arrangement. He can't come within a hundred yards of this place."

My sisters seemed to think it was over. After the officers left, they dispersed, heading to the library, to classes, to their boyfriends' places.

I stayed in our living room, staring at the beige wall. I could no longer see the words, but I knew they still existed and always would.

Just as they would always reverberate in my head.

You killed her.

My future had seemed bursting with possibilities before that fall. I'd been dreaming about cities where I might move after graduation, considering them like a hand of cards: Savannah, Denver, Austin, San Diego . . . I wanted to teach. I wanted to travel. I wanted a family.

But instead of racing toward my future, I began making plans to run away from my past.

I counted down the days until I could escape from Florida. New York, with its eight million residents, beckoned. I knew the city from my visits to Aunt Charlotte's home. It was a place where a young woman with a complicated past could start anew. Songwriters composed passionate lyrics about it. Authors made it the centerpiece of their novels. Actors professed their love for it in late-night interviews. It was a city of possibilities. And a city where anyone could disappear.

On graduation day that May, I donned my blue robe and cap. Our college was so large that after the commencement speeches concluded, students were divided up according to their majors and awarded diplomas in smaller groups. When I walked across the stage of the Education Department's Piaget Auditorium, I looked out into the audience to smile at my mother and Aunt Charlotte. As I scanned the crowd, someone caught my eyes. A young man with red hair, standing off to one side, away from the other graduating students, even though he also wore a shiny blue robe.

Maggie's brother, Jason.

"Vanessa?" The dean of our department thrust my rolled-up diploma into my hand as a camera flashed. I walked down the steps, blinking from the light, and returned to my seat. I could feel Jason's eyes boring into my back for the rest of the ceremony.

When it ended, I turned to look at him again. He was gone.

I knew what Jason was telling me, though. He'd been biding his time until graduation, too. He wasn't allowed to come within a hundred yards of me at school. But there were no rules about what he could do after I left campus.

A few months after graduation, Leslie emailed a newspaper link to a few of us. Jason had been arrested for drunk driving. The ripple effects of what I'd done were still spreading. A tiny selfish burst of relief went through me, though: Maybe now Jason wouldn't be able to leave Florida and find me.

I never found out more—whether he went to jail or rehab or was simply let off with a warning again. But about a year later, just before the doors of my subway car closed, I saw a slim frame and shock of red hair—someone was hurrying through the crowd. It looked like him.

I burrowed deeper into the cluster of people on my subway car, trying to hide myself from view. I told myself that the phone was in Sam's name, that I'd never changed my driver's license to a New York one, and that since I was renting, he wouldn't be able to find a paper trail that led to me.

Then, a few days after my mother surprised me by placing an engagement announcement in my local Florida paper that listed my name, Richard's name, and where I resided, the phone calls began. No words, just breathing, just Jason telling me he'd found me. Reminding me in case I'd forgotten. As if I could ever forget.

I still had nightmares about Maggie, but now Jason entered my dreams, his face twisted in fury, his hands reaching out to grab me. He was why I never listened to loud music when I jogged. His was the face I saw the night our burglar alarm blared.

I became acutely aware of my surroundings. I cultivated my sense of gaze detection, to avoid becoming prey. The sensation of static rising over my skin, the instinctual lifting of my head to search out a pair of eyes—these early-warning signs were what I relied upon to protect me.

I never made the connection that there could have been another reason why my nervous system became exquisitely heightened immediately after my engagement to Richard. Why I obsessively checked my locks, why I started getting hang-ups from blocked numbers, why I'd pushed Richard away so hard when my loving, sexy fiancé had held me down to tickle me on the night we watched *Citizen Kane*.

The symptoms of arousal and fear can be muddled in the mind.

I was wearing a blindfold after all.

CHAPTER
THIRTY

I EXIT SAKS for the last time, avoiding the security guard's eyes when he checks my bag, then I begin to walk to Emma's apartment. I try to tell myself that it is also for the last time. That after this, I will leave her alone. I will move on.

Move on to what? my mind whispers.

Ahead of me on the sidewalk, a couple strolls hand in hand. Their fingers are interlaced, and their gaits are in sync. If I had to make a snap determination of the quality of their relationship, I would say they are happy. In love. But, of course, those two feelings are not always intertwined.

I consider how perception has shaped the course of my own life; how I saw what I wanted to—needed to—during the years I was with Richard. Maybe being in love carries the requirement of filtered vision; perhaps it is so for everyone.

In my marriage, there were three truths, three alternate and some-times competing realities. There was Richard's truth. There was my truth. And there was the actual truth, which is always the most elusive to recognize. This could be the case in every relationship, that we think we've entered into a union with another person when, in fact, we've formed a triangle with one point anchored by a silent but all-seeing judge, the arbiter of reality.

As I stride past the couple, my phone rings. I know who it is before I even see Richard's name flash.

"What the fuck, Vanessa?" he says the moment I answer.

The fury I'd felt earlier when I looked at Duke's photo comes roaring back to me. "Did you tell her to stop working, Richard? Did you tell her you'd take care of her?" I blurt out.

"Listen to me." My ex-husband bites off each word. In the background on his end, I can hear honking. He obviously just received the photograph, so he must be on the street outside his office. "The guard told me you tried to deliver something to Emma. Stay the hell away from her."

"Bought her a house in the suburbs yet, Richard?" I can't stop goading him; it's as though I'm letting out everything I was forced to repress during our marriage. "What are you going to do the first time she makes you mad? When she isn't your perfect little wife?"

I hear a car door slam, and suddenly the background sounds on his phone—the city's ambient noises—cease. There's a hush, then a distinct voice I recognize as one that runs on a loop on New York Taxi TV: "Buckle up for safety!"

Richard is adept at being a move ahead of me; he must know exactly where I'm going. He's in a cab. He's trying to get to Emma first.

It's not even noon; traffic is light. From Richard's office to Emma's apartment is maybe a fifteen-minute drive, I estimate.

But I'm closer to it than he is; my trip to Saks took me in the direction of her place. I'm just ten blocks away. If I hurry, I'll beat him. I quicken my pace, feeling for the letter in my purse. It's still there. A breeze tingles across the light perspiration on my body.

"You're insane."

I ignore this; those words from him no longer have the power to derail me. "Did you tell her you kissed me last night?"

"What?" he shouts. "*You* kissed *me!*"

For a moment my pace falters, then I recall what I said to Emma the first time I confronted her: *Richard does this! He confuses things so we can't see the truth!*

It took me years to figure that out. Only by writing down all the questions that were battering my mind did I begin to see a pattern.

I started about a year after my mother's death. I began to keep a secret diary that I hid under the mattress in the guest room. In my black Moleskine notebook, I logged all the statements Richard made that could be construed in more than one way. I recorded the supposed lapses in my memory—big discrepancies, such as my wanting to live in a house in the suburbs, or the morning after my bachelorette party, when I'd forgotten Richard was flying to Atlanta—as well as smaller ones, such as my supposedly mentioning I wanted to take a painting class, or thinking lamb vindaloo was Richard's favorite dish.

I also painstakingly documented unsettling conversations I couldn't ask my husband about—such as how he knew I'd gone to see someone other than my aunt when I'd secretly traveled into the city. I wrote down some of what had happened during that first clandestine meeting. After I'd introduced myself to the sympathetic-looking woman who'd ushered me inside, she'd gestured for me to sit on the couch across from an aquarium filled with colorful fish. She took the upholstered straight-back chair to my left and told me to call her Kate. *What would you like to talk about?* she asked. *Sometimes I worry I don't know my husband at all,* I blurted. *Can you tell me why you think Richard is trying to keep you off-balance?* she asked toward the end of our discussion. *What would his motivation be for this?*

That was what I'd tried to puzzle out during the long, empty days when Richard was at work. I'd pull out my notebook and ponder how my cell phone hang-ups had begun immediately after Richard and I had gotten engaged and only seemed to occur when he wasn't around. I wrote about how I was certain I'd told Richard I regretted insisting Maggie had to wear the blindfold, how much that particular detail—that I'd made her cover her eyes—had bothered me. I added, *So why would he give me a blindfold to wear when we drove to the new house?* I chronicled how I'd found the heirloom cake topper that had been manufactured years after Richard's parents had gotten married. The words on my page smudged from my tears as I recalled Duke's mysterious disappearance.

When my insomnia struck, I'd ease out of bed and tiptoe down the hall so I could fill pages with the insistent thoughts that invaded my brain in the darkest hours of night, my handwriting growing sloppy as my emotions grew heightened. I underlined certain notes, drew arrows connecting thoughts, and scribbled in the margins. Within months, my ink-stained notebook was more than half full.

I spent so many hours writing, my words unspooling across the pages, and in the process, unraveling my marriage. It was as if my relationship with Richard was a gorgeous, hand-knit sweater, and I'd found a tiny thread that I kept worrying between my fingertips. I'd slowly tugged on it, twisting and turning it, erasing patterns and colors and distorting the shape with every question and inconsistency I laid bare in my diary.

He's, left foot, *wrong,* right foot. The words fill my brain as my legs churn even faster. I must reach Emma before he does.

"No, Richard. You kissed me." The only thing Richard hates more than being challenged is being wrong.

I pass Chop't and turn the corner, glancing behind me down the street. A dozen cabs are heading my way. He could be in any one of them.

"Are you drinking?" He is so good at shifting the focus, at exposing my vulnerabilities and putting me on the defensive.

But I don't mind as long as he keeps talking. I need to keep him on the phone so he doesn't warn Emma that I am coming.

"Have you told her about the diamond necklace you gave me?" I taunt him. "Do you think you'll have to buy her one someday?"

I know this question is the equivalent of throwing a bomb through the window of his cab, and that's exactly what I intend. I want to enrage Richard. I want his fists to clench and his eyes to narrow. That way, if he reaches Emma first, she will at last understand what he has so adeptly concealed. She will see his mask.

"Dammit, you could have made that light," he shouts. I picture him coiled on the edge of the taxi seat, hovering behind the driver.

"Have you told her?" I ask again.

He is breathing heavily; I know from experience he is on the verge of losing control. "I'm not engaging in this ridiculous conversation. If you come near her again, I'll have you locked up."

I press *End Call*. Because right in front of me is Emma's apartment.

I have wronged her so deeply; I've preyed on her innocence.

Just as I was never the wife Richard thought I was, I am also not the woman Emma believed me to be.

On the first night I met my replacement at the office holiday party, she rose from behind her desk in a poppy-red jumpsuit. She flashed that wide, open smile and extended her hand to me.

The gathering was as elegant as everything else in Richard's world: A wall of glass overlooking Manhattan. Ceviche in individual tasting spoons and mini lamb chops with mint being offered by waiters in tuxedos. A seafood station with a woman shucking briny Kumamoto oysters. Classical music soaring from the strings of a quartet.

Richard headed to the bar to get us drinks. "Vodka and soda with a twist of lime?" he asked Emma.

"You remembered!" Her eyes followed him as he walked off.

It all began in that moment: A new future materialized in front of me.

For the next few hours, I sipped mineral water and made polite conversation with Richard's colleagues. Hillary and George were there, but Hillary had already begun to distance herself from me.

The entire night, I felt the surge of energy arcing between my husband and his assistant. It wasn't that they exchanged private smiles or ended up side by side in the same conversational group; on the surface, they were perfectly appropriate. But I saw his eyes slide to her as her throaty laugh spilled out. I *felt* their awareness of each other; it was a tangible, shimmering link joining them across the room. At the end of the party, he ordered a car to see her safely home, despite her protestations that she could hail a cab. We all walked out together and waited for her Town Car to arrive before we got into our own.

"She's sweet," I said to Richard.

"She's very good at her job."

When Richard and I arrived home from the holiday party, I began to climb the stairs toward the bedroom, looking forward to rolling down the elastic band of the stockings that were cutting into my stomach. Richard extinguished the hallway light and began to follow me. The moment I stepped into the bedroom, he spun me around to face the wall. He kissed the back of my neck and pressed himself against me. He was already hard.

Usually Richard was a tender, considerate lover. Early on, he'd savored me like a five-course meal. But that night, he grabbed my hands and used one of his own to trap them over my head. With his free hand, he yanked down my stockings. I heard a ripping sound and knew they had torn. When he entered me from behind, I gasped. It had been so long, and I wasn't ready for him. He thrust against me as I stared at our striped wallpaper. He came quickly with a loud, raw groan that seemed to echo through the room. He leaned against my body, panting, then turned me around and gave me a single kiss on the lips.

His eyes were closed. I wondered whose face he was seeing.

A few weeks later, I saw her again when she arrived at the cocktail party Richard and I hosted at our home in Westchester. She was as flawless as I'd remembered.

Not long after our soirée I was supposed to go to the Philharmonic with Richard. But I came down with a stomach bug and had to cancel at the last minute. He took Emma. Alan Gilbert was conducting; Beethoven and Prokofiev would be played. I imagined the two sitting side by side as they listened to the lyrical, expressive melodies. At intermission, they would likely get cocktails, and Richard would explain the origin of Prokofiev's dissonant style to Emma, just as he had once instructed me.

I took to my bed and fell asleep to images of them together. Richard stayed in the city that evening.

I have no way of knowing for certain, but I imagine that was the night of their first kiss. I see her staring up at him with her round blue eyes as she thanks him for a wonderful evening. They hesitate, reluctant to part. A moment of silence. Then her lids sweep shut as he bends down, closing the distance between them.

Shortly after the Philharmonic, Richard flew to Dallas for a meeting. By then I was making it a point to keep better track of his schedule. This was an important client to Richard. Emma would accompany him. I was not surprised by this: Diane had traveled with him on occasion, too.

But Richard didn't call or text me to say good night.

I was certain their affair was under way after that trip. Call it a wife's intuition. I went into the city a few weeks later. I wanted another look at Emma. I lingered in the courtyard outside their building, shielding my face with a newspaper. That was the day Richard, gently touching the small of her back, held the door for my replacement as they came outdoors. She wore a blush-pink dress that matched the tinge on her cheek as she looked up at my husband from beneath her eyelashes.

I could have confronted them. Or I could have called out, feigning enthusiasm, and suggested we all have lunch together. But I simply watched them go.

Now I frantically press all the intercom buttons belonging to the residents of Emma's building, hoping someone will let me in. I hear the door buzz a second later and I burst inside the modest small lobby. I glance at the row of mailboxes, grateful that her last name reveals her floor and apartment number: 5C. As I run up the stairs, I wonder if she will take Richard's name. If we will be linked in that way, too.

I stand in front of her apartment and knock loudly.

"Who is it?" she calls.

I stand to one side so she can't see me through the peephole. If Emma recognizes my voice, she may not read my note. So I just push the envelope through the crack at the bottom of her door. I watch my note disappear, then I run back down the hallway to the stairs, hoping I'll get out before Richard arrives.

I picture her unfolding my letter, and I think of all the things it didn't say.

Like how I faked my stomach flu the night of the Philharmonic.

"Why don't you take Emma?" I had suggested to Richard when I called him to cancel. I made sure my voice sounded weak. "I remember being young and poor in the city. It would be a real treat for her."

"Are you sure?"

"Of course. All I want to do is sleep. And I'd hate for you to miss it."

He agreed.

The moment we hung up, I made myself a cup of tea and began to think about my next move.

I knew I had to be careful. I couldn't afford a single mistake. My attention to detail needed to be as scrupulous as Richard's always was.

When I went to bed that evening, I put a bottle of Pepto-Bismol on my nightstand, next to my water.

I paced myself. I didn't even mention her for weeks, but when Richard closed a big deal, I suggested he thank Emma for her help by giving her a generous gift certificate to Barneys.

For a moment, I worried I'd gone too far. He paused in shaving and looked at me carefully. "You never reminded me to do anything for Diane."

I shrugged and reached for my hairbrush. Trying to cover, I said, "I guess I identify with Emma. Diane was married. She had a family. Emma reminds me of myself when I first came to New York. I think it would go a long way toward making her feel appreciated."

"Good idea."

I slowly released the breath I'd been holding.

I imagined her opening the certificate, her eyebrows rising in surprise. Perhaps she'd go into his office to thank him. Maybe, a few days later, she'd wear to the office a dress she'd bought with his certificate and show it to him.

The stakes were so high. I tried to continue with my usual routines, but adrenaline flooded me. I found myself constantly pacing. My appetite evaporated and weight fell off me. I lay awake beside Richard at night, mentally reviewing my plan, searching for holes and weaknesses. I was desperate to hurry things along, but I forced myself to bide my time. I was a hunter in a blind, waiting for my prey to wander into position.

My big break came when Emma called me one evening from Dallas, saying Richard needed to catch a later flight because his meeting was running long.

I'd prayed for an opportunity exactly like this one. Everything hinged on what would happen next; I had to play my part seamlessly. Emma couldn't suspect I'd been creating a house of cards; that I was poised to set the final one in place.

"Poor guy," I'd said. "He's been working so hard. He must be exhausted."

"I know. This client is really demanding!"

"You've been working hard, too," I said as if it had just occurred to me. "He doesn't need to rush. Why don't you suggest he have a nice dinner and book a hotel? Just come back in the morning. It'll be easier on both of you." *Please, take the bait.*

"Are you sure, Vanessa? I know he wants to get home to you."

"I insist." I faked a yawn. "To tell you the truth, I'm looking forward to watching some trashy television and vegging out. And he'll just want to talk about work."

The idle, dull wife. That was how I'd wanted her to think of me.

Richard deserved better, didn't he? He needed someone who could appreciate the intricacies of his job; who would take care of him after a rough day. Someone who wouldn't embarrass him in front of his colleagues. Someone who was eager to be with him every night.

Someone exactly like her.

Please, I'd thought again.

"Okay," Emma had eventually replied. "I'll just check with him, and then if he agrees, I'll let you know what time we land tomorrow once I switch the flights."

"Thank you."

As I hung up the phone, I realized that, for the first time in a long while, I was smiling.

I'd found my perfect replacement. Soon Richard would be done with me and I'd finally be free.

Neither of them knew what I'd orchestrated. They still don't.

PART
THREE

PART
THREE

CHAPTER
THIRTY-ONE

I TEAR DOWN THE STAIRS, slipping as I round the corner to the third floor. My hip smacks against the edge of a step before I can catch myself on the railing, sending pain radiating up the left side of my body. Yanking myself upright, I press on with barely a pause. If Richard decides to take the stairs rather than the elevator, we will run right into each other.

The thought propels me even faster, and I burst out of the stairwell into the lobby just as the elevator doors press themselves together. I want to watch the numbers flash on the panel above the elevator to see if it stops on Emma's floor. But I can't risk taking even a few seconds to check. I race onto the street, where a cab is pulling away from the curb. I bang on the trunk and the red brake lights flash.

Scrambling in, I lock the door before collapsing against my seat. I open my mouth to give the address of Aunt Charlotte's apartment, but my words catch in my throat.

The aroma of lemons surrounds me. It winds through my hair and permeates my skin. I can feel the sharp citrus notes invading my nose and trickling down into my lungs. Richard must have just exited this cab. Whenever he was agitated—when his features tightened and the man I loved seemed to disappear—his scent always grew stronger.

I want to flee again, but I can't afford to wait for another taxi. So

I roll down the window as far as it will go as I give the driver my destination.

My letter is only a page long; it will take just a minute for Emma to scan it. I hope she has time to do so before Richard makes it to her door.

The driver turns onto the next block, and after a final glance out the window assures me that Richard isn't following, I lean my head back against my seat. I wonder how I'd missed the flaw in my plan to escape my husband. I had so much time to formulate it; after his office holiday party, it became my full-time job, then my obsession. I was so careful, and yet I'd made the greatest possible miscalculation.

I didn't think about how I would be sacrificing an innocent young woman. I could only desperately latch onto my getaway. I'd almost given up hoping it might be possible. Until I realized he'd never let me go unless he believed it was his idea.

I was certain of this because of what he'd done to me before when he'd thought I was trying to leave him.

I had begun to withdraw from my marriage right before the Alvin Ailey gala. I was still relatively young and strong. I hadn't yet been broken.

Immediately after the gala, when Richard confronted me in the kitchen, he'd looked down at my right wrist, which was turning white in his strong hands. It was as if he didn't even realize he was twisting it; as if someone else were responsible for the birdlike cry of pain that had escaped from my lips.

Richard hadn't hurt me bad before that night. Not physically, anyway.

At times he'd paused at the brink of what I now recognize as the edge. I'd recorded each of those episodes in my black Moleskine notebook: in the cab after I'd kissed Nick at my bachelorette party; at Sfoglia when a man at the bar had bought me a drink; and on the evening when I'd confronted Richard about Duke's disappearance. At other times he'd come even closer. Once he'd thrown our framed

wedding picture to the floor, shattering the glass and also hurling a ludi-
crous accusation at me: that I'd been flirting with Eric, the scuba
instructor, during our honeymoon. *I saw him stop by our room,* Richard
had yelled at me, as I recalled how my husband had left bruises on my
upper arm after helping me out of the boat. Another time, shortly after
one of our visits to the fertility doctor, when he'd lost a big client,
Richard slammed the door of his office so hard a vase fell off an étagère.

He'd also seized my upper arm on a few more occasions, squeezing
it too tightly, and once when he was questioning me about my drinking and I dropped my eyes, he grabbed my jaw and yanked my head
upright so I was forced to look at him.

In those instances, he'd always been able to contain his fury; to retreat into a guest room or to leave our home and come back once his
anger was spent.

The night after the Alvin Ailey gala, it seemed at first as if my high-
pitched whimper had cut through to him.

"I'm sorry," he'd said as he released my wrist. He'd taken a step
back. Run a hand through his hair. Exhaled slowly. "But why the fuck
did you lie to me?"

"Aunt Charlotte," I whispered again. "I swear I just went to see
her."

I shouldn't have said that. But I worried that admitting I'd gone to
talk to someone about our marriage might cause him to erupt further—
or ask questions I wasn't prepared to answer.

My repeated lie made something snap within him. He lost the
struggle.

The sound of his palm against my cheek was like a gunshot. I fell
onto the hard tiled floor. Shock suppressed my pain for a moment as I
lay there in the gorgeous dress he'd given me, now crumpled around
my thighs. I stared up at him, holding my hand to my face. "What—
how could you—"

He reached down and I thought he was going to help me to my
feet, to beg my forgiveness, to explain he'd meant to strike the cabinet
behind me.

Instead he grabbed my hair in his fist and yanked me upright.

I stood on my tiptoes, clawing at his fingers, desperate for him to release me. It felt as if he were tearing my scalp from my skull. Tears streamed out of my eyes. "Stop, please," I begged.

He let go but then leaned in to pin me against the edge of the counter. He wasn't hurting me now. But I knew it was the most dangerous moment of the night. Of my life.

Everything in his face compressed. His narrowed eyes darkened. But the eeriest part was his voice. It was the only piece of him I still recognized; it was the voice that had soothed me on so many nights and had vowed to love and protect me.

"You need to remember that even when I'm not there, I'm always with you."

He stared at me for a moment.

Then my husband reemerged. He took a step back. "You should go to bed now, Nellie."

Richard brought me a breakfast tray the next morning. I hadn't slept nor had I moved from the bed.

"Thank you." I kept my voice quiet and even. I was terrified of setting him off again.

His glance fell on my right wrist, which was already bruised. He left the room and returned with an ice pack. Wordlessly, he placed it on the injury.

"I'll be home early, sweetheart. I'll pick up dinner."

I obediently ate the granola and berries. Even though my face was unmarked, my jaw felt tender and chewing was painful. I went downstairs and rinsed my bowl, wincing when I unthinkingly pulled on the dishwasher door using my hurt arm.

I made the bed, being careful to not jar my wrist when I tucked in the corners. I took a shower, flinching when the heavy spray hit my scalp. I couldn't bear to shampoo my hair or aim a blow-dryer at it, so I left it damp. When I opened my closet door, I found the Alexander McQueen dress hanging neatly right in front. I couldn't remember even taking it off; the rest of the night had been a blur. I only recalled the sensation of trying to shrink; of wanting to become as physically small as possible. Of willing myself to be invisible.

I walked past the dress and reached for layers: leggings and thick socks, a long-sleeved T-shirt and a cardigan. From a high shelf my suitcases beckoned. I stared at them.

I could have packed some of my things and walked out then. I could have booked a hotel or gone to my aunt's place. I could even have called Sam, though we hadn't spoken in a long time, since a rift had cleaved us apart. But I knew leaving Richard wouldn't be that easy.

When he'd departed that morning, I'd heard the beeps that meant Richard was activating our alarm, then the thud of the front door closing behind him.

But what I heard loudest of all was the echo of his words: *I'm always with you.*

The doorbell rang while I was still staring at the suitcases.

I raised my head. It was such an unfamiliar sound; we almost never had unannounced visitors. There was no need for me to answer; it was probably a delivery person leaving a package.

But the bell chimed again, and a moment later the house phone rang. When I lifted the receiver, I heard Richard's voice. "Baby, where are you?" He sounded worried.

I looked at the clock on the nightstand. Somehow it was already eleven. "Just getting out of the shower." I could hear someone knocking.

"You should go answer the door."

I hung up and descended the stairs, feeling my chest growing tight. I used my good arm to deactivate the alarm and unlatch the lock. My hands were shaking. I had no idea what was on the other side, but Richard had told me what I needed to do.

I shivered as the winter air blew against my face. A courier stood there, holding an electronic clipboard and a small black bag. "Vanessa Thompson?"

I nodded.

"Please sign here." He extended the clipboard toward me. It was hard to grip the pen. I wrote my name gingerly. When I looked up, I saw that he was staring at my wrist. Bruises the color of an eggplant were peeking out from beneath the sleeve of my cardigan.

The courier caught himself quickly. "This is for you." He handed me the package.

"I was playing tennis. I had a fall."

I could see the relief seep into his eyes. But then he turned and glanced at the snow blanketing our neighborhood, and he looked back at me.

I closed the door quickly.

I untied the ribbon on the bag and saw a box inside. When I lifted the lid, it revealed a thick gold cuff from Verdura, at least two inches in diameter.

I reached into the box and held it up. The bracelet Richard had sent would perfectly cover the ugly bruises ringing my wrist.

Before I even had the chance to decide if I would ever be able to wear it, we got the call that my mother had died.

For years, I have allowed fear to dominate me. But as I sit in the cab, I realize another emotion is rising to the surface: anger. It felt cathartic to unleash my rage at Richard after absorbing his for so long.

I suffocated my feelings during our marriage. I doused them with alcohol; I buried them in denial. I tiptoed around my husband's moods, hoping that if I created a pleasing enough environment—if I said and did the right things—I could control the climate of our household, just as I used to Velcro a smiling sun to the weather chart in my Cubs' classroom.

Sometimes I was successful. My collection of jewelry—the Verdura cuff was the first of the items Richard had delivered to me following what he called our "misunderstandings"—reminds me of the times I was not. I didn't consider packing those pieces when I left. Even if I sold them, the money I received would feel tainted.

During my marriage and even beyond it, Richard's words would echo in my mind, causing me to constantly second-guess myself, and limiting my actions. But now I remember what Aunt Charlotte said to me just this morning: *I'm not afraid of storms, for I'm learning how to sail my ship.*

I close my eyes and inhale the June air streaming through my open window, clearing away the last of Richard's scent.

It's not enough that I've escaped from my husband. And I know it won't be enough to simply stop the wedding. Even if Emma leaves Richard, I am certain he'll just move on to another young woman. Yet another replacement.

What I must do is find a way to stop Richard.

Where is he at this exact moment? I see him folding Emma into a hug, telling her how sorry he is that his ex is targeting her. He pulls the letter out of her hand and scans it, then crumples it into a ball. He is angry—but perhaps she thinks it is justified given my actions. What I hope, though, is that I've convinced her to reexamine their past, to look at their history through a new lens. Maybe she is recalling times when Richard's reactions had seemed slightly off. When his need for control revealed itself in subtle ways.

What will be his next move?

He will retaliate against me.

I think hard. Then I open my eyes and lean forward.

"I've changed my mind," I tell the cabdriver, who is taking me to Aunt Charlotte's apartment. "I need to make a different stop." I pull up an address on my phone and recite it.

He drops me off in front of a Midtown Citibank branch. It's where Richard keeps his accounts.

When Richard left me the check, he told me to use the money to get help. He even alerted the bank that I'd be depositing it. But with my delivery of Duke's photo and the letter to Emma, I've shown him I'm not going to quietly disappear.

I suspect he will try to stop payment on the check today. This is how Richard will begin my punishment; it's a relatively easy way for him to signal he won't tolerate my insubordination.

I need to cash his check instead, before he has a chance to tell the bank he has changed his mind.

There are two free tellers; one is a young guy in a white shirt and tie. The other is a middle-aged woman. Although the man is closer to me, I approach the woman's window. She greets me with a warm smile. Her name tag reads BETTY.

I reach into my wallet for Richard's check. "I'd like to cash this."

Betty nods, then glances at the amount. Her brow furrows. "Cash it?" She looks back at the piece of paper.

"Yes." My foot begins to tap against the floor and I still it. I worry Richard may be phoning the bank as I stand there.

"Can you take a seat? I think it would be better if my supervisor helped you with this."

I glance at her left hand. She isn't wearing a wedding ring.

It isn't difficult to dodge questions once you learn the tricks. Tell colorful, drawn-out stories that deflect attention from the fact that you aren't actually sharing anything. Avoid specifics. Be vague. Lie, but only when completely necessary.

I lean as close to the window as possible. "Look, Betty . . . Wow, that is, I mean it *was*, my mother's name. She passed away recently." This lie is necessary.

"I'm sorry." Her expression is sympathetic. I chose the right teller.

"I'm going to be honest with you." I pause. "My husband— Mr. Thompson—is divorcing me."

"I'm sorry," she repeats.

"Yeah, me, too. He's getting remarried this summer." I smile wryly. "Anyway, this check is from him, and I need the money because I'm trying to rent an apartment. His pretty, young fiancée has already moved in with him." As I speak, I picture Richard jabbing the bank's numbers on his phone.

"It's just that it's such a large amount."

"Not to him. As you can see, our last names match." I reach into my bag and pass her my driver's license. "And we still have the same address, although I've moved out. I'm in a dingy little hotel a few blocks away from here now."

The address on the check is our Westchester home; any New Yorker knows that suburb is exclusive.

Betty stares down at my license and hesitates. The photo was taken several years ago, roughly the time I first planned to leave Richard. My eyes were bright and my smile genuine.

"Please, Betty. Tell you what. You can call the manager at the branch on Park Avenue. Richard alerted him that I'd be cashing this check."

"Excuse me for a moment."

I wait while she steps to the side and murmurs into the phone. I feel light-headed from the strain, wondering if Richard has outmaneuvered me yet again.

When she returns, I can't read the expression on her face. She clicks on her computer keyboard, then finally looks up at me. "I apologize for the delay. Everything is in order. The manager confirmed the check was authorized. And I see that you and Mr. Thompson used to have a joint account here that was closed only a few months ago."

"Thank you," I breathe. When she comes back a few minutes later, she holds several stacks of cash. She runs the money through the bill counter and then tallies each one-hundred-dollar bill twice as my insides clench. At any moment I expect someone to hurry toward her and pull it all back. But then she slips the money through the shallow opening beneath the window, along with an oversize, padded envelope.

"Have a nice day," I say.

"Good luck."

I zip my purse shut, feeling the reassuring heft against my ribs.

I deserve this money. And now that I've lost my job, I need it more than ever to help my aunt.

Besides, it is exquisitely satisfying to think of what Richard's reaction will be when a bank official tells him his money is gone.

He kept me off-balance for years; whenever I displeased him, I suffered consequences. But he also clearly relished being my savior and comforting me when I was upset. The dueling sides of my husband's personality made him an enigma to me. I still don't completely understand why he needed to control everything in his environment as precisely as he organized his socks and T-shirts.

I've regained a bit of the power he took away from me. I've won a minor battle. I am filled with exhilaration.

I imagine his rage as a tornado, swirling and rotating outward, but at the moment, I am beyond its reach.

I exit onto the sidewalk and hurry to the nearest Chase branch office. I deposit the cash into my new account, the one I opened after Richard and I separated. Now I'm ready to go back to Aunt Charlotte's. But not to the safety of my bed; I am determined to shed that defeated woman like a husk.

I am suffused with energy at the thought of what I will do next.

CHAPTER
THIRTY-TWO

"I AM TWENTY-SIX YEARS OLD. I'm in love with Richard. We are getting married soon," I whisper as I look in the mirror. *More lipstick,* I think, reaching into my cosmetics case. "I work here as an assistant." I am wearing a blush-colored dress that I bought just this afternoon at Ann Taylor. It isn't an exact replica, but it's close, especially with my new padded bra.

My posture isn't quite right, though. I pull back my shoulders and lift my chin. *That's better.*

"My name is Emma," I say into the mirror. I smile—a wide, confident grin.

Anyone who knows her well wouldn't be fooled. But all I need to do is get past the cleaning crew at Richard's office.

If one of his colleagues is working late tonight, it will be over. And if Richard happens to still be here—but no, I can't even let myself think about that or I won't have the courage to go through with this.

"My name is Emma," I repeat again and again, until I am satisfied with the throaty timbre of my voice.

I walk to the door of the bathroom and crack it, peeking out. The hallway is empty and the lights are dim; I can't see around the corner to the double-glass doors that lead to Richard's firm. I know they will be locked, as they are every evening. Few people have the keys. The financial information of hundreds of clients is contained on the company's computers. They are all protected by passwords, plus I'm certain the company's cyber-security experts would be alerted if anyone tried to hack the system.

What I'm after isn't an electronic record, though. I need a simple document from Richard's office, one that would have no importance to anyone else at the firm.

Even if Emma had the chance to read my letter, and even if a few fleeting doubts have begun to form in her mind, I know she is a savvy, logical young woman. Who will she believe in the end—her accomplished, perfect fiancé or his crazy ex-wife?

I need proof to sway her. And Emma is the person who revealed to me how to obtain it.

When I confronted her outside her apartment building, I told Emma to ask Richard about the missing Raveneau that he sent me to retrieve from our wine cellar the night of our cocktail party. *Who do you think placed the order?* she asked just before dismissing me and leaving in a cab.

It was a brilliant move on Richard's part to have Emma, as his assistant, order that wine for our party.

He hadn't needed to punish me in a long time. I'd been on my best behavior for months, rising early with him and exercising every morning, and cooking us healthy dinners at night. These acts of service made Richard feel benevolent toward me. By this point in my marriage, I was under no illusions about how dangerous my husband could be when he feared my love was slipping away.

So I anticipated that I would pay severely when I altered my hair a few days before our cocktail party. First I asked my stylist to dye it caramel brown. She'd protested, saying that women paid her hundreds of dollars to re-create my natural hue, but I was resolute. When she finished darkening it, I instructed her to lop off five inches, resulting in a shoulder-length bob.

On the day we met, Richard had told me to never cut my hair. That was the first rule, masked as a compliment, that he'd set down.

I'd obeyed it throughout our marriage.

But by then I'd met Emma. I knew I had to give my husband reasons to get rid of me, no matter what the repercussions.

When Richard saw my hair, he'd paused for a moment, then told me it was a nice change for the winter. I understood he wanted my old style back by summertime. After that brief exchange, he worked late every night until our party.

Richard had asked Emma to order the wine so he could build his case against me.

And now I can use it to build my case against him.

Hillary was standing at the makeshift bar with Richard in our living room at the Westchester house that night. The caterers were late, and I'd been murmuring apologies for the wheel of Brie and wedge of cheddar I'd set out.

"Honey? Can you grab a few bottles of the '09 Raveneau from the cellar?" Richard called to me from across the room. "I ordered a case last week. They're on the middle shelf of the wine fridge."

I moved in what felt like slow motion toward the basement, delaying the moment when I'd have to tell Richard, in front of all of his friends and business associates, what I already knew: There was no Raveneau in our cellar.

But not because I drank it.

Everyone thought I did, of course. That had been Richard's intention. This was our pattern: I challenged Richard by trying to assert my independence, and he made me pay for my transgression. My punishments were always proportional to my perceived crimes. On the night of the Alvin Ailey gala, for example, I knew Richard had told his partner Paul that he needed to get me home because I was drunk. But that wasn't true; Richard was angry that Paul had offered to help me find a job. And more than that, my husband already knew I'd snuck into the city for a secret meeting, one that I eventually explained away as a visit to a therapist.

Making me look bad in public—having other people view me as unstable and, worse, causing me to question myself—was one of

Richard's default ways to discipline me. It was especially effective given my mother's struggles.

"Honey, there isn't any Raveneau," I said when I returned from the cellar.

"But I just put a case down there—" Richard cut himself off. Confusion swept across his face and was quickly replaced by obvious embarrassment.

He was such an adroit actor.

"Oh, I'm happy with any old white wine!" Hillary said too brightly.

Emma was across the room. She wore a simple black dress, belted to show off her hourglass figure. Her luxuriant blond hair curled loosely at the ends. She was as perfect as I'd remembered.

I needed to accomplish three things that night: Convince everyone at the party that Richard's wife was a bit of a mess. Convince Emma that Richard deserved better. And most important, convince Richard of the same.

I felt dizzy from anxiety. I looked at Emma for courage. Then I did some acting of my own.

I linked my arm through Hillary's. "I'll join you in that," I said gaily, hoping Hillary couldn't feel my ice-cold fingers through her sleeve. "Who says blonds have more fun? I love being a brunette. Come on, Richard, open us up a bottle."

I dumped my first glass down the kitchen sink when I went to get more cocktail napkins, making sure Richard was within earshot when I asked Hillary if she needed a refill. Her glass was still half full. I saw her eyes drift to my empty one before she shook her head.

A moment later, Richard handed me a glass of water. "Shouldn't you call the caterers again, sweetheart?"

I looked up their number and dialed the first six digits, moving far enough away from Richard so he wouldn't pick up on the unnatural cadence of a one-sided conversation. I nodded to him after the call and said, "They should be here any second now." Then I put down my water.

I was on my pretend third glass of wine when the caterers arrived.

While servers began setting up a buffet, Richard motioned the head caterer into the kitchen. I followed them.

"What's going on?" I asked before Richard could say a word. I didn't make any effort to keep my voice down. "You guys were supposed to be here an hour ago."

"I'm sorry, Mrs. Thompson." The man looked down at his clip-board. "But we showed up when you instructed us to."

"That can't be. Our party started at seven-thirty. I'm sure I told you we wanted you here at seven."

Richard was by my side, ready to unleash his complaints about the company's error.

The head caterer wordlessly turned around his clipboard and pointed at the time—*8 p.m.*—then my signature on the bottom of the page.

"But . . ." Richard cleared his throat. "What happened?"

My response had to be perfectly delivered. I needed to convey both my ineffectualness, and my lack of concern about the agitation I'd caused him.

"Oh, I guess it's my fault," I said easily. "Well, at least they're here now."

"How could you—?" Richard choked back the rest of his sentence. He exhaled slowly. But the tightness in his face didn't relax.

I felt nausea rise in my throat and knew I couldn't sustain my per-formance much longer, so I hurried to the powder room. I splashed cold water on my wrists and counted my breaths until my heartbeat finally evened out.

Then I exited the bathroom and surveyed our gathered guests.

I hadn't quite accomplished all I needed to yet.

Richard was chatting with one of his partners and a golf buddy from the club, but my tingling skin alerted me that his eyes kept returning to me. My hair, my drinking, my reaction to the caterers—I was acting like a very different woman from the one who'd scrupulously reviewed every detail of the party with him during the preceding weeks. We'd spent hours going over our guest list, with Richard reminding me of personal details about his associates so I could more easily mingle and introduce people. We'd discussed flower choices for our arrangements. Richard had instructed me to avoid ordering shrimp because one of our guests was allergic, and I'd told him I'd double-check that we had enough hangers so no one's coat would have to be splayed across a bed.

Now it was time to check off another item on my private list, the one I kept only in my head and reviewed when Richard left for work: *Talk to Emma.*

A server passed by and offered me a warm Parmesan crostini from his tray. I forced myself to smile and take one, but I folded it into a napkin.

I paused for a moment, until the same server reached the group that contained Emma, then I approached.

"You have to try these," I gushed. I forced a laugh. "You've got to keep up your strength if you're working for Richard."

Emma briefly frowned, then her face cleared. "He does work long hours. But I don't mind."

She took a crostini and bit into it. I could see Richard begin to approach us from across the room, but George intercepted him.

"Oh, it's not just the hours," I said. "He's very particular, isn't he?"

She nodded and quickly popped the rest of her appetizer into her mouth.

"Well, I'm glad everyone finally has something to eat. You'd think the caterers would at least show up on time with what they charge." I spoke loudly enough so that the middle-aged man holding the platter of food could hear, and more important, so Emma would think I'd lobbed the harsh comment at him. I could feel my cheeks burn, but I hoped Emma assumed it was from too much wine. When I met her eyes, I saw disdain in them for my rudeness.

Richard extracted himself from George, walking directly toward us. Right before he arrived, I pivoted and headed in the opposite direction.

Give them one more reason. I knew I had to do it now or I'd lose my nerve.

Every step was a struggle as I slowly crossed the room. My pulse throbbed in my ears. I could feel a thin film of cold sweat gathering on my top lip.

All of my instincts were screaming at me to stop, to turn around. I forced myself forward, weaving through the clusters of smiling people. Someone touched my arm, but I pulled away without a glance.

Only the thought of Emma and Richard watching propelled me forward.

I knew I wouldn't have another chance to be near her anytime soon.

I reached the iPod that was attached to our speakers. Richard had carefully arranged a playlist, alternating jazz with some of his favorite classical compositions. The elegant music soared through the room.

I clicked to the Spotify app and selected seventies disco music, as I'd practiced doing. Then I cranked up the volume.

"Let's get this party started!" I shouted, raising my arms into the air. My voice cracked, but I continued, "Who wants to dance?"

The murmured conversations halted. Faces turned toward me in unison, as if they'd been choreographed.

"Come on, Richard!" I called.

Even the caterers were staring at me now. I caught a glimpse of Hillary averting her eyes, then of Emma gaping at me before quickly turning to look at Richard. He strode toward me quickly and my insides clenched.

"You forgot our house rule, honey," he called, his voice filled with a forced merriment. He turned down the volume. "No Bee Gees until after eleven!"

Relieved laughter cut through the room as Richard flipped the music back to Bach and reached for my arm and led me into the hall-way. "What is wrong with you? How much have you had to drink?" His eyes narrowed and I didn't have to conjure the panicked note of apology in my voice.

"I can't—just a couple glasses, but—I'm sorry. I'll switch to water right now."

He reached for my half-full goblet of Chardonnay and I quickly relinquished it.

For the rest of the night, I felt my husband's glare. I saw his fingers clenching his glass of Scotch. I tried to remember the sympathy mixed with admiration on Emma's face when he'd smoothed over the scene I'd created; that was what got me through the rest of the party.

I'd accomplished everything I'd set out to do.

It was worth it, even though my bruises didn't heal for two weeks.

Richard never sent me a new piece of jewelry to make amends for that misunderstanding. This was confirmation he was no longer as invested in us; his focus was shifting.

"I'm in love with Richard," I say a final time as I peer into the empty hallway. "I am supposed to be here."

It wasn't difficult to get into Richard's office building. Just a few floors below his firm was an accounting company that handled high-net-worth individuals. I made an appointment, explaining that I was a single woman who had recently come into an inheritance. It wasn't far from the truth. After all, I still had the receipt from Richard's check in my wallet. I booked the last appointment of the day, six o'clock, and sailed past the guard's desk with my visitor sticker attached to my new dress.

After my appointment, I took the elevator to Richard's floor and walked quickly to the ladies' room. The code hadn't changed, and I slipped into the end stall. I already looked as much like Emma as possible on the outside; my new red lipstick and fitted dress and curled hair completed my physical transformation. I tore my visitor's pass into a dozen pieces and buried it in the trash can. I spent the next couple of hours practicing her voice, her posture, her mannerisms. A few women came in to use the bathroom, but no one lingered.

Now it is eight-thirty. I finally see the three-person cleaning crew emerge from the elevator, pushing a cart filled with supplies. I force myself to wait until they reach the door of Richard's firm.

I am confident.

"Hello!" I call as I stride briskly toward them.

I am poised.

"Nice to see you again."

I belong here.

Surely this crew must have encountered Emma on nights she worked late with Richard. The man who has just unlocked the double glass doors gives me a hesitant smile.

"My boss needs me to check something on his desk." I gesture to the corner office I know so well. "I'll just be a minute."

I hurry past them, taking longer steps than I would normally. One of the cleaning women picks up a duster and follows me, which I expected. I pass Emma's old cubicle, which now holds a potted African violet and a flowered tea mug. Then I open the door to Richard's office.

"It should be right here." I walk behind the desk and open one of the two heavy lower drawers. But it is empty save for a squeezable stress reliever, a few PowerBars, and an unopened box of Callaway golf balls.

"Oh, he must've moved it," I say to the cleaner. I can feel her energy heighten; she's clearly a little nervous now. She moves closer to me. I can read her mental process. She is telling herself I must belong here or I could never have gotten through the guard. And she doesn't want to offend an office employee. But if she's wrong, she could be jeopardizing her job.

My salvation is staring at me: a silver-framed photograph of Emma on the corner of Richard's desk. I pick it up and show it to the cleaning woman, making sure to hold it a couple of feet away from her. "See? It's me." She breaks into a relieved smile, and I'm glad she doesn't think to ask why my boss keeps a photo of his assistant on his desk.

I pull open the second drawer and see Richard's files. Each has a typewritten label.

I find the one marked AmEx and leaf through his statements until I find the itemized one for February. What I'm searching for is right at the top: Sotheby's Wine, $3,150 refund.

The cleaning woman has turned toward the windows to dust the blinds, but I can't allow myself even the briefest of celebrations. I slip the piece of paper into my purse.

"All done! Thank you!"

She nods and I start to exit the office. As I round the edge of the desk, I reach out and touch Emma's photo again. I can't resist. I twist it so she faces the wall.

CHAPTER
THIRTY-THREE

THE NEXT MORNING, I awaken feeling more refreshed than I have in years. I've slept straight through for nine hours without the aid of alcohol or a pill. Another small victory.

I can hear Aunt Charlotte puttering in the kitchen as I approach. I walk up behind her and envelop her in a hug. Linseed and lavender; her scent is as comforting to me as Richard's aroma is unsettling.

"I love you."

Her hands cover mine. "I love you, too, honey." Surprise threads through her voice; it's as if she can sense the shift within me.

We have hugged dozens of times since I moved in. Aunt Charlotte embraced me as I sobbed after a cab left me on her building's doorstep. When I was unable to sleep as the memories of the worst times in my marriage tormented me, I felt her slip onto the bed and wrap me up in her arms. It was as if she wanted to absorb my pain. For every page in my notebook that I filled with descriptions of Richard's deceit, I could write an equal number recounting times throughout my life when Aunt Charlotte has buoyed me with her steady, undemanding love.

But today I'm the one reaching out to her. Sharing my strength.

When I let go, Aunt Charlotte picks up the pot of coffee she has just brewed, and I pull the cream out of the refrigerator and hand it to her.

I crave calories—nourishing food to fuel my newfound fortitude. I crack eggs into a pan, scramble in cherry tomatoes and shredded cheddar cheese, and slide two pieces of whole-grain bread into the toaster.

"I've been doing some research." She looks up at me and I can tell she knows exactly what I'm talking about. "You are never going to be alone in this. I'm here for you. And I'm not going anywhere."

She stirs the cream into her coffee. "Absolutely not. You're young. And you are not spending your life taking care of an old woman."

"Too bad," I say lightly. "Like it or not, you're stuck with me. I found the best macular degeneration specialist in New York. He's one of the top guys in the country. We're seeing him in two weeks." The office manager has already emailed me the forms that I'll help Aunt Charlotte fill out.

Her wrist moves in more rapid circles, and the coffee is in danger of sloshing over the edge of her mug. I can tell she's uncomfortable. I'm sure that as a self-employed artist, she doesn't have a great health-care plan.

"When Richard came by, he gave me a check. I have plenty of money." And I deserve every cent of it. Before she can protest, I reach for a mug of my own. "I can't argue about this before I have coffee." She laughs, and I change the subject. "So, what are you doing today?"

"I thought I'd go to the cemetery. I want to visit Beau."

Usually my aunt makes this trip only on their wedding anniversary, which is in the fall. But I understand she is seeing everything anew now, fixing familiar images into her memory bank to revisit them when her eyesight is gone.

"If you're up for company, I would love to join you." I give the eggs a final stir and add salt and pepper.

"You don't have to work?"

"Not today." I butter the toast and slide the eggs out of the pan, dividing them between two plates. I serve Aunt Charlotte, then take a sip of coffee to buy some time. I don't want to worry her, so I come up with a story about storewide layoffs. "I'll explain it to you over breakfast."

———

At the cemetery, we plant geraniums by his headstone—yellow, red, and white—as we trade some of our favorite Beau stories. Aunt Charlotte recounts how the first time they met, he pretended to be the blind date she was meeting at a coffee shop. He didn't reveal the truth until a week later, on their third date. I've heard this story many times, but it always makes me laugh when she tells the part about how relieved he was to no longer have to answer to the name David. I share how I loved the little journalist's notebook he kept in his back pocket with a pencil threaded through the spirals. Whenever I came to New York with my mother to visit, Uncle Beau gave me a duplicate one. We'd pretend to report on a story together. He'd take me to the local pizza parlor, and while we waited for our pie, he'd tell me to record everything I saw—the sights, the smells, what I overheard—just like a real reporter. He didn't treat me like a little kid. He respected my observations and told me I had a sharp eye for detail.

The midday sun is high in the sky, but the trees shade us from the heat. Neither of us is in any rush; it feels so good to be sitting in the soft grass, chatting comfortably with Aunt Charlotte. In the distance I see a family approach—a mother, father, and two kids. One of the little girls is riding on her father's shoulders, and the other is holding a bouquet of flowers.

"You were both wonderful with children. Did you ever want to have any?" I'd posed the same question to my aunt once before, when I was younger. But now I'm asking as a woman—as an equal.

"To be honest, no. My life was quite full, with my art and Beau traveling on assignment all the time and me joining him. . . . Plus, I was lucky enough to get to share you."

"I'm the lucky one." I lean over to briefly rest my head on her shoulder.

"I know how much you wanted children. I'm sorry it didn't happen for you."

"We tried for a long time." I think of those slashing blue lines, the Clomid and resulting nausea and exhaustion, the blood tests, the doctor's visits. . . . Every single month, I felt like a failure. "But after a while, I wasn't sure if we were meant to have kids together."

"Really? It was that simple?"

I think, *No, of course not, it wasn't simple at all.*

It was Dr. Hoffman who finally suggested to me that Richard should have a second semen analysis. "Didn't anyone tell him that?" she'd asked as I sat in her immaculate office during one of my annual physicals. "There can be errors in any medical test. It's standard to repeat the sperm analysis after six months or a year. And it's just so unusual for a healthy young woman like yourself to be having this much trouble."

This was after my mother had died; after Richard had promised things would never get bad again. He'd made an effort to come home by seven o'clock several nights a week; we'd taken a long weekend trip to Bermuda and another to Palm Beach, where we golfed and sunbathed by a pool. I'd recommitted to our marriage, and after about six months, we'd agreed to start trying anew for a baby. The job Paul had suggested never came through, but I continued my volunteer work with the Head Start program. I'd told myself I'd been partly to blame for Richard's violence. What husband would be happy to learn his wife was sneaking into the city and lying about it? Richard had told me that he'd thought I had a lover; I reasoned he would never have hurt me otherwise. As time passed and my sweet, attentive husband brought me flowers just because and left love notes on my pillow, it became easy to rationalize that all marriages had low points. That he would never do it again.

Just as my bruises faded, so, too, did the small, insistent voice inside me that cried out for me to leave him.

"My marriage was kind of . . . uneven," I tell my aunt now. "I began to worry about bringing a child into such an unstable environment."

"You seemed happy with him at first," Aunt Charlotte says carefully. "And he clearly adored you."

Both statements are true, so I nod. "Sometimes those things aren't enough."

When I told Richard what Dr. Hoffman had said, he immediately agreed to get retested. "I'll make the appointment for Thursday at lunch. Think you can keep your hands off me for that long?" We'd learned the first time that he had to wait two days to build up a good number of mobile sperm.

At the last minute, I decided to join Richard for this test. I thought back to how he was always beside me at my fertility appointments. Besides, I didn't have much else to do that day and figured it might be nice to spend the afternoon in the city, then meet him after work for dinner. At least those were the reasons I told myself.

When I couldn't immediately reach my husband on his cell phone, I called the clinic. I remembered the name from the first time Richard had gone years earlier—the Waxler Clinic—because Richard had joked that it should really be called the Whack-Off Clinic.

"He just phoned to cancel a little while ago," the receptionist said.

"Oh, something must have come up at work." I was grateful I hadn't begun the journey into the city.

I'd assumed he'd go the following day, and I planned to suggest at dinner that I accompany him.

That night, when I greeted him at the door, he folded me into a hug. "My Michael Phelps boys are still going strong."

I remember time seemed to shudder to a stop. I was so stunned I couldn't speak.

I pulled back, but he just hugged me tighter. "Don't worry, sweetheart. We're not going to give up. We'll get to the bottom of this. We'll figure it out together."

It took everything I had to look him in the eye when he released me. "Thank you."

He smiled down at me, his expression gentle.

You're right, Richard. I will get to the bottom of this. I will figure this out.

The next day, I bought my black Moleskine notebook.

My aunt has been my confidante for much of my life, but I will not burden her with this. I reach into my purse for the bottles of water I brought along and give one to her, then I take a long sip from mine. After a little while, we stand up. Before we leave, Aunt Charlotte slowly runs her fingertips across the engraved letters of her husband's name.

"Does it ever get easier?"

"Yes and no. I wish we'd had more time. But I'm so grateful I had eighteen wonderful years with him."

I link my arm through hers as we walk home, taking a long route.

I think of what else I can do for her with Richard's money. My aunt's favorite city in the world is Venice. I decide that when this is all over—when I've saved Emma—I will take my aunt to Italy.

After we arrive home and Aunt Charlotte goes into her studio to work, I am ready to execute my plan to get the AmEx statement to Emma. I know how I'm going to do it, because Emma never changed the cell phone number she used as Richard's assistant. I will photograph the document and text it to her. But I need to transmit it when Richard won't be near, so she can absorb the full implications of what she is seeing.

It was too early when Aunt Charlotte and I left this morning; they might have still been together. But by now he should be at work.

I take the statement out of my purse and smooth it open. The AmEx is Richard's business card, the one he keeps for his sole use. Most of the charges on this statement are for lunches, taxis, and costs associated with a trip to Chicago. I also see the fee for the caterers for our party; I signed the contract and specified the details, but since it was primarily a business function at our home, Richard had said to use the AmEx card they had for us on file. The four-hundred-dollar charge from Petals in Westchester covered the cost of our flower arrangements.

The Sotheby's wine refund is at the top of the statement, a few lines above the charge for the caterers.

I use my phone to take a photograph of the entire page, making sure the date, the name of the wine store, and the amount stand out clearly. Then I text it to Emma with a one-line message:

You placed the order, but who canceled it?

When I see that it has been delivered, I put down my cell. I didn't use my burner phone; there's no longer any need to conceal what I'm doing. I wonder what Emma's memory will reveal when she looks back at that night. She thinks I was drunk. She believes Richard covered for me. She is under the impression that I polished off a case of wine in a week.

If she realizes one of those things is not true, will she question the others?

I stare at my phone, hoping this will be the thread she begins to worry between her fingertips.

CHAPTER
THIRTY-FOUR

EMMA'S RESPONSE ARRIVES the next morning, also in the form of a single-line text message:

Meet me at my apartment at 6 tonight.

I stare at the words for a full minute. I cannot believe it; I've been trying to reach her for such a long time, and now she is finally welcoming me in. I've created the necessary doubts in her mind. I wonder what she already knows, and what she will ask me.

Exhilaration floods my body. I don't know how long of an audience she will grant me, so I write down the points I must make: I can bring up Duke, but what proof do I have? Instead I write *fertility questions.* I want her to ask Richard why we weren't able to become pregnant. He'll surely lie, but the pressure will build in him. Maybe she'll see what he fights to keep hidden. *His surprise visits,* I write. Has Richard ever shown up unexpectedly, even when she hasn't told him her schedule for the day? But that won't be enough; it certainly wasn't for me. I will need to tell her about the times Richard physically hurt me.

I have never shared with anyone what I am about to reveal to Emma. I need to harness my emotions so they don't overwhelm me and reinforce any lingering suspicions she might have that I'm unbalanced.

If she listens to me with an open mind—if she seems receptive to what I am saying—I must explain to her how I meticulously crafted a plan to free myself. That I set her up, but that I had no idea it would go this far.

I will beg for her forgiveness. But more important than my absolution is her own. I will tell her she has to leave Richard, immediately, tonight even, before he ensnares her.

When I last saw Emma, I tried to craft the image I wanted her to see: that we were interchangeable versions of each other. Now I strive for plain honesty. I shower and put on jeans and a cotton T-shirt. I don't fuss with my makeup or hairstyle. To burn off nervous energy, I plan to walk to her apartment. I decide to leave at five o'clock. I cannot be late.

Be calm, be rational, be convincing, I repeat to myself. Emma has seen the act I've put on; she has heard Richard's rendering of my character; she knows of my reputation. I need to reverse everything she believes about me.

I am still practicing what I will say when my cell phone rings with a number I don't recognize. But I know the area code well: it's in Florida.

My body tenses. I sink onto my bed and stare at the screen as the phone rings a second time. I must answer this.

"Vanessa Thompson?" a man asks.

"Yes." My throat is so dry I cannot swallow.

"This is Andy Woodward from Furry Paws." His voice sounds hearty and affable. I've never spoken to Andy before, but I began to anonymously donate to the shelter in Maggie's honor following her death, since she'd volunteered there in high school. After Richard and I married, he suggested that we increase my monthly contribution substantially and fund the shelter's renovation. As a result, Maggie's name is on a plaque by the door. Richard has always served as the contact to the shelter; he suggested it, saying it would be less stressful for me.

"I got a call from your ex-husband. He told me the two of you have decided that in light of everything, you can no longer afford your charitable gifts."

Here is my punishment, I realize. I took Richard's money, so this is how he'll extract revenge. There's a symbolic flourish to it, a balancing of the scales, that I know Richard is relishing.

"Yes," I say when I realize the silence has stretched on too long. *This was for Maggie, not for me,* I think furiously. "I'm really sorry. If it's okay, I can still contribute a small amount each month. It won't be the same, but it's something."

"That's very generous of you. Your ex-husband explained how terribly he feels about this. He said he would personally call Maggie's family to let them know what happened. He asked me to relay that to you so you didn't have to worry about any loose ends."

Which of my actions is Richard retaliating for? Am I being punished for the photograph of Duke, my letter to Emma, or cashing the check?

Or does he also know I've texted the AmEx statement to Emma?

Andy doesn't understand; no one does. Richard would have been charming when they chatted. He'll be the same way when he calls Maggie's family. He will make sure he speaks to them all individually, including Jason. Richard will mention my maiden name—it will seamlessly slip into the conversation—and perhaps he'll say something about how I've moved to New York City.

What will Jason do?

I wait for the familiar panic to set in.

It doesn't.

Instead, I am struck by the realization that since Richard left me, I haven't thought of Jason at all.

"The family will be delighted to have a chance to thank you both personally," Andy says. "Of course, they write notes every year that I forward to your husband."

My head jerks up. *Think like Richard. Stay in control.* "I don't—you know, my husband didn't share those notes with me." Somehow my tone is casual and my voice remains steady. "I was really affected by Maggie's death, and he probably thought it would be too painful for me to read them. But I'd like to know what they said now."

"Oh, sure. They mostly sent emails for me to forward. I remember the content, if not the exact words. They always expressed how grateful they are to you, and how they hoped to meet you one day. They visit the shelter occasionally. What you've done has meant so much to them."

"The parents come to the shelter? And Maggie's brother, Jason?"

"Yes. They all do. And Jason's wife and his two children. They're a lovely family. The kids cut the ribbon on opening day after the renovation."

I take a half step backward and nearly drop the phone.

Richard must have known this for years; he intercepted the correspondence. He *wanted* me to be afraid, to be his nervous Nellie. He needed to pretend to be my protector because of some depravity within him. He cultivated my dependence upon him; he preyed upon my fear.

Of all of Richard's cruelties, this is perhaps the worst.

I sink down onto my bed at the realization. Then I wonder what else he did to pique my anxiety when we were together.

"I would like to call Maggie's parents and brother, too," I say after a moment. "May I have their contact information?"

Richard must be on edge; he should have realized Andy might mention the emails and letters to me. My ex-husband is the one who isn't thinking clearly now.

I've never pushed him this far before, not even close. He is probably desperate to hurt me, to make me stop. To erase me from his tidy life.

I say good-bye to Andy and realize I need to get to Emma. It is almost five o'clock, the time I'd planned to leave. But I'm suddenly overwhelmed by the worry that Richard is waiting outside. I can't walk there, after all. I will take a cab, but I still need to get to one safely.

A second exit in the back of the building leads to a narrow alley where trash cans and recycling bins are kept. Which door will Richard expect me to use?

He knows I suffer from mild claustrophobia, that I loathe being trapped. The alley is narrow and usually empty, penned in on both sides by high buildings. So that's the route I choose.

I change into sneakers, then I wait until five-thirty. I take the elevator downstairs and fumble with the latch on the fire door. I ease it open and look out. The alley appears vacant, but I can't see behind the tall plastic waste containers. I take a deep breath and push away from the door, sprinting down the passageway.

My heart is exploding. I expect his arms to shoot out and grab me at any moment. I push myself toward the sliver of sidewalk I see ahead. When I finally reach it, I whip around in a full circle, gasping, as I scan my surroundings.

He isn't here; I am certain I would be able to feel his predatory gaze upon me.

I lift my arm to signal passing cabs as I hurry down the street. It doesn't take long for one to pull over, and the driver expertly weaves through rush-hour traffic toward Emma's place.

When we arrive at her corner, I see it's four minutes before six. I ask the driver to keep the meter running while I mentally rehearse a final time what I need to say. Then I exit the cab and walk to the door of Emma's building. I press the buzzer for 5C and hear Emma's voice through the intercom: "Vanessa?"

"Yes." I can't help it; I glance behind me a final time. But no one is there.

I take the elevator to her floor.

She opens the door as I approach. She is as lovely as ever, but she looks worried; her brow is creased. "Come in."

I step over the threshold and she shuts the heavy door behind me. At last, I am alone with her. I feel a rush of relief so intense I am practically giddy.

Her apartment is a small, neat one-bedroom. A few framed photographs are on the wall, and a vase of white roses is on a side table. She gestures toward the low-backed couch and I perch on the edge. But she remains standing.

"Thank you for seeing me."

She doesn't respond.

"I have wanted to talk to you for so long."

Something seems off. She isn't looking at me. Instead she is glancing over her shoulder. Toward her bedroom door.

Out of the corner of my eye, I see that door begin to open.

I recoil into the couch, my hands instinctively flying up to protect myself. *No,* I think desperately. I want to run, but I cannot move, just like in my nightmares. I can only watch as he approaches.

"Hello, Vanessa."

My eyes shift to Emma. Her expression is inscrutable.

"Richard," I whisper. "What are—why are you here?"

"My fiancée told me you texted her some nonsense about a wine refund." He continues moving toward me, his gait fluid and unhurried. He stops next to Emma.

Some of the terror eases out of my body. He isn't here to hurt me. Not physically, anyway; he would never do that in front of anyone. He is here to put an end to this by defeating me in front of Emma.

I rise to my feet and open my mouth, but he wrests away control of the situation. The element of surprise is on his side.

"When Emma called me, I explained to her exactly what happened." Richard longs to close the distance between us. His narrowed eyes tell me so. "As you well know, I realized that wine wasn't technically a business expense since I wasn't sure we'd drink any of it at the party. The ethical thing to do was to cancel the AmEx payment and put it on my personal Visa. I remember telling you this when Sotheby's delivered the Raveneau to the house and I stored it in the cellar."

"That's a lie." I turn to Emma. "He never ordered the wine at all. He's so good at this—he can come up with explanations for anything!"

"Vanessa, he told me instantly what happened. He didn't have time to concoct a story. I don't know what you're after."

"I'm not after anything. I'm trying to help you!"

Richard sighs. "This is exhausting—"

I cut him off. I am learning how to anticipate his line of attack. "Call the credit-card company!" I blurt. "Call Visa and confirm that charge while Emma listens in. It'll take thirty seconds and we can settle this now."

"No, I'll tell you how we're going to settle this. You've been stalking my fiancée for months. I warned you last time what would happen if this continued. I'm sorry about all your issues, but Emma and I are filing restraining orders against you. You've left us no choice."

"Listen to me," I say to Emma. I know I only have this final chance to convince her. "He made me think I was crazy. And he got rid of my dog—he left the gate open or something."

"Jesus," Richard says. But his lips are tightening.

"He tried to convince me it was my fault we couldn't have kids!" I blurt.

I see Richard's hands curl into fists and I reflexively flinch, but I press on.

"And he hurt me, Emma. He hit me and he knocked me down and he almost strangled me. Ask him about the jewelry he gave me to cover my injuries. He will hurt you, too! He will ruin your life!"

Richard exhales and squeezes his eyes shut.

Can she sense how close he is to the edge? I wonder. *Has she ever seen Richard disappear into anger before?* But perhaps I've said too much. She might've believed some of what I've told her, but how can she reconcile my outlandish accusations with the solid, successful man standing beside her?

"Vanessa, there is something deeply wrong with you." Richard pulls Emma close to him. "You are never to come near her again."

The restraining order means Richard will have an official record of my being a menace to them. If there is ever a violent confrontation between us, the evidence will support his side. He always controls the perception of our narrative.

"You need to leave." Richard walks over and reaches for my elbow. I flinch, but his touch is gentle. He has vanquished his anger for now. "Should I take you downstairs?"

I feel my eyes widen at his words. I shake my head rapidly and try to swallow, but my mouth is too dry.

He wouldn't do anything to me in front of Emma, I assure myself. But I know what he is insinuating.

As I walk past Emma, she folds her arms across her chest and turns away.

CHAPTER
THIRTY-FIVE

I WISH I COULD have given my Moleskine notebook to Emma along with the Raveneau receipt. Maybe if she had the chance to leaf through the pages, she would detect the undercurrent churning together these seemingly disparate events.

But that notebook no longer exists.

By the time I wrote my last entry, my journal contained pages and pages of my recollections and, increasingly, of my fears. After the night when Richard told me he'd gone for the sperm analysis and I vowed to get to the bottom of what had really happened, I could no longer suppress my intuition. My notebook served as a courtroom, with my words arguing both sides of every issue. *Perhaps Richard went to a different clinic to have his semen tested,* I'd written. *But why would he do that when he'd scheduled an appointment at the original one?* I'd hunch over in bed in the guest room, the dim bulb in the nightstand light illuminating my scribblings as I tried to puzzle out other confusing encounters, going back to the very beginning of our marriage: *Why did he tell me the lamb vindaloo I made was delicious, then leave more than half of it on his plate and send me a gift certificate for cooking lessons the following morning? Was it a thoughtful gesture? Was he trying to convey a subtle message about the inadequacy of the meal? Or was it a punishment for my revelation that day at Dr. Hoffman's office that I'd gotten pregnant in college?* And, a few pages before that: *Why would he suddenly appear the night of my bach-elorette party when he hadn't been invited to join us? Did love or control propel him?*

As my questions mounted, it became impossible for me to continue to deny it: Something was either deeply wrong with Richard, or deeply wrong with me. Both possibilities were terrifying.

I had been certain Richard sensed the change between us. I couldn't help withdrawing from him—from everyone. I dropped out of all my volunteer work. I rarely went into the city. My friends from Gibson's and the Learning Ladder had moved on with their lives. Even Aunt Charlotte was away; she and a Parisian artist friend had arranged a six-month apartment exchange, something they'd done several times in the past. I had felt steeped in loneliness.

I explained to Richard that I was depressed because we couldn't have a baby. But not being pregnant was a blessing now.

I escaped into alcohol but never around my husband. I needed to be sharp in his presence. When Richard noted the amount of wine I was consuming during the day and asked me to stop drinking, I agreed. Then I began driving a few towns over to buy my Chardonnay. I hid the empty bottles in the garage and sneaked out on early-morning walks to bury the evidence in a neighbor's recycling bin.

The alcohol made me sleepy, and I napped most afternoons, sober-ing up in time for Richard's return from work. I craved the comfort of soft carbohydrates and soon dressed only in my forgiving yoga pants and loose tops. I didn't need a psychiatrist to tell me that I was trying to add a protective layer to my body. To make me less attractive to my trim, fitness-conscious husband.

Richard didn't directly say a word about my weight gain. I'd shed and put on the same fifteen pounds several times throughout our mar-riage. Whenever my weight ticked upward, he made a point of re-questing that I cook broiled fish for dinner, and when we went to restaurants, he eschewed bread and asked for his salad dressing on the side. I followed his lead, ashamed that I lacked his discipline. On the night of my birthday dinner with Aunt Charlotte at the club, I'd grown agitated, but not because I thought the waiter had made a mistake with my salad. By that birthday my old clothes no longer fit. My husband had refrained from commenting on this.

But the week before the celebratory dinner, he'd bought a new, high-tech scale and had set it up in our bathroom.

One night I woke up in our Westchester house desperately missing Sam. I'd realized the previous afternoon that it was her birthday. I wondered how she was celebrating. I didn't even know if she still worked at the Learning Ladder and lived in our old apartment, or if she'd gotten married. I turned to see the clock announce it was almost three A.M. This wasn't unusual; I rarely slept through the night anymore. Beside me in bed, Richard was like a statue. Other women complained about their husbands snoring or hogging the blankets, but Richard's stillness always camouflaged whether he was deeply slumbering or on the verge of waking up. I lay there for a few moments, listening to his steady exhalations, then I slipped out from beneath the covers. I padded quietly to the door, then glanced back. Had my movements awoken him? In the darkness it was impossible to tell if his eyes were open.

I eased the door closed behind me, then headed to the guest room. I'd blamed Sam for our rift, but now that I was reevaluating everything, I'd begun to wonder where the fault truly lay. After our dinner at Pica, we'd drifted further apart. Sam had invited me to a going-away party for Marnie, who was moving back home to San Francisco, but Richard and I already had dinner plans at Hillary and George's house for the same evening. When I showed up at the party late, bringing Richard with me, I recognized disappointment on my best friend's face. We stayed for less than an hour. For much of it, Richard stood in the corner on his phone. I saw him yawn. I knew he had an early meeting the next morning, so I made our excuses. A few weeks later, I called Sam to see if she wanted to meet for a drink.

"Richard isn't going to come, is he?"

I lashed back, "Don't worry, Sam, he doesn't want to spend time with you any more than you do with him."

Our argument escalated, and that was the last time we spoke.

As I entered the guest room and reached under the mattress to retrieve my notebook, I wondered if I'd been so hurt and angry because Sam seemed to know something I wouldn't allow myself to accept— that Richard wasn't the perfect husband. That our marriage only looked good on the surface. *The Prince. Too good to be true. You're dressed like you're going to a PTA meeting.* She'd even called me Nellie once in a tone that felt more mocking than joking.

I lifted the mattress with my right hand and stretched out my left arm, sweeping it back and forth on top of the box spring. But I couldn't feel the familiar edges of my journal.

I eased down the mattress and turned on the nightstand lamp. I dropped to my knees and hoisted the mattress even higher. It wasn't there. I checked under the bed, then began to peel back the comforter, then the top sheet.

My hands stopped moving when I felt static rise over my skin. I detected Richard's stare before he spoke a word.

"Is this what you're looking for, Nellie?"

I slowly rose to my feet and turned around.

My husband stood in the doorway, wearing boxers and a T-shirt, holding my notebook. "You haven't been writing this week. Although I guess you've been busy. You went to the grocery store on Tuesday right after I left for work, and yesterday you drove to the wineshop in Katonah. Sneaky, aren't you?"

He knew everything I was doing.

He lifted up the journal. "You believe I'm the one who can't get us pregnant? You think there's something wrong with me?"

He knew everything I was thinking.

He moved closer to me and I cowered. But he merely took an object off the nightstand behind me. A pen.

"You forgot something, Nellie. You left this here. I saw it the other day." His voice was different, more high-pitched than I'd ever before heard it, and the cadence was almost playful. "Where there's a pen, there must be paper."

He riffled through the pages. "This is fucking insane." His sentences tumbled out faster and faster. "Duke! Lamb vindaloo! Turning your picture around! *I* set off the house alarm!" With every accusation, he tore out a new page. "My parents' wedding photo! You snuck into the storage unit! You're wondering about my parents' cake topper? You've been going into the city to talk about our marriage to some stranger? You're psychotic. You're even worse than your mother!"

I didn't realize I was backing up until I felt the nightstand hit the back of my legs.

"You were a pathetic waitress who couldn't even walk down the street without thinking someone was going to come after you." He dragged his hands through his hair, and part of it stood up. His T-shirt was rumpled and stubble coated his jawline. "You ungrateful bitch. How many women would kill to have a man like me? To live in this house, to vacation in Europe and drive a Mercedes."

All the blood seemed to rush out of my head; I felt dizzy with fear. "You're right, you're so good to me," I began to plead. "Didn't you see the other pages? I wrote how generous you were in paying for the animal shelter renovation. How much you helped me when my mom died. And how much I love you."

I wasn't reaching him; he seemed to be looking through me. "Clean up this mess," he ordered.

I dropped to my knees and gathered the pages.

"Tear them up."

I was crying now, but I obeyed, gathering a handful and trying to rip them in half. But my hands were shaking and the stack of pages was too thick for me to shred.

"You're so fucking incompetent."

I sensed a metallic change in the air; it felt swollen with pressure.

"Please, Richard," I sobbed. "I'm so sorry. . . . Please . . ."

His first kick landed near my ribs. The pain was explosive. I curled into a ball and pulled my knees into my chest.

"You want to leave me?" he shouted as he kicked me again.

He climbed on top of me, forcing me onto my back and pinning my arms with his knees. His kneecaps ground into my elbows.

"I'm sorry. I'm sorry. I'm sorry." I tried to twist away from him, but he was sitting on my abdomen, trapping me in place.

His hands closed around my neck. "You were supposed to love me forever."

I gagged as I thrashed and kicked beneath him, but he was too strong. My vision became spotty. I wrenched one hand free and clawed at his face as I grew light-headed.

"You were supposed to save me." His voice was soft and sad now.

Those were the last words I heard before I blacked out. When I came to, I was still lying on the floor. The pages of my notebook had vanished.

Richard was gone, too.

My throat felt raw and desperately parched. I lay there for a long time. I didn't know where Richard was. I rolled onto my side, my arms encircling my knees, shivering in my thin nightgown. After a while I reached up and pulled the comforter around me. Fear immobilized me; I couldn't leave the room.

Then I smelled fresh coffee.

I heard Richard's footsteps coming up the stairs. There was nowhere to hide. I couldn't run, either; he was between me and the front door.

He walked unhurriedly into the room, holding a mug.

"Forgive me," I blurted. My voice was hoarse. "I didn't realize . . . I've been drinking and I haven't been sleeping. I haven't been thinking clearly. . . ."

He just stared at me. He was capable of killing me. I had to convince him not to.

"I wasn't going to leave you," I lied. "I don't know why I wrote those bad things. You're so good to me."

Richard took a sip of coffee, keeping his eyes on mine over the rim of his mug.

"Sometimes I worry I am becoming like my mother. I need help."

"Of course you wouldn't leave me. I know that." He had regained his composure. I'd said the right words. "I acknowledge I lost my temper, but you pushed me," he said, as if he'd merely snapped at me during a minor spat. "You've been lying to me. You've been deceiving me. You are not acting like the Nellie I married." He paused. He patted the bed and I hesitantly climbed up to sit on its edge, keeping the comforter around me like a shield. He sat down next to me, and I felt the mattress sink beneath his weight, tilting me toward him.

"I've thought about it, and this is partly my fault. I should have recognized the warning signs. I indulged your depression. What you need is structure. A routine. From now on you'll get up with me. We'll work out together in the morning. Then we'll eat breakfast. More protein. You'll get fresh air every day. Rejoin some committees at the club. You used to make an effort with dinner. I'd like for you to do that again."

"Yes. Of course."

"I am committed to our marriage, Nellie. Do not ever make me question whether you are again."

I quickly nodded, even though the motion hurt my neck.

He left for work an hour later, telling me he would phone me when he got to the office and that he expected me to answer. I did exactly as he said. I could only swallow some yogurt for breakfast because of my throat, but it was high in protein. It was early fall, so I took a walk in the cool fresh air, keeping the ringer on my cell phone turned up as high as possible. I put on a turtleneck to cover the red, oval imprints that would turn into bruises, then went to the grocery store and selected filet mignon and white asparagus to serve to my husband.

I was in the checkout lane when I heard the cashier saying, "Ma'am?" I realized she'd been waiting for me to pay for my groceries. I looked up from the bag of food I was starting at, wondering if he already knew what I was buying for his dinner. Somehow Richard was aware of every time I left the house; he'd found out about my secret journey into the city, the liquor store I frequented, the errands I ran.

Even when I'm not there, I'm always with you.

I looked at the woman at the next register over as she appeased a cranky toddler who wanted to be lifted out of the cart. I glanced up at the security camera near the door. I saw the pile of red baskets with gleaming metal handles, the display of tabloid magazines, the candy in bright, crinkly wrappers.

I had no idea how my husband was constantly watching me. But his surveillance was no longer stealth. I could not deviate from the more stringent new rules of our marriage. And I could certainly never try to leave him.

He would know.

He would stop me.

He would hurt me.

He might kill me.

A week or two later, I looked up from the breakfast table and watched Richard select a crispy piece of turkey bacon that I'd prepared along with our scrambled eggs. His face was still slightly flushed from our morning workout. Steam curled from his cup of espresso; *The Wall Street Journal* was folded by his plate.

He bit into the bacon. "This is perfectly cooked."

"Thank you."

"What are your plans for today?"

"I'm going to shower and then head over to the club for the used-book drive. Lots of sorting to do."

He nodded. "Sounds good." He wiped his fingertips on his napkin, then snapped opened the newspaper. "And don't forget Diane's retirement luncheon is next Friday. Can you pick up a nice card and I'll put the cruise tickets inside?"

"Of course."

He bent his head and began to scan the stocks.

I stood up and cleared the table. I loaded the dishwasher and wiped down the counters. As I ran the sponge over the marbled granite, Richard approached me from behind and wrapped his arms around my waist. He kissed my neck.

"I love you," he whispered.

"I love you, too."

He put on his suit jacket, then picked up his briefcase and walked toward the front door. I followed him, watching as he headed to his Mercedes.

Everything was exactly as Richard wished it to be. When he came home tonight, dinner would be ready. I'd have changed out of my yoga pants into a pretty dress. I'd entertain him with a funny story about what Mindy had said at the club.

Richard looked up at me through the big bay window as he walked toward the driveway.

"Good-bye!" I called, waving.

His smile was wide and genuine. He radiated contentment.

I realized something in that moment. It felt like glimpsing a pinpoint of sunlight in the cottony, suffocating gray pressing in on me.

There was one way my husband would let me go.

It would need to be his idea to end our marriage.

CHAPTER
THIRTY-SIX

I AM UPDATING my résumé on my laptop when my cell phone rings.

Her name flashes across the screen. I hesitate before answering. I worry this could be another of Richard's traps.

"You were right," says the husky voice I've come to know so well. I remain quiet.

"About the Visa bill." I fear that even my slightest utterance will cause Emma to stop talking, change her mind, hang up. "I called the credit card company. There was no wine charge from Sotheby's. Richard never ordered the Raveneau."

I can hardly believe what I have just heard. Part of me still worries Richard may be behind this, but Emma's tone is different from in the past. She no longer sounds contemptuous of me.

"Vanessa, the way you looked when he said he would escort you downstairs . . . that's what convinced me to check. I thought you were jealous. That you wanted him back. But you don't, do you?"

"No."

"You're terrified of him," Emma says bluntly. "He actually hit you? He tried to strangle you? I can't believe Richard would—but—"

"Where are you? Where is he?"

"I'm home. He's in Chicago on business."

I'm grateful she's not at Richard's apartment. Her place is probably

safe. Although her phone may not be. "We need to meet in person."
But this time it will be in a public place.

"How about the Starbucks on—"

"No, you have to stick to your routine. What do you have planned
today?"

"I was going to take a yoga class this afternoon. And then go pick
up my wedding gown."

We won't be able to talk in a yoga studio. "The bridal shop. Where
is it?"

Emma gives me the address and time. I tell her I will meet her there.

What she doesn't know is that I'm going to arrive early to make
sure I'm not ambushed again.

"What a perfect bride," Brenda, the boutique's owner, exclaims.

Emma's eyes meet mine in the mirror as she stands on the raised
platform in a creamy silk sheath. She is unsmiling, but Brenda seems
too busy surveying the final fit of the dress to notice Emma's somber
mood.

"I don't think it needs a single tweak," Brenda continues. "I'll just
steam it and we'll messenger it to you tomorrow."

"Actually, we can wait," I say. "We'd like to take it with us." The
dressing area is empty, and in a corner are several armchairs. It's private. Safe.

"Would you care for some champagne, then?"

"We'd love some," I say, and Emma nods in agreement.

As Emma slips out of the dress, I avert my gaze. Still, I see her
reflection—smooth skin and lacy pink lingerie—in a half dozen angles
in mirrors around the room. It is an oddly intimate moment.

Brenda takes the gown and carefully places it onto a padded hanger
while I impatiently wait for her to leave the room. Before Emma can
even finish fastening the button on her skirt, I head to the chairs. This
bridal shop is one place where I can be certain Richard won't unexpectedly show up. It's practically forbidden for a groom to see his
fiancée in a wedding gown before the ceremony.

"I thought you were crazy," Emma says. "When I worked for Richard, I used to hear him on the phone with you, asking what you'd eaten for breakfast and if you'd gotten out for some fresh air. I had access to emails he sent asking where you were. Saying he'd phoned four times that day but you hadn't answered. He was always so worried about you."

"I can see how it seemed that way."

We fall silent as Brenda returns with two flutes of champagne. "Congratulations, again." I'm worried she will linger and chat, but she excuses herself to check on the dress.

"I figured I had you sized up," Emma tells me bluntly once Brenda is gone. She looks at me carefully, and I see an unexpected familiarity in her round blue eyes. Before I can place it, she continues, "You had this perfect life with this great guy. You didn't even work, you just lounged around in the fancy house he paid for. I didn't think you deserved any of it."

I let her continue.

She tilts her head to the side. It's almost as if she is seeing me for the first time. "You're different than I imagined. I've thought about you so much. I wondered what it would feel like for you to know your husband was in love with someone else. It used to keep me up at night."

"It wasn't your fault." She has no idea how true that statement is.

A loud ding emanates from Emma's purse. She freezes with the flute almost touching her lips. We both stare at her bag.

She pulls out her phone. "Richard texted me. He just arrived at his hotel in Chicago. He asked what I'm up to and wrote that he misses me."

"Text him and tell him you miss him, too, and that you love him." She raises one eyebrow but does what I ask.

"Now give me your phone." I tap on it, then show it to Emma. "It's tracking you." I point to the screen. "Richard bought it for you, right? His name is on the account. He can access your phone's location—*your* location—at any time."

He did the same thing to me after we got engaged. I eventually figured it out after that day in the grocery store when I wondered if he already knew what I'd be serving him for dinner. It was how he discovered my clandestine visit into the city, and to the wine store a few towns over.

Richard was also responsible for the mysterious hang-ups that began after I met him, I've realized. Sometimes they served as punishment, such as during our honeymoon, when Richard thought I'd been flirting with the young scuba instructor. Other times I believe he was trying to keep me off-balance; to unnerve me so that he could subsequently reassure me. But I don't tell this part to Emma.

Emma is staring at her phone. "So he pretends he doesn't know what I'm doing even though he does?" She sips her drink. "God, that's sick."

"I realize it's a lot to take in." I recognize this is an extraordinary understatement.

"Do you know what I keep thinking about? Richard showed up right after you slipped that letter under my door. He immediately tore it up, but I keep remembering this one line you wrote: 'A part of you already knows who he is.'" Emma's eyes grow unfocused and I suspect she is reliving the moment when she began to see her fiancé anew. "Richard wanted to—it was like he wanted to *murder* that letter. He kept ripping it into smaller and smaller bits, then he shoved them in his pocket. And his face—it didn't even look like him."

She lingers in the memory for a long moment, then shakes it off and stares directly at me. "Will you tell me the truth about something?"

"Of course."

"Right after the cocktail party at your house, he came in with a bad scratch on his cheek. When I asked him what happened, he said a neighbor's cat did it when he tried to pick it up."

Richard could have covered the scratch or come up with a better story for it. But conclusions would be drawn after my sloppy conduct at our party; it was more proof of my instability, my volatility.

Emma is very still now. "I grew up with a cat," she says slowly. "I know that scratch was different."

I nod.

Then I inhale deeply and blink hard. "I was trying to get him off me."

Emma doesn't react initially. Perhaps she instinctively realizes that if she shows me sympathy, I'll crumple into tears. She simply looks at me, then turns away.

"I can't believe I got this so wrong," she finally says. "I thought you were the one . . . He's coming back tomorrow. I'm supposed to spend the night at his place. Then Maureen's coming to town. We're meeting at my apartment so she can see my dress . . . then we're all going to taste wedding cakes!"

Her chatter is the only sign that she's nervous, that our conversation has thrown her.

Maureen is an added complication. I'm not surprised Richard and Emma are including her in the wedding preparations, though; I remember wanting to do the same. Along with the butterfly-clasp necklace I gave her, I sought out her opinion on whether Richard would want black-and-white or color photographs in the album that was my wedding gift to him. Richard also called her and put her on speakerphone while the three of us discussed entrée options for the meal.

I put my arm around Emma. At first her body is rigid, but it softens for a brief moment before she pulls away. She must be holding back a tidal wave of emotions.

Save her. Save her.

I close my eyes and recall the girl I couldn't save. "Don't be scared. I'm going to help you."

When we arrive at Emma's place, she lays her wedding gown across the back of her sofa.

"Can I get you anything to drink?"

I barely touched my champagne; I want my thoughts to remain clear so I can figure out how Emma can safely extract herself from Richard. "I'd love some water."

Emma bustles about her galley kitchen, anxiously chattering again. "Do you take ice? I know my place is a little messy. I was going to do laundry and then all of a sudden I just felt like I had to check on the Visa charge. He added me to that account after we got engaged, so all I had to do was call the number on the back of my card. I've got some grapes and almonds if you want a snack. . . . Usually I reviewed his AmEx statements before submitting them to Accounting for reimbursement, but a couple of times, he told me he'd handle it himself. That's why I never saw the refund." Emma shakes her head.

I absently listen to her as I look around. I know she is grasping for ways to blunt the impact of what she has learned about Richard. The champagne she quickly drank, the frantic energy—I recognize the symptoms too well.

As Emma cracks ice cubes into our glasses, I study her small living room. The couch, the end table, the roses that are now slightly wilted. Nothing else is on the end table, and I suddenly realize what I'm looking for.

"Do you have a landline?"

"What?" She shakes her head and hands me my glass of water. "No, why?"

I am relieved. But all I say is "Just figuring out the best way for us to communicate."

I am not going to tell Emma everything yet. If she learns how much worse the reality could be, she may shut down.

There's no need to explain that I am certain Richard was somehow eavesdropping on calls I made from our house phone during our marriage.

I finally made the connection after I saw the pattern emerge on the pages of my notebook.

When our burglar alarm erupted in the Westchester house and I fled to cower in my closet, I was initially reassured that the video cameras posted by our front and back doors showed no evidence of an intruder. Then I realized Richard had checked the cameras. No one else had verified what they might reveal.

And immediately before the siren had blared, I was on the phone with Sam. I'd made a joke about bringing guys home after a night of barhopping. I now believe Richard had set off the alarm. It was my punishment.

He feasted on my fear; it nurtured his sense of strength. I think of the mysterious cell phone hang-ups that began shortly after our engagement, how he'd booked a scuba dive for his claustrophobic new bride, how he always reminded me to set the burglar alarm. How he'd enjoyed comforting me, whispering that he alone would keep me safe.

I take a long drink of water. "What time is Richard coming back tomorrow?"

"Late afternoon." Emma looks at her gown. "I should hang this up."

I walk with Emma into her bedroom and watch as she hooks the gown on the back of her closet door. It appears to be floating. I can't pull my gaze away from it.

The bride who was supposed to wear this exquisite dress no longer exists. The gown will remain vacant on her wedding day.

Emma straightens the hanger slightly, her hand lingering on the dress before she slowly pulls it away.

"He seemed so wonderful." Her voice is filled with surprise. "How can a man like that be so brutal?"

I think of my own wedding dress, nestled in a special acid-free box in my old closet in Westchester, preserved for the daughter I never had.

I swallow hard before I can speak. "Parts of Richard *were* wonderful. That's why we stayed married for so long."

"Why didn't you ever leave him?"

"I thought about it. There are so many reasons why I should have. And so many reasons why I couldn't."

Emma nods.

"I needed Richard to leave me."

"But how did you know he ever would?"

I look into her eyes. I have to confess. Emma has already been devastated today. But she deserves to be told the truth. Without it, she will be trapped in a false reality, and I know exactly how destructive that can be.

"There's one more thing." I walk back to the living room and she follows me. I gesture to the couch. "Can we sit down?"

She perches rigidly on the edge of a cushion, as if steeling herself for what is to come.

I reveal everything: The office holiday party when I first spotted her. The gathering at our house when I pretended to be drunk. The night I faked illness and suggested Richard take her to the Philharmonic. The business trip when I encouraged them to stay overnight.

She is holding her head in her hands by the time I finish.

"How could you do this to me?" she cries. She leaps to her feet and glares at me. "I knew it all along. There really is something wrong with you!"

"I am so sorry."

"Do you know how many nights I lay awake wondering if I'd contributed to the demise of your marriage?"

She didn't say she felt guilt, but it's natural that she would have; I am certain their physical relationship began while Richard and I were still married. Now all of Emma's memories with Richard are doubly tainted. She must feel like a pawn in my dysfunctional marriage. Maybe she even thinks we deserved each other.

"I never thought it would go this far. . . . I didn't think he would propose. I thought it would just be an affair."

"*Just* an affair?" Emma shouts. Her cheeks flush with anger; the passion in her voice surprises me. "Like it's some innocuous little thing? Affairs destroy people. Did you ever consider how much I would suffer?"

I feel battered by her words, but then something ignites in me and I find myself pushing back at her.

"I *know* affairs destroy people!" I shout, thinking of how I'd curled up in bed for weeks after learning about Daniel's deception, after seeing his tired-looking wife. It happened almost fifteen years ago, but I can still visualize that little yellow tricycle and pink jump rope behind the oak tree in his yard. I still remember how my pen had trembled across the page when I signed in at the Planned Parenthood clinic.

"I was deceived once by a married man in college," I say, more softly now. This is the first time I've ever revealed this particular piece of my story to anyone. The rush of pain that hits me is so fresh, it's as if I'm that heartbroken twenty-one-year-old all over again. "I thought he loved me. He never told me about his wife. Sometimes I think my life could have been so different if I'd only known."

Emma strides across the room. She yanks open her door.

"Get out." But the venom is gone from her tone. Her lips are trembling and her eyes shine with tears.

"Just let me say one final thing," I plead. "Call Richard tonight and tell him you can't go through with the wedding. Tell him I came over again and it was the last straw."

She doesn't react, so I continue quickly as I begin to walk toward the door. "Ask him to announce to everyone that the engagement is off; that part is really important," I stress. "He won't punish you if he gets to control the message. If he comes out with his dignity."

I pause in front of her so she cannot miss my words. "Just say you can't deal with his psycho ex-wife. Promise me you'll do that. Then you'll be safe."

Emma is silent. But at least she is looking at me, even though it is with a cold, appraising stare. Her eyes rake across my face and down my body, then back up again.

"How am I supposed to believe anything you say?"

"You don't need to. Please go stay with a friend. Leave your cell phone here so he can't find you. Richard's anger always passes quickly. Just protect yourself."

I step over the threshold and hear the door close sharply behind me.

I hover in the hallway, staring down at the dark blue carpet beneath my feet. Emma must be reevaluating everything I've told her. She probably doesn't have any idea who to trust.

If Emma doesn't follow the script I've given her, Richard may unleash his rage on her, especially if he can't find me. Or worse, he may convince her to change her mind and go through with the wedding.

Maybe I should not have told her of my role in this. Her security should have trumped my need to unburden my guilt, to be scrupulously honest. Her faulty perception would have left her less vulnerable than this dangerous truth.

What will be Richard's next step?

I have twenty-four hours until he returns. And I have no idea what to do.

I slowly walk down the hallway. I am so reluctant to leave her. I am about to step into the elevator when I hear a door open. I glance up and see Emma standing in her threshold.

"You want me to tell Richard I'm calling off the wedding because of you."

I nod quickly. "Yes. Blame it all on me."

Her brow furrows. She tilts her head to one side and looks me up and down again.

"It's the safest solution," I say.

"It might be for me. But it isn't safe for you."

CHAPTER
THIRTY-SEVEN

"I've MISSED YOU so much, sweetheart," Richard says.

At the love and tenderness filling his voice, something in my chest twists.

My ex-husband stands not nine feet from me. He returned from Chicago a few hours ago and stopped by his place to change into jeans and a polo shirt before arriving here, at Emma's apartment.

I am crouched down, staring through an old-fashioned keyhole in her bedroom closet. It is the only place that gives me both cover and a vantage point into the room.

Emma sits on the edge of her bed in sweatpants and a T-shirt. A package of Sudafed, a box of tissues, and a cup of tea rest on her night-stand. I thought of those touches.

"I brought you chicken soup and fresh-squeezed orange juice from Eli's. And some zinc. My trainer swears by it to kick summer colds."

"Thank you." Emma's voice is feeble and soft. She is convincing.

"Can I get you a sweater?"

My insides clench as Richard's form fills my vision, blotting out the rest of the room. He is approaching my hiding place.

"Actually, I'm too warm. Could you bring me a cool washcloth for my forehead?"

We didn't practice those lines; Emma improvises well.

I don't exhale until I hear his footsteps reverse themselves as he heads to the bathroom.

I shift slightly; I've been kneeling for several minutes and my legs are aching.

Emma hasn't looked my way even once. She is still reeling from my revelation; she doesn't seem to completely trust me. I don't blame her.

"You don't get to orchestrate my life any longer," she'd said to me yesterday as I stood in her hallway, by the elevator. "I'm not going to end things with Richard on the phone just because you told me to do it. I'll decide when to call my wedding off."

But at least she is allowing me to remain close by tonight with my cell phone in hand. Watching him. Protecting her.

We both predicted Richard would insist on visiting when Emma told him she was sick. Faking illness solves a multitude of problems. If Richard is tracking Emma's movements, it would explain why she skipped her yoga class. Why she wants to sleep at her own place. And why she can't even kiss him, let alone have sex with him. I wanted to spare her that.

"Here you go, baby," Richard says, coming back into the room.

I glimpse him bending over the bed, then his back blocks me from seeing his movements. Still, I imagine him holding the damp wash-cloth to Emma's forehead and smoothing back her hair. Looking at her with so much love.

My kneecaps feel as if they are grinding against the hardwood floor. My thighs are burning; I am desperate to stand up and shake out my legs. But Richard might hear.

"I hate for you to see me like this. I'm a wreck."

If I didn't know the truth, I would be certain she was innocent of any ulterior motives.

"Even when you're sick, you're the most beautiful woman in the world."

I still know Richard so well. He genuinely means every word. If Emma expressed a craving for a strawberry sorbet or cozy cashmere socks, he'd scour Manhattan to get her the best. He'd sleep on the floor next to her if she said it would make her feel better. This is the part of my ex-husband's nature that is the most difficult to expunge from my heart. At this moment, just like his profile through the keyhole, it is all I can see.

I squeeze my eyes shut.

Then I immediately force them open. I've learned the danger of failing to observe the things I don't want to behold.

If Emma didn't live up to Richard's expectations—and it was inevitable that she would fail to—there would be consequences. If she wasn't the wife of his fantasies, he would hurt her, then give her jewelry to smooth it over. If she didn't provide the family or create the kind of home he desired, he would systematically assault her reality and twist it until it became unrecognizable even to her. And worst of all, he would take away whatever or whomever she loved the most.

"I'll tell Maureen you need to cancel tomorrow," Richard says to Emma.

Perfect, I think. This delay could buy us some more time to figure out how to best extract Emma.

But instead of agreeing, Emma says, "No, I'm sure I'll be better if I just get some rest."

"Anything you want, my love, but the most important thing is you."

Even through the closet door I can feel the magnetic pull of his charisma.

I was holding on to the hope that Emma would begin to create distance between her and Richard tonight. But after only a few minutes in his presence, she seems to be wavering.

Through the keyhole, I can see their clasped hands. His thumb is gently stroking her wrist.

I want to leap out of the closet and wrench them apart; he is swaying her. Luring her back to him.

"Besides, Maureen has to come over so I can show her my wedding dress." That dress is now hanging six inches to my left; Emma tucked it in here so Richard wouldn't see it. "Plus we have those fun wedding errands. You don't think I'm going to let you do the cake tasting alone, do you?" she continues in a playful voice.

This is the opposite of what should be happening. The Emma of right now is a completely different woman from the one of twenty-four hours ago who asked me, as we stood in this same room, how Richard could be so wonderful yet so brutal.

I cannot hold my position any longer. I slowly lift my right knee off the floor and plant my foot gently down. I repeat the motion with my left leg. Inch by agonizing inch, I rise. Dresses and shirts engulf me, silky fabrics sliding across my face.

A hanger clinks against the metal rod, the sound as delicate and precise as a wind chime striking a single note.

"What was that?" Richard asks.

I cannot see anything.

His citrus scent surrounds me, or am I imagining it? I suck in a shallow inhalation. My heart pounds violently. I am terrified I will pass out, my body thumping against the closet door.

"Just my creaky old bed." I hear Emma shift, and miraculously, the bed squeaks. "I can't wait until I only sleep in yours."

Again, I am stunned by her lightning-quick subterfuge.

Then Emma says, "But there is one thing I need to tell you."

"What's that, sweetheart?"

She hesitates.

I sink back down to peer through the keyhole again. I wonder why she's drawing out their conversation. She knows how clever Richard is; doesn't she want him out of the apartment before he figures out she isn't really sick?

"Vanessa called me today."

My eyes widen and I barely suppress a gasp. I can't believe she has set me up again.

Richard barks an expletive and violently kicks the wall next to Emma's dresser. I feel the vibrations through the floorboards. I see his fists clench and unclench.

He stands facing the wall for a few moments, then he turns around to look at Emma.

"I'm sorry, baby." His voice is strained. "What bullshit did she tell you this time?"

Emma has chosen to believe Richard. The act she has been putting on was to trick me. I can call 911, but what will the police think if Emma and Richard tell them I broke in here?

Emma's clothes are suffocating me. There's no air in this small closet. I'm trapped. I feel the grip of claustrophobia descend as my throat tightens.

"No, Richard, it wasn't like that. Vanessa apologized. She said she's going to leave me alone."

My head is swimming. Emma is so far off any script I could have anticipated that I can't even guess at her intentions.

"She's said that before." I can hear Richard breathing heavily. "But she keeps calling and coming to my office and writing letters. She won't stop. She's insane—"

"Honey, it's okay. I really believe her. She sounded different."

My legs feel as if they've turned to liquid. I have no idea why Emma created this pretense.

Richard exhales. "Let's not talk about her. I hope we never have to again. Can I get you anything else?"

"All I want to do is sleep. And I don't want you to get sick. You should go. I love you."

"I'll pick you and Maureen up at two tomorrow. I love you, too."

I stay in the closet until Emma opens the door a few minutes later. "He's gone."

I bend and unbend my legs and wince. I want to ask her about the unexpected turn in her conversation, but her face is so expressionless that I know she only wants me out.

"Can I wait a few minutes before I leave?"

She hesitates, then nods. "Let's go into the living room." I catch her sneaking appraising looks at me. She's wary.

"What are we going to do next?"

She frowns. I can tell my use of the word *we* chafes her. "I'll figure it out." She shrugs.

Emma doesn't get it. She doesn't seem to feel any urgency to call off the wedding. If Richard can be this compelling in a brief visit, what will happen when he feeds her bites of cakes, his arm wrapped around her waist, and whispers promises of how happy he'll make her?

"You saw him kick the wall," I say, my voice rising. "Don't you see what he is?"

This is so much bigger than just Emma. Even if Richard lets Emma go—which I'm not convinced he'll do—what about all the many ways in which Richard hurt me? And the woman before both of us, the dark-haired ex who couldn't bear to keep that gift from Tiffany's? I am now certain he hurt her, too.

My ex-husband is a creature of habit, a man ruled by routines. Whatever stunning piece of jewelry that glossy blue bag contained was his apology; his attempt to literally cover up an ugly episode.

Emma does not know that I intend to save any woman who could become Richard's future wife.

"You have to end it soon. The longer it goes on, the worse it will be—"

"I said I'll figure it out."

She walks to the door and opens it. I reluctantly step past her.

"Good-bye," she says. I have the distinct feeling she plans to never see me again.

But she's wrong about that.

Because by now I know I need a plan of my own. The seed of an idea was planted as I watched Richard's explosive flash of anger at the mention of my name, my fictitious call. It takes shape in my mind as I walk down the blue-carpeted hallway, following the path Richard took only minutes ago.

Emma thinks Maureen is coming over to see the wedding gown tomorrow, then they'll go cake tasting with Richard.

She has no idea what will really happen.

CHAPTER
THIRTY-EIGHT

THE PAGES OF MY BRAND-NEW life insurance policy unspool from the printer.

I clip them together, then slide them into a manila envelope. I have made sure to select a plan that covers not only my demise from natural causes, but also death and dismemberment from an accident.

I place it on my desk, beside the note I've penned to Aunt Charlotte. It is the hardest letter I have ever written. In it I've left information about my bank account with my swollen new balance so she can easily access it. She is the sole beneficiary of my life insurance policy as well.

I have three hours left.

I pick up my to-do list and mark off that task. My room is clean, my bed neatly made. All of my belongings are stored in my wardrobe.

Earlier today I also checked off two other items. I telephoned Maggie's parents. And then I called Jason.

At first he didn't recognize my name. It took him a few moments to remember. I paced during the pause in which he made the mental connection, wondering if he would acknowledge our past encounters.

Instead, he thanked me profusely for the donations to the animal shelter, then caught me up on his life since college. He told me he'd married the girlfriend he'd met on campus. "She stuck by me," Jason said, his voice thickening with emotion. "I was so angry at everyone, but mostly at myself for not being there to help my little sister. When I got arrested for drunk driving and went to rehab—well, my girl-friend was my rock. She never gave up on me. We got married the next year."

Jason's wife was a middle-school teacher, he said. She'd gradu-ated the same year as me. That was why he went to her ceremony at the Piaget Auditorium and stood in the corner. He was there to sup-port her.

My guilt and anxiety had concocted a lie. It was never even about me.

I couldn't help but feel sad for the woman who let all that fear shape so many of her life choices.

I am still very afraid, but it is no longer constricting me.

Only a few items remain on my list now.

I open my laptop and clear my browser history, wiping away evi-dence of my recent investigations. I double-check to make sure my searches into airline tickets and small, non-chain motels are no longer visible to anyone who might access my computer.

Emma does not understand Richard as I do. She cannot grasp what he is truly capable of. It's impossible to imagine what he becomes in his worst moments.

Richard will simply move on unless I stop him. He'll be more care-ful, though. He will find a way to rotate the kaleidoscope and sweep away the current reality, forming a bright, distracting new image.

I lay my outfit on my bed and take a long, hot shower, trying to ease the tightness in my muscles. I wrap myself in my bathrobe and clear the fog from the mirror above the sink.

Two and a half hours left.

First my hair. I brush back the damp strands into a tight bun. I care-fully apply makeup and select the diamond stud earrings Richard gave me for our second anniversary. I fasten my Cartier Tank watch around my wrist. It's essential that I am able to keep track of every second.

The dress I've selected is one I wore when Richard and I went to Bermuda. A classic snow-white sheath. It could almost serve as a wedding dress for a simple beachside ceremony. It is one of the outfits he sent back to me a few weeks ago.

I've chosen it not only for its history, and for its possibilities, but also because it has pockets.

Two hours remain.

I slip on a pair of flats, then gather the items I will need.

I tear up my list into tiny bits, then flush them down the toilet. I watch as they swirl away, the ink blurring.

A final act I must do remains before I leave. It is the most wrenching item on my list. It will require every bit of strength and all of the acting expertise I have accumulated.

I find Aunt Charlotte in the extra bedroom that serves as her studio. The door is open.

Canvases are stacked three deep throughout the room. Splatters of succulent colors layer the soft wood floor. For a moment, I surrender to the beauty: cerulean skies, clinquant stars, the horizon in the ephemeral moment before dawn. A rhapsody of wildflowers. The weathered grain of an old table. A Parisian bridge spanning the Seine. The curve of a woman's cheek, her skin milky white and creased by age. I know this face so well; it is my aunt's self-portrait.

Aunt Charlotte is lost in the landscape she is creating. Her strokes are looser than they have been in the past; her style more forgiving.

I want to capture her like this in my memory.

After a few moments she looks up and blinks. "Oh, I didn't see you there, honey."

"I don't want to disturb you," I say softly. "I'm heading out for a bit, but I've left lunch for you in the kitchen."

"You look nice. Where are you off to?"

"A job interview. I don't want to jinx it, but I'll tell you about it tonight."

My eyes fall on a canvas across the room: a laundry line hanging outside a building above a Venetian canal, the shirts and pants and skirts billowing in a breeze I can almost feel.

"You have to promise me one thing before I go."

"Bossy today, aren't you?" Aunt Charlotte teases.

"Seriously. It's important. Will you go to Italy before the end of the summer?"

The smile fades from Aunt Charlotte's lips. "Is something wrong?"

I desperately want to cross the room and hold on to her, but I fear if I do, I might not be able to leave.

This is all in my letter, anyway:

Remember that day when you taught me about how sunlight contains all the colors of the rainbow? You were my sunlight. You taught me how to find rainbows. . . . Please go to Italy for us. You will always carry me with you.

I shake my head. "Nothing's wrong. I was planning on taking you as a surprise. But I'm worried if I get this job, we won't be able to go together. That's all."

"Let's not think about that now. You just focus on your interview. When is it?"

I check my watch. "Ninety minutes."

"Good luck."

I blow her a kiss and imagine it landing on her soft cheek.

CHAPTER
THIRTY-NINE

FOR THE SECOND TIME in my life, I stand in a white dress at the end of a narrow swath of blue, waiting for Richard to approach.

The elevator doors close behind him. But he is motionless.

I feel the intensity of his gaze all the way down at my end of the hallway. I've been deliberately stoking his anger for days, coaxing it from the place where he struggles to keep it buried. It is the opposite of how I taught myself to behave during my marriage.

"Are you surprised, sweetheart? It's me, Nellie."

It is precisely two o'clock. Emma is a dozen yards from where I stand, in her living room, with Maureen. Neither of them knows I am here; I snuck into the building an hour ago by trailing a deliveryman through the door. I knew exactly when the uniformed man carrying the long rectangular box would arrive. It was I who placed the order for a dozen white roses to be sent to Emma this afternoon.

"I thought you were out of town," he says.

"I changed my mind. I wanted to have another chat with your fiancée."

My hands are touching a few different objects in my pockets. Which I pull out first will depend on Richard's reaction. Richard takes a step onto the carpet runner. It is almost impossible for me to avoid shrinking back. Despite the summer heat, his dark suit, white shirt, and gold silk tie appear creaseless and elegant. He isn't unhinged yet, not the way I need him to be.

"Really? And what do you intend to say to her?" His voice is dangerously quiet.

"I'm going to start with this." I pull out a piece of paper. "It's your Visa bill showing you never ordered the Raveneau." He's too far away to see the fine print and realize it's actually one of my own statements.

I need to press on before he demands to see the proof. I smile at Richard, though my stomach is churning. "I'm also going to explain to Emma that you are tracking her through her phone." I keep my voice as low and steady as his. "Just like you did to me."

I can almost feel his body clench. "You've gone over the edge, Vanessa." Another measured step. "This is my fiancée you're messing with. After everything I went through with you, you're trying to ruin this now?"

Out of the corner of my eye, I gauge the distance to Emma's apartment door. I tense my body in preparation.

"You lied about Duke. I know what you did with him, and I'm going to tell Emma." This isn't true—I never found out what happened to my beloved dog, although I truly don't think Richard actually harmed him—but it hits its target. I see Richard's face compress in rage.

"And you lied about the sperm analysis, too." My mouth is so dry it's difficult to form the words. I take a step backward, toward Emma's door. "Thank God you couldn't get me pregnant. You don't deserve to have a child. I took photos after you hurt me. I collected evidence. You didn't think I was smart enough, did you?"

I've carefully chosen words I know will incite my ex-husband.

They are working.

"Emma is going to leave you when I tell her everything." I can no longer keep my voice from shaking. But the truth it contains is undeniable. "Just like the woman before me left you." I take a deep breath and deliver my closing lines. "I wanted to leave you, too. I was never your sweet Nellie. I didn't want to stay married to you, Richard."

He explodes in fury.

This I expected.

But I miscalculated how quickly he would lose all control, how fast he would be.

He is upon me before I have taken more than a few running steps toward Emma's door.

Richard's hands tighten around my throat, cutting off my supply of oxygen.

I thought I'd have time to scream. To bang on the door and summon Emma and Maureen, so they could witness Richard's transformation. Richard would never be able to explain this violence away; it would be the physical proof that couldn't be found in a notebook or a filing cabinet or a storage unit. This was the other insurance policy I needed to save us all—me, Emma, and the women in Richard's future.

I was also counting on Richard to halt his attack when Maureen and Emma appeared—or that, at least, they would be able to stop him. Now there is no reason for him to deny himself his need to extinguish me.

My windpipe feels as if it is being crushed into the back of my neck. The pain is agonizing. My knees buckle.

My left arm helplessly stretches out toward Emma's door, though I know it's futile. She is twirling in her wedding gown for her future sister-in-law. Completely unaware of what is happening on the other side of her living room wall.

Richard's assault is nearly silent; a gurgling noise wrenches free from my throat, but it is not loud enough to reach her or anyone else who may be home on this floor.

He thrusts me back against the wall. His hot breath brushes my cheeks. I see the scar above his eye, a silvery crescent, as he leans closer.

I am engulfed by dizziness.

I fumble for the pepper spray in my pocket, but as I pull it out, Richard bangs my head against the wall and I lose my grip on it. It tumbles to the carpet.

My vision recedes; it is being hemmed in by black borders. I frantically kick at his shins, but he is unaffected by my blows.

My lungs are burning. I am desperate for air.

His eyes blaze into mine. I claw at his body and my hand hits something hard in his suit jacket pocket. I wrench it free.

Save us.

I summon the last of my strength and smash the object against his face.

Richard releases a cry.

A splash of bright red blood erupts from the wound by his temple.

My limbs grow heavy and my body begins to relax. A calmness I haven't felt in years—perhaps ever—overtakes me. My knees give way.

I am fading into the blackness when the pressure abruptly disappears. I collapse and draw in a ragged breath. I cough violently, then I retch.

"Vanessa," a woman calls from what seems a great distance away.

I am splayed on the carpet, one of my legs bent beneath me, but I feel as if I am floating.

"Vanessa!"

Emma. All I can do is roll my head to one side, bringing broken pieces of porcelain into view. I see jagged pieces of china figurines—a serenely smiling blond bride and her handsome groom. It was our cake topper.

And beside them is Richard on his knees, his expression blank, a rivulet of blood streaming down his face and staining his white shirt.

I suck in a painful breath, then another. All of the menace has leached out of my ex-husband. His hair has fallen forward into his eyes. He is immobile.

Fresh oxygen returns a little strength to my body, though my throat feels so swollen and tender I can't swallow. I manage to edge backward and pull myself into a sitting position, slumping against the hallway wall.

Emma hurries to my side. She is barefoot and, like me, clad in a white sheath. Her wedding gown. "I heard someone yell—I came out to see—but then . . . What happened?"

I can't speak. I can only suck in shallow, greedy breaths.

I see her eyes drift down to my neck. "I'm calling an ambulance."

Richard doesn't react to any of this, not even to the gasp of surprise Maureen gives as she suddenly appears in the doorway.

"What is going on?" Maureen stares at me—the woman she dismissed as unstable, as her brother's cast-off wife. Then she looks at Richard, the man she helped raise and loves unconditionally. She goes to him. She reaches out and touches his back. "Richard?"

He raises a hand to his forehead, then stares at the streak of red on his palm. He seems oddly distant, as if he's in shock.

I hate the sight of blood. That was one of the first things he'd ever said to me. I suddenly realize that in all of the ways Richard hurt me, he never once made me bleed.

Maureen hurries into the apartment and returns with a wad of paper towels. She kneels next to him and presses the towels to his wound. "What's going on?" Her words grow sharper. "Vanessa, why are you here? What did you do to him?"

"He hurt me." My voice is hoarse and every syllable feels as if one of the shards of porcelain is rubbing against the inside of my throat.

I need to finally say these words.

I grimace as I make my voice louder. "He choked me. He nearly killed me. Just like he used to hurt me when we were married."

Maureen gasps. "He wouldn't—no, not—"

Then she falls silent. She is still shaking her head, but her shoulders sag and her face collapses. I am certain that even though she hasn't yet seen the fingerprint-shaped marks that I know are blooming on my neck, she believes me.

Maureen straightens up. She pulls the paper towels away from Richard's face and examines his injury. When she speaks again, her tone is brisk, yet caring.

"It isn't so bad. I don't think you need stitches."

Richard doesn't react to this, either.

"I'll take care of everything, Richard." Maureen gathers up the shattered pieces of porcelain. She cups them in one hand, then wraps her arms around her brother and tilts her head close to his. I can just barely make out her whispered words: "I always took care of you, Richard. I never let anything bad happen to you. You don't have to worry. I'm here. I'm going to fix everything."

Her utterances are bewildering. But what shocks me most is the strange emotion infusing them. Maureen doesn't sound angry or sad or confused.

Her voice is filled with something I can't identify at first, because it is so out of place.

I finally realize what it is: satisfaction.

CHAPTER
FORTY

THE BUILDING BEFORE ME could be a Southern mansion, with its grand columns and wraparound porch lined with a tidy row of rocking chairs. But to gain access to the grounds, I have to pass through a gate manned by a security guard and show photo identification. The guard also searches the cloth bag I'm carrying. He raises his eyebrows when he sees the items inside, but merely nods for me to continue on my way.

A few patients at the New Springs Hospital are gardening or playing cards on the porch. I don't see him among them.

Richard is spending twenty-eight days at this acute mental-health facility, where he is undergoing intensive daily therapy sessions. It is part of the deal he made to avoid being prosecuted for assaulting me.

As I climb the wide wooden steps toward the entrance, a woman unfolds herself from a chaise lounge, her limbs sharp and athletic looking. The bright afternoon sun is in my eyes and I can't immediately identify her.

Then she moves closer, and I see it is Maureen. "I didn't know you'd be here today." I shouldn't be surprised; Maureen is all Richard has left now.

"I'm here every day. I've taken a leave of absence from work."

I look around. "Where is he?"

One of his counselors passed along Richard's request: He wanted to see me. At first I was unsure if I would comply. Then I realized I needed this visit, too.

"Richard is resting. I wanted to talk to you first." Maureen gestures to a pair of rocking chairs. "Shall we?"

Maureen takes a moment to cross her legs and smooth a crease in her beige linen pantsuit. Clearly she has an agenda. I wait for her to reveal it.

"I feel terrible about what happened between you and Richard." I see Maureen glance at the faded yellow discoloration on my neck. But there is a disconnect between her words and the energy she is conveying. Her posture is rigid and her face is devoid of sympathy.

She doesn't care for me. She never has, even though early on I'd hoped we would become close.

"I know you blame him. But it isn't that simple. Vanessa, my brother has been through a lot. More than you ever knew. More than you can ever imagine."

At this, I can't help blinking in surprise. She is casting Richard as the victim.

"He attacked *me*," I almost shout. "He nearly killed me."

Maureen seems unaffected by my outburst; she merely clears her throat and begins again. "When our parents died—"

"In the car accident."

She frowns, as if my remark has irritated her. As if she has planned for this to be less a conversation than a monologue.

"Yes. Our father lost control of their station wagon. It hit a guardrail and flipped. Our parents died instantly. Richard doesn't remember much, but the police said skid marks showed my dad was speeding."

I jerk back. "Richard doesn't remember—you mean he was in the car?" I blurt.

"Yes, yes," Maureen says impatiently. "That's what I'm trying to tell you."

I am stunned; he concealed more of himself than I ever realized.

"It was horrible for him." Maureen words are almost rushed, as if she wants to hurry through these details before she gets to the important part of her story. "Richard was trapped in the backseat. He hit his forehead. The frame of the car was all twisted and he couldn't get out. It took a while for another driver to pass by and call for paramedics. Richard had a concussion and needed stitches, but it could have been so much worse."

The silvery scar above his eye, I think. The one he said was caused by a bike accident.

I picture Richard as a young teenager—a boy, really—dazed and in pain from the crash. Crying out for his mother. Failing to rouse his parents. Trying to wrench open the upside-down station wagon's doors. Beating his fists against the windows and yelling. And the blood. There must have been so much blood.

"My dad had a temper, and whenever he got mad, he drove fast. I suspect he was arguing with my mother before the crash." Maureen's cadence is slower now. She shakes her head. "Thank God I always told Richard to wear a seat belt. He listened to what I said."

"I had no idea," I finally respond.

Maureen turns to look at me; it's as if I've pulled her from a reverie. "Yes, Richard never talked about the accident with anyone but me. What I want you to know is that it wasn't just when he was driving that my father lost his temper. My father was abusive to my mother."

I inhale sharply.

My dad wasn't always good to my mom, Richard had told me after my mother's funeral as I sat shivering in the bathtub.

I think back to the photograph of his parents Richard hid in the storage unit. I wonder if he needed to literally bury it to suppress the memories of his childhood, so they could yield to the more palatable story he presented.

A shadow falls over me. I instinctively whip my head around. "I'm sorry to interrupt," a nurse in blue scrubs says, smiling. "You wanted me to let you know when your brother woke up."

Maureen nods. "Can you ask him to come down, Angie?" Then Maureen turns to me. "I think it would be better for you two to talk here rather than in his room."

We watch the nurse retreat. When the woman is out of earshot, Maureen's voice turns steely. Her words are clipped. "Look, Vanessa.

Richard is fragile right now. Can we agree that you will finally leave him alone?"

"He's the one who wanted me to come here."

"Richard doesn't know what he wants right now. Two weeks ago, he thought he wanted to marry Emma. He believed she was perfect"— Maureen makes a little scoffing sound—"even though he barely knew her. He thought that about you at one time, too. He always wanted his life to look a certain way, like the idealized bride and groom on the cake topper he bought for my parents all those years ago."

I think of the mismatched date on the bottom of the figurines. "Richard bought that for your parents?"

"I see he didn't tell you about that, either. It was for their anniversary. He had this whole plan that we'd cook them a special dinner and bake them a cake. That they'd have a wonderful night and start loving each other again. But then the car crash happened. He never got to give it to them.

"It was hollow inside, you know. The cake topper. That's what I thought when I saw it broken in the hallway that day. . . . I guess he was bringing it to the tasting to show the cake designer. But Richard really has no business being married to anyone. And it's my job now to make sure that it doesn't happen."

She suddenly smiles—a wide, genuine grin—and I'm completely unnerved.

But it isn't for me. It's for her brother, who is approaching us.

Maureen stands up. "I'll give you two a few minutes alone."

I sit beside the man who both is and is no longer a mystery to me.

He wears jeans and a plain cotton shirt. Dark stubble lines his jaw. Despite the fact that he's been sleeping so much, he appears tired and his skin is sallow. He is no longer the man who enthralled me, then subsequently terrorized me.

He appears ordinary to me now, somehow deflated, like a man I wouldn't look at twice as he waited for a bus or bought a cup of coffee at a street kiosk.

My husband kept me off-balance for years. He tried to erase me.

My husband also hugged my waist on a green sled while we sped down a hill in Central Park. He brought me rum raisin ice cream on the anniversary of my father's death and left me love notes for no reason at all.

And he hoped I could save him from himself.

When Richard finally speaks, he says what I have wanted to hear for so long.

"I'm sorry, Vanessa."

He has apologized to me before, but this time I know his words arc different.

At last they are real.

"Is there any way you could give me another chance? I'm getting better. We could start over."

I gaze out at the gardens and rolling green lawn. I had envisioned a scene much like this when Richard first showed me our Westchester house: The two of us side by side on a porch swing, but decades into our marriage. Connected by memories we'd constructed together, each of us layering in our favorite details with every retelling, until we'd created a unified recollection.

I'd expected to be angry when I saw him. But I only feel pity.

By way of an answer to his question, I hand Richard my cloth bag. He pulls out the top item, a black jewelry box. In it are my wedding and engagement rings. He opens the box.

"I wanted to give these back to you." I have spent so long mired in our past. It is time to return them to him and truly move on.

"We could adopt a child. We could make it perfect this time."

He wipes his eyes. I have never seen him cry before.

Maureen is between us in an instant. She takes the bag and the rings from Richard. "Vanessa, I think it's time for you to go. I'll see you out."

I stand up. Not because she told me to, but because I am ready to leave. "Good-bye, Richard."

———

Maureen leads me down the steps toward the parking lot.

I follow at a slower pace.

"You can do whatever you want with the wedding album." I gesture to the bag. "It was my gift to Richard, so it's rightfully his."

"I remember. Terry did a nice job. Lucky that he was able to fit you in that day after all."

I stop short. I'd never told anyone how close we'd come to not having a photographer at our ceremony.

And it has been nearly a decade since our wedding; even I couldn't come up with Terry's name that quickly.

As Maureen meets my stare, I recollect how a woman had phoned to cancel our booking. Maureen knew which photographer we were using; she had suggested I include black-and-white shots when I emailed her a link to Terry's website and sought her opinion about Richard's gift.

Her icy-blue eyes look so much like Richard's in this instant. It is impossible to gauge what she is thinking.

I recall how Maureen came to our house for every holiday, how she spent her birthdays with her brother engaged in an activity she knew I didn't enjoy, how she never married or had children. How I cannot remember her mentioning the name of a single friend.

"I'll take care of the album." She stops at the edge of the parking lot and touches my arm. "Good-bye."

I feel cold, smooth metal against my skin.

When I look down, I see she has slipped my rings onto the fourth finger of her right hand.

She follows my gaze. "For safekeeping."

CHAPTER
FORTY-ONE

"Thank you for seeing me today," I say to Kate as I settle into my usual spot on her couch.

Though I haven't been here in months—since when I was still married—the room is exactly the same, with magazines fanned on the coffee table and a few snow globes on the windowsill. Across from me, in the large aquarium, two angelfish languidly wind around a leafy green plant, while orange-and-white clown fish and neon tetra swim through a rock tunnel.

Kate is unchanged, too. Her eyes are large and sympathetic. Her long dark hair is brushed back behind her shoulders.

Richard caught me the first time I snuck into the city to meet Kate. I didn't return for quite a while. When I did, I made sure to tell him I was going to visit Aunt Charlotte. Then I deliberately left my phone at her place while I rushed the thirty blocks here.

"I'm divorced," I begin.

Kate smiles slightly. She has always been so careful to avoid letting me know how she feels, but even though we've met only a few times, I've learned to read her.

"He left me for another woman."

The smile disappears from Kate's face.

"But she's not with him anymore, either," I add quickly. "He had a kind of breakdown—he tried to hurt me and there were witnesses. He's getting help."

I watch Kate as she processes all of this.

"Okay," she finally says. "So he is . . . no longer a threat to you?"

"Correct."

Kate cocks her head to the side. "He left you for another woman?"

This time it's me who smiles slightly. "She was the perfect replacement. That's what I thought the first time I saw her. . . . She's safe now, too."

"Richard always did like everything to be perfect." Kate leans back in her chair and crosses her right leg over her left, then absently massages her ankle.

The first time I met Kate, she'd merely asked me a few questions. But the queries helped me untangle the twisting thoughts in my mind: *Can you tell me why you think Richard is trying to keep you off-balance? What would his motivation be for this?*

The second time I came to see Kate, she'd reached for the box of tissues on the side table between us, even though I hadn't been crying.

She'd stretched out her arm to pass them to me, and my gaze had fallen on the thick cuff bracelet on her wrist.

She'd held her arm still, letting me take it in. But she hadn't said a single word.

Seeing that distinctive cuff shouldn't have come as a surprise. After all, collecting information was part of the reason why I'd sought out Richard's ex, the dark-haired woman he'd been with before me.

It hadn't been difficult to find her; Kate still lived in the city and was listed in the phone book. I was so careful. I never even mentioned her by name when I wrote about our meetings in my Moleskine notebook, and when Richard discovered I'd snuck into the city, I told him I'd been to see a therapist.

But Kate was even more careful.

She listened to me thoughtfully, but she didn't seem willing to share the story of what had happened during the years she and Richard were together.

I believe I discovered why during my third visit.

During our previous meetings, Kate had moved to one side after letting me into her apartment, gesturing for me to walk ahead of her toward the living room. When she stood up to signal our conversations had concluded, she motioned for me to go first and then followed to see me out.

On our third visit, though, when I wondered aloud if I should simply try to leave Richard and go stay with Aunt Charlotte, Kate abruptly stood and offered me tea.

I nodded, confused.

She walked into the kitchen while I stared after her.

Her right foot dragged along the floor; her body compensating for it by tilting down and up, gathering momentum to propel her forward. Something had happened to her leg, the one she massaged at times during our talk. Something that had left her with a pronounced limp.

When she returned with the tray of tea, she merely said, "What was it you were saying?"

I shook my head when she tried to hand me a cup. I knew my hands were trembling too violently for me to hold it.

I looked at the intricate platinum necklace she was wearing, that cuff bracelet, and the emerald ring on her right hand. Such exquisite, expensive pieces. They stood out against her simple clothing.

"I was saying . . . I can't just leave him." I choked out the words.

I rushed out a few moments later, suddenly terrified that Richard was trying to call my cell phone. That was the last time I'd seen Kate until today.

"There's a police record of the incident. And Maureen has stepped in to watch over Richard," I say now.

Kate closes her eyes briefly. "That's good."

"Your leg . . ."

When Kate speaks, her voice is emotionless. "I fell down some stairs." She hesitates and shifts her gaze to stare at her fish gliding through the aquarium. "Richard and I had argued that night because I was late to an important event." Her voice is much softer now. "After we got home and he went to bed . . . I left the apartment. I was carrying a suitcase." She swallows hard and her hand begins to massage her calf. "I decided to take the stairwell instead of the elevator. I didn't want anyone to hear the chime. But Richard . . . he wasn't asleep."

Her face crumples for an instant, then she recovers. "I never saw him again."

"I'm so sorry. You're safe now, too."

Kate nods.

After a moment, she says, "Be well, Vanessa."

She stands and walks me to the door.

I hear her lock click behind me as I start down the hallway. Then my head snaps back to look toward her apartment, a connection firing in my brain as I recall a long-ago vision.

The woman in the raincoat who'd stood outside the Learning Ladder, staring while I packed up my classroom. She had turned away with an odd jerking motion when I approached the window.

It could have been a limp.

FORTY-TWO

I AWAKEN TO FEEL RICH sunlight pouring through the slats of the window blinds, warming my body as I lie in bed in Aunt Charlotte's spare room.

My room, I think, spreading out my arms and legs like a starfish so I take up the entire bed. Then I stretch out my left hand and turn off my alarm before it can blare.

Sleep still eludes me on some nights, as I turn over in my mind all that has happened and try to put together the pieces that remain a mystery to me.

But I no longer dread mornings.

I rise and wrap myself in my robe. As I walk toward the bathroom to take a quick shower, I pass my desk, where the itinerary for our trip to Venice and Florence rests. Aunt Charlotte and I leave in ten days. It's still summertime, and I won't begin work teaching pre-K students in the South Bronx until after Labor Day.

An hour later, I step out of the apartment building into the warm air. I'm not in a rush today, so I stroll down the sidewalk, taking care not to smudge the chalk hopscotch squares a child has drawn. New York City is always quieter in August; the pace seems gentler. I pass a cluster of tourists taking photos of the skyline. An elderly man sits on the steps of a brownstone, reading the paper. A vendor fills buckets with clusters of fresh poppies and sunflowers, lilies and asters. I decide I'll buy some on my way home.

I reach the coffee shop and pull open the door, then scan the room.

"Table for one?" a waitress asks as she passes by with a handful of menus.

I shake my head. "Thanks, but I'm meeting someone."

I see her in the corner, lifting a white mug to her lips. Her gold wedding band glints as it catches the light. I pause, staring at it.

Part of me wants to run to her. Part of me wants more time to prepare.

Then she looks up and our eyes meet.

I walk over and she stands up quickly. She reaches out unhesitatingly and hugs me.

When we draw back, we wipe our eyes in unison. Then we burst into laughter.

I slide into the booth across from her.

"It is really good to see you, Sam." I look at her bright, beaded necklace and smile.

"I've missed you, Vanessa."

I've missed me, too, I think.

But instead of speaking, I reach into my bag.

And I pull out my matching happy beads.

EPILOGUE

V ANESSA WALKS DOWN THE CITY sidewalk, her blond hair loose around her shoulders, her arms swinging free at her sides. Her street is quieter than usual in the waning days of summer, but a lone bus lumbers by the spot I've staked out. A few teenagers loiter on the corner, watching as one spins on a skateboard. She passes them and pauses at a flower stand. She bends down, reaching for a generous cluster of poppies in a white bucket. She smiles as the vendor makes change, then continues on toward her apartment.

All the while, my eyes never stray from her.

When I've watched her before, I've tried to gauge her emotional state. Know thy enemy, Sun Tzu wrote in *The Art of War*. I read that book for a college course and the line resonated with me deeply.

Vanessa never realized I was a threat. She only saw what I wanted her to see; she bought into the illusion I created.

She thinks I am Emma Sutton, the innocent woman who fell into the trap she laid to escape her husband. I'm still stunned by Vanessa's admission that she orchestrated my affair with Richard; I thought I was the one spinning a web.

Apparently we were unwitting coconspirators.

Vanessa has no idea who I really am, though. No one does.

I could walk away now, and she'd never be privy to the truth. She looks completely recovered from all that has happened to her. Maybe it's best for her not to know.

I look down at the photograph I am clutching. The edges are worn from age and frequent handling.

It is a picture of a seemingly happy family: a father, a mother, a little boy with dimples, and a preteen girl with braces. The photo was taken years ago, when I was twelve, back when we lived in Florida. A few months before our family shattered.

It was after ten P.M. and I should have been asleep—it was past my bedtime—but I wasn't. I heard the doorbell ring, then my mother call, "I'll get it."

My father was in his room, probably grading papers. He often did that at night.

I heard the murmur of voices, then my father scrambling down the hallway toward the stairs.

"Vanessa!" he cried. His voice sounded so strained it propelled me out of my room. My socks slid silently along the carpeted floor as I crept past my younger brother's bedroom, to the top of the stairs, and huddled there. I could see everything unfolding directly below me. I was a spectator in the shadows.

I witnessed my mother fold her arms and glare at my father. I witnessed my father gesture with his hands as he talked. I witnessed my little calico cat wind between my mother's legs, as if trying to soothe her.

After my mother slammed the door, she turned to my dad.

I will never forget how her face looked in that moment.

"She came on to me," my father insisted, his round blue eyes, so like mine, widening. "She kept showing up during my office hours and asking for extra help. I tried to turn her away, and she kept— It was nothing, I swear."

But it wasn't nothing. Because a month later, my father moved out.

My mother blamed my father, but she also blamed the pretty coed who'd enticed my dad into an affair. She would throw out the name Vanessa during their fights, her mouth twisting as if those three syllables tasted bitter; it became shorthand for everything that went wrong between them.

I blamed her as well.

After I graduated from college, I came to New York for a visit. I looked her up, of course; she was Vanessa Thompson by now. My name was different, too. After my father left, my mother reverted to her maiden name, Sutton. When I became an adult, I changed mine to it also.

Vanessa lived in a big house in an affluent suburb. She was married to a handsome man. She was gliding through a golden life, one she didn't deserve. I wanted to see her close up, but I couldn't find a way to get near her. She rarely left her home. There was no way we could naturally intersect.

I almost cut my trip short. Then I realized something.

I could get close to her husband.

It was easy to find out where Richard worked. I quickly learned that he liked double espressos from the corner coffee shop every afternoon around three. He was a creature of habit. I brought my laptop and camped out at a table. The next time he came in, our eyes met.

I was used to men hitting on me, but this time I was the pursuer. Just as I imagined she had been with my father.

I'd given him my brightest smile. "Hi. I'm Emma."

I'd expected him to want to sleep with me; men usually did. That would have been enough, even if it was just for one night; eventually, his wife would have found out. I'd have made certain of that.

The symmetry of it appealed to me. It felt like justice.

Instead, he suggested I apply for a job as an assistant at his company.

Two months later, I replaced his secretary, Diane.

A few months after that, I replaced his wife.

I look down at the photo in my hand again.

I was so wrong about everything.

About my father.

I was deceived once by a married man when I was college, Vanessa had said on the day we'd met at the bridal salon. *I thought he loved me. He never told me about his wife.*

I was wrong about Richard.

If you marry Richard, you will regret it, she'd warned me when she confronted me outside my apartment. And later, while Richard stood beside me, she'd tried again, even though she was visibly scared: *He will hurt you.*

I think of how Richard pulled me to his side, wrapping his arm around me, after Vanessa uttered those words. The gesture seemed protective. But his fingertips dug into my flesh, creating a little trail of plum-colored marks. I don't even think he knew he was doing it; he was glaring at Vanessa in that moment. The next day, when I met Vanessa at the bridal salon, I made sure to keep her on my other side.

And most of all, I was wrong about Vanessa.

It is only fair that she knows she was wrong about me, too.

I make myself visible as I cross the street and approach her.

She turns around even before I call her name; she must have sensed my presence.

"Emma! What are you doing here?"

She was honest with me, even though it wasn't easy. If she hadn't fought so hard to save me, I would have married Richard. But she didn't stop there. She risked her life to expose him, preventing him from preying on yet another woman.

"I wanted to say I'm sorry."

Her brow creases. She waits.

"And I wanted to show you a picture." I hand it to her. "This was my family."

Vanessa stares at the photograph as I tell my story, beginning with that long-ago October night when I was supposed to be asleep.

Then her head snaps up and she searches my face. "Your eyes." Her tone is even, measured. "They seemed so familiar."

"I thought you deserved to know."

Vanessa hands back the picture. "I've been wondering about you. You seemed to materialize out of nowhere. When I tried to look you up online, you didn't exist until a few years ago. I couldn't find much more than your address and phone number."

"Would you rather not have known who I really was?"

She considers this for a moment.

Then she shakes her head. "The truth is the only way to move forward."

And then, because there is nothing more for either of us to say, I signal for an approaching cab.

I climb into the taxi and twist around to stare out the back window. I lift my hand.

Vanessa stares at me for a moment. Then she raises her palm, her movement a mirror image of my own.

She turns and walks away from me at the exact moment the cab begins to move, the distance between us growing greater with each breath.

ACKNOWLEDGMENTS

From Greer and Sarah:

We are grateful every day for our editor and publisher, Jennifer Enderlin at St. Martin's Press, whose brilliant brain has made this a much better book and whose unparalleled energy, vision, and savvy have launched it higher and farther than we ever dreamed.

We are lucky to have an outstanding publishing team behind us, which includes: Katie Bassel, Caitlin Dareff, Rachel Diebel, Marta Fleming, Olga Grlic, Tracey Guest, Jordan Hanley, Brant Janeway, Kim Ludlam, Erica Martirano, Kerry Nordling, Gisela Ramos, Sally Richardson, Lisa Senz, Michael Storrings, Tom Thompson, Dori Weintraub, and Laura Wilson.

Thank you to our amazing, smart, and generous agent, Victoria Sanders, as well as her fabulous crew: Bernadette Baker-Baughman, Jessica Spivey, and Diane Dickensheid at Victoria Sanders and Associates. Our gratitude also to Mary Anne Thompson.

To Benee Knauer: We are so appreciative of your spot-on early edits, most especially teaching us the true meaning of "palpable tension."

Many thanks to our foreign publishers, notably our dreamy dinner partner Wayne Brookes at Pan Macmillan UK. Our deep appreciation also to Shari Smiley at the Gotham Group.

From Greer:

Simply put, this book would not exist without Sarah Pekkanen, my inspiring, talented, and hilarious co-author—and cherished friend. Thank you for being my partner in crime on this wondrous journey.

In my twenty years as an editor, I learned a tremendous amount from the authors I worked with, especially Jennifer Weiner and also her agent, Joanna Pulcini. I also want to thank my former colleagues at Simon & Schuster, many of whom I also regard as dear friends, especially my mentor at Atria Books, Judith Curr; the sublime Peter Borland; and the most talented young editor in the business, Sarah Cantin.

From elementary school through graduate school I was fortunate to have teachers who believed in me, most remarkably Susan Wolman and Sam Freedman.

I am deeply grateful to our early readers, Marla Goodman, Alison Strong, Rebecca Oshins, and Marlene Nosenchuk.

I am gifted with many friends—both in and outside of the publishing industry—who cheered me on from the sidelines. Thank you to Carrie Abramson (and her husband, Leigh, our wine consultant), Gillian Blake, Andrea Clark, Meghan Daum (whose poem to me inspired Sam's), Dorian Fuhrman, Karen Gordon,

Cara McCaffrey, Liate Stehlik, Laura van Straaten, Elisabeth Weed, and Theresa Zoro. A special shout-out also to my Nantucket book club.

Thank you to Danny Thompson and Ellen Katz Westrich for keeping me physically and emotionally fit.

And my family:

Bill, Carol, Billy, Debbie, and Victoria Hendricks; Patty, Christopher, and Nicholas Allocca; Julie Fontaine and Raya and Ronen Kessel.

Robert Kessel, who always motivates me to break down walls.

Mark and Elaine Kessel, for passing on their love of books, serving as my earliest readers, and always telling me to "go for it."

Rocky, for keeping me company.

Extra-special gratitude to Paige and Alex, who encouraged their mother to pursue *her* childhood dream.

And finally to John, my True North, who not only told me that I could and should, but held my hand every step of the way.

From Sarah:

Ten years ago, Greer Hendricks became my editor. Then she became my beloved friend. Now we are a writing team. Our creative collaboration has been a singular joy, and I am so grateful for the way she supports, challenges, and inspires me. I cannot wait to see what the next ten years have in store for us.

My appreciation to all of the Smiths for their assistance through this process: Amy and Chris for the encouragement, laughter, and wine; Liz for her early read of the manuscript; and Perry for his thoughtful advice.

Thanks to Kathy Nolan for sharing her expertise on everything from marketing to websites; to Rachel Baker, Joe Dangerfield, and Cathy Hines for always having my back; the Street Team and my Facebook friends and readers who spread the word about my books with fun and flair; and my vibrant, supportive community of fellow authors.

I'm grateful to Sharon Sellers for keeping me strong enough to climb that next mountain, and to the wise, witty Sarah Cantin. My appreciation also to Glenn Reynolds, as well as Jud Ashman and the Gaithersburg Book Festival crew.

Bella, one of the great dogs, sat patiently by my side as I wrote.

Love to the incomparable Pekkanen crew: Nana Lynn, Johnny, Robert, Saadia, Sophia, Ben, Tammi, and Billy.

Always, and most of all, to my sons: Jackson, Will, and Dylan.